PRAISE FOR MARTIN L. SHOEMAKER

"Martin Shoemaker is a rare writer who can handle the challenges of dealing with future technology while touching the human heart."
—David Farland, *New York Times* bestselling author

"Martin Shoemaker's 'Black Orbit' is a more conventional *Analog* adventure, and a very good example of such . . . A really solid story."
—Rich Horton, Locus Online

"['Bookmarked'] is an exceptional example of how to discuss deep moral and philosophical issues while maintaining a tight narrative that brings the reader along. This story will be added to the required readings for my SF classes."
—Robert L. Turner III, Tangent Online

"In 'Brigas Nunca Mais,' Martin L. Shoemaker presents one of the best tales in the issue. A framed narrative about a love relationship told through the voice of the groom at a wedding on board a space ship, this tale delights by featuring dance as a central image and metaphor . . . A very enchanting story."
—Douglas W. Texter, Tangent Online

"What I did particularly enjoy [about 'Murder on the *Aldrin* Express'] was the excellent character development, and the heart and emotional depth brought to the story by its romantic aspect."
—Colleen Chen, Tangent Online

THE
LAST
CAMPAIGN

ALSO BY MARTIN L. SHOEMAKER

The Last Dance

Today I Am Carey

THE
LAST
CAMPAIGN

MARTIN L. SHOEMAKER

47NORTH

Text copyright © 2020 by Martin L. Shoemaker
All rights reserved.

No part of this book may be reproduced, or stored in a retrieval system, or transmitted in any form or by any means, electronic, mechanical, photocopying, recording, or otherwise, without express written permission of the publisher.

Published by 47North, Seattle

www.apub.com

Amazon, the Amazon logo, and 47North are trademarks of Amazon.com, Inc., or its affiliates.

ISBN-13: 9781542091404
ISBN-10: 1542091403

Cover illustration and design by Mike Heath | Magnus Creative

Printed in the United States of America

For Jack McDevitt,
inspiration, mentor, and friend.
You asked for "The Adventure of the Martian Tomb,"
and the rest followed.

Contents

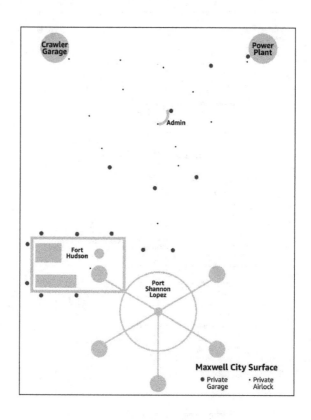

Maxwell City Surface

● Private Garage   · Private Airlock

Crawler Garage

Power Plant

Admin

Fort Hudson

Port Shannon Lopez

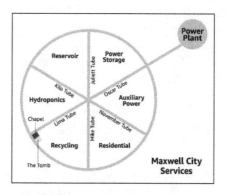

Maxwell City Services

Power Plant

Reservoir

Power Storage

Juliett Tube

Kilo Tube

Oscar Tube

Hydroponics

Auxiliary Power

Chapel

Lima Tube

Mike Tube

November Tube

Recycling

Residential

The Tomb

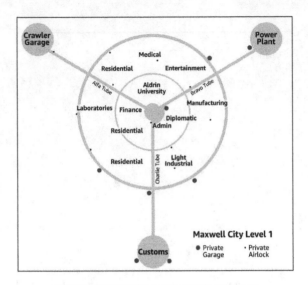

Maxwell City Level 1

● Private Garage   • Private Airlock

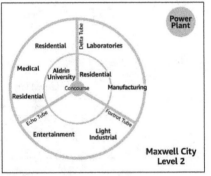

Maxwell City Level 2

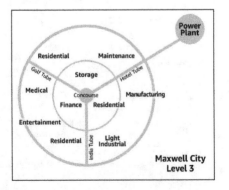

Maxwell City Level 3

1. THE ADVENTURE OF THE MARTIAN TOMB

When I squeezed down to the bottom of the crevasse, there was no doubt about it: Simons was dead. I tapped my suit comm and called up to the top where Nick waited, "Helmet's cracked, Nick." I didn't describe the desiccated skull behind the shattered plexi. There was no need to. Nick had spent far more time on Mars than I had, and he had seen his share of corpses.

"Photograph everything, Rosie," Nick called back. "Let's not have anyone doubt our thoroughness."

"Space it, Nick, I know how to do my job," I replied with a sigh; but I smiled as I said it. Nick and I had competed since our first meeting, when I had been the new recruit from Brazil and Nick had been the arrogant spacer from America. After all these years, sparring with Nick over an investigation was just a pleasant game. Our spats spiced up the romance and kept things interesting.

But then I remembered that in this incident, we had a dead Mars settler on our hands. Jacob Simons, age thirty-seven, had gone out on a scientific mission and had never returned. On Mars, past a certain number of days missing, you are presumed dead. But São Paulo Mutual wouldn't pay Simons's widow on a presumption. At best, they would pay her a fraction of the policy value, enough to keep her in air until she got her life in order.

So Nick and I had volunteered to search for Jacob. It had not been easy. Mars is more complex geologically than people of Earth assume. In some places vehicles and people leave easy-to-follow tracks in the sand; but in others, long stretches of rock show no signs of passage. And frequent dust storms can bury tracks in minutes. If Jacob had stayed with his crawler, we could have tracked that by its transponder; but he had set out on foot and seemed to have deviated far from the course he had registered in the expedition office. It had taken Nick and me three days to confirm his half-buried tracks and to trace them back to this small offshoot of the West Candor Chasma system of valleys and crevasses.

So now we would be able to bring back Jacob's body, and Althea would be able to file for full survivor benefits. Not that that would make up for losing Jacob. Althea and Jacob were one of the closest couples I'd met on Mars. But at least there'd be something to help support her while she tried to rebuild. Maybe even something to invest in a fund like the Red Planet League and get some continuing income.

I videoed the body from every angle, dictating notes as I did so. Nick watched through my helmet cam. The crevasse blocked my signal from reaching Maxwell City. If Jacob had called for help, no one would have known. But Nick was straight overhead, so he could pick it up. He made suggestions as I worked, and I pointed out that I was already ahead of him on most of them, while acknowledging when he made good points.

When we were both satisfied with my work, I shut down the camera, and I called up, "All right, let's get him out of here. Take him home."

I had elected to go down into the crevasse. Although Nick is not the tallest of men, I'm still smaller than he is and able to fit into smaller places while suited up for the Martian surface. When we had spotted the body from above, I had swapped out my oxygen pack for just a single small tank. This had made it easier to negotiate the crevasse, but now I had only ten minutes of oxygen left before I was down to suit reserves. That should be enough; but if not, Nick could throw down a spare to me. A tank would be easy enough to catch in the light Martian gravity.

But smaller or not, I was still cautious. I wanted to get away from Jacob's body before Nick pulled the crawler up closer to the edge. The ground had seemed solid enough from up there, but Mars could surprise you. If anything came crashing down, Jacob was past caring, but I wasn't. So I crept a good ten meters from Jacob's body, to where the crevasse started to narrow. Any farther, and even I might worry about getting stuck. I was glad to have a modern Mars suit, so much lighter and more maneuverable than suits from the early days of space exploration. I could never have navigated the crevasse with another hundred kilos of environment pack.

Nick backed the crawler closer to the edge, unfolded the legs for the winch, and extended the winch boom out over the crevasse. Then he attached a harness to the cable, and he turned on the motor to lower it down. While the harness descended, Nick tested the edge, both with his own weight and with the crawler's deep radar. When he seemed satisfied, Nick said, "Let's hook him up."

I crawled back, watchful for any sign of falling rock or dust. When I saw none and I was sure it was safe enough, I lifted Jacob's body and slipped the harness around his arms and legs. Then I called up to Nick, "He's hooked up."

"Everything free?" Nick called back.

"Yep. I lifted him off the ground, and nothing is wedged."

"All right, go back to your safe spot, and I'll haul him up." Nick left nothing to chance. That was how Nick and his crew had survived on their mission to Mars, the ill-fated second *Bradbury* expedition. This was one of the things that had first attracted me to him. As difficult as he could be sometimes, he didn't miss details.

Oh, he missed *human* details, sometimes. He could be infuriating, not recognizing what someone was feeling or thinking. But he could be attentive in his own unique way. If he knew something mattered to me, it mattered to him. He would never forget, and he'd make sure that any job I needed got done right.

So I went back to my safe spot, and I watched as Jacob's body rose into the air.

And then I cursed under my breath. I liked Nick's attention to detail, but I hated it when he was right about something going wrong. Dust started to fall from the crevasse wall, followed by small pebbles. The added weight of Jacob and his suit out on a long moment arm was proving just enough leverage to stress the rock and soil of the crevasse wall.

"Nick—"

"Stay back, Rosie!"

"If you're going to get him up, you had better hurry."

"Working on it!"

And then Nick swore, something he usually saved for when things were really falling apart. A single Portuguese word I had taught him: "*Porra*. Rosie, get out of there. The whole wall's starting to crumble. It's going to take the crawler with it if I don't—"

"Move, Nick!"

They tell me that today, rock climbing is an optional subject for the kids, only for those who elect to attend Martian survival school. But on my first assignment to Mars, it had *all* been Martian survival school. Now that we had returned, Nick and I still climbed a lot for recreation. With the crevasse as narrow as it was there at my safe spot, it was an easy climb in the light Martian gravity. I could just press against both sides and walk myself up, hands and feet.

Then I felt the wall on the crawler side tremble, and I saw the whole face start to fall. I quickly scrambled for hand- and footholds on the other wall as I shouted up, "Fall, Nick! Move!" I scaled the wall as fast as I could, daring one quick look back as the rocks came crashing down, filling the crevasse. It was a strange thing to watch. Even after all my years on Mars, I still expected such an accident to create a large crashing sound. But my external audio picked up almost nothing. Sound didn't propagate very far or very fast in the thin atmosphere of Mars. Only the lowest of rumbles reached me across the distance. So I felt more than heard the collapse.

Through the dust, I saw Jacob's body rising quickly, more quickly than the winch motor operated. Nick had to be driving the crawler away from the edge. So Nick had gotten away. I was relieved.

Even if he hadn't, there would have been nothing I could do about it. I would have had to walk back to Maxwell City to get help.

No, scratch that idea. I would never make that trip on one air bottle with only ten minutes left. If Nick had not survived, I would not have either. So I was glad my husband was a survivor.

I scaled to the top of the wall, and I stuck my head up. As soon as my helmet cleared the edge, I heard Nick shouting on the comm. "Rosie! Answer, Rosie!"

"I'm all right, Nick." I pulled myself over the edge, lying on the ground. "I am up."

"*Graças a Deus!* I would never forgive myself if I lost the best spacer on Mars. Now get clear."

I scrambled to my feet, and I made some distance between me and the edge. Then I looked back. Nick was on the far side of the crevasse, leaning against the crawler at a safe distance. He had already folded back the winch legs. Jacob's body lay on the ground near the crawler treads. "I was wondering if I'd have to come get you," Nick said.

"That will be the day, love," I said. But I knew he would have if he had had to. "Jacob would be really disappointed in us," I continued. "Look what we have done to a perfectly good geological site." Though Jacob ran other experiments under contract, geology was his specialty, his passion.

5

"I know," Nick said. "Plus now we can't finish our investigation. I wanted videos of the crevasse without him in it."

"Nick, it's not like it is a crime scene."

"I know. But accident scene, crime scene, details matter. They always matter."

"I *know*." If Nick was nagging me, he was calming down. I looked around. The crevasse was pretty big. I checked my air. "Nicolau, you will have to toss me a spare air bottle. It will take a while to walk around this crack in the ground. We need to get Jacob's body back to Althea, so let's not waste time."

☾

While Nick drove us back to Maxwell City, I called ahead to let them know that we had found Jacob, and I arranged to deliver the body. In our unspoken division of labor, that was my responsibility. On a good day, Nick could be caring and considerate—if you knew how to read him. On a bad day, he could be utterly unaware of another person's suffering when he thought it was irrelevant to getting work done. I did not know that this would be a bad day, necessarily, but I had learned that breaking bad news was just something that I did better than Nick did.

As we neared the city, the lifeless sands of Mars gave way to more signs of human habitation: crawlers, a few suited figures, and a scattering of structures. Most of Maxwell City proper lay below the surface, with only a few airlocks, the crawler garage, and the upper three floors of the Admin Center showing above the ground. But far to the south were the control towers and the ground facilities of the largest spaceport on Mars. As I looked, a hopper leaped into the thin Martian air. Hoppers are ballistic aircraft that can launch between points on the Martian surface, with limited course correction abilities. They are one of the fastest ways to travel on Mars, but not cheap. The only faster way is fully powered flight; but Mars's thin atmosphere made gliding nearly impossible, so powered flight burned fuel the entire way.

Most surface travel was via crawlers like ours: slow but reliable. The city had a fleet of public crawlers for rent, most based in the big crawler garage northwest of town. We pulled into the garage airlock, and then waited for the door to seal behind us and the lock to pressurize. When the cycle was done, we pulled into the main garage. Althea was there waiting for us. With her was Adam Simons, Jacob's brother and his partner in the scientific survey business. Nick pulled the lever to drop the rear end of the crawler, lowering the wheels so that the rear was practically touching the ground. Then I got out, went to the back, opened the rear door, and wheeled out the stretcher. Once the stretcher was clear, I closed the hatch, and Nick drove the crawler away to its charging bay. He would continue home from there, while I would handle the personal matters.

Adam and Althea came up to me, Althea quietly sobbing and dabbing her nose with a handkerchief, while Adam tried to look stoic. At least I think that is what he was trying, but it wasn't working. His jaw muscles were trembling.

I held up my hand before they got close. "Althea," I said, "you do not have to do this. It's not like anybody else was out there. We know it is him, and Dr. Costello can do a DNA test to confirm. He looks pretty bad. You don't have to identify him."

Althea wiped her nose, and then her eyes. She looked at me. "Yes, I do. When your time comes, you'll understand."

I stepped back, and I gently folded down the sheet to uncover Jacob's face. Althea peered through the cracked plexi, and she began sobbing loudly. Adam pulled her in, held her close to his chest, and nodded to me. I covered Jacob back up.

"He shouldn't have been out alone," Adam said. "We were trying to get ahead on contracts." Then Adam started sobbing as well.

As we stood there, I silently anticipated what would happen next. I knew it would be awkward for me; and then I was ashamed, because my discomfort was insignificant compared to Althea's pain. But that did not change how I felt, and I was just glad that Nick was not there to get involved.

As if on cue, the access tube opened, and Marcus stepped into the garage, leading a gurney drone. He walked up to us; and in a carefully controlled voice, I said, "Dr. Costello."

Marcus nodded at me. "Admiral," he said, using the title I was no longer legally eligible to claim. He didn't smile. The occasion was not one for smiling anyway, but I had not seen him smile in years. Not at me, anyway.

I turned back to Althea and Adam. "Althea," I said, "Dr. Costello is here. He needs to . . ."

Althea looked up, tears streaking her face. Marcus finished my thought. "I need to take Mr. Simons now, Mrs. Simons. We have to prepare him for interment."

Althea buried her face again, but Adam nodded. I held out a tablet to Marcus, and he signed it. Then with my help, he transferred Jacob's body from the crawler's stretcher to the gurney drone. He turned back to the tunnel, and the drone followed. The three of us did as well.

"Adam," Althea said. "He . . ." But she could not put words to what she wanted to say.

"I know," Adam said. "It's the rules."

"I know." Althea sniffed.

"Mother and Father can't be here," Adam said. Of course not. They were on Earth. Months away, even if they left right now, even if there was a vessel to bring them right now. Adam continued, "But they might like to come see a grave someday. Rosalia, Mayor Holmes likes you. Do you think we could get an exception for the burial? Just once?"

I shook my head. "You know there is no such thing as just once. If we bury Jacob, we shall have to bury everybody, and the Commission has not authorized that yet here on Mars. And you know: we need the organics, and we cannot wait for them to come back in a natural cycle." Maxwell City was growing rapidly. The initial settlers, fewer than a dozen, had been Nick and his crew when they had been stranded here on Mars and struggled to survive. Since that day, Maxwell City had grown to nearly fifty thousand people. But it had grown at such a fast rate that infrastructure development was still racing to keep up. And in particular, organics production lagged behind. Martians were starting to produce their own topsoil through dedicated nano plants; and water was turning up everywhere we looked, more than the twentieth century or even the early twenty-first had ever suspected. But still, for the foreseeable future, Maxwell City had a 100 percent recycling goal. All organics had to go through the city cycler for reuse. And that included human bodies.

This was no news to old space hands. Nick's crew had had to recycle Shannon Lopez—the first person to die on the surface—plus the lower section of Fadila van der Ven's leg. Space exploration was not for the squeamish. But the latest wave of Martian colonists were not trained astronauts. They were scientists, researchers, construction teams, and prospectors, plus administrators and merchants and families. A few were even tourists. And the new people just did not appreciate the importance of recycling, even after it had been explained to them over and over.

Mayor Holmes had found a compromise. One of the recyclers on the Services level at the bottom of the city had been modified to produce soil, or a reasonable facsimile of it. The Tomb was open to all faiths and burial traditions to bury their dead there and let them rest for a brief time in a biodegradable coffin, dressed in biodegradable burial wear, until finally the recycler was activated and the remains were broken down. The resultant rich soil was offered to the family for gardens, and to the community as well. Nick used some for his bonsai trees.

Adam nodded, but the look in his eyes was pleading. I inclined my head as well, but it was only a polite courtesy. Anthony Holmes could only change this policy with the whole city council on board. With the election coming, he was unlikely to rock the boat. His Libertist Party needed the support of the Saganists, a minor party, in a coalition against the Realist opposition; and the Saganists protested any new development, any growth beyond the limits of the Mars Compact. If they could, they would drastically *reduce* human presence on Mars, in order to protect undiscovered Martian life.

We reached the ramp down to the underground levels of Maxwell City. "I'll see you at the service," I said. I let them and Marcus proceed without me down Alfa Tube and into the main city. By now, I knew, Nick would be filing his first round of reports on the accident and our discovery of Jacob's body. I might as well do the same. It is important to capture observations when they are still fresh.

I was glad Nick had left. He and Marcus would never get along well, and I hated to be caught in the middle of that storm—especially since I had created it.

I opened my comp, worked through my photos and notes and videos, and sorted them into piles. Then I pushed them over to my filing agent app, which knew how to process them from there.

Next I dictated more notes on what I remembered. I had learned that from Nick. Your perception on the scene and then hours later and days later are all different. But it is wrong to assume that your immediate perceptions are correct. The mind does not work that way. Sometimes you notice something at the moment, but you only get the context to make sense of it later. That is when it connects in your mind. So I dictated, and I tried to think about what I might have missed. Even though it was a routine accident site, it was good to go through the drill anyway. And it let me give Nick time to decompress in his own way.

C

When I got back to our apartment, Nick was in his closet workshop, trimming trees. I found things to busy myself while I waited.

Mars had grown wealthy compared to its founding days, but luxuries were still scarce and measured. Each family had to decide what to do with spare air, spare organics, and spare space. And spare time. Nick and I had an apartment in a residential district down on the third subsurface level of the city, just above the Services level. Friends found that odd: it was a working-class neighborhood, not up to their expectations for a founder of the city. But Nick hated to be treated as a founder, even if there was some truth to it; and the rent was lower that deep. That let us afford a little more space.

And that gave us room for Nick's trees. And our small private hydroponics plots, of course, but the trees were most important. Few even of Nick's friends ever saw his bonsai work. It was not a hobby, more a coping mechanism. He had learned from Emilia Oliveira Correia, a master from Bonsai do Campo, the leading bonsai firm in South America. In Nick she had found a willing, eager, meticulous pupil—as his duties in the Space Corps permitted. And in bonsai, Nick found peace. When he was angry or stressed, he poured that energy into bending and trimming trees, planting cuttings, even just cleaning the waste. The whole process was so precise, yet so organic.

And so private. After five years together, Nick tolerated me in his workshop; but after a day like this, I gave him his time alone.

When Nick emerged from the workshop at last, I wrapped my arms around him, and I felt him shake all over. I held him close, shaking myself. I felt sad, but at the same time, special. No one ever saw this side of Nick either. We had been together for years before *I* ever saw it. Nick is the bravest man I have ever met, in the moment, when it is needed. But that is only because he shoves the fear and the grief deep inside. After, he takes to his trees. And to me.

"Was it bad?" Nick asked.

I sighed. "No worse than I expected," I said. "Althea is pretty strong." I did not mention Marcus, of course.

"Yeah," Nick said. "Jacob always told me that."

We sat on the couch, holding each other. Staring at nothing, saying nothing, for nearly an hour before Nick stood up.

And that was it. He had had his release, and he was back to old reliable Nick. He recorded a voice report for São Paulo Mutual. Then he mixed up caipirinhas for both of us, and he started finding dinner.

While Nick prepared the Martian equivalent of bauru sandwiches—vat-grown roast beef with cultured mozzarella, but at least we had real tomatoes from our own garden—I sipped at my caipirinha. The lime juice was a chemical substitute, but the cachaça was good. The cool taste of lime and sugary liquor over ice soothed my nerves.

When I was sufficiently calm, I called Anthony. His face appeared on the screen quickly. I could guess that he already knew the news.

"Admiral," he said.

"Anthony . . . ," I said.

He held up a hand. "I'm sorry, old habits. Rosalia, I've heard the news about Jacob."

"Yes, pretty much exactly what we feared. He was too eager to get work done, and he paid for it."

Anthony looked down at his hands. "I wish we could force everybody to take a refresher course in Martian survival. People are getting sloppy."

"You are the mayor. Couldn't you get the city council—"

Anthony waved his hands in the air. "No, no, no. People are already riled up about one thing after another. They say we're too heavy handed as it is. But still . . ." He smiled a little. "It would sure be nice to have Commander Adika give some of them a little remedial instruction."

But Chukwunwike Adika, of course, wasn't on Mars. Chuks was still in charge of security for the *Aldrin*, the cycler ship for which Nick and I had thrown away our careers. It had been a good trade, we were convinced of that. Aldrin City was the largest, safest route to Mars that humanity could take. Nick had an almost mystical conviction that the future of humanity depended on that ship. And when he talked about it, I could believe it myself.

"Well, we do not have Chuks," I said. "But we do have the next best thing. There are few accidents around here, thankfully enough, so Nick gets pretty bored sometimes. Maybe we should open up an advanced survival school."

"Funny you should mention boredom," Anthony said. "I'd like to talk to Nick, if I could."

"He's getting dinner, but he should be free in a moment. In the meantime . . ." I talked to Anthony about a real burial on Mars for Jacob, but it was strictly pro forma. I had known his answer before he told me no.

Nick came in, kissed me on the forehead gently, and handed me a bauru sandwich on a plate. Then he turned to walk away, but I grabbed his arm. "No, Anthony wants to talk to you." I moved out of the camera zone, and I bit into the sandwich. The cheese was perfectly melted, flowing in and around the tomato wedges. My man had not lost his touch.

Nick sat down with his own sandwich and caipirinha. "So is this Mr. Mayor?" he asked. "Or is this Anthony the kid?"

Anthony grinned. "This is whichever one has the most pull with you, Nick. I need a big favor."

"Oh?"

Anthony paused. "All right, here goes. This election's tighter than I expected, Nick. The Realists are making a strong push, with big money behind them. Their candidate, Carla Grace, is the first real competition I've had since we started holding elections."

"Nothing wrong with that," Nick said. "If you're smart, you'll bow out. Let Grace and the Realists have the headaches, she deserves them.

You have no idea what a relief it is not to have to make all the decisions every day."

I managed not to laugh at that. Yes, Nick had adjusted to life after the *Aldrin*, as an independent contractor with no one to order around. But I knew him too well. He had thrived as captain of the *Aldrin*, making sure that Earth–Mars transport was done properly and safely. Governor Carver of Aldrin City still ran things Nick's way more often than not in all the major particulars.

Anthony wasn't as reserved as me. He laughed. "Nick, maybe when I'm your age, I'll be ready to retire to a nice, cushy contract job. But right now, if I didn't make sure Mars was managed successfully and safely, I'd be a disappointment to my mentor."

"Your mentor doesn't give a damn," Nick said. "I say run it the way you want."

"Who said anything about you?" Anthony smiled. "I was talking about Chuks."

And then I did lose my composure. I curled up on my end of the couch, laughing until my sides hurt. Even Nick managed a smile.

When my laughter subsided, Nick said, "So how can I help you in this?"

Anthony took another breath, and I knew this was something that Nick would not like. "Nick, I'm getting dinged a lot in the polls because of the rising crime rate."

Nick snorted. "You get fifty thousand people in close quarters, you're going to have crime. That's as predictable as Phobos setting in the east."

"I know, Nick. But I'm getting blamed for it anyway. I need to take a positive stand. We've been relying on Initiative Security for way too long, and they're not really trained for policing, which is what we need. So next week I'm going to announce our new police department."

"That is hardly news," I said. "Many people are talking about it. They say it will be a new division of Public Safety."

Anthony shook his head. "The rumor mill gets it wrong again. This will be a whole new department, separate from the Department of Public Safety. But we're recruiting heavily from their ranks, and we've already started basic training."

"So what does this have to do with me?" Nick asked.

"Rosie's right," Anthony answered. "It's a pretty open secret; but I can't make an official announcement until I can show a solid team that people can trust. I need a leader they'll have confidence in. Nick, I want to announce you as my new police chief."

Nick's eyes widened. It was rare that someone surprised him, especially someone he knew as well as Anthony.

I thought of what a great idea this would be. It would give Nick more to do to prevent his boredom. And it would give us a more steady income than these insurance investigations did.

So I was surprised when Nick shook his head. "No, sorry. Pass," he said.

Anthony held his hands out, pleading. "But why not, Nick? It would really help the credibility of our police force to have one of the founders in charge."

"Well, that's reason one right there," Nick said. "I've got no patience with this 'founders' crap. I did a job, one mission, over twenty years ago. A lot more people have built Maxwell City since then, and they deserve the credit. *You've* done more to build Mars than I have. I get tired of feeling like I stepped out from some sort of legend. People have only recently stopped greeting me as 'Founder' everywhere I go. If you bring that all back up as part of some publicity campaign . . ."

"All right, all right," Anthony said. "I'll cut out any mention of founders in the campaign material. I can't help what people say, though, and let's face it: today, a lot of people know you as the founder of Maxwell City."

"Yeah," Nick said, "another reminder I'd rather not have. But that's not the major reason. I wasn't kidding, Anthony. It's a relief not to be in charge of anything. All that burden-of-command rhetoric that you always read about? It's real. I spent my time making sure two thousand people never made a mistake that could get the entire ship killed, or an entire Mars colony left with no supplies. I did a good job, and I'm proud of it, but I'm done. It's a relief to wake up in the morning and know that I have to worry about me, and Rosalia, and our latest insurance contract, and nothing more."

"Nick, no one could do this better than you," Anthony said.

"No," Nick replied, "but here's something else you learn eventually as a leader: There's someone else out there who will do it different than you, but good enough. And someday, they'll be as good as you ever were. Maybe better. But only if you get out of their way. There comes a time to pass the baton. And I've passed mine."

"I hope you'll reconsider this, Nick," Anthony said. "I have officers in training. I need you to shape them up."

"There's nothing to consider. Anthony, you're a good friend, and I'm proud of the man you've become. And I really hope Maxwell City is smart enough to elect you mayor for another term, and beyond, if you're determined to run. I'll even"—Nick glanced at me—"I'll even campaign for you as a founder, if you think it will help. But no. We've got our own life now. Mars doesn't need me."

☾

The next time we saw Anthony was two days later at Jacob's funeral. Anthony attended not as the mayor, nor as a candidate, but as a family friend. Althea worked in the mayor's office.

Carla Grace, though, had less excuse to be there. She barely knew the Simons brothers, and she did not know Althea at all. I was sure she would deny it, but I was also sure that she was there strictly for publicity for her campaign. If there was any chance that Anthony was going to end up in the news, then Carla wanted to be there as well.

The service was held in an ecumenical chamber adjacent to the Tomb, down in the Services level at the bottom of the city. Some designer had really gone the extra kilometer on that chapel. Most of Maxwell City was finished in plastic, with much of the more recent plastic manufactured on Mars from local materials. The chapel, however, was carefully fashioned from raw Martian rock, diligently sealed to prevent air leaks. Even the pews had been carved directly from the native rock, all of one piece with the floor itself. On Earth, stone pews might have been uncomfortable to sit on; but in the low Martian gravity, they were more comfortable than any wooden pew back on Earth, even without cushions. And the simple, polished stone everywhere gave the chapel a sense of timelessness.

Althea sat in the front, squeezing Adam's hand and weeping quietly. She and Jacob had had no children, and Ilse had left Adam two years ago. She had booked passage back to Earth, packed up, and left. Rumor had it she had told him that she loved him just as much as ever; and if he loved her, he would return with her, but she could not take Mars anymore. Instead, Adam had stayed; and thus he was the only family Althea had within two AUs. With nothing else in his life, he had thrown himself deeper into the business he had founded with Jacob.

Althea had asked Anthony to sit in the pew behind her, and so Nick and I found ourselves there as well. Anthony had insisted that we join him. I scanned the rest of the room. In that sense, I am as incorrigible as Nick. We had first met in astronaut training back in São Paulo, where we had competed to see who was the best incident investigator. Nick usually won, because for me it was a game, but for him it was an obsession. He would always go one step further than was needed. But I had held my own, and that training had served me well in my career in the Space Corps. And you do not lose a decades-old habit just because you retire, especially when that habit is useful in our insurance contracts today. So scanning an area and making mental notes is second nature to me, even in a venue as inappropriate as a funeral.

I recognized a few friends, one or two of whom I had not even realized had known Jacob. Fifty thousand people is getting pretty large, so you cannot know everybody, but Maxwell City still had the feel of a small town. Everybody was still connected across just a couple of links. A few of them were Anthony's supporters, prominent Libertists. Nick and I weren't party members, but our sympathies lay with them. It was uncommon to find Mars surface explorers who were not Libertists, though some leaned more toward Saganists.

I also recognized a few who I suspected were more Jacob's clients than friends. Maxwell City was home to a number of Martian scientific efforts: some pure research, some commercial, some government oversight bodies—though they seldom contracted individual firms like Simons Brothers Labs. The likely clients were all clustered near the rear of the chapel, whispering among themselves.

Also in the rear were Carla Grace, her entourage, and a small pool of reporters. I could not be sure whether Carla hung back out of respect, or just to be closer to the cameras. But I knew which way I would bet.

No, I did not particularly like Carla. Maybe that wasn't fair. I didn't really know her. But I had heard her speeches, pure Realist dogma. I think what bothered me most was that she made their timid platform sound reasonable, and that made me want to shout at the video screen.

I glanced back to the row in front of Carla, to a face I had almost missed. Marcus. I had forgotten that he knew Jacob and Adam. I seldom ran into him anymore. Again, fifty thousand people. Plenty of room for a couple of exes to miss each other. Or was it to avoid each other? Not that there were problems there—I didn't know of any, at least. But Marcus still did not get along with Nick. And the feeling was mutual, and Nick was worse at hiding it. So I hoped he would not notice Marcus back there.

I need not have worried. Nick was concentrating on the scene ahead. He kept reaching up to touch the yarmulke on his head and to scratch under it. I slapped his hand.

"But it itches," he whispered.

"Scratch later," I said. "What would Grandma Ruth say?" That was a low blow—Grandma Ruth had been the only family member Nick had loved, and he had run away from home right after her funeral—but it was effective. Nick stopped scratching.

Then Rabbi Miller strode to the front, and I pressed Nick to sit back in the pew as the rabbi gave the service. I had never been to a Jewish funeral before, so I could not tell if it was Orthodox or not. What did Orthodox even mean on Mars? But it was sincere and moving.

In the middle, Adam got up and told a few stories from his brother's life. He ended with, "Today we bury a great scientist and a loving husband. My partner, my friend, my . . ." Adam swallowed. "My brother." He held a hand out to a camera, which was recording the service for his parents back on Earth. "Mother, Father, I wish you could be here to sit shiva with us. But I feel your love. I know nothing can erase this pain, but please remember . . ." Adam started to cry. "Jacob died doing what he loved. Something important for every life here on Mars. All of Mars will remember him for that. Shalom, my brother."

I had told myself I wasn't going to cry. As a former admiral, I had seen my share of deaths in the line of duty. But Adam's tribute touched me, and I started to weep.

Then I looked down, and Nick was holding out a handkerchief to me. I wrapped my arm around him and pulled him close. "Thank you, Nico," I whispered.

2. SHIVA

After the service, we swung by our apartment to pick up Nick's contribution to shiva: a large batch of kosher Brazilian cheese bread, *pão de queijo*—or at least kosher as far as Nick knew. It was hard to tell sometimes with Martian ingredients. Nick pulled the pan from the oven and set it on the work top, filling the apartment with the toasty smell of bread and hints of cheese. Once I was sure Nick's hands were free from the hot pan, I wrapped my arms around his waist, pulled him close, and leaned in. Pão de queijo had been what Mrs. Quintana had brought to Grandma Ruth's funeral nearly half a century ago. In Nick's mind, it was comfort food.

While we waited for the pão to cool, I turned on a news stream. When I saw Carla Grace, I almost turned it off again; but Nick waved a hand. Since Anthony's call, Nick had paid closer attention to the news.

From the background, I could see that Grace was speaking from the corridor just outside the Tomb. As I had suspected, the *cachorra* was using Jacob's death to promote her campaign.

"It's a very sad day for Maxwell City, of course," she said to the camera. "We can't afford to lose a good scientist like Jacob Simons."

"Can't afford?" a female voice asked from off screen.

"We can't afford to lose *any* trained personnel. We're still too small, too interdependent."

"And too dependent on the Initiative," the journo added—a response surely planted by Grace's campaign.

"Far too dependent," Grace continued. "We still have to—" She caught herself, as if choked up. "We can't even bury our dead. We have to recycle them in the Tomb. We can't spare the organics. We're not ready for independence."

"*Porra*," Nick said, turning off the stream himself. "Aldrin City recycles more tightly than we do, and they're independent. That's a phony argument."

"Phony," I agreed. But I remembered Althea's face when they had interred Jacob in the Tomb. It carried emotional weight. *"We can't even bury our dead."*

☾

We left our apartment and navigated the local tunnels to India Tube. Levels 1 to 3 of the city were laid out as discs, each surrounded by a ring tube. Three tubes (Golf, Hotel, and India on our level) ran from the ring to the center, and smaller tunnels divided the cubic between the tubes into neighborhoods and apartments.

We stepped aboard the slidewalk in India, and it carried us inward to the Concourse, the large commons area in the center of the city. On the levels above, the Concourse was a stack of ring-shaped balconies; but here on level 3 it was a round park a hundred meters across, filled with decorative plants engineered for high oxygen production. Children bounded through the paths in the natural-spectrum light from LED banks three levels up. The youngest wore anchor rings, weighted circles on fabric skirts, to hold them to the ground and keep them from jumping too high and injuring themselves. Those older than toddlers, though, moved with a freedom and grace that Earth-born children might never know, bouncing with ease from ground to trees to walls in what might have been a game of tag. I smiled to see them at play, a little joy in a sad day.

We skirted the edge of the park to the nearest elevator and punched the button for level 1. We felt a brief increase in weight, almost a full G, as the car sped us to the top. Then we stepped out into the ring-shaped mall, lined with shops and restaurants and VR parlors. A quick turn to our left took us into another residential district between Alfa and Charlie Tubes. It was a more prestigious neighborhood, being just below the surface; but the side tunnels were smaller, and the rents were higher.

We reached Jacob and Althea's apartment—Althea's apartment now; I would have to get used to thinking of it that way. Adam let us in. Nick offered the basket of warm bread.

"Thank you, Rosalia," Adam said. "Thank you, Nick. This is a mitzvah." Adam took the basket. Nick shook Adam's free hand, and I reached in close to hug him.

I had done only a bit of research on sitting shiva. I knew it was a seven-day period of mourning; and during that time, the respectful thing to do in the home was to sit silently unless one of the family spoke to you first, and then to share stories of the departed. So I found a corner to sit in.

The apartment was not large by modern Maxwell City standards. Maxwell is known for having the smallest cubic per person of any planet-bound city in the solar system. It was still that new, and space was still at a premium. This was one of the older apartments; and it appeared that, in preparation for shiva, Althea had borrowed low stools from somewhere to provide plenty of places for people to sit. A center island naturally divided the space into four corner conversation nooks. The island made the apartment even smaller.

Nick followed Adam into the kitchen. I was sure he would volunteer to help with food. It would give him something to do in a situation where he was powerless to make things better.

Soon Anthony came in, carrying a clear covered plate with fruit. From my vantage point, I could not tell for sure, but it looked fresh from the hydroponics gardens, not reconstituted. Althea took the fruit off to the kitchen, and Anthony came over and joined me. He nodded silently, respecting shiva, and I did the same. His assistant, Alonzo Gutierrez, stood silently behind him.

Then to my surprise, a video screen lit up in the wall beside me. On the screen was an older gentleman who looked very much like Jacob and Adam. He spoke in a soft voice. "Forgive the unusual nature of this call," he said. "We programmed this screen to play this message when someone sat nearby. This is not a normal shiva ritual; but then, this is not a normal shiva. Normally I would introduce myself as Isaiah, Jacob's father, and share my thanks with you for joining us, taking your hand and thanking you. I cannot take your hand; but please, I would be honored if you would record an answer. Please tell me who you are, and share with me a memory of Jacob."

I turned to the screen. The arrangement made sense. The current light-speed delay between Earth and Mars was thirty minutes round trip. Isaiah must have recorded this message fifteen minutes ago. Now, when we told our memories, it would be fifteen minutes before those got back to him.

"I am so sorry for your loss, Mr. Simons," I said. "I am Rosalia Morais, a resident of Maxwell City. I was . . ." I swallowed hard. "I was the one who found his body. Along with my husband, Nicolau Aames." I cringed at that. Nick was famous across the solar system, both for his Mars mission and for his purported mutiny aboard the *Aldrin*. I did not want Mr. Simons to think I was name-dropping in the middle of his mourning. But there was nothing I could do except continue. "I do not think he suffered."

Anthony tapped my arm, shaking his head, and I remembered the tradition. A story . . . "There are many stories about Jacob. He was one of the earlier permanent residents here. I think my favorite story is when

Nick and I first arrived. Jacob was one of the first residents to greet us, and he said— Let me think, I want to get his words correct. He said, 'Welcome to Mars. Your new life begins here. You're one of us now, and that's all that counts.' And he meant it. He helped us find work for a while, helped us find a home, and helped us move into larger quarters once we established our own business and could afford it. And . . ." I had trouble continuing. "And he was so kind to my Nick. You may have heard stories. So many people judge Nick before they ever meet him, based on what they have heard—most of which is lies. They see a revered founder, or a major scoundrel, or a demanding martinet. But to Jacob, Nick was just a friend. We lost touch as the city grew, and our business and his took us in different directions. We saw each other at parties now and then. But I shall never forget. He made us welcome on Mars."

Anthony gripped my shoulders, and I leaned into him, sobbing. I knew this was wrong. I knew that I was supposed to help Mr. Simons with his grief, not indulge my own. But I'm only human. It had suddenly hit me how we had let time and business pull us away from a friend, and now we would never have the chance to reach back out to him.

Then Anthony told a story as well. He had been here longer than Jacob and Adam, from the very first voyage of the *Aldrin*. He had come down as a spoiled billionaire's son; but with a lot of determination and with help from Nick and Chuks and Connie, he had turned himself into a damn fine Martian scientist. And that is what he spoke of: Adam and Jacob and how much they had added to the science effort on Mars. Also how sorry he had been to see them take off on their own, but how happy he had been for them as well.

By the time Anthony was done, Nick had joined us. I introduced him to Isaiah Simons, and I explained that the gentleman was hoping for stories about Jacob. Nick being Nick, he told a work story. It was short, typical Nick.

"I wish you could be here to hear this in person, Mr. Simons," Nick said. "My top story about Jacob and Adam is when they formed their own business. That was early in the era of Martian settlement. Independent operations were still rare, not like the numbers we have today, and were considered high risk. Jacob and Adam sought business insurance from São Paulo Mutual, one of the prime underwriters of ventures here on Mars. I often do contract investigations for SPM, and they asked me to audit the facilities, to make sure the business was fit for underwriting. That's boring work, no challenge at all. I just go through the facility, and I write up all the discrepancies that I find. Then I give a final recommendation of whether the business can remediate the discrepancies and operate in a safe function compatible with underwriting. Can they figure out Mars? Can they survive, and thrive, or will they get somebody killed?" Anthony looked at Nick with curious eyes; but I had heard this story before, and I knew where it was heading. Nick went on, "But with Simons Brothers Labs, I had a challenge all right: finding any discrepancies to report. I looked. I looked hard. I spent extra time. And I *always* find discrepancies."

I added, "He does."

Nick continued, "The entire time, they just stood, leaning back against the lab table, arms crossed as they watched me. If they'd had smug looks on their faces, I would've made something up, just to shock them out of their complacency. But no: they were patient, they were confident, and they were pleasant. Mr. Simons, in my entire career, I have never given out a 100 percent on an inspection report. Except that one. You raised your sons to pay attention to details. You can be proud of their work. You can be proud of Jacob, and of Adam."

I noticed the far corner of the room had another video screen, and Mrs. Simons looked out from there, talking to Alonzo and a couple of researchers. Others had come in while we had been speaking to the video screen. I realized that other people might have stories to tell as well; so I reached out to the screen, touching it as if I could reach through to touch Mr. Simons. "We shall let someone else come talk to you now, sir. Again, we are very sorry for your loss. And Mars's loss as well."

I stood up and moved to the third corner, the one opposite the kitchen, and Nick and Anthony followed me. As I passed through the room, I saw Althea standing by the kitchen door, talking to . . . The woman turned, and I saw that I was right, it was Carla Grace. I did not think she had ever met Jacob or Althea, but I could be wrong. I hoped that the woman had the class not to be politicking here; but after her tactless interview . . .

Beside Carla stood her campaign manager, Françoise Merced—though he usually went by Francis here on Mars. He was watching the conversation carefully, and unobtrusively making notes on his comp as he did. So maybe politicking, maybe not: Merced was not the type to let any information go to waste if it might prove useful to the campaign. Oh well. Jacob was dead, Althea was in mourning, but life on Mars went on.

We sat. Shortly Adam came by to join us. We told him more stories. I was surprised to find how few stories were only Jacob stories, and how many were Adam stories as well. The two had been inseparable through much of their time on Mars.

But that had changed when Ilse had left, and Adam had thrown himself more into the business, heavily marketing their services while Jacob did solo missions that they never would have taken before. They had gotten overconfident; but that was not something to bring up now.

So instead I told of the time I drove Jacob out for a core sample survey where some new settlements had been proposed. Anthony told of the time that Jacob had run against him for mayor. It had been the most unusual election Anthony had ever sat, because they had been such good friends that neither would speak out against the other. It was also the closest race Anthony had ever run on Mars—until this one.

Nick told a brief story about introducing Jacob to caipirinhas and how they had had so many, Jacob had ended up sleeping on our couch. In the morning, Jacob had insisted on repaying the hospitality by making an incredible breakfast. A better breakfast than Nick makes, and Nick is a pretty good cook.

Adam smiled weakly, and we sat in silence for a while until he drifted away. I wondered how mechanical this whole process felt to him and Althea: us moving from station to station in the room, like a choreographed dance, to wait our turn to pay respects to each surviving family member. I wondered if we had been in a house on Earth, with more rooms and more conversation nooks, would it have had the same choreographed flow? Or would it be more random?

But then I thought that in this case, "mechanical" might be a synonym for "ritual." The purpose might be to let the visitors comfort each mourner in their own time, but organized so that that time was today, the day of the burial.

Whether by design or not, eventually we drifted over to the corner where Althea sat. Her eyes were dry now, but red and weary. We sat silently as she reached over and took my hand; but she said nothing, and so we honored the ritual in that respect as well. Until she chose to talk, we would sit in silence.

But others were not so observant. From the corner over by Adam came voices—not raised voices, but too loud for this occasion. Peering around the center island, I saw someone I did not recognize: an older man, gray haired, wearing expensive, well-tailored clothes. I heard him say, "We have to have those reports, Adam." Adam murmured something, and the man replied, "What do you mean a week?" Again Adam kept his voice low, and he waved his hand to try to get the speaker to lower his voice as well.

I gently pulled my hand free from Althea's, I strode across the room, and I put my hand on the large, loud man's shoulder. The fabric felt like silk. Who wears silk on Mars? "This is a day of mourning," I whispered. "Lower your voice! Show some respect."

"I don't give a damn about respect," the man said. I glared at him. When I had been an admiral, that glare had silenced many a junior officer. It was nice to see I still had the touch. The man lowered his voice before he continued, "I don't care. I need those reports. Adam promised me I'd have them by today."

"And you are . . . ?"

"Philippe Trudeau," the man said.

I did not know his face, but I recognized the name. "Trudeau Labs." Trudeau was a leading scientist and a vocal Saganist.

"Yes," he answered.

I glanced at Adam. "Adam, do you want him to leave?"

"Yes." Adam's eyes were moist, almost ready to tear. "Please, Philippe, please leave. Come back in a week."

"I don't have a week," Trudeau answered.

"They are sitting shiva, Monsieur Trudeau," I said. "That is a seven-day ritual. They cannot transact business during those seven days."

"Preposterous!" Again his voice rose. "We should let the scientific exploration of Mars fall behind for some primitive superstition? The body is buried, man, move on."

There were gasps around the room. Grace and Merced looked up from the screen near them. Their eyes were wide, their faces shocked. Adam looked ready to punch Trudeau. Over by Nick and Anthony, Althea broke into tears again.

I crouched slightly, sliding my hand from Trudeau's shoulder until my forearm crossed his windpipe. Just a little pressure, and I would crush his trachea. "I think you should leave now, Monsieur Trudeau."

"Get your—"

I squeezed. Just enough to make him gag, not enough to do permanent damage. He said no more.

"I am going to walk you to the door," I continued. "You will not disturb this grieving family anymore. You will wait a week for whatever you are expecting; or so help me, it will be a week before you can talk again."

Using my right arm, I nudged him to his feet. We crossed the room, and I shoved him out the door.

As the door slid closed, I turned, and Nick was behind me. He had my back. Always. I didn't have to say anything. I just touched his shoulder, and he gripped mine.

After that scene, though, the mood in the room changed. An awkward cloud hung over everything. By ones and twos, visitors started slowly making their good-byes and leaving. Nick and Anthony and I were the last to leave. We stood at the door, and Adam saw us out. "If you need anything, Adam," I said, "just call."

"Thank you," he answered. "Now we must be alone. We must reflect and remember. We shall rejoin the world in a week."

3. Consequences

The next day, I got another call from Anthony. "Hello, Anthony. Let me get Nick."

"No, Rosalia," Anthony answered. "I'm afraid my business is with you this morning."

"What?"

"Philippe Trudeau has filed an assault complaint against you."

"Oh, that! The man was being an ass, and you all saw it."

"We saw it. There are plenty of witnesses who will testify that what you did was entirely appropriate; but technically, he's right. You threatened to crush his larynx, and that's assault. You laid hands on him. That's battery. And I hate to involve you in politics, but he's a prominent Saganist. Everyone knows you and Nick are my friends, and this doesn't look good. Alonzo says if the Saganists think I'm going easy on my friends, it could endanger our coalition. They won't trust me."

"Nonsense," I said. "This has nothing to do with politics."

"*Everything* is political at this point, Rosie. The story is already on the smaller news streams, and the others may pick it up. I can make this go away, in time; but for now, I need you to come down to Admin and make a statement."

I sighed. "Is this the path of least resistance, Anthony?"

"I'm afraid so. Cooperation is the fastest way to get this behind us."

"All right. Nick and I were going to scout locations for survival school, but that can wait, I guess. I shall be there as soon as I can."

☾

I found Nick in the bath stall, showering. On the shelf by the door was a small blue box, an e-reader and music player that was Nick's only tangible legacy from Grandma Ruth. It was an ancient bit of technology, but Nick kept it working. It was playing an old popular street song from our youth in São Paulo, and Nick was singing along. Badly. Nick was an excellent dancer, but singing was never one of his talents.

I paused the music. "Nico," I said, "I'm afraid I have a change of plans." I explained Anthony's call, and Nick grew livid. Someone else might not ever notice. You would have to know him as well as I do to realize that he was angry. We had had a plan. He knows plans have to change—despite his reputation, Nick is anything but hidebound—but to change just for social reasons or bureaucratic idiocy never sat well with him.

"I don't know what this Trudeau wants that's so all-fired important," he said, "but there goes our day."

"I know. But maybe you can take care of some of the paperwork?" I said hopefully. I did not expect him to like that suggestion. Inspection reports and audits were Nick's forte, but permits and licenses did not interest him. He saw those as bureaucratic interference in our work, so they usually fell to me.

"I suppose," he said, "but maybe I should check on Althea and Adam and see if they need anything. They can't leave their apartment."

I almost laughed. Thoughtfulness does not come easily to Nick. He's just not that good at understanding people, unless he knows them very well. He has an instinct for secrets and lies and the steps people take to conceal them, but other motivations can elude him. In this case, though, being thoughtful would get him out of paperwork. "All right,"

I agreed, and then I headed out to India Tube and up the Concourse to the Admin Center.

☾

There are very few actual buildings in Maxwell City. Most of it is underground; but the Admin Center has three stories sticking out from the Martian surface, with actual windows to give views of the Coprates quadrangle. Anthony's office was a whole quarter of the top floor, suitable for entertaining dignitaries and visitors. By Martian standards, it was pure opulence, though it would have been only a large family room back on Earth. Alonzo showed me in and brought me a glass of water. I sat and waited.

Anthony showed up a few minutes later. "Thank you for coming in, Rosalia," he said as he sat. "Let me get Alonzo to act as a court reporter."

Anthony glanced at the ceiling—"talking" to his subcutaneous comp, I knew, though a casual observer might not notice. I had never liked the idea of implanting a computer in one's skull. It gave me shivers. I knew the argument, that it was no different from an old-style pacemaker or an artificial joint. And some people prized having data directly in their minds, fed to audio and optic nerves on demand. But I did not like being *that* connected. It was too much like changing my mind. My *self.*

But Anthony found the subcomp convenient. It helped him to manage things and recall data easily. Nick had told me that as a young man Anthony had been opposed to embedded technology, therapy nanos in particular; but by the time subcomps became available to the public, Anthony had had a change of heart. He got his when they were still new and quite expensive. Today they were more common.

Alonzo came back in, sat down, and started recording.

"All right," Anthony continued, "I've taken the liberty of filling in most of the statement form for you already." He pushed the form to my comp, and I looked it over. He knew my contact information and other administrivia as well as I did. "Alonzo will record your statement and attach it and a transcription to this form. Do you see any inaccuracies in the information?"

"None, Mr. Mayor."

"All right. Do you solemnly swear that the statement that you're about to give is true and accurate in your best memory?"

"I do." A signature box appeared in front of me, and I signed.

"Now that that's done . . . ," Anthony said. "Please tell me of your encounter yesterday with Monsieur Philippe Trudeau in the home of Althea Simons."

I stated the simple facts, careful not to embellish. When I was done, Anthony asked, "And at any time, did you actually intend to crush Monsieur Trudeau's windpipe?"

"No, I would not have had to. A little pressure there is enough to scare any sane person into cooperating."

Anthony's face grew pale, and he signaled Alonzo to pause the recording. When Alonzo signaled back, Anthony said to me, "You're not helping your case, Rosalia."

I shrugged. "The truth is the truth."

"Nick's rubbing off on you." Anthony sighed and signaled Alonzo to resume. Then he continued, "So you threatened, but you did not intend to carry out the threat. Why did you see the need to threaten him?"

"Because the family is in mourning. He was being disrespectful, and he refused to leave when asked."

Again Anthony signaled for a pause. "We have witnesses who say you grabbed him before you asked him to leave."

"Check with those witnesses. Adam asked him to leave before I got there."

"Are you sure?" Anthony asked. I nodded, and he signaled to restart the recording. "Continue," he said.

"I was in the best position to see him out without disrupting things any further," I explained.

"And by what authority did you act?"

"My authority as a citizen of Mars. Call it a citizen's arrest, if you would like."

Anthony shook his head. "That statute hasn't been invoked in years."

"But it is still in the Mars Compact," I said. All of our "laws" are just regulations under the authority of the Compact. "Citizen's arrest requires a reasonable explanation in plain language why the person needs to cooperate for the good of the city or the peace thereof, and how they are violating it. It then allows any citizen to apply the least force necessary to restore peace in the area. I had tried lesser force, and it had failed. I then escalated the least amount possible. But I was ready to escalate further, because otherwise Adam—"

"That's Adam Simons," Anthony cut in. "For the record."

"Yes. Adam, or my husband, Nicolau Aames, might have felt the need to step in. They might have acted in a much more aggressive fashion, him being—"

"Him, meaning Trudeau," Anthony said.

"Yes."

"So your actions were carefully calculated to restore the peace and ensure his own safety?"

"Yes."

Anthony signaled Alonzo. "You really plan to sell this, Rosie?" he asked.

"It is the truth," I answered. "Adam was furious. And Nick was ready to throw the man through the door. Possibly without opening it first."

"All right. Continue, Alonzo." Then to me he said, "Do you have anything further to say?"

I grinned. "Not for the record, no."

"Alonzo, strike that." Anthony frowned at me. "Do you have anything further to say?"

"No."

"Very well. End recording." When Alonzo signaled we were clear, Anthony added, "You couldn't resist that comment about Nick, Rosie?"

"Trudeau was being an ass. It would have served him right if I had let Nick bounce him out of there."

Anthony smiled sheepishly. "I would've done it myself, but Grace would've made an issue of that in the media for sure. And I might've lost the Saganists."

"Is that what this is all about?" I asked. "The election?"

Anthony grimaced. "It's close, Rosie. And Grace is sniffing around for any scandal to turn the tide—or any way to split off the Saganists. I have to be extra careful in everything that comes out of this office now. I hate it! I just want to get the job done."

"So is there anything else you need, Anthony?"

"Company for lunch, if you'd like."

I checked my comp. Nick had left a note saying he was out shopping for supplies for our scouting mission, so I had some time free. "That sounds good."

"Should I order in, sir?" Alonzo asked.

"No," Anthony answered. "It's good for me to be seen out in public. If you could make some reservations for us, that would be fine."

☾

We lunched at Zeb's, a Cajun place—or so Zeb claimed. Zeb had a prime location off the first level of the Concourse, the largest retail and entertainment space in Maxwell City. It was directly across the Main Dome from the Admin Center, and popular with city workers, shoppers, and scientists. And with tourists, if they made it this far, but most tourists were happy to stay in the port district.

Zeb was a former Mars explorer, had learned under Chuks himself, but restaurateur was his calling. I did not have enough experience with Cajun food to know how close Zeb's food came, but I had always liked his fare. I ordered the jambalaya, along with Martian Springs, a local mineral water. The meal was delicious, as usual. The jambalaya was just spicy enough; and it even had real shrimp, one of the few animals we farmed on Mars.

Anthony and I talked, and he danced around the topic of a police force and the police chief position again. I did not take the bait. When Nick said no, I knew he meant no. If Anthony wanted to press Nick, he would have to do it himself. I was not going to get in the middle.

When I got back to our apartment, Nick was still gone. So I sat down and accepted the inevitable: I started filling in license requests and permit applications for our survival school. I could do this myself faster than I could cajole Nick into doing it. We were as close together as we had ever been, but he was still just as stubborn with me as he was with anyone else.

I was working on the last form when Nick returned. He gave me a good excuse to set the form aside. I got up, greeted him with a kiss, and looked into his face. There were subtle traces of worry there. "How's Althea?" I asked.

Nick walked past me and into the room. "What can I say? She buried her husband yesterday, that's how she is. She's contemplating the meaning today, her and Adam."

"He is not back in his apartment?"

"No."

I was unsure how that sat with the shiva rituals. I had read that they were not allowed to travel out of their homes except for certain conditions, emergencies and such. That wasn't Adam's apartment; but if he had not been there, Althea would have been alone. And so would he. I was no rabbi. It was not my call, but it made sense to me.

"It's probably good that he's there," Nick said. "Somebody's going to have to help her eat all that food."

"Oh?"

"I brought over some bauru, some Martian Springs, and some frozen vegetables. I'd wanted to make sure that they had plenty to eat, but I was surprised by how much they had. I don't remember guests bringing that much food yesterday, but I guess some must've slipped by."

Slipped by Nick? I had never seen that happen. "Well, they cannot shop for food for seven days," I said. "They probably stocked up before the service."

"That makes sense," Nick said. "There's at least a week's worth of food there, and I might guess two."

"It will not go to waste," I said. "She can store it. But now we need to look at this." I pulled him over to the couch and to the paperwork. "I have most of this done, but we need to discuss a few things."

So we filled out the last form, and then we went over all of my earlier work. That lifted my spirits a little. Even on a small task like that, we made a good team. When we were done with the paperwork, we pulled up maps of the quadrangle, and we started plotting out locations for our Martian survival lessons.

4. EXPEDITIONS

While Nick was lax about filling out paperwork, he was a master at pushing it through the system. He would follow each piece relentlessly through the bureaucracy. At every step, he would call and check out how it was going, telling the clerks how to do their jobs. Once upon a time, he had written the protocols for this sort of work; and although his regulations had been mostly superseded, he still knew how the system worked. When he had to, he would hound a clerk until they finished the paperwork just to get rid of him.

So it was only four days later that we had our freshly printed certificate of operations for the business as well as our expanded permits for Martian surface operations. Back on Earth, at least in the free societies, people went where they wanted, when they wanted, and worked at what they wanted. The closer a country got to that ideal, the more comfortable I was. But on Mars, under Initiative jurisdiction and the Mars Compact, conditions were different. Every resource had a cost, and the loss of it could potentially affect the survival of others. Every expedition could lead to a rescue operation if things went wrong, putting other lives at risk in the process. We had seen that just recently with Jacob. It had taken Nick and I three days to find him; and when we had, it had almost resulted in an accident of our own.

Plus there were scientific protocols to be observed, lest we contaminate some new discovery that could only be made on Mars. That was the constant concern of the Saganists. Before an area could be exploited for commercial purposes, there had to be proper surveys and research. So between the Initiative and the Saganists, only authorized personnel had true freedom of movement outside the city. There were a number of small, independent surveyors and prospectors, but they operated under strict mission rules. The Libertists chafed under these rules, and sometimes bent them—occasionally broke them, leading to flare-ups with the Saganists that Anthony and Alonzo had to tamp down. So Anthony was taking extra care to enforce the protocols.

But with our new certificates, Nick and I had free rein across all of Coprates quadrangle. In exchange, any research team could ask us to conduct experiments while we were out. And our reputation for thoroughness preceded us: it was not ten minutes after the arrival of our certificates before the first email arrived, asking about our plans for future expeditions and where they might go, along with our availability for performing experiments.

When I saw the name on the email, I could not help laughing. Nick looked over and asked, "What is it?"

"It's from Philippe Trudeau."

"Really?"

"Well, not him, but one of his assistants."

"You tell him—"

"Wait! Down, Nico. He starts by informing me that all charges have been dropped. He then asks me if we can do a series of core samples—the ones that Adam promised."

"That's simple enough work."

"You have not heard the rest. He wants to know if we can start today. It looks like about two days of work, and he would really like to have it in three."

"We don't need that business," Nick said. "I see no reason to hurry on his account."

"There is one more point. Listen: 'Monsieur Trudeau is willing to pay the rate that he agreed upon with the Simons brothers, plus an additional premium because of the short schedule. And he adds that if this work is done on time, he will find it within his heart to avoid a breach of contract suit against Adam Simons.'"

"That *sacano!*"

"He wants it fast," I said, "and Adam cannot do it. This would be a favor for Adam and Althea. The last thing they need right now is a legal battle. And it would help Anthony with the Saganists."

Nick looked over my shoulder, reading the request for proposal. "We can do that in two days. Ask Adam to send us the mission profile—if that doesn't break shiva. We'd better get moving."

C

Core samples are finicky work. It depends on the soil. When it was soft, we could practically push the bore in. When it was hard, it was a delicate balancing act to push the drill through, but not push so hard as to dull the bit or break the bore.

But Nick and I had done plenty of these in our time. We were just pulling up our fifth core and wrapping it for analysis when Nick stopped and looked around. "He was nowhere near here," he said.

"What?" I asked.

"Jacob. Whatever he was working on, it wasn't part of this survey."

I nodded, a pointless gesture in a helmet. "Adam never said what they were working on, but it must have been a different project. You know what their business had been like. They had taken on so many projects, plus they had expansion plans in the works. I had never heard of any out in this area, but we just have not kept in touch like we used to. Maybe it wasn't a project at all, just long-term planning."

"Still," Nick said, "he was a long way from his crawler when we found him. I wonder what drew him to the crevasse."

"We may never know," I said, "now that it has collapsed."

Nick sighed, and then went silent, staring off into the distance as if he could see the crevasse from here. After all these years, I could guess what he was thinking: there were unanswered questions, and he himself had unwittingly buried the answers. He would kick himself for that for a long time.

We finished our scheduled core samples for that day early, so we got in three more before the sun set over Phoenicis Lacus quadrangle. Then we went into the crawler, took off our suits, and settled in for a nice meal of tofu and tomatoes. I was very proud of our tomato crop that year. Our bedroom was half-full of Lada units. The Russian-designed hydroponic systems produced a lot of fresh vegetables in a very small space, and without breaking our consumables budget. The loss of bedroom space was worth it to have fresh tomatoes whenever we wanted them. They reminded me of *mamãe's* garden when I was a child. We had been poor, but we were seldom hungry, thanks to the garden she had kept. The tomatoes were always my favorite, and Nick knew that, so he had surprised me with the Lada units on our first anniversary. Between the tomato plants and Nick's bonsai, our apartment was very green.

After a night in the crawler, we got back to work. Again we finished the core samples early. We got them back to Maxwell City, and we handed them over to a tech from Trudeau's lab. Then we went home to scrub off two days of suit dirt.

With a little free time in our schedule, I had an idea. "Should we go check in on Althea, see how she is doing?"

Nick looked at his comp. "It's too soon," he said. "I think she's still sitting shiva. Let's give her one more day."

"Is she?" I wondered. "Is she supposed to sit for seven Earth days? Or seven Martian days? In the Hebrew tradition, the day starts at sunset. I know that is local sunset, but does that apply here?"

"I asked Jacob about that once," Nick said. "Given the importance of the calendar and the Sabbath, I wondered if Jewish rituals followed the twenty-four hours, thirty-nine minutes, and thirty-six seconds of the Martian day or the twenty-four hours of the Earth day. He said when the first Jewish settlers came to Mars, they consulted with the rabbis; and he said that as usual, when you have two rabbis, you get three opinions. Some argued that in the Torah it is written about sunrise and sunset, not about twenty-four hours. Others argued that if you're going to base your calendar on local astronomical phenomena, then you would have to base your month on the waxing and waning of Martian moons. Even if you went with Deimos, that would end up with a month of only thirty and one-third hours. You might as well call that a day. And they also argued that bar mitzvahs and bat mitzvahs would happen much later because of the longer Martian year. Why should the children have to wait that long to become adults?"

"So what did they decide?"

"Like so many other human traditions, there are different points of view, and they try to get along. They use lunar months, and where it matters, lunar years. They use Martian days for everything else. There are some in the community who see it differently, but I know that's how Jacob and Althea practiced. So they're still in their seventh *Martian* day of shiva."

"All right," I said, "we can stay in and eat then." And we did. Nick made an excellent tofu salad, with pão de queijo on the side. It was simple, but better than survival rations. And then we went to bed.

☽

We woke to find a recorded message from Adam, thanking us for fulfilling his contract with Trudeau and apologizing that we had been drawn into the unpleasantness. We stopped by briefly to see Althea. She offered us a light lunch and some coffee. I took the coffee out of courtesy, but I still could not enjoy Martian-grown beans. Brazil had spoiled me for what coffee should taste like: rich, strong, and earthy.

Then we left, and we resumed planning our scouting expedition. Nick was eager to get out on the Martian surface again—not for core sampling, just pure exploration. He had spent so many years on the *Aldrin*, safeguarding travelers to Mars while never getting to go himself. So many had traveled in his footsteps, to explore the planet that he had helped open up. Now he was not part of any official mission. The System Initiative would sooner see him in prison than on a Martian team. But we still filed our own reports, and we had been published in several astronomical journals. Since he had been a very little boy, Nick had craved being out here, discovering, and setting his own course. And Mars still had plenty of opportunities for that.

The next day, we packed up enough food, water, and air for two Martian weeks. We only expected to be out for one, but we both believed in planning for the worst. Then we signed out a crawler and went out for our first real exploration in almost a Martian year.

Exploring Mars was as close as we ever got to the honeymoon we never had. Exploration was in my blood, too, and we both had a passion to do it right and safely. Nick, at least, had been on the second *Bradbury* mission. Even with all its troubles, he had had time to explore Mars as part of an official mission. But he and I had both gotten sidetracked for decades. When I was stationed here, I had been the admiral in charge of orbital traffic control. A flag-rank officer in many ways has less freedom than the newest enlisted personnel. I was free to explore Mars as much as I wanted—between all of my official duties. That meant that on a really good day, I could have gotten as far as two hours away from my command post. And most of the time I had been stationed on orbit.

But now we were civilians, virtual exiles on Mars, and we no longer had official duties. So anytime we got to explore Mars for real, well, it brought back our youth. It made both of us feel like kids again; but older, wiser kids, who understood how many ways Mars could kill you.

We spent the first three days in travel, back and forth across the Coprates quadrangle. In the morning, while Nick drove, I made observations, took videos, and annotated maps. Then in the afternoon, we traded places, Nick climbing up on top of the crawler while I drove. Every night, we went over our maps and videos, identifying points of interest and sorting them into three different categories. One was places that looked like good opportunities for further surveys we might turn into research papers for publication. The second was places that would provide interesting obstacles that would challenge the survival school students, but hopefully not kill them. Killing your customers is never a good idea—but neither is making them so weak and foolish that they cannot survive on their own. And we both knew that accidents happened in training. If we could not live with that, we should scrap our business plans now.

The third category was locations for a special project that we never discussed with anyone else: São Paulo, a Martian homestead that we would build for ourselves, far away from anyone else's rules. It was just a dream at that point, but a shared dream. A vision we both had had since our first arrival on Mars. Someday . . .

At the end of our fourth day, we made our first camp. We were both tired of being stuck in the crawler, so we broke out the Mars shelter, set it up, and tested it out. This was a self-inflating model similar to those used on the Azevedo expedition to Mars, where the professor had gotten himself killed, all those years ago; but it had many improvements designed by people who had actually lived on Mars for a decade and more, and who understood the territory better. Once we had it secured to the ground and tested for leaks, we climbed inside and out of our pressure suits. It was nice to have so much room after sleeping on the narrow floor of the crawler for three nights.

When we were sure that the dome was secure and would shelter us for a night, we broke out a picnic lunch: feijoada made with black beans and shrimp, and *pastéis* filled with cheese. It was simple fare, reheated in a small radiant oven; but after four days of survival rations, it was heavenly.

As I sat back and enjoyed one last pastéi, Nick stood and walked to the dome wall. He found a zipper for the privacy cover, and he started unzipping. "What are you doing, Nico?" I asked.

"There should be stars" was all he said as he peeled back the opaque cover, revealing the transparent outer layer of the dome. The sun had set, and yes, there were stars. Everywhere. When there were no storms, night on Mars was almost as beautiful as being in space.

Then Nick returned to his backpack and pulled out a surprise: Grandma Ruth's old blue e-reader. He pushed a button, and I heard the familiar opening guitar notes of "Brigas Nunca Mais." Our song: "Never fight again."

"May I have this dance, *meu amor*?" Nick asked, holding out his arms.

In one smooth motion, I leaped from the ground and into his arms. Nick caught me with perfect timing, and we danced. We could not do the Coriolis leap that we had mastered back on Farport Station. There was no significant Coriolis effect on a planet, and the dome roof was too low. Plus even in Martian gravity, we were getting a little old for that. But Nick had lost none of his grace, and the weariness seeped from my bones as the music enveloped us. We danced for hours: every old song, every memory. For one night, Mars was just the two of us.

Later we made love in the starlight. Afterward I lay back on top of him. In the low gravity, he was the softest, warmest pillow, with his strong, hairy arms clasping me to him, close and safe. Then with his right arm, without saying a word, he pointed out Deimos passing overhead. I knew Phobos was soon to follow, and I spotted it first. Then we spotted objects in the deep black sky, stars and planets and man-made satellites. A few galaxies, even. We whispered their names to each other. Canopus. Acrux, Mimosa, Gacrux, and Delta Crucis. Rigel and Betelgeuse and Bellatrix. Andromeda and the Magellanics—not to mention our own Milky Way. Plus Jupiter and the Galileans, beckoning across the AUs. These names were beautiful poetry shared between us. We lay there, sharing the night sky. Sharing the closeness, and what followed after.

5. THE EDGE OF THE CREVASSE

So we passed the time in our outing: In the days we planned out simulated emergencies, and in the evenings we planned the academic side of the training. And every night, we lay beneath our stars.

Toward the end, I noticed that Nick was taking an odd route back. I was riding on the roof again, making sightings, and I noticed something up ahead. I checked the map. Then I called down over the comm, "You are going back to the crevasse."

"Yes, we are," Nick said. "From the other side."

"Do not get too close, Nico. We already saw that the ground is unstable."

"We saw that one side was unstable. Assuming can get you killed out here. It can also make you blind to details."

"I know, Nick, I am not some greenhorn! But I think we should keep our distance. That is the best way to make sure we get home."

"I have to do it, Rosie," he said. And I knew that tone in his voice very well. He was not kidding, it was a compulsion: when he had a question, he had to know the answer.

"So what are we looking for?" I asked.

"I screwed up last time," he said. "I was so glad to get you out alive, and so sad at finding Jacob. I had so much adrenaline running through me from almost falling into the crevasse that I never thought: we only searched one side of it."

"That was the side from which he would have approached from the crawler," I said.

"But that was too long of a trip for one person to make on foot," Nick said. "He'd have to have extra oxygen packs, maybe even some water tanks. We didn't find any of that."

"So what do you think we shall find on the other side?"

"No," Nick said. "We're not guessing, we're investigating." I had heard him give that answer to his teams many times over the years.

So we continued toward the crevasse until we got within one hundred meters. Then fifty meters. "All right, Nick," I said.

The crawler stopped immediately. "What's the matter, Rosie?"

"We are here," I said. "We can go the rest of the way on foot. And with safety lines. I do not trust that edge."

"I don't think he did, either," Nick said.

"He? He, who?"

"I've been watching," Nick said. "Head over to the port side of the crawler. Look down."

I looked over the side as instructed. There, only slightly obscured by the sand whipped up by the wispy Martian winds, were crawler tracks that stopped about where ours had. Looking more closely, it looked like the crawler had backed out on the same path.

"This was recent," I said. "Hard to tell how recent, the Martian weather has been pretty mild lately. Two, maybe three weeks."

"Let's say four weeks," Nick said. "About the time Jacob went missing. It's not proof, but it's suspicious."

As I climbed down, Nick got out of the crawler. We both hooked up safety lines, and then we proceeded toward the crevasse, carefully avoiding obscuring any tracks, and videoing every step along the way. Now that we knew where to look, we found boot prints. The wind would cover them soon enough; but for now they were too deep for that.

Deep. "Nick, these are too deep," I said. "As if someone were carrying a heavy load."

"Almost double," he agreed. "But look very closely." Nick took out a laser pointer, and he outlined a second set of tracks coming back. These were shallower, already mostly buried by the wind.

"Nick, you cannot mean . . ."

"Somebody went out there, massing roughly twice that of a suited explorer. They came back with normal mass." Nick paused for a moment. "I blew it, Rosie. I should've had you video more around Jacob's body before we lifted him. I didn't realize that the ledge was going to fall."

"Do not be so hard on yourself, Nico." But I knew better. Nick's crew had always known that he expected perfection from them, but he expected more from himself.

"So someone ran Jacob out here, and then threw him in the crevasse," I continued.

"We don't know that," Nick said. "We don't have any way to tell now. All the evidence is buried. But all the indicators lead to that hypothesis. Jacob was murdered, and someone tried to hide his body."

We videoed all of the evidence, including 3D scans of the tracks, both human and crawler. Nick was damnably thorough this time: it took us the rest of the day, and I only pulled him away when it was getting too dark to work. When we got back in the crawler, I wanted to rest so that we could make an early drive back; but there was a recorded message from Anthony waiting for us on the comm: "Nick, I know you turned down that police chief position, but can I at least hire you as an investigator? It's bad, Nick. Really bad, more important than my campaign. We've got people sick. One dead already, and more may be dying. At first, we thought it was an illness, but there are no obvious connections between the victims. Yeah, we're a closed environment, but a big one. Fifty thousand people. It takes too much time for something to spread through a populace that large, so we looked for something environmental. Dr. Costello has identified it as some sort of industrial compound, very toxic. It strikes people at random. Nick, I'm afraid we've got some kind of lunatic here killing people in Maxwell City. Your city. I know you can't let that stand. Please, wherever you are, come back. We need your help."

"Nick," I said, "what could be happening?"

But Nick was already on the comm. As soon as he connected to the Admin Center, he said, "Give me Mayor Holmes." He did not bother identifying himself. For once, being recognized as a founder worked to his advantage. The communications clerk treated him as if he had authority that he really did not, and she pushed his call straight through.

When Anthony's face appeared on the screen, Nick wasted no time. "Anthony, it's in the food supply. Shut down the Tomb, now! Shut it down, seal it off, and don't let any more organics from it into the city's nutrition system. Issue a recall notice for any food grown from organics dated from Jacob's funeral forward. But whatever you do, *don't* let them flush the Tomb or dispose of any organics that you got from it. We need that as evidence."

Anthony's eyebrows rose. "Nick, are you investigating from out on the Martian plains?"

"I'm telling you how to save lives. Tell Marcus the concentration should be low, so he's going to have to look for traces in the food." Despite Nick's feelings, he respected Marcus as a medical examiner. "You're probably all getting a dose, but it's so low you don't notice it. But some people are more sensitive. Some fatally so."

Anthony got the faraway look that indicated he was sending instructions through his subcomp. Then his eyes focused back on us. "Nick, this is going to really hamper our food production."

"How much food do dead people produce? Shut down all the restaurants. Shut down all production from hydroponics until we have a chance to clean the whole system. Tell everyone they're going to have to settle for emergency rations for a while."

"Are you sure?"

"Damn it, Anthony! Move, before someone else dies. And one more thing . . ."

"What's that?"

Nick's voice caught, but he said what he had to say: "Arrest Althea and Adam Simons. Suspicion of murder."

☾

We drove through the night, violating at least a dozen safety protocols that Nick himself had written. As we drove, Nick told me what he had deduced. "Althea and Adam had tried to have Jacob buried in the ground because they knew that otherwise, the poison in his system would get out into the Maxwell City food supply. It would be dilute, as I told Anthony, but still a risk to those with weakened systems or with a sensitivity."

I saw his point. "But then when they failed to stop the recycling, they took advantage of the shiva ritual to stock up on food that they knew would be safe. Jacob's body would not be recycled until a week after burial."

Nick nodded. "They planned to simply eat stores until it was safe to eat city food again."

A little later, Anthony called again. "We've had two more deaths, but Dr. Costello has identified the compound. It's a synthetic solvent, highly soluble in water. It's a minor irritant to most, but it triggers something akin to anaphylaxis in those who are more sensitive. Depends on their genetics."

"So if Adam knew that Jacob was sensitive, he could guess that he was, too," I said.

"But less likely for Althea," Nick replied. "Anthony, I need to talk to her."

6. MISSING PIECES

We found Althea in a holding cell in the lower levels of the Admin Center. Maxwell City did not really have a prison, although the Initiative base at Fort Hudson had a stockade. For anything longer than overnight, the city usually transferred prisoners there. Maxwell City had never had enough crime to need jails of its own.

But maybe that had changed.

As we came in, Althea rose from a small plastic chair. "Nick! Rosalia!" she said, tears running down her face. "They're talking crazy things! They're talking . . . They say that I . . . they say that I killed my Jacob!"

Nick did not blink as he looked into her eyes and asked, "How long have you been sleeping with Adam?"

Suddenly the desperation in Althea's face changed to rage, and she slapped Nick. He did not react, he just stared, and he continued, "Was it before Ilse left? Is that why she left, because you and Adam were having an affair?"

Althea's eyes flared; but then, suddenly, she deflated, and she flopped back down onto the plastic chair. "That woman was like a sister to me," she said. "I would never hurt her. But when she . . . abandoned Adam . . ."

"What?" I asked. "You just had to comfort him?"

"It wasn't like that! Jacob was out so much. In the field, doing work. And Adam—"

"Oh, spare me," I said. "You are going to tell me how lonesome he was. How kind, how sensitive. Was he good in the sack? Was that why you killed Jacob?"

"Killed?" Althea broke down, crying. It seemed genuine to me.

I pulled Nick aside, and I whispered, "Nick, I do not think she is lying. I think Jacob's death surprised her. I do not think she ever considered that Adam might have killed his brother."

"I don't see it."

"I know, Nico. You don't see it. But . . ." I looked back at Althea sobbing, practically slumping off the chair. This woman was suffering a loss all over again. She and Jacob may have had problems, but she had not wanted him dead. "Trust me on this, Nick. It is my area."

I stared into Nick's face as he stared into Althea's. He would see it eventually. I took his hand and pulled him toward the door. "Come on, Nick, let us go see Anthony."

As the cell door closed behind us, Nick said, "Adam was out in the city, drumming up business, while Jacob went out on the surface to carry out the experiments. It was a perfect opportunity for Adam to get closer to his own brother's wife while he ensured that Jacob was away."

"It happens, Nick," I said.

"I know it happens, but I liked Adam." Nick punched his comm. "Anthony, where is Adam? We need to talk to him next."

"We're still looking for him, Nick," Anthony answered. "As best we can tell, he disappeared before we even started looking for him."

"Are you sure? He's not in his lab?"

Anthony consulted his subcomp. "We've locked it down. He's not in there, so we need to sweep it for evidence."

Nick looked at me, and he asked, "Do you need the help of two expert incident investigators?"

Anthony grinned, but it was a sad effort. There wasn't much to smile about. "I thought you'd never ask."

☽

There were two Maxwell City Public Safety officers standing guard in front of the lab entrance on level 2. We walked up, and the taller of the officers stood straighter, crossing her arms across her chest. She was a large, muscular blonde woman who reminded me a little bit of Nick's old bosun, Smitty. Her badge read *Vile*. "I'm sorry, Founder, but no one is allowed in without authorization by Mayor Holmes."

"We have mayoral authorization," Nick said, "to go in and investigate the labs. Haven't you received the authorization yet?"

"No, sir."

"Then check already, Vile. Why are you wasting our time?"

Vile tapped her comp, and then she nodded. "We're to let you in and render any assistance you require."

"Thank you," Nick answered. "Just keep everyone out. We don't want to be disturbed."

The guards opened the door to Simons Brothers Labs. Nick and I stood just on the threshold and looked in. The labs were dark, just as Anthony had said. I shined my light inside.

The fake wood wall panels soaked up the light, leaving the room mostly in shadow. Beyond the entry, desk drawers were pulled out, chairs ripped open, decorations smashed.

Nick and I did not waste time on the obvious: someone had been here before us, searching; but it was too soon to speculate on who or why. Instead we spent the morning videoing everything from every angle. I used a tiny borescope to view inside of small openings. Nick used chemical sensors to search for organics and toxins in the air. We took every measurement we could while touching nothing.

Then after a quick lunch, we went back to work, this time opening every drawer and compartment, lifting and looking under every piece of debris. There were dozens of places that Nick and I identified where information could be hidden. Whoever had searched the place had been an amateur.

I pointed at a wall panel that lay on the floor, apart from other debris, as if to draw attention to itself. It was a double-sided panel, the kind often used in spacecraft—but almost never in subsurface construction. The hollow middle is designed to hold vacuum resin, a compound that seals and hardens when exposed to vacuum. The labs were deep underground, with no need for vacuum seals.

I pointed at the panel, and Nick lifted a corner. "Look at this," he said. I looked closely at the edge. There was a thin crack between front and back. Vac panels were supposed to be sealed.

As I videoed, Nick pulled out his knife and carefully pried apart the edges of the panel. Inside was a thin compartment filled with clear plastic sleeves for data chips. Five sleeves were empty; but in the last, we found a single data chip. On it, in Adam's handwriting, was a single word: *Nick.*

"It's too easy," Nick said. "Does he think I'm stupid?"

"He was not hiding it from you, Nick," I answered. "He wanted to keep it from"—I waved around at the mess—"whoever did this."

Nick shook his head. "For all we know, *he* did this to mislead us, then hid this message in such an obvious place."

I touched Nick's arm. "Obvious to you, Nick. Adam did not really know you, though. Jacob would have known better, but Adam thinks he is too smart for us."

"He was. We have four dead to prove that." He sighed. "I suppose we'd better find out what he wanted to tell us."

Nick pulled the chip from the sleeve, put it in his comp, and ran a security scan. When the light turned green, Nick tapped "Play," and Adam's face and voice came from the comp. "Mayor Holmes, Nick, whoever finds this . . . I've done a terrible thing. I've committed the crime of Cain. And now because of me, others have died as well. You have to believe me, I didn't expect that. I tried. I really tried to get you to bury Jacob's body but . . ." Adam gathered himself up to look straight at the camera. "This is my confession. I, Adam Simons, murdered my brother, Jacob Simons, in cold blood. I poisoned his water before he went out on his last expedition. I knew how much reserves he carried, and how the toxin would build up and kill him before he could notice. I knew the combination would be quick and lethal. Then I went out in a crawler, and I found his body. I switched out his comp and his water tanks, so that even though I didn't expect anyone to ever find his body, it would look like he had an accident. I should have known, Nick, that you would find him. You never give up."

Adam looked around. "I have embarrassed my friends. I have shamed the Libertists. And for what I have done to my family, there is no forgiveness. You won't find me. This is my crime only. Althea didn't know. She was weak, I took advantage of that, but she is a good woman. Her hands are clean of this blood. She did not know. Jacob had only started to suspect that I had been keeping double books. That I had skimmed from the business and billed clients for services that we had never delivered, giving them only fraudulent reports. Some have found out, and they wanted satisfaction. But they shall not have it. All of my records, all of my private accounts, shall be lost with me."

Adam leaned closer, and I saw tears in his eyes. "Please, tell my mother, my father . . ." The recording of Adam shook his head. "No, there's nothing you can tell them. They'll never forgive me for this. Nor should they, nor Althea. Nor Ilse. I'm going out to the farthest areas that we have studied. You won't find the body this time. I won't get even a Martian Tomb, and no one will sit shiva for me. I don't deserve it." Then the image of Adam reached forward, and the recording cut off.

☾

Three days later, we were in our apartment, planning our survival school. Without either of us saying it, throwing ourselves into the school gave us something to take our minds off the Simons tragedies.

We were surprised out of our work when the door announcer said, "Mayor Anthony Holmes is here."

Nick and I both rose. "Let him in," I said.

The door slid open, and Anthony came in. "Nick, Rosie, I . . ."

I reached out and took Anthony's hand. "'Good to see you' does not seem right these days, does it?" I said.

"There's nothing good," Anthony answered. "Can I sit down?"

We all sat back around the worktable. Anthony looked at our holographic model of survival school. "Interesting. This is based on Chuks's designs."

"We started there," Nick said. "He laid down the principles, but we know so much more about Mars now, decades later. So many ways that Mars can kill the unwary."

I glanced at Anthony's face. I doubted that Nick would have noticed the shadow that passed over it. Anthony made a good show of covering it up by concentrating on the model. "It makes me wish I had time to go through it again," he said. "But this campaign takes up so much of my time. And now . . . Adam was a prominent Libertist. There's no obvious connection from the murder to the party, but that hasn't stopped the journos from searching for it. I barely have enough left to govern the city."

"You'll always be welcome," Nick said. "You name the class, we'll make room for you. We'll even give you an alumnus discount." But Nick had never been good at small talk and frivolities. That overture had exhausted his capacity, and he changed the subject to one that interested him more. "So what's the word on Adam?" he asked.

Anthony looked down at his feet. "Still no sign of the body. We found the crawler out on the flat basalt plains. No tracks. Nothing anywhere within walking distance. I'm ready to declare him dead."

"Did he take a lot of air with him?" Nick said.

"Yeah," Anthony answered. "Enough to walk far away and get lost, but not enough to walk to another settlement. No, I'm convinced he wanted to die on Mars, on his own, where no one would find him. And not have to face anyone again even in death."

"And Althea?" I asked.

Anthony frowned. "Adam's confession exonerated her."

"If he was telling the truth," Nick said.

"We've got no way to prove otherwise," Anthony said. "A lot of people have suspicions, but I think she's innocent." Then after a pause, Anthony added, "Either way, it's pointless. She can't take the suspicious stares. She's been ostracized. She put in for a hardship transport to Earth, and the Initiative has agreed under the usual terms: all of her property here is forfeit, up for auction to cover her transport costs."

Nick's eyes gleamed. "Including the labs?"

"Including the labs, yes," Anthony said, "and I know what you're thinking. That might be a good reason someone searched the labs. They thought there was incriminating evidence there."

"So there might still be conspirators," I said.

"It seems that way." Anthony sighed. "That's part of why I'm here today. After the events of the past two weeks, I'm more convinced than ever that Maxwell City needs a police chief, a chief investigator. I need someone who knows Mars, knows the city, and knows how to ferret out the truth. And someone who hates loose ends as much as you do."

Nick firmly planted both feet on the ground, his hands on his knees. "I told you, Anthony, I'm not interested."

Anthony looked at Nick; and for the first time since he had arrived, he really smiled. "Who said I was talking to you, Nick? I've decided: a former admiral is as good as a founder to me." From his pocket, Anthony pulled out a shiny gold-hued badge. On it was stamped the image of Mars's eastern hemisphere, Phobos and Deimos crossing the middle. Along the top it said, ROSALIA MORAIS; around the bottom it said, CHIEF OF POLICE, MAXWELL CITY. "What do you say, Rosie?"

I looked at Nick. His face was blank, more so than usual. This would interfere with our survival school plans, but it was also important to both of us. Nick was leaving the decision up to me; but I saw only one choice.

"Yes."

7. NEW SHERIFF IN TOWN

I looked at my image in the camera screen. "Looking good, Rosalia," I said to myself. Nick wandered from the tree room toward the kitchen. I had been fishing for a compliment, knowing he could hear me, but he wasn't biting.

It did not matter. I had always liked the way I looked in a uniform; and I had not worn one since I had given up my admiral's bars, and Nick had given up the captaincy of the *Aldrin* to preserve the independence of the ship and its crew. And I knew Nick liked it, too, even if he was too stubborn to admit it.

This was a different uniform, of course. The Maxwell City Chief of Police uniform was red. Designers never tired of red when they were designing things for Mars. After all these years, it seemed pretty unimaginative to me; but that was what they had come up with, a dusky maroon color with darker-red piping. It complemented my color nicely. Even living in the underground world of Maxwell City, I never lost my tan, thanks to my Brazilian blood.

Nick came back out of the kitchen. I planted myself in front of him, blocking the workroom. "Nicolau Aames, you will give me a compliment on this uniform, and that is an order."

Nick curled a lip. "I don't think you can order that. I haven't broken any laws."

"Disturbing the peace," I said.

"If that's the sort of crime we have around here, then Anthony's wrong: we don't need a police department and a police chief. So why don't you stop playing dress-up, and help me plan our survival school? It was your idea, after all."

I let out a long, slow breath. "It was my idea, Nico, to give you something to do, so you would not be bored. But as much as I enjoy exploring Mars, I have done my time as boot camp instructor. Sooner or later, you find yourself competing with a younger, stronger person to show them that they are not as good as they think they are; and you win out in the end because you are craftier. You know how to train, and you know the game. But you go to bed aching in every bone in your body; and the next morning, you have to get up and do it again, and you realize you are not getting younger. That may be your idea of fun, but not mine. I am glad Anthony made me police chief. I am looking forward to this."

"I don't know why," Nick answered.

I could explain, but not without hurting his feelings. I love Nico with all my heart, but this was something I was doing as *me*, not as Nick Aames's wife and partner. If I said that to him, he would think I was rejecting him. But I wasn't! I was rejecting the way I was perceived by other citizens of Maxwell City, as just the founder's wife and a disgraced admiral. In fact, I was not rejecting at all, I was standing up. I was accepting my responsibility to my city.

But I did not try to explain that. I just gently kissed Nick on the cheek and walked away, trusting that he knew better than to keep up the argument. And he did. Over the years, I had become one of the few people he really understood. So many others were a mystery to him, but he read my moods more often than not.

I went to the Admin Center. Anthony had planned a media conference to announce the police department as a new branch of the civil service, separate from the Department of Public Safety, and he needed his police chief front and center as he made his point.

When I arrived, my police force was there, impossible to miss. We had not filled every post yet—far from it!—but lieutenants, sergeants, and over ninety patrol officers had already been hired and had passed their first rounds of training. They overflowed the anteroom of the first-floor auditorium and into the surrounding hallways, all waiting for Anthony. Most of them had been interviewed and hired before I had accepted my new position, so I had spent much of the last four days reviewing their files and issuing new training assignments. Anthony and I had spent several hours going over officer appointments, but most of those were still unfilled. It was challenging to build an entire organization from the ground up.

I knew it would be difficult. On the plus side, most of the candidates came from the Department of Public Safety, while others were recent émigrés transferred from the System Initiative with time spent in security. They all had some experience in policing methods and had been training for at least a month. Now Anthony's plan was to build on that with advanced training while simultaneously deploying them for immediate duty. Much of their training had gone on in the background before he had ever approached me to lead the department. I had resisted the idea of deployment while training as impractical; but Anthony— with help, strangely, from Nick—had persuaded me that it was possible.

While we waited, I weaved my way between the bodies and gave my force an inspection. For a bunch of mostly civilians they did not do too badly; but my orders from Anthony were to train them to be observers and investigators of the highest order, and I could not do that without setting an example.

I turned to the nearest officer, a muscular blond man who seemed a little too casual for the occasion. I read his badge. "Flagg!"

He straightened. "Yes, ma'am."

I looked him over. "That is a brand-new uniform. How did you get it so wrinkled?"

"Ummm . . ."

"Never mind. Next time you show up for muster, I want it pressed."
I looked to the next officer. "Willis! Button those cuffs. People, you
need to look sharp, dress sharp. It gives the public confidence."

I continued my inspection, citing every single discrepancy in their
uniforms, and I filed a report for every one of them. When the inspection was done, I stood in the anteroom near the entry, and I addressed
them. "I expect better. Next time, you *will* do better." I checked my
comm, but only for effect. "There is no time to send you back for tailor-
ing and stitching now, so this will have to do." I said that last remark as
I saw Anthony's private elevator showing the floor count rising. I had
properly chastised my troops; but I had done it in private, not in front
of the big boss.

When the door dinged open, Anthony came out, in deep conversation with Alonzo. Then he saw me, squeezed through the crowd to
my side, and shook my hand. "Ms. Morais, what do you think of your
police force?"

I looked around, and in a loud voice I hoped that every one of them
could hear, I said, "They will do, Mr. Mayor. A lot of potential here. I
think you have done an excellent job hiring."

"Thank you," he said, and then turned to the nearest officers. "I
agree. You men and women look good, and your records look good as
well. Maxwell City is counting on you. We're having growing pains, and
we need to manage that growth. Having a police force will be a whole
new experience for the residents, so I'm counting on you to help smooth
things out. I want them to see you as on their side, not as some hostile
other. You're here to keep the public safe, yourself included. Your next
priority right behind safety is *trust*. They go hand in hand. If they don't
trust you, they won't be safe, and you won't be either."

Then he turned back to me. "Ms. Morais, is your force ready to be
introduced to the city?"

"Yes, sir, Mr. Mayor," I said, snapping to attention. "Do you want
us to march into the auditorium behind you?"

Anthony carefully looked around, and then he grinned. "March? In those red paramilitary clothes? You'd look like a conquering army. No, Ms. Morais, my orders are to amble, stroll, come in at your own pace. Don't worry about ranks and files. You're casual. You're at ease. But when you're all in, *then* form a line. Well, three lines, or you won't all fit on the stage, but you get my point. You're a wall, you're strong. And smiles, everyone, smiles!"

With that the curtains of the auditorium spread open, and Anthony strolled out casually to the microphone. After the Main Dome and the Concourse, the auditorium was the second-largest room in Maxwell City, and it was nearly full with journos and other onlookers. A giant holographic Mars globe hung in the air behind and above Anthony, rotating once per minute. Sparkling dots indicated Maxwell City, Tholus Under, and Alpheus Base. Smaller pinpoints indicated the Gander and Azevedo settlements, as well as numerous smaller registered settlements.

The force followed Anthony, taking our time working through the anteroom, obviously civilian, not military. And yet, when we finally found our places, we *were* that red line backing him up.

Anthony began his remarks. He had no visible notes, of course, but he did not need them with his subcomp. "Ladies and gentlemen of the media, citizens of Maxwell City, you're all familiar with the Department of Public Safety. DPS seals leaks. They search for lost personnel. They put out fires. They deliver emergency medicine. They see you home if you've been out too late and enjoyed yourself too much." A laugh rolled through the crowd. "And they keep the peace. But we're experiencing growth: we're a city of fifty thousand now, and going up. And unfortunately, being a bigger city brings big-city problems. DPS will still be here to help with emergencies and to respond to traffic incidents; but we need to expand our enforcement and investigation capacity. The time has come for me to introduce to you"—he turned to his left, waving his arm at half of our line, and then turned to wave at the other half—"the new Maxwell City Police Department."

Questions flooded from the audience of media people. I wanted to shake my head, but I kept my cool. None of this was a surprise. The police force had been discussed and approved in multiple council sessions. Even the uniform designs had been gone over in detail to try to soften them and make them less military.

But many of our citizens never paid attention to government unless it paid attention to them. For some of them the police force was going to be a complete surprise. They were a large subset, and the journalists were pandering to them. They asked questions that had been answered in council half a dozen times before: "Why do we need a police force?" "Is this a vote of no confidence in the Department of Public Safety?" "What sort of laws will they enforce?" "What sort of punishment?"

I swear: Had *none* of these people studied our system of government? They did not seem to know the first thing about how law and order ran around here. We still operated under the authority of the System Initiative, the international body created to oversee human exploration of space. Not everyone was happy with that: Anthony's Libertist Party led a bloc of smaller parties, in Maxwell City and the other Martian settlements, that wanted to press for Martian independence. But until the situation changed, our "laws" were Initiative regulations, with a limited local autonomy layered on top. The System Initiative was "taking the future status of Mars under advisement," meaning that we might *someday* be free cities when we had earned back enough to pay for the investments in our infrastructure and had demonstrated that we were functioning as a cohesive, self-sufficient community.

Then came a question that Anthony had warned me to expect, one which threw the question of independence versus Initiative wide open: "Are they going to have guns?" The reporter, Tara Rockford, was a stringer who sold most of her stories back to Earth. Lately she had reported extensively on the Carla Grace campaign and the Realist Party, the bloc that wanted stronger ties with the Initiative. Grace's charisma and quick mind made this the first seriously contested race Anthony had ever faced; and Rockford's stories had been slanted against Anthony.

Anthony looked at Rockford and said, "I'll leave that question up to my police chief. Most of you are familiar with the nearly three-decade-long space career of Rosalia Morais: first on the construction crew for Farport Station; later an admiral in charge of Martian traffic control; and more recently a citizen of Maxwell City and a valued member of our community." There was polite applause. "I have asked Ms. Morais to serve as police chief because I have complete confidence in her ability to keep the peace and to lead investigations into issues that may cross over into criminal. I need not tell you of her involvement in the resolution of the recent poisoning scandal. So she is the perfect person to establish the practices and responsibilities of the police chief's office. Ms. Morais."

There was more applause as I stepped to the microphone. I waited it out, and then I turned to Rockford. "Ms. Rockford, as I know you are aware, we have no native predators here on Mars. The only purposes for weapons here is for use against other human citizens. And so the official System Initiative policy is that firearms are not permitted on Mars."

Then I looked out over the crowd. "Now, pardon me, but as a former officer of the System Initiative, I can tell you that sometimes they are blind to realities out in space. I have heard tales that on Earth weaponsmithing is a hobby some skilled people pick up. On Mars, skill—all kinds of skill—is how we survive. Other than you, Ms. Rockford, if there is a person in this room who could not build a functioning firearm with a machine shop and a few hours . . ." I looked over the crowd. "If that is any of you, please do not tell me. I do not want to lose respect for you."

The crowd laughed, and I continued, "So yes, we plan to be armed when we think circumstances warrant, *in full violation of official Initiative policy.* They encourage us to govern and police ourselves, because they do not have enough personnel and enough logistics to run things from twenty light-minutes away." I was cribbing from Libertist boilerplate, but it was *good* boilerplate. "They do not have the personnel necessary to disarm all of Mars, so I cannot believe they'll waste time trying to disarm the police. And you can quote me to your viewers back on Earth. Ms. Rockford: we do not plan to use the arms if we do not have to; but when you have to, it is too late to arm yourself then."

And then I turned out to the crowd. "Ladies and gentlemen, if an armed police force worries you, there is one simple way to solve that issue. Do not use weapons anywhere in Maxwell City, and we shall not have to use ours."

Rockford stood and reached the microphone closer to me, making sure she would be heard throughout the room. "Ms. Morais, are you under orders of Mayor Holmes to willfully disobey an Initiative regulation? Is Chief Hogan aware of this?"

I looked straight into her camera. "It is not my place to speak for Chief Hogan. I only say that if the Initiative regulators came here, they would see things the way they are, and then they would make the same decision I have. For a long time now, the people of Mars—certainly the people of Maxwell City—have understood that we must make our own rules because *we* are the ones who live or die by them. That truth goes all the way back to before the founding of the city, back to the *Bradbury* expeditions. We will comply where it makes sense, but we shall do what we have to do to run things here and to survive. We always have, and I do not expect that to change now that we have a police force."

I turned the microphone back over to Anthony. The rest of the questions were tame after that one. Again, everything had been discussed in council meetings. There was no new information to divulge. Even the fact that we were an armed police force was nothing new. Rockford was just playing up the drama of the moment, or so it seemed to me, trying to generate speculation about conflict with the Initiative.

When Anthony took another break, I introduced some of my senior officers and let each of them tell of their experience on Mars.

Some were former Initiative personnel, while others came from various local industries: shipping, manufacturing, exploring, hydroponics, trading, and more. And of course, Public Safety: I recognized Officer Erica Vile from our encounter a week ago.

After five officers had told their stories, Anthony took the microphone again. "We could tell more. We could talk for hours. These are your fellow citizens. They understand your life here on Mars. They're here to protect it." He turned to me. "Ma'am."

I snapped to attention, and my force did as well. We did not look military, but we looked a whole lot more disciplined than when we had walked in. We were transformed. We were something new. We were the police.

I looked them over. "Ladies, gentlemen, to your patrols. Let us go meet Maxwell City, and keep it safe."

My force broke ranks. Some filed back through the curtain, while others strode through the crowd and out the other exits. They set off toward their assigned patrols.

8. THE SQUAD ROOM

Maxwell City being mostly underground, it was a city of slidewalks, elevators, drop tubes, and walkways. A fast person who knew their way around could cross the city in under twenty minutes. But I had told the force I did not want them walking fast. I wanted them meeting the people. It was crucial that we build rapport.

Anthony and I had debated on whether I should lead a squad or not; but I had insisted, and eventually I had won out. "I do not want to be a figurehead," I had said. "You wanted me for my powers of observation, and I am happy to jump in wherever I am needed. But those powers are best put to use on the street with the people."

I was no stranger to policing, though it had been a long time since I had done so at a personal level. When I had been admiral in charge of Martian traffic, that had made me a de facto head of a policing organization—in some sense, a traffic cop. A major part of that job had been ensuring that traffic was in safe orbits that would not intersect other traffic and would not threaten any facilities, on orbit or on the ground; but a secondary part had been enforcing customs and contamination regulations.

I had to laugh when I thought of Rockford asking me about the dangers of firearms in the hands of the police. I had once had the power to order ships blown out of the sky if they failed to move to a safe orbit. A ship in the wrong orbit can be lethal to other vessels, as Nick had learned on the second *Bradbury* expedition when a runaway lander had destroyed his ship. On occasion through the years, I had had to sacrifice one ship to save another, and then justify it to my higher-ups. By comparison, firearms were a small threat.

My intransigence about commanding a squad threw a monkey wrench into Anthony's plans for my office. He had intended to give me a room on the same floor as his, where I could easily make progress reports on cases. As we left the media conference, he brought it up again. "I talked with Alonzo. I can move his office into my reception room, and you can turn his old office into your squad room."

"No," I said. "Unless you expect high crimes in the Admin Center, we need to be out in the city."

"I haven't leased any space for a squad in the district. I hadn't thought we'd need it."

"Well, count on needing it now. You should be able to negotiate a lease in a few days. In the meantime, I shall go to Zeb and see if we can take up residence in his back room."

I went out and found my command squad standing around gossiping while waiting for me. I walked up slowly until I was close enough to surprise the nearest one. "Schippers," I said. "Here!" I pointed to a spot. "Ammon, here!" I pointed to another. Two young women moved to the locations I had indicated. "Monè," I said. A young Indian man jumped to where I indicated. "Flagg!" The man sauntered over. "Look alive. Byrne!" A shorter man moved into place. "Vile!" Vile took her spot. I snapped my fingers twice, trying to remember the next name. "Um, um, Wagner!" A short older man stepped into place. "And . . ." But I drew a blank on the final name.

The last officer, a tall, dark-haired man, opened his mouth and held up a hand. "Hulett, ma'am," he said.

"All right," I said. "I shall dock myself one point for that. But the rest of you, I remembered your names from a five-minute inspection this morning. Do you think you could do that?"

Hulett shook his head. "No, ma'am."

"That is why I am the police chief, because I am right and you are wrong. You all *will* learn to observe this well, and you *will* learn to remember the details. I am going to teach you if it means drilling you every night until you drop. Even if it means playing stupid cadet games, tracking points earned and lost. You were all chosen for this squad because you already knew Public Safety and other departments inside and out. You demonstrated aptitude to do better. I do not know what your habits were in DPS, but here we have to be proactive."

"What?" Vile asked. "Arrest people for things they haven't done yet?"

"No, Vile, but learn to be aware of what might happen and what you might do if it does happen. I am counting on you eight to be my test case to show the rest of the force what can be done. And then you know what your reward will be?"

"No, ma'am," Ammon said.

"I shall break this command squad up and send you out to lead other squads and have you train them and prove to me that you are better trainers than I am. We've already established a squad post in each district, and each of you has been assigned a command office in a district. You'll divide your time between here and your squad post according to schedules you'll receive. You shall all have promotions and the gratitude of the city, because it will be a safer place because of you."

Flagg looked at me. I thought I saw calculation behind his eyes. "It sounds like boot camp. I didn't sign up for no boot camp."

I inclined my head toward the door. "There is your way out. Your records show all of you are the best we have, but this is not a draft. You can leave anytime you want . . . but you will be leaving one of the most important jobs in the city, and you shall not be welcome back. Go back to DPS if you want, but from this day forward this is the hardest job you will ever have—and the best. If you quit, you will spend the rest of your life knowing you could not be the best. So, any quitters here?"

I stared at Flagg. He stared back, but then turned away. No one looked at the door. "All right, let us go find a squad room."

C

We entered Zeb's Place. Zeb stood behind the bar. He saw me and waved. "I saw you on the news. Congratulations."

"Thank you, Zeb."

"And these are your police force?"

"These are some of my officers. My command squad." I introduced them.

"Come, we must celebrate," Zeb continued. "I will make lunch for you and your entire squad."

I shook my head. "That is not why we are here, Zeb. I want to talk to you about the long-term rental on your back room."

"Long term. Hmmm. I would have to consider the cost on that lost opportunity."

"I will have someone from the mayor's office talk to you about the details. I just want to look it over to see if it will fit our needs."

"Indeed, I understand. We are not making cubic fast enough around here. Sometimes you have to make do with what you can find."

I could see the gleam in his eyes. He was absolutely right. The city was overdue for some expansion. He seemed like a nice enough guy, but I could also see the calculation going on. He could charge me pretty well for this space. I had seen the back room on my last visit to Zeb's, and it was spacious enough for our needs. Now we looked it over, checking the power, communications capabilities, and lighting.

Ammon looked toward the back. "We could add some partitions in here. Some soundproofing. You can have a couple of interview rooms."

"Not bad," I said. "We will need more than that, though. We will need holding. That will have to go across the Concourse in the Admin Center."

As we inspected, Zeb came in with a plate of spicy soy wings and a pitcher of sweet tea. "Officers, police duty must work up an appetite."

Ammon and Monè immediately grabbed for the plate. I said, "Halt." Zeb's eyes lifted in surprise. "Zeb, please, first I need an invoice for this."

"But this is my treat. I want to show my appreciation for the police."

"An invoice, Zeb. We shall talk about it later. And, please, we need to be alone."

Zeb left, the door sliding shut behind him. I looked at Monè and Ammon and then at the rest of them. "All right, I do not know how things were run in Public Safety, but this was covered in your briefing. I know that. No gratuities. No gifts. No exceptions."

"But, ma'am . . . ," Ammon said.

"No 'buts.' You are going to be paid well for this work. There is no need for you to be taking free lunches. It will only end up getting us into trouble eventually. Rockford and the rest of the journos are going to be watching us, looking for trouble. This is a new experiment in Martian self-governance, and I am not going to see it messed up because somebody wanted some free wings."

There was some grumbling, the first sign I had seen that I was going to have to watch this group carefully. And these were the *best* that Anthony had hired. I had my work cut out for me.

When I got home that night, Nick was working on simulated emergencies he could create. I tried to talk to him about how my day went, but he really was not paying attention, so I turned to my crime reports. I had not realized until Anthony had approached me how much small crime there could be in a city of fifty thousand. Simple stuff like fights arising out of minor disputes, property damage, bored kids, or drunkards. But also some petty thefts. I was even surprised to see a couple of muggings.

And the squad assigned to Port Shannon Lopez had a number of customs reports. Those made me uncomfortable. There is a constant debate within the Martian community on free trade versus regulated trade with tariffs to support the operation of government facilities. Philosophically I was a free trader; but officially, well, I had to enforce the regulations. The trade rules mostly involved issues of safety and resource management. We had to have inspections to make sure no diseases were brought in.

We had to worry about what went out too. As we found more water supplies, Mars was slowly becoming self-sufficient in terms of air and water and organics, but we still had to have the tightest recycling to keep a safety buffer. If any Martian exports included net water or net organics, then like it or not tariffs were the answer to make sure we were compensated for the loss.

The customs reports were really a mess: people trying to slip past the inspection point, and shippers trying to shade the organics declarations on their customs papers. Plus there were reports of a possible customs shakedown that Wagner was investigating. And the port district had the highest rate of pickpocketing and other petty larceny in the city. It was clear that we had some lowlifes who thought tourists and ships' crews were easy marks.

I was frankly surprised at the overall amount of crime, so I started researching the older records. I was alarmed to find out how much had been going on under Public Safety that we had just never noticed. Nick and I lived in a poorer part of the city, but still a safe neighborhood, and we had not even known there were unsafe parts; but if you looked around the port area, organics processing, and some of the older, smaller excavations, there were surprising pockets of violence and larceny that you never would have known if you did not see the reports.

And now I would be seeing them every day. It was a new side to my adopted home city, and I did not particularly like it.

9. The New Routine

The next morning when I woke up, Nick had breakfast ready. He set my plate down as I came in from the shower still buttoning the sleeves of my uniform.

"It smells good, Nico," I said.

"Hot off the grill, and just the way you like the eggs," he said. I noticed they were real eggs. Well, vat-grown eggs, but not soy eggs. Nick had splurged on this breakfast.

"So what is the occasion?"

"Occasion?"

"Real eggs?"

"I just thought you ought to start your day with a good meal."

"You are not very convincing, Nick. If that is the truth, it is not the whole truth."

"Well, just thought I'd find out when your days off are, so we could go out and inspect some expedition sites in more detail."

I sighed and set my fork down. "Nick, I will not have days off for a while."

"You can't work your people that much."

"I am going to work them pretty hard, but I shall work myself harder. I must watch my squad and keep on top of what is going on in the other squads until we get a routine established across the city. Some of the squads out there are falling back into their Public Safety habits.

They are not doing a decent job of investigating at all. They are not out patrolling, they are lounging around. I shall have to do a lot of surprise inspections. You remember those?"

"Understood. If you need, I could do some for you."

I took his hand. "No, you cannot, Nico. This is my job. You turned it down. You are a civilian, and I envy you that, but that means that you cannot do anything to help me on this. You keep working on the school, and leave the police work to me."

I headed off to Zeb's, and my command squad was gathered there. Our first day had been largely orientation and going out to meet the public. Now I had to make shift and neighborhood assignments for my command squad. Then I had to spend the other half of the day dropping in on each squad to see if my interim commanders there had their schedules and squad assignments in order.

It was long after dinner when I finally got home. I brought a bucket of gumbo from Zeb's to share with Nick; but he had already eaten and was working on his trees. So I had a bowl of gumbo, stored the rest, and went back to my reports.

That became my routine: morning meeting with my squad, follow up on any cases that they brought in that needed work, afternoon training and inspection tours, then dinnertime meeting with my night-shift squad to keep up with what they were up to. Then home for reports. We expected a lot from the department, learning on the job, so I expected even more from myself.

Soon I settled into a rhythm with it. It was a couple weeks before I realized that Nick was no longer trying to find time with me. He had settled into a routine where we had breakfast together, dinner rarely, and spent most of our time at home wrapped up in our responsibilities—with him spending more time on trees than on exercises. I made a note to find some time off, with a question mark after it. I did not know where the time would come from.

10. Trouble in the Ranks

In my third week as police chief, I shook up my inspection schedule. I figured the squads had gotten used to me showing up at particular times, so I needed to find out how they behaved when they did not expect me—starting with my command squad. I popped into Zeb's during the dinner rush on Tuesday, waiting until there was a lot of noise that could cover my entrance. When I walked into the squad room, I found Monè and Ammon both behind their desks, leaning forward over steaming plates of jambalaya. When they saw me, they both sat straighter, pulling away from the food.

I looked up. "You had better have paid for those meals."

"Sure we did, Ms. Morais," Monè said.

"So if I go and ask Zeb for the receipts, it will show draws out of both of your accounts, right?"

Ammon pushed the plate away. "Oh, come on, ma'am, it's just a little food. Zeb's just showing appreciation that we're keeping the place safe."

"'Showing appreciation' is how graft is always excused. You two are on report, and we are going to discuss this with the mayor tomorrow morning, 0900 sharp. If Rockford and, God help us, Grace get ahold of this, the force would be a complete embarrassment to the mayor; and they would be right to raise a stink. So I want you to explain this to the mayor and let him decide whether to give you walking papers or not. But do not expect me to stand up for you. If you cannot figure it out yet: this is wrong."

"But, ma'am . . . ," Ammon said.

"No 'buts.' Where are Flagg and Schippers?"

Monè answered, "Out on call, ma'am."

"They have patrol officers with them?"

"Yes, and the rest have been reporting in."

"Kind of a busy night. It seems like folks are getting riled up about all this election business. There are a lot more minor assaults than usual. Maybe I need to put you two on double shifts to keep you busy, since you have nothing better to do than embarrass me and the mayor."

Monè looked at his feet. "We're sorry, ma'am."

"You should be. But for now I shall cover the desk here. You go out and you pay Zeb for this. You will make me regret I found this decent space. Here you have room to work around each other without stepping on each other, but you abuse it. Maybe I should go back and find us a broom closet at the Admin Center. Would you like that better?"

"No, ma'am," Monè answered.

"No, ma'am."

"All right. Go pay Zeb. As soon as I get Flagg and Schippers back from the field, I want you two out there, and I want you out on patrol every night this week. Understood?"

"Yes, ma'am."

"Dismissed."

I thought I had been clever, finding a space that we could get without having to worry about rearranging the Admin Center or displacing any tenants. But space was not the problem. Somehow I had to get thorough to my squad and the whole force that we were *not* going to put up with graft. I knew it was a concern for police forces everywhere, but my standards were higher than that. I would not let people believe that *my* force could be bought.

The next morning Anthony chewed out Monè and Ammon. He did it on an open circuit to all squads so they could all hear how serious he was about it. Then he confirmed my order putting them on patrol for the week and informed all of the squads watching that graft was not going to be tolerated.

Afterward we met in his office. "So what do I do, Rosalia?" he asked. "Do I need monitor cams in every squad room?"

"It would not help," I said. "The transfers can be arranged outside of the sight of the cams. And you will never get approval for more thorough monitoring, that is too much privacy violation. Even if it prevents corruption, it will cause resentment."

"So, what, we need an internal affairs department?"

"Same problem. We might need one eventually, but they cause as much strife as they solve. The officers hate feeling like their own people are watching them."

"So what do we do?"

"Be vigilant, and be very visible and swift in punishing problems when they are exposed. Our force has to learn that we are serious and we shall not put up with this."

Anthony shook his head. "This almost never happened on the *Aldrin*. How did Nick do it? What does he have that we don't have?"

I smiled at him. "Nick's secret was no secret. He hounded out anyone who could not live up to his standards, and replacements were assigned. He just kept weeding them out until he had the best. You do not have that luxury. The only pool you can draw from is people already living here who are willing to be police. You cannot just fire people who are not fitting in, you have to find a way to make them fit. Even if they are not perfect, firing has to be a last resort."

"You think we can fix this?"

I frowned. "We shall try. Nothing is perfect. We will do pretty good."

Before I could leave, Alonzo rushed into the office. "Mr. Mayor," he said, "you're going to want to see this."

"See what?"

Alonzo flipped on the big video screen, and there was Tara Rockford. "Repeating, our top story this noonday is a lecture from Mayor Holmes to his own police force regarding issues of graft that have come up in the department."

"No," I said.

What came next on the screen was the entire message we had broadcast out to other squads and recorded for the second shifts.

"No," I said again. "How did she get this so fast?"

"I don't know," Anthony said. "I've had some suspicion she's got a mole somewhere in Admin."

"It did not have to be in Admin," I said. "We sent this out encrypted to the other squads; but someone there could have decrypted, recorded, and delivered it to her. So we cannot really know who, but somebody is feeding her information."

Rockford came back on the screen. "This comes on top of revelations of a year-long Public Safety investigation into a rising tide of crime and violence in Maxwell City, something which Mayor Holmes and his people quietly swept under the rug. But now in this exclusive report we can tell you—"

Anthony squinted, and the screen turned off. "God damn it, I didn't cover anything up. The reports were right there, publicly available. We even discussed them in open council—which was why we instituted a police force."

"To be fair, Anthony," I said, "it is a surprise to me, and I thought I had been paying attention."

"I understand," he said. "The trend crept up on us slowly, and we only recently realized just how out of control it was. Ms. Morais, you'd better get back on top of your squads. Alonzo and I need to figure out how we're going to respond to this, and we'd better make it fast."

"Yes, Mr. Mayor," Alonzo and I said in unison as he sat down and I got up and left.

☾

I was later than ever getting home that night, worrying over who had leaked our recording. Either we had been hacked, or one of our own police force had passed it along. I did not know which it was, so I had to go out and talk to every squad face-to-face to see if I could pick up anything or anyone who seemed to be hiding something.

I cursed Rockford for putting me in that position. I was too new in the job to be suspecting my own people. That was stress that I did not want to deal with. If Nick had been in charge, he would have gone and confronted them, bawled them all out, maybe gotten into a few fights. He had a knack for finding the answer that way. By ordering people around and observing how they behaved, he would pick up on anomalies. Plain, ordinary human behavior often confused him; but behavior under stress? He was good at analyzing that. Me, I had come up empty.

I wished I could talk it over with him. Maybe he could give me some new insight. He always made a good sounding board for my problems; but he was fast asleep by the time I got home. There was a container with a bauru sandwich in the fridge, with instructions on how to reheat it. I sat and ate alone. I wondered why I had ever taken this job.

11. The Fire

When I woke, Nick was already gone and a note on my comp read: *Meeting with SPM. Dinner?* SPM was São Paulo Mutual, the insurance company we had sometimes done investigations for.

I could not tell from the words of the note if Nick was angry I had been so late. But that was silly. We were both driven workaholics, as the Americans described it. We understood that about each other. When the job had to be done, you did it. So if I looked at a few words on a screen from Nick and saw something there, it was probably something that I was reading into myself, not something he had put there. I made myself a note that no matter what came up, I would be home on time for dinner that night.

Later I would come to remember the old Yiddish proverb: "Man plans. God laughs."

☾

The first hint of trouble was a report of a fire at a commercial chamber being handled by DPS, and they sent us a request for crowd control. Part of me rankled at the thought. We were police, we were investigators, we were not crowd control; but we were, when needed. It was all part of the job—I knew that—just a less glamorous part. So, I sent over

Vile, Ammon, and some patrol officers to help reroute traffic around the district, while DPS fought the fire and treated any injuries.

It was twenty minutes later when I got the next call from Vile herself. "What is it, Vile, crowd problems? Do you need more officers?"

"Well, ma'am, it's not a crowd, it's just one person causing us trouble."

"And you cannot handle one person?"

"Ma'am, I think you'd better come down here," she said. "It's the founder." Nick.

I made my best speed to the fire site on level 2. The traffic in the area was pretty congested, as people routed around the district. By now the fire had to have been controlled. One advantage of a sealed environment is you can evacuate an area, cut off the pressure, pump in suppression gas, and smother the fire. It is not as easy as it sounds, but it is a technique DPS has mastered over the years. As long as you do not get anybody caught in an evacuated area, you are fine; but it still takes time, and it requires being able to work without civilians getting in the way and getting into trouble.

When I had worked my way through a crowd of onlookers, I saw what had them all so interested: a face-off with Nick on one side, and Vile and Ammon on the other. Vile had more than a head of height advantage over Nick, and she was more muscular to boot, but I had no doubt who would win in a fight. Nick had years more practice on her, and he fought dirty.

I cut my way through the crowd. "Excuse me, this is police business. Excuse me, excuse me." Once I got up to the confrontation, I said, "All right, break it up. Public Safety does not need whatever is going on here."

Nick said, "Rosie, I have to—"

"It is Ms. Morais, Founder, and you have been told to move along."

"Oh, give me—"

"*You have been told to move along.* Come with me, sir!" I grabbed Nick's arm and pulled him away, and I found a maintenance shaft down to the next level. My police chief's credentials opened the shaft. "Get down there, Nick, right now," I said, "before I stuff you in there myself." He climbed into the shaft, and I climbed down behind him, sealing it above me. "Over to the left." I pointed to the maintenance access for the space that ran between the levels. "Nick," I said, but he interrupted me.

"Rosie, I—"

I interrupted him in turn. "You 'Rosie' me one more time on duty, and I will have you thrown into the brig!"

"I'm sorry, Ms. Morais," he said, dripping sarcasm.

"And do not pull that on me either. The condescension is no better. I am on duty as police chief, and I have a responsibility, and I cannot have you undermining it."

Nick opened his mouth to say something more, but then he stopped. He thought better of it, I hoped, and then he tried again in a lower, more relaxed tone. "I'm sorry, Ms. Morais, but I need to get in there. Public Safety is destroying all the evidence."

"Evidence?"

"This fire was not an accident, I'm sure of it."

"How so?" I could not help myself. I wanted to know the truth as much as he did, no matter how angry I was.

"That fire is in MMC, Martian Machine Co-Op. They're a group of specialists who pooled their funds for tools, so that they could bid on bigger machining jobs and share the work back and forth. Lately São Paulo Mutual says there has been an unusually high rate of industrial accidents in there. They can't pin it down, but they're sure somebody in the co-op has been having a severe run of bad luck—too much to be random."

"So you think this fire was staged?"

"I'm not guessing—"

I cut him off. "You're investigating, I know. But that is what you are thinking."

"If it is, they've escalated. Everything up to now has been small claims of broken equipment, lost time, personal injury; and they kept it very close to the edge of plausible, so São Paulo had nothing the computers would flag as a problem. But their human auditors grew suspicious, and they asked me to take a look."

"I thought you were planning the survival school?"

"Let's not talk about that right now. This is more important." I could tell from his look and his tone that he had something to say about the school, but I did not push it.

"Look," I said, "we need to worry about safety first. We cannot have you in there while DPS is still securing the place."

"They can loan me a hazmat suit, and I can go in and be just as safe as them."

I shook my head. "You know better. They have insurance risks to worry about, too, and you are not covered on-site, hazmat suit or no."

"But damn it, ma'am, they're spraying fire foam! They're evacuating the place, tromping all around, dragging hoses around. Is there anyone on that team who has ever even investigated an arson?"

There was not, I had to admit, so I shook my head. But then I said, "Nick, that is not part of my responsibility. First I have to worry about the safety of the city. Second, I have to worry about the safety of anyone caught in the fire. Third, I have to worry about the safety of Public Safety personnel. Fourth, I have to worry about civilians in the area, you included. Preserving evidence is way down the list on my priorities."

"I thought you were the police chief," he said. "Chiefs investigate."

"Chiefs protect and serve. Protect is first."

Nick looked at me for several seconds. "I'm not going to change your mind on this, am I?"

"No, Nick, I am sorry."

"All right," he said, "But as soon as they're done, I want access to that site."

"Space it, you are *not* giving orders here."

"All right, Ms. Morais, I request access to the MMC facilities as soon as I may safely be allowed."

"I will *consider* it, as soon as the site is declared safe, and my people have performed whatever investigations we need." I tried to smile. "Since a reliable source tells me this might be a crime scene."

Nick looked at me. He does not smile easily, and he did not even try, but at least his tone was conciliatory. "Could that reliable source assist in the investigation?"

I did not want to cause trouble with Nick. "I think he can accompany the investigation if he keeps within his boundaries. I do have some pull with the mayor's office for that."

It took more than two hours for the head of Public Safety, Harrison Wright, to declare the MMC complex safe and the fire contained. City planners and civilian architects tried to reduce the amount of flammables in a Martian city—generations later, everyone in space still knew the legends of the Apollo 1 fire—but it was simply not practical. Virtually everything is flammable under the right conditions. And too many compromises had to be made, so fire was always a concern. A city carved in rock did not have to worry about buildings burning down, but the contents could be extremely flammable.

When Wright finally gave me the okay to investigate, Nick was standing at my shoulder, practically bouncing with energy to get in. We followed the DPS inspectors in. The MMC facility was three levels of mills and lathes and assembly lines and stereoliths and other equipment, rising through the maintenance space between levels and up to city level 2. Wright gave us a walkthrough of what his team had found so far.

"It looks like the ignition started here," he said, "in this waste bin. Paper and film used to wrap raw materials during shipping. It looks like from there, hot gas escaped upward." We had started at the MMC office, where the different partners in the co-op met and organized. "From there, hot gases, not quite incandescent, boiled up above. They pooled under some flooring." He pointed up to where the flooring had burned through. "It's just grid flooring with a carpet laid down for appearance, and the carpet went up. And that spread rapidly throughout that floor, then bits of hot carpet dropped back down. And after that, it was a mess."

Nick looked at the carpet underneath our feet. "This is pretty burned too. No one was in here to notice any of this?"

I glared at Nick. I did not want to chew him out now, but later . . .

Wright answered, "Founder, there has been a slowdown and a lot of the partners were off doing other work. So the whole facility had been shut down for maintenance. We're thinking maybe some part of that caused a spark in the first place."

Nick shook his head. "You're reading the fire wrong."

"What?"

"The carpet up there is the same as down here, right?"

"Yeah."

"Up there, quick, hot ignition went through and just gobbled up carpet. Dripping pieces came down here." Nick pointed around. "Right?"

"Yeah."

"But look at the carpet here. It's barely singed." Nick pointed at the ground. "It's in a small area, almost like a path. And if you look closely, you can see the direction of propagation is toward the waste bin, not away."

"How can you tell that?"

Nick frowned. "Thirty years of investigating fires, Wright. Trust me, that fire came from those offices over there."

"We haven't even been in there yet," Wright said. "The offices were sealed, and there are no working cameras in there."

"That's suspicious," Nick replied. "Wright, get your people to check the offices. Rosie, I told you we needed those hazmat suits. All right, everybody who's not in a suit, back away!" Nick looked around. "Let's get over into that testing chamber! Move, move, move! You too, Wright. When your people crack that office, I don't want anybody outside without a suit. Tell them to be ready, it might still be hot."

"Do it," I said.

So we all crowded in the testing chamber, Nick sealed the door, and Wright's people opened the office door. When they did, a big flash of light blinded us through the testing lab window. Wright's team were ready, quickly doing fire suppression and putting the flames out.

"How'd you know?" Wright said.

Nick answered, "I was pretty sure that something had burned in there; and what's left would be hot, pressurized gas without enough oxygen to ignite. When you opened it, poof. Someone lit a fire in there and sealed it up to make sure it did its job. In the meantime, they lit the rest of the fire to cover things up."

"You can't know that," Wright said.

"I can't, but that's where we'll start investigating."

"No, Nick," I said. "That is where *I* shall start investigating. You are here as a courtesy, remember."

"Yes, Ms. Morais," he said. "But the office should be clear now. We should go look in there."

I glared at Nick, opened the test lab door, and went out. We looked in the office. It was a mess, but I had seen enough fire investigations myself to know that Nick was right. The quick flash we had seen had been a secondary ignition. Everything in the office had burned pretty badly before then. Including the corpse we found.

12. THE CRIME SCENE

"So it was arson?" Anthony looked at Nick as he asked the question, and I bit back my urge to shout.

"Yes," I said firmly. "Indicators are that it is arson, and *your police force* is investigating it."

"I'm sorry, ma'am," Anthony said. The three of us sat in his office, looking out over the surface of Mars. "You're right. Still, I'm happy that you have expert civilian assistance."

What could I say? That I did not need any help? That I would turn down an expert? A founder? Even here in private, just the three of us, that was the wrong thing to say. "I will take any assistance we can find, Mr. Mayor."

"I'm happy to hear it," Anthony said. "Arson makes that death murder. That's two in three months here in Maxwell City, plus the accidental deaths from the poisoning incident. That's more than we've had in almost the past decade. Tara Rockford is already having a field day with this; and her interview with Grace, it was brutal. Do we know who the victim was?"

I checked my comp. "No reports from the lab yet, Anthony."

"Tell them to run a DNA test for Manuel Ramos," Nick said.

"Ramos?" Anthony said. "He was the organizer of the co-op, right?"

"Yes, and he pretty much ran the place, and he worked in that office. He'd be the first one to test. If it's not him, then we can go through the others; but I've been looking for Ramos as part of my investigation, and he's proving difficult to find, so . . ."

"So that is a pretty good first place to check," I agreed, trying to ignore Nick's trampling in my area.

Anthony was confused, but I knew things he did not. He looked at Nick and asked, "Your investigation? What investigation is that?"

So Nick explained about the high rate of insurance claims.

"Really?" Anthony said. "It does sound connected. All right, ma'am, you need to start digging into Ramos and that side of things. Nick, I'm going to have to ask you to step aside from it for now."

"What?" Nick asked.

"This is now an active police investigation. You're familiar with the rules regarding that. You need to give Rosie"—he caught himself— "Ms. Morais and her people room to work. So any questioning you're going to do, any investigation, you're going to have to clear it with her. Stay out of her way, and anything you find you report to her."

Nick did not look at me, keeping his eyes on Anthony as he answered, "Yes, Mr. Mayor."

"All right. Ma'am, I guess this is where your career really takes off," Anthony said. "Find out what's happening, please. We need to shut this down fast."

"Yes, Mr. Mayor."

Nick and I got up and left. We got in the elevator to go down into the main city, but I stopped it at the first floor.

"Come with me," I said. "We need to talk. Alone." Before he could raise an objection, I grabbed his sleeve and pulled him over to the small municipal garage next door to Admin. I went up to the dispatch desk. "We are signing out a crawler," I said.

"You don't have suits," the clerk behind the desk answered.

"A short trip. My responsibility. Do it." He looked like he was about to object again. I just stared at him. "Do it."

He got us the crawler. We climbed in, waited for the garage lock to cycle, and drove out onto the Martian surface. As soon as we cleared the driveway area, I stopped the crawler, shut down the comps, and turned to Nick, my face feeling hot. "Stop it, Nick," I said.

"I don't—"

"Stop it! You know damn well what I am talking about."

"Rosie, I was just trying to help."

"You were not. You were trying to run things. You were trying to take charge just like you always do. Apparently I was not clear enough before. You are a damn good investigator, Nicolau Aames, but I am better. And this is my responsibility and my case."

"It's a big enough case that it needs both of us."

"It does, but I am the one who has to direct it. You would never have put up with this on your ship. You shot down admirals who tried to usurp your command."

"And we see how that turned out for me."

"It turned out exactly the way you planned it, so do not give me that bullshit. You heard what Anthony suggested. If you are going to go out and investigate this, and I know I cannot stop you, you *are* going to keep me in the loop for everything. You are *not* going to keep any secrets. You are *not* going to follow up on any special leads that you tell me about later. You shall tell me about it as it happens, or you can go back and work on survival school . . . which is what I thought you were doing in the first place. What is up with that?"

"What's up with that," Nick answered very coldly, "is that I've gone as far as I can by myself. This was supposed to be an *us* project, not a *me* project, and it's not safe for me to take the next steps without a partner. My partner has gone and gotten herself another job."

"That was not my choice. Anthony needed me. Maxwell City needs me."

"You always had a choice," Nick said.

"You are saying I made the wrong one?"

"No, damn it. I'm saying that the one you made has consequences. The choice you made has costs, and our survival school is one of them. That was a wonderful dream. I was looking forward to it. And now . . . ?"

Nick did not answer his implied question, and I did not have an answer either. We just stared at each other.

Finally I looked away. "And now I have a job to do. A murder to solve. We shall talk about this later." I turned the crawler around and took us back into Maxwell City.

☾

The next day, I burrowed into the MMC investigation. As angry as I was at Nick, I also knew he knew his job. And that was only confirmed when Marcus's report came in: the burned corpse was Manuel Ramos.

Anthony had hired a science team, and he told me to walk them through the basics of arson investigation. I was surprised how ill-prepared Maxwell City was for the level of crime that we actually experienced. There had never been arson here before that we knew of; but without investigators, how could you really tell? We needed chemists to analyze traces from all the surfaces from the fire. A number of labs in the city could do the testing, but they needed to gather the evidence according to proper forensic procedure.

We had never had a forensics department before. Marcus's position as coroner was as close as we came; but until recently, his work had been more administration than investigation. It was time to change that, and it was my reluctant duty to instruct him.

I arrived at the entrance to MMC. It was a completely different scene from the day before: no crowds, and no Nick. But one thing was the same. "Hello, Lieutenant Vile."

"Hello, Ms. Morais." Vile pointed at the patrol officer blocking the door behind her. "Lawson and I have the door here covered. The other doors are bolted, as per your orders."

"Good work, Vile. How are the electronic screens?"

Vile tapped her comp. "All probes negative. Nothing's getting in."

I almost smiled at her naivete. A skilled hacker could bypass any screen, given time. But ours were pretty good, certified for forensic containment.

I looked around. "Any sign of the examiner and his team?"

She shook her head. "Not yet." So I waited, trying to calm my nerves. Punctuality had never been one of Marcus's strong points.

A few minutes later, Marcus walked up, followed by the lab technicians Anthony had contracted: a digital specialist, a videographer, a chemist, an engineer, and a field investigator. An inspector from Public Safety joined them.

"Ms. Morais," Marcus said, extending his hand.

"Dr. Costello," I said, shaking his hand as I nodded to the technicians. "It is good to see you." It was a polite lie: it *was* good to see him, a brief flare of nostalgia; but at the same time it was uncomfortable after the way things had ended between us.

"Good to see you," Marcus answered. "Sorry I was late. I was reviewing reports from Mr. Wright's team. Shall we begin?"

"Right this way." I led the technicians to the entrance. Taylor, the digital specialist, plugged into Vile's comp to examine the data screen and verify that the systems within MMC were still isolated. Meanwhile Swanson, the engineer, examined the door seals to make sure they were secure as well. Later she would examine the seals on the other entrances.

Nick had been right, of course: fighting the fire had seriously compromised the investigation. But Nick was also wrong, in a way, because in the past he had not usually performed *criminal* investigations. During our Initiative service, we had investigated accidents, cover-ups, and incompetence, but seldom crimes for a court. A compromised chain of evidence was normal for arson, where safety and containment were the first concerns. There were so many ways that the chain of evidence could *not* be established, with so many people rushing through the facility without regard to investigations. Circumstances gave you no choice; you just did your best and sealed the area afterward. Any evidence you found might not survive a court challenge, but you could only do so much. Attorneys and courts would argue the rest.

Once Taylor and Swanson were satisfied that the scene was contained, I used my access code to unlock the entrance. The group stepped forward, but I held up a hand. "Not yet. Videos and inspection first. We need to capture the scene before you start to work. The rest of you keep studying the exterior."

"Studying for what, Ms. Morais?" Swanson asked.

"If we knew that, we would be done already."

The videographer, Priest, stepped forward, followed by the DPS inspector. Marcus joined them. I had not mentioned him, but I was not up to arguing. This was his team. If he wanted to accompany them, that was his decision.

We entered the facility, and I guided them through the areas we had examined the day before. Donihue, the inspector, led the way. He wore a backpack remote sensing package: a thermal imager, a focused sonograph, a terahertz scanner, multiple chemical sensors, a micro EMP projector, a lidar unit, and a spectrophotometer. It was a lot for one package, but light enough in Martian gravity. With these instruments, Donihue probed ahead, looking for stressed metal, hot spots, hazardous chemicals, or any other danger. I set the course, but Donihue cleared it. Priest followed behind, capturing complete video, from IR to UV and at multiple magnifications; and his fleet of scan bots swarmed through the air around us, building a rich 3D model of the environment. Marcus brought up the rear, dictating notes, as I guided us through the factory and the offices.

It took most of the morning for us to record the facility as is. Then Marcus called in the rest of the technicians. O'Neil, the field investigator, led them in gathering samples and evidence. His work on surface science expeditions had prepared him well for the rigorous standards of forensic evidence. I made a few suggestions here, a few warnings there. I answered questions and reminded them of proper procedures. But on the whole I was pleased with O'Neil and their team. Their examination was thorough, and their documentation was meticulous. Nick could have done better, but this team had potential.

And I was . . . well, not pleased with Marcus, but relieved. At ease. He was even pleasant, almost the man I remembered from before. He had none of the sullen anger he had fallen into after I had broken our engagement, none of the withdrawal that had followed. Maybe the tension I feared was all in my head.

The investigation continued on all through the day, well into second shift. I stepped out a few times to get outside the digital containment so I could check my messages. Things seemed routine, and my command squad had things under control; yet the sheer volume of reports kept me busy with follow-ups and approvals. So I found myself answering questions both from the forensics team and from my squad throughout the day.

It was after 2000 by the time the team was done for the day. There was still more work, but they had convinced me that they could carry on without my help. I ushered everyone out. "Good work, everyone," I said. "Pick back up tomorrow." Then I turned to reseal the facility.

When I turned back, the technicians were gone, but Marcus was still there. "Quite a day, ma'am."

I straightened. "A good day. For a team so hastily assembled, they did good work."

"Not *that* hasty." He smiled. "Mayor Holmes and I have been reviewing candidates for a while now. They've been doing online coursework. We hadn't gotten to arson techniques yet, but they're good people. They learn quickly."

"I am glad," I said. "We need them. And you." I sighed. "What have I gotten myself into? Trying to build a police department from nothing. And all under the eye of the media in the middle of an election."

"We'll make it," Marcus answered. "Mayor Holmes is a smart administrator. He has a good plan, and we'll do our parts." He looked at his comp. "It's pretty late, and we missed lunch. You hungry?"

I checked my own comp. 2011. And plenty of messages. But none from Nick. He had to have eaten by then.

"Yes. Very. Let us get some dinner."

C

We settled on Zeb's. We both had reports to file, so it made sense to dine on the Concourse. Marcus's office was right across the dome, and mine was in the back room.

We placed our orders—rice and gravy for me, andouille for Marcus, a glass of wine for each of us—and discussed the day's investigation while we waited. When the waitress set down our plates, Marcus leaned over his and inhaled deeply. "Ahhh, meat . . . A big change from Phobos Base, eh, Rosalia?"

"Hey, we had meat on Phobos! Vat-grown, but so is this."

"Yes, but we didn't have Zeb." He smiled as he speared a slice of sausage. "We didn't have a lot of things there. Or here, for that matter." Marcus waved his fork in a circle. "Mars has really changed since then."

I tried my rice. "Oooh . . . spicy!" I drank some water. "It has, but so gradually. It is hard to remember how it used to be. I never spent much time on the surface then."

"I did," Marcus answered. "After . . ." But then he stopped, stuffing a large forkful of sausage into his mouth.

I suddenly found my rice fascinating. I knew what he had not said: *After we broke up.* He had put in for a transfer to Fort Hudson. I had understood: it was as far away from me as he could get at the time. If he had stayed at Phobos, we would have served months in the same cramped base before he might get a reassignment and transportation back to Earth–Luna space.

So instead he had transferred to Mars. I eventually transferred as well, back to Earth orbit for a prime post in traffic control—the post I eventually sacrificed to protect Nick from the Admiralty's machinations. So Marcus might have found his way back to Phobos. Instead, after his tour had ended, he chose not to reenlist, and instead applied to emigrate to Maxwell City. The city had needed doctors then—still did—so they had courted him heavily. He had been accepted immediately. Perhaps it had been an easy way for him to avoid me, serving in the Admiralty, and Nick on the *Aldrin*.

And then our careers had crashed, and we had landed on Mars. And from there it was only a matter of time before Marcus and I found ourselves dining at Zeb's.

We ate in silence. I glanced occasionally at Marcus, while he remained focused on his food. It was ridiculous that two adults could not have a conversation just because of matters years past. How would we ever work together?

Work. That was the key. I cleared my throat. "If it will not . . . spoil your dinner . . ."

I paused, and Marcus looked up from his food. "I'm a doctor. My stomach's pretty strong."

I half smiled. "So . . . what have we learned about Manuel Ramos? Do we have a cause of death?"

Marcus swallowed a last bite of sausage, and he shook his head. "Not yet, but close. He . . . It appears he was stabbed. Repeatedly. The damage to his lungs shows he was still breathing when the fire started. So it's a toss-up: Did he bleed to death or asphyxiate? We should have the lab results tomorrow, and then I can sign off on the cause of death; but either way, it was murder and arson."

"Clumsy arson," I replied. "Trying to hide the murder, but they did a poor job of it. They left easy signs for a professional investigator to track down."

Marcus looked down at his empty plate. "And lucky for us, we have a professional."

"Marcus . . ."

He looked up, waving his hand. "I'm sorry, Rosalia. That was over the line."

"Marcus." He looked at me. "Is this going to be a problem with us? We could not work together on Phobos, but that was over eight years ago."

"I . . ." He paused. "No, there's no problem, ma'am. I slipped up, and I'm sorry. It's the wine talking."

I doubted that. Marcus was a big man; one glass of wine had never affected him. But it gave him an excuse, so I let it pass.

Instead, I tried for a conciliatory tone. "That is good. We need you." His eyebrows rose. "*Maxwell City* needs you. As a doctor, and as a coroner, you are the best we have."

"And we couldn't ask for a better police chief." He smiled; and for an instant I saw the old Marcus, the man I had been engaged to, before Nick had . . . had what? Stolen me away, Marcus would say, but that was not correct. Nick had tried to break up our engagement with a grand romantic gesture; but in the end, *I* had made the decision. And I did not regret it.

"Thank you, Marcus. But this police chief has work still tonight and an early day tomorrow, so I had better get moving."

13. GRAFT

Nick was still up when I got home, but I was in no mood to discuss the case with him—and certainly in no mood to discuss Marcus. My silence seemed fine with him. He barely grunted at me as he worked at his station. I sat, going through my notes on my comp.

Finally, Nick turned to me. "Well, Ms. Morais, you wanted to know what I found out, so here it is." He pushed a report to my comp. "It's been going on a lot longer than we realized. Only it took this long for São Paulo Mutual to put the pieces together. Accident payout rate and crime payouts are all in the high end of average, nearly a standard deviation up. Not quite enough to flag their alerts; but finally it added up to enough payouts that somebody noticed. This has been going on for almost three years. Somebody's been milking them."

I looked at the file. It was as thorough as ever. I could not fault Nick for shoddy work, but that did not put me in a better mood. "This is a pretty wide range of reports."

"I know," he said. "And some of them are likely legitimate, but we can't really be sure which ones. We're going to have to go back and reopen every one of those."

I looked at the report. "It is a long list."

"Yeah. It's by no means just MMC, although they're one of the biggest culprits."

"So you think someone there got greedy?"

"Greedy, or a guilty conscience," Nick said. "Maybe Ramos knew something and someone didn't want it getting out."

"That makes sense," I said. "All right. I shall work with my team to put together a citywide investigation into this." I looked at him. "Thank you, Nick."

"Just following orders," he said. But he was still tense. He did not show his anger easily, but I could tell he needed some time to come around. So I went to bed.

C

When I woke in the morning, I found Nick's side of the bed undisturbed. He had slept out on the couch and was gone before I woke.

Going through two-year-old insurance claims—even with the help of the best computing technology in the city—was a time-consuming process. I sent my command squad out to all the other squads to lead the effort and report to me directly. The problem was that the evidence, such as it was, was all statistical, circumstantial, making it difficult to press anybody involved in any of the claims.

And then it got worse when I got a call from Mayor Holmes. "Ms. Morais," he said, "I've received some complaints that the police force is harassing businesspeople in the community."

I sighed and looked at the screen. "Mr. Mayor, this is a delicate matter. We probably should not discuss it over a comm channel."

"That's fine. I'll see you in my office. Five minutes."

Anthony did not look angry, but he did look on edge. So I made best speed to his office. He was waiting for me at the door. Alonzo stood behind him, fidgeting. I came in and sat down, and I explained what Nick had uncovered. Anthony stared into space for a few seconds, and then he looked at me.

"This is pretty bad, Rosie."

"I know. But it is solid. You know Nick. He would not bring it up if it were not."

"I know. But some of the people were upset. They're already whispering."

Alonzo added, "Some of them were already leaning toward Grace in the campaign. This is pushing them further her way."

I almost lashed out; but instead I held back and asked very carefully, "Mr. Mayor, am I supposed to find the truth, or am I supposed to support your campaign?"

Anthony winced. "I hear what you're saying, and I want the truth, of course. But the timing is lousy."

"I know. I shall ask my people to be extra polite, but statistics say something is there. We just do not know where." I looked back and forth between the two. "We are on a fishing expedition, Anthony, we have to be. And fishing expeditions make waves."

"All right. Should I talk to these people and try to calm them down?"

"Oh, hell no!" I answered. "It would not do you any good, and it would only alert them to what we are up to. I assume that if any of them are actually involved, they have figured that out already; but still, let us not make it obvious."

"So what do you know so far?"

I had been asking myself that question already, looking over the reports. And I had not liked what I had seen. "This is bad. Really bad. Whatever is going on, it involves more than just the people filing the reports."

Alonzo's eyes widened. "How so?"

"The reports are too good, if that makes any sense. The paperwork, everything. Whoever did this knows how to work the system. It is too professional . . . meaning, I do not know yet. I have suspicions . . ."

Anthony grinned. "But you're just like Nick: you don't guess, you find out."

100

"Yes." I nodded. "And until then, any guess could give too much away." I leaned forward, gripping the desk. "You wanted a police force, Mr. Mayor. This is what a police force does."

Alonzo frowned. Anthony sighed and said, "All right. But let me know more as soon as you can."

C

I did have a guess, of course, a pattern I was starting to see. But it was not clear enough yet. If I was wrong, it was going to cast suspicion on good people who did not deserve it. The only person I could trust to discuss it with—and not get ahead of themselves and run with it—was the person who was not talking to me right then, space it!

So I went to my office and started going through the reports again from a different angle. And the more I looked, the more I was sure this was an inside job. Inside where? was the question.

I needed to get out in the city, see if I could observe anything to support my hunches. Every member of my command squad was still out attached to other squads, driving the data-gathering operation. I had given them Anthony's instructions to soft-pedal as best as they could; but space it, I had to have the facts! Now I wanted to see what was going on in those offices, so I made my way through the city.

I started with the farm district, where Wagner was busy collating data from his investigations. I pulled him aside and looked at it myself. He was doing pretty much the work I would do—making some mistakes, which I pointed out, but he seemed to be on the right path.

Next was Ammon in the port district. When I stepped into her office, she shut the door and said, "I'm sorry, Ms. Morais."

"Sorry?" I asked.

"For getting in a confrontation with the founder. I shouldn't have made a spectacle of the whole thing."

I smiled and patted her on the arm. "Nick does that to people, Ammon, it is not your fault. I cannot count how many times I have wanted to pop him one myself."

At that she grinned, and then she giggled and said, "Really?"

"Thought it once or twice. We have a long history with plenty of our own ups and downs, so do not worry about it. Next time try to keep it cooler in public, but I do not blame you for it. So show me what you have on the insurance situation."

We went over her reports—which were not as good as Wagner's. She was trying, but he was more thorough; so I pulled down a copy of his for her to look at as an example.

I moved on to the manufacturing district, not too far from MMC, where Vile was overseeing the investigation. She was nowhere to be seen. A couple of officers were manning the place, Brooks and DeHaven. They stood to attention when I came in. "Good afternoon, Ms. Morais," said Brooks.

"Good afternoon," I said. "Just dropping in." They were used to it, of course. I made enough regular inspections for that. "Carry on."

I went back to Vile's desk and saw a pile of virtual papers showing on the display screen. I also saw an envelope next to it with a hand-lettered label. *Lieutenant Vile, Private,* it said. Private. That raised my curiosity, but I did not open it. I was unsure whether I could make a case for that or not. It was on police property during police hours; but still, privacy rights were pretty strong in Maxwell City. The Initiative thought otherwise, but the populace wanted their rights to privacy respected.

I stuck my head out into the main office. "Any idea when Vile is supposed to be back?"

Brooks checked her comp. "Soon, about ten minutes if she's on schedule."

"I will wait, thanks." I sat and went through my notes, and I pulled up Vile's work history at DPS. Not long after, she came rushing in.

"Ms. Morais," she said. "I'm sorry, I would have been here if I had known you were coming."

"I expect you would," I said, then pointed at the envelope. "What is that?"

"Ma'am . . . what?" She looked at the envelope. "That's . . . I have never seen that before."

"I see. Then you would not mind opening it."

"Ma'am, honest. I have never seen that before."

"Well, will you open it then, or should I?"

"Ma'am, I . . ."

I was bluffing. If she did not want me opening it, there would be a stink if I did; but I hoped she would fold.

And she did. "Go ahead. I want to know too."

I opened it up, and inside were blockchips, voucher cards commonly used in interplanetary commerce. They could be tendered for goods and services on Earth, Mars, and Luna. "What is this?" I asked.

Vile looked at the chips. "Ma'am, I have never seen those before."

"They are just on your desk with your name on them."

"Ma'am, I swear—"

"Vile, you are suspended immediately. Give me your badge and your weapon."

"But, ma'am—"

"Now! Or do I need to call Brooks and DeHaven in to take you into custody?"

She removed her badge and her weapon and handed them over. "Ma'am, this is some sort of mistake."

"Oh, it is a mistake, all right." I hit my comm. "Brooks, I need you to escort Vile to an interrogation room in Admin."

I would have to keep an eye on Brooks. She showed promise: she did not hesitate, she did not stammer, she just said, "Yes, ma'am." And like that she was in the room taking Vile by the elbow and leading her out.

I called through the door, "DeHaven, evidence bag, please." He was not quite as quick as Brooks; but then it was a more unusual request. Who ever needed an evidence bag in the squad room? But he showed up with one quickly enough, and I sealed the envelope back up and dropped it in the bag.

Then I turned to DeHaven and asked, "Did you see where this envelope came from?" He stared down at the desk. "Come, man, spit it out. Whatever it is, we need to clear this up."

"Well, a courier came in with a . . . delivery from the Merchant's Association."

"A delivery? And you did not find that suspicious?"

He still did not look up from the desk. "Ma'am, it wasn't the first time. They bring by a little bit of food now and then, sometimes a recreation voucher."

"Space it! What do I have to do to get through to you people?"

Finally he looked up at me. "Permission to speak freely, ma'am?"

I had to know what was going on in my own force, so I had to build a rapport with them. "Yes. This is off the record."

"Ma'am," he said, "you're trying to change an ingrained culture. We understand what you're trying to do, but little gifts of appreciation are the way it's always been in Public Safety. And it's so easy to accept small stuff as a sign of appreciation, so we just kind of don't question it."

"Small stuff," I said, looking at the bag; but DeHaven probably did not know what was in the envelope. "I will tattoo this on your foreheads if I have to. Spread the word, I mean *no gratuities*. You can all get on board with that, or you can all put up with being watched at every moment. And you do not want that."

"No, ma'am, we don't."

"All right, expect another meeting on this. In the meantime, get back to work. Somebody has to cover the squad room."

DeHaven left Vile's office, and I sat back down behind Vile's desk, turning over this latest event in my head. I did not like it. It was too pat. I had been an investigator for much of my career, and an admiral for longer. I had seen cover-ups, both official and amateur. And this one was on the amateur end. Paper envelopes in plain sight? Someone wanted me to find this, someone who could keep tabs on my schedule. I could not believe Vile was taking a bribe. I would have to make her suffer for a while as if believing she was guilty. I would make it up to her somehow. The real problem had to be someone close. Until I knew who had the evidence to back it up, I would have to pretend that I was fooled.

But I had started to *like* Vile, and that could blind me. I needed to muster my objectivity. Not guessing, investigating. Maybe Vile was corrupt *and* stupid.

I went back over my numbers, but I was distracted by what DeHaven had said. *"An ingrained culture."* That was what my guess had been too. I went through all the insurance reports. Every one of them had followed the same basic procedure: a claim of a loss, sometimes with a claim of a crime as well, investigated by the Department of Public Safety—or more recently by the police department—signed off by DPS as to the amount of the loss and the items recorded as lost.

I was still looking at those numbers when I got a call from Nick. "Ms. Morais," he said, "I have some information for you."

Sigh. He had been investigating without telling me, but now was not the time to chew him out about that. "Go ahead, Nick."

"I've been looking into some of the losses claimed. Precision machine parts, valves, raw materials, some pretty expensive stuff with high value went in for claims. SPM paid them off, because all of the paperwork was proper. But I've been looking at the business records of the people who filed the claims. They still met all their contracts."

"What?"

"I don't have full access. I don't have police powers to investigate this; but if I did, I would subpoena records that I'm pretty sure would show that these claims for lost parts"—he pushed a file over to me—"were followed not long after by jobs completed by the claimants. Jobs that required those missing parts. I can't subpoena those closed records, but you can. Nail them, Rosie!"

I went through Nick's reports, and I ran a quick correlations algorithm to tie them to what I was looking at. I found that in all of the cases, the Public Safety officers who had signed off on the insurance loss claims were Monè and Vile, including the cases since the force had started up. Damn.

I packed up to head to Monè's office. I was just passing through the residential district when I got a call from Flagg.

"Yes, Lieutenant?" I asked.

"Ma'am, I've got a problem," he said.

"Make it fast," I said. "I am on the way to the metro district office."

"I'm there right now, ma'am. I had some errands to run over here, and I stopped into the squad room to check in and . . . well . . ."

"Spit it out!"

"Ma'am, this is going to make me the least favorite person in the squad for turning on one of our own, but I found an envelope on Monè's desk."

"An envelope?"

"Uh-huh. I think you'll want to look at it."

"I think I will at that. Is Monè there?"

"No."

"All right, get your evidence. Do not let him touch it. Get it down to the Admin Center, and don't tell anyone."

Then I hung up with Flagg and called Nick back. "Nick, we need to meet and compare notes. We have an explosive situation on our hands."

☾

Nick and I arrived at the Admin Center. The evidence in my comp, based on his notes and mine, could put this case to bed. I had called ahead and reserved a large meeting room, and I had also put some patrol officers on as guards. They brought in all the parties concerned: Vile, Monè, Flagg, Ammon, Schippers, Byrne, Wagner, Hulett, Brooks, and DeHaven. I also called up to Anthony's office to ask if we could borrow Alonzo as a court reporter; and Anthony trailed along out of curiosity. When everyone was settled, I had Brooks and DeHaven tell the story of the envelope on Vile's desk.

Vile tried to object. "That's not the way it happened at all!"

From behind the large table Anthony said, "You'll have your chance to explain your side of things, Lieutenant. In the meantime, let the police chief continue her interrogations."

Then I turned to Flagg, swore him to honest testimony, and asked him, "Explain to me about this envelope that you found on Monè's desk."

Monè stood. "Envelope on my desk?"

"Lieutenant Monè," Anthony said, and Monè sat.

Flagg said, "Ms. Morais, Mr. Mayor, I was visiting the metro squad room for some errands."

I held up a hand. "What would those errands be?"

"Just some questions about some reports that had come in that I wanted to confirm."

It was vague, but I let it go. "Go on."

"I went into Lieutenant Monè's office, and I found this." He took an envelope out of his jacket pocket.

I offered him an evidence bag. "In here, please."

"What?"

"In here, please. Now, Lieutenant!"

He dropped the envelope into the bag. I sealed it up and handed it to DeHaven. "Take this to the lab. They are waiting for it. All right, go on, Lieutenant," I said.

Flagg continued, "Well, it looked suspicious. A delivery with Monè's name."

"What was suspicious about that?" I did not say that I had similar suspicions myself.

"There . . . have been rumors that Monè was on the take."

Monè shouted, "Ma'am, that's a lie! I'm not—"

I raised my hand. "Silence! Lieutenant Flagg, you had not reported those rumors to me?"

"No, ma'am. If I was wrong, I would've ruined the reputation of a good man."

"That is a pretty serious charge you are making," I said. "What proof do you have?"

"Informants, ma'am. People I can't bring in or they'll clam up. So like I said, I have nothing I can prove."

I checked my comp. The lab was nearly done with the evidence. "And do you have any other reports of wrongdoing by Lieutenant Monè?"

"Ms. Morais—" Monè objected again; but Nick waved a hand to stop him.

Flagg looked at Nick, and his face got a little green. "Well, ma'am, I was following up on that investigation you assigned us. There were some irregularities in some reports, some insurance claims."

I looked over at Nick, knowing. "Oh, really?"

"Most of the suspicious reports were filed by Monè when he was in DPS."

"Ma'am!"

"Hush, Lieutenant Monè." I turned back to Flagg. "Most?"

Flagg swallowed and looked away. "The rest . . . The ones I looked at . . . The rest were by Vile."

"You can't believe that, ma'am!" Vile said.

I smiled at her. "Sit down, Lieutenant," I said. "I do not believe it. But if I had acted like I did not, the real guilty party would have known I was suspicious, and would have fled. They would not have been here in this room where I need them."

At that, most of my squad sat straighter. No one spoke, but there was a tension in the air. Everyone stared at me, except for Flagg. He remained casual, unconcerned. Was he the one?

I checked my comm, and I saw a message from DeHaven. "Alonzo," I said, "could you let Officer DeHaven in?"

Alonzo was as quiet and efficient as always, reaching the door before I had finished my request. He opened the door to the outer chamber, and Officer DeHaven came in. I held out my hand, and he handed over the envelopes, now in larger clear sleeves with the report attached.

But the reports were just there for the chain of evidence. I did not need to read the paper, I had the reports on my comm already. I looked them over, paused, and then continued my exposition: "These are the results from the lab. The blockchips in both envelopes were untraceable, naturally, and they add up to a nice haul: confirmed 3,500 Lunars, in an unlocked condition. Legal tender here, on Luna, or anywhere in space; and convertible for a small fee in most jurisdictions on Earth."

I tapped the reports. "It is a nice little haul, but still not enough to risk your career over. Not unless you are getting this on a regular basis. I hope that if one of you is for sale, you do not sell yourself so cheaply.

"Now as for the envelope . . . The lab found that clean of any fingerprints except mine"—I looked at Vile—"and yours."

"Ma'am—"

"Relax, Vile. As frames go, this was pretty ugly." I turned around and looked at the squad, pausing at Flagg. Still he did not look up. "Pretty stupid, in fact. Mine are on it because I picked it up to look at it, of course. DeHaven's are not. I made him use an evidence bag. And the courier, whoever that was, must have used gloves. But this thing is spotless, no prints whatsoever, except Vile's. And she had not been there to pick it up!"

At that, Flagg glanced at me; when he saw me looking back, he turned back to studying the floor. Vile, meanwhile, half rose and said, "You're right!"

I smiled. "You will find I usually am, given time. And the other envelope has only Flagg's prints, since he . . . *found* it.

"But there is more. Stratigraphic analysis shows my prints, a layer of skin oils, over top of yours. That would indicate that you touched the envelope *before* I did—and then were stupid enough to leave it out where somebody could find it." Vile started to speak, but I continued, "You're not that stupid. I have read your file. Besides, a chemical analysis of 'your' prints shows skin oil mixed with elements of an adhesive."

Vile's eyes narrowed. "Adhesive?"

"Yes." I paced before the squad. "I am disappointed in whichever of you did this. Not just that you are corrupt, but that you're *stupid*! This trick was old in the twentieth century. It is my fault, I guess, I should institute a proper police academy and teach you all better investigative techniques." I turned back to Vile. "Someone with access to something you touched lifted your prints with an adhesive and laid them down on the envelope. I suspect we will find Monè's sticky prints on the other envelope. It was a pretty clumsy effort."

"But who?" Vile asked, staring suspiciously at her squad mates.

"That is what we are here to answer," I said. I tapped my comm, pushing reports to the big screen on the wall behind Anthony. "Let us review. There have been a number of suspicious accidents in the city, what we believe to be fraudulent insurance claims. Most of those pre-dated our department, but were investigated by Public Safety; and you all were part of Public Safety then, right?" They nodded. "So looking at these reports, we see"—I zoomed in on a relevant line—"that all of them were investigated and signed off on by the same people: Erica Vile and Arun Monè."

"What? I never—"

"Relax, Monè. That is what is in the official records here in the Maxwell City offices. But apparently our security needs some work. Someone has gotten access. But who?" I smiled at Flagg. We would see how well his cool held up. "Someone who could *not* access the records filed with São Paulo Mutual, and could not imagine we would ever check there." I turned to Nick. "But we did. Mr. Aames, what did we find?"

Nick rose from his chair and took a step behind Flagg. "Ma'am," he said, "I just got the results back from São Paulo, and they're the same in every case: every one of those reports was signed off on originally by Jordan Flagg."

I watched Flagg, wondering if he would bolt, deny, or try to bluff. Nick was ready if the man became violent.

But he surprised me. Without looking up at me, he said in a calm, measured voice, "My name is Jordan Flagg, and I am a citizen of Bettendorf, Iowa. I demand to have my case heard by a representative of my government."

14. Port Shannon

"He cannot do that!" I said.

"Of course he can, Ms. Morais," Nick said. "It's in the Compact."

"Space the Compact!" I said.

Anthony glanced around his office, as if worried who might have heard me. But the room was practically empty. I had asked Vile and Monè to join us in the mayor's office, but the rest of my squad had escorted Flagg down to the holding area. It was just Anthony, Nick, Vile, Monè, Alonzo, and me.

But Anthony still seemed nervous. "You have to watch that kind of talk, Rosie," he said. "You're going to give the Realists ammunition."

"Space the Realists," I replied. "That man is an accessory to murder."

"Probably," Anthony answered. "But the Mars Compact is the overriding authority here. The international signatories that chartered our settlement all agreed that any member of any mission or settlement could choose the jurisdiction of their home nation over that of local authorities."

"But that is ridiculous," I answered. "That has not been invoked in . . . in years. In a decade or more."

Alonzo cleared his throat. "I'm afraid you're wrong there, ma'am. It gets invoked all the time on minor matters. I'm afraid it's something of a standard way to settle labor disputes. A worker threatens to invoke the Compact, and that makes the boss decide just how big of an issue some disciplinary matter really is. Most of the time, they drop it. Sometimes, though, they press it; and then the worker invokes the Compact."

"And then what? We wait nine months for someone from Earth to get up here to handle things?"

Anthony sat, scowling. "No," he said with a sigh. "What happens is the government in question first decides whether they accept the jurisdiction. Sometimes they don't. Sometimes they decide that the citizenship claim is invalid. And then usually they delegate their authority in the case to the Initiative representatives here on Mars."

"Oh, great," I replied. "That means Chief Hogan and Admiral Etough."

Anthony nodded. "It's not as bad as it sounds. Etough delegates to Hogan unless it's a high-profile case, and Hogan can be reasonable. Sometimes the employer's in the wrong. Those he settles pretty consistently for the employee. Sometimes the employee's in the wrong, and they're surprised to learn that Hogan finds for the employer, and they have to face sanctions dictated up from Earth. But sometimes I think Hogan just likes to stick it to us."

"One more argument for the Libertists," Alonzo interjected.

I looked around the room. "So our hands are tied?"

"Yes, tied," Anthony said. "We can't touch Flagg. We're going to have to turn him over to Hogan. We can't take too long at it either. He frowns on that."

I sighed. "All right. But, at least that bastard's out of my squad." Then I remembered the other officers in the room. I turned to them. "Vile, Monè, I apologize for what I just put you through."

"It's all right, ma'am," Vile said. Monè nodded.

"No." I shook my head. "It was necessary, but it was not all right. I was sure you were being framed; but I was equally sure that if I let anyone know that, the person behind it would be impossible to catch. By acting like I had a case against you, I fooled Flagg so he would hang around to see how it played out. I had to use you, and I am sorry for that."

Vile relaxed a bit in her seat. "It *is* all right, ma'am," Monè said.

I shook my head again. "I do not buy it. I saw your faces as the accusations mounted. You were angry, right?" They sat in silence. "Right?"

As I persisted, I saw the color returning to Vile's cheeks. "Yes," she said at last.

"Angry because you were innocent?"

Monè answered, "Angry because I couldn't prove the truth!"

I heard Nick chuckle softly behind me, but I kept my focus on Vile and Monè. "So which is it? Is it about you, or about the truth?"

"Both!" Vile said.

"Good!" That puzzled them. "Vile, Monè, I think Flagg picked you two because he thought you would be easy marks. Of all my squad, you are the most cooperative. The most pliant. You go along with things."

"I'm trying to be a good officer, ma'am," Vile said.

"A good team member," Monè answered.

"Good for you both; but you cannot let anyone steamroll you just because you are trying to be cooperative." I tilted my head back over my shoulder. "Vile, you let Mr. Aames bully you at the fire investigation site until you had to call for backup."

"He's . . . insistent, ma'am."

I managed to keep from smiling. "He is that, Lieutenant." I turned to Alonzo. "Please record commendations for Vile and Monè on this date." Then I turned to Anthony. "Any objections?"

"None, ma'am. I trust your judgment."

I turned back to the lieutenants. "And I trust yours; but can I trust you to stand up for it? Not question yourself just because somebody with authority or just bullheadedness pushes back?"

Slowly Vile nodded. "Yes, ma'am." She paused, then added, "I'll . . . work on that."

"*We* will," Monè confirmed.

I turned back to Anthony. "So we have commendations to announce. Do you think that will counter any rumors that Flagg may have spread about them?"

Anthony looked at Alonzo. "Don't ask me, ask Alonzo. He's the PR expert. I'm just a policy guy, a glorified Mars explorer."

I turned to Alonzo.

"I'm already handling it, ma'am," he said. "I think it will all go over fine. It's going to be a mess no matter what we do, and we can be sure that Grace will use this to her advantage in her ads. Nothing we can do about that. But I think Vile and Monè will come out looking pretty good."

I could have foisted my next responsibility off onto one of my subordinates. I was not looking forward to the visit to Fort Hudson, but it had to be done. Someone had to effect prisoner transfer to the Initiative command; and after what I had just been through, I was reluctant to trust anyone with the job but myself.

It hurt that the team I thought I had been building into a good, reliable squad had harbored a traitor. It happens, but I thought I had known better. This was not my first command.

And if I was unsure who I could trust, then I needed to see to Flagg's delivery personally. I took DeHaven as an escort—it would not do to use Vile or Monè, no sense in putting them in a position of responsibility for the man who tried to frame them—and we set out to Charlie Tube and the slidewalk to Port Shannon.

Traffic was light that morning. Much of Maxwell City's population was at work at that hour. DeHaven did a good job of breaking traffic for us as I pushed Flagg ahead and onto the slidewalk.

Flagg was silent but cooperative. He must have decided that Initiative authority would be more tractable. But I had him cuffed anyway. I was taking no chances.

We passed the off-slide for two residential districts, and then one for a light industrial district. Next was the outer ring, including drop tubes for the Services level.

After that came the long slidewalk out to the port. Traffic was even lighter there. When there were no ships in, there was not a lot of commuting to and from the port. And there had been no ships in port for almost a week.

The slide stopped at the port, and we stepped off. Flagg stumbled—accidentally, I think, though I could not be sure—but I caught him before he fell. "Watch your step, Flagg," I said.

He grunted back at me, and we marched him up to the Customs area. Beyond that lay Port Shannon Lopez, named for the first crewmember lost on Nick's mission that had founded the city. The port was a neutral zone, jointly administered by Maxwell City and the Initiative. That was something of a legal fiction, unless the Libertists got their way, as Maxwell City was ultimately under Initiative control; but we had enough autonomous rule and separate departments to require a small bureaucracy just to manage joint operations between us and the Initiative. And Customs was part of that bureaucracy, the demarcation between joint control and local control.

DeHaven and I marched Flagg up to a kiosk where a guard waited to check credentials. She looked bored, almost half-asleep with so little traffic coming through. Her skin was nearly as dark as her black Admiralty uniform, and she wore her hair in short, tight curls. Her expression was bland as she looked up. "Can I help you?"

"I am Police Chief Rosalia Morais," I answered. "We are supposed to effect prisoner transfer for Jordan Flagg of Bettendorf, Iowa."

"Yes, ma'am," she said. There was just a slight emphasis on my title. Was she mocking it? It would not surprise me. I had been on both sides of this desk, long before she had been stationed here, no doubt. Back when I had been an admiral in charge of orbital traffic for all of Mars, many in the Admiralty had expressed open contempt for the idea of Martian independence; and I had seen that contaminate the forces under them. I had done my best to curtail that simply for practical reasons: contempt breeds resentment, and resentment breeds trouble. If anything, Admiralty attitudes were pushing more people into the Libertist camp as a very predictable reaction. It also made joint operations, such as Customs, much trickier because no one was inclined to cooperate with someone they resented.

But I responded as I had back then: with professionalism, even congeniality—until someone took advantage of it. "Thank you, Spacer," I said. "So do we take him through?"

She shook her head. "My instructions are that you are to wait in the anteroom"—she pointed to a door at the side of the tunnel—"until Chief Hogan arrives to take custody of the prisoner."

That was unacceptable, but it was not the spacer's fault. I would have to take that up with Hogan—exactly the confrontation I would have rather avoided.

The anteroom door slid open at our approach, and DeHaven stepped in, scanning the area. Then he looked back at me. Like myself, DeHaven was formerly with the Initiative, working in security. That was another reason I had chosen him for this assignment: I knew he could handle trouble if Flagg gave us any. DeHaven gave a thumbs-up. "All clear, ma'am." He stepped inside, and I nudged Flagg through the door.

As the door slid shut behind us, I heard a solid click. We were secure inside. Since this was still the Maxwell City side of Customs, this should be under our jurisdiction, and my police chief's credentials should work on the door. I thought of testing it but decided not to make an issue. No sense ruffling Hogan's feathers any further.

The room was sparse, with an empty desk, two chairs in front of it, one behind. Without waiting for instruction, Flagg flopped himself down in the left chair. I remained standing, as did DeHaven.

Our wait was only a few seconds before the door clicked again, sliding open and letting Chief Hogan enter. With four of us plus the desk and chairs, the room was pretty crowded, so I squeezed aside to let him in. I noted approvingly that DeHaven did as well, while keeping Flagg always in sight.

"Excuse me," Chief Hogan said as he snuck behind the desk. Then he turned back to us, holding out his hand. "Ms. Morais."

There was a slight sardonic tone in his voice. You would have to know him to pick up on it, but I did. Ignoring it, I shook his hand. "Good afternoon, Chief Hogan. We are here for the prisoner transfer. There seems to be some problem?"

Hogan shook his head, and he looked at Flagg. "No problem, ma'am, just procedure. Prisoner, stand up."

Flagg stood, staring from me to Hogan and back again.

Hogan tapped a button on his comm, and the record light came on. "I need your statement for the record, please."

Flagg kept his face neutral. "My name is Jordan Flagg, and I am a citizen of Bettendorf, Iowa. I demand that my case be processed by a representative of my government."

Hogan leaned forward to speak clearly into his comm. "I am Chief Ralph Hogan, commander of Fort Hudson, speaking on behalf of the System Initiative in representation of the United States of America and the city of Bettendorf, Iowa. I have confirmed Jordan Flagg's citizenship claim, and I am taking him into custody from Police Chief Rosalia Morais of Maxwell City." Then he glanced at me.

I spoke up for the comm. "I am Police Chief Rosalia Morais of Maxwell City, and I am formally transferring Jordan Flagg to your custody. Charges and details have already been transferred to your system."

Hogan spoke again. "I accept your transfer of the prisoner, and I acknowledge receipt of the necessary paperwork regarding all charges against this man and his surrender of all claims territorial, property, and intellectual in the project known as Maxwell City, Mars. All of the paperwork appears to be in order, so we accept custody of the prisoner." He tapped off the recorder and pressed the signal button. "This is Chief Hogan. You can take the prisoner now."

The door clicked again and slid open, and a large, armored Rapid Response Team trooper stepped in. Another stood behind him, but the anteroom had no more cubic, especially for another one that big. Hogan nodded at Flagg, and the trooper in the room took Flagg's arm and tugged him toward the door. Flagg did not resist.

The door remained open after the troopers left, and I started toward it; but Hogan cleared his throat. "Ma'am, a word if I may?"

DeHaven looked at me, a question on his face; but I shook my head. "You can go back to your duties, DeHaven." Then I thought I should add something. "Good work today." This whole affair was going to play hell with department morale, so I would have to start reinforcing it.

This time when the door slid shut, there was no security click. Hogan sat behind the desk. "Have a seat, Police Chief."

I slid lightly into the nearest chair. "You do not have to say 'chief' like it is an insult."

His eyes narrowed. "It *is* an insult, Rosie. You were an admiral. Second-in-command of all of Mars. Now you're just a . . . a rent-a-cop for a bunch of Downies."

I shook my head. "The term is 'Martians,'" I said firmly. "I taught you better than that. Show some respect."

"Respect? For what? For this bunch of tunnel rats?"

"They are settlers. Scientists and engineers. Explorers."

He shook his head. "Explorers! Damn few of them. The real explorers are out on the surface, mapping and measuring and sampling. This place is just a hick town in space, just like any other hick town near a spaceport. You— They came all the way out here just to be Downies. They could've stayed home for that."

I sighed. His was a common attitude. I had shared it myself, back when I had been in charge of traffic. I had kept it quiet better than he did, but I had shared it.

But I had not understood then, and he wouldn't either. You had to live on Mars, with a real commitment to make it your new home, before you really got the mindset of Maxwell City. As an assignment, it was pretty pathetic, like the worst downside duty; but as a life, it mattered to me. "We are building something here."

He sat back. "And that's enough for you?"

I glanced down at the badge on my chest. "More than enough. This is not some experiment. This is a home. A new home for humanity."

He snickered. "You sound like a Libertist."

I smiled. "I have to be. I have nowhere else to go."

At that, his eyes turned down. "Thanks to that bastard Aames."

I glared. "That bastard is my husband, Chief. And a better spacer than you will ever be."

His eyes grew wide, and I could see he knew he had gone too far. "Sorry, ma'am."

I knew he was not sorry. Nick had made a lot of enemies in the Initiative. A few friends had let me know privately that they thought Nick had done the right thing, and that Aldrin City was working out well for Earth, Mars, and the investors. But most of them followed the party line: Nick was persona non grata; and because I had chosen to back him up, I was a pariah as well.

But in this new role, I was going to have to deal with the Initiative again, with Hogan. So, it was time to build some bridges. "I accept your apology." Then I added with a smile, "So is that why you kept me here? To talk old times? To talk dirt about the dirt diggers?"

"No. I wanted a chance to talk to you privately. Personal matters." Then he reached down and turned off his comm.

I raised my eyebrows. "Personal?"

"Yes."

I turned off my comm as well. Then in a lower voice I asked, "Is this room secure?"

He smiled. "That's why I wanted to do the transfer here, Rosie. I can't talk on the other side of Customs, too many listening places. I needed to talk to you, as a friend."

"Are we still friends?"

"Yes, damn it! I'll never understand what you did, but I'm still your friend. Officially, I have to keep things formal. But off the record"—he glanced at his comm—"I don't want you blindsided."

"By?"

"By some people very high up who are taking an interest in this election of yours."

"High up in the Initiative?"

He nodded. "And not just them. There's money behind it too. There's a real push to make sure your Realists prevail."

"I thought you agreed with the Realists?"

"I agree with fair elections, following the polls, and letting events take their course. I think the Realists are right, you all are not ready for independence; but that's got to be your decision. I don't get a say in it, and neither should anyone else off-world. There's a process for this, and there shouldn't be interference."

"But there is."

"But there is. I wish I had details for you, but I'm still tracking them down myself. I just wanted to let you know there are a lot of things going on behind the scenes, and you need to watch your back."

15. Table of Organization

By the time I was done with Hogan, the biweekly transport had reached orbit, and Port Shannon was coming alive with workers. A steady stream of people passed through the express security lane, where port credentials cleared them for the scanners as fast as they could go through. A longer, slower line passed through the Customs station. Scans there were mostly perfunctory, identification and DNA checks. These were not port workers, but they were merchants and agents and brokers who knew the routine. Sprinkled among them were just enough tourists and researchers to gum up the works with their confusion about the routine.

The transports carried high-ticket luxury goods and VIP passengers, people and goods that just could not wait for the slow but economical transport of Aldrin City and the *Collins*. These fusion-powered rockets cost nearly twenty times more per kilo delivered than the *Aldrin* did, even after you factored in the lower life-support costs due to the shorter trips. So these were the mainstay of the port economy, the goods and people with money to burn; and our people were there, ready to take that money. If anything ever interfered with this commerce, Maxwell City would not be viable, not at its current size.

That was a strong argument on the Realist side: that Maxwell City, that all of Mars was not yet self-sustaining. But it was more complicated than that. Manhattan on Earth could not feed itself, nor could São Paulo, Moscow, or London. But they could do enough commerce to keep the food coming. Aldrin City had already proved net self-sufficiency and had been granted independence. The Libertists argued that our research and tourism economy was solid, dependable, able to sustain Mars into the future as we slowly built up our own agricultural capabilities. They had the charts and graphs to back them up; but did they have the confidence of the people?

I weaved my way through the lines and to the slidewalk back to the city proper. The slide was full of tourists and researchers, plus a few local merchants. The latter moved at two speeds: slow and dejected, or fast and triumphant. Micro fortunes were made every day at Port Shannon. And more were lost.

With a practiced eye, I could tell tourists from researchers more often than not. Researchers were here for longer stays. Whether corporate, government, or academic, the cost to bring them out here was high; so no one sent them for short journeys. And it could be a career killer to waste the trip, to become injured or ill or manic and have to go home early. So as a group the researchers took their conditioning more seriously: they took their nanotherapy to stave off bone loss and radiation risks, yes; but they also followed the strict training regimen to prepare themselves for the local gravity. They were the ones who walked the slide almost with the ease of locals. But not the tourists. A few of them could fool me, the eager would-be explorers who took everything seriously. But the rest, the ones for whom a trip to Mars was a lark, were finding that Martian gravity was more of a challenge than they expected. They overcorrected, taking very small steps, or they undercorrected and bounced. After a few mishaps, you would find them clinging to the safety rail on the slide. There were always a few injuries as people learned safety lessons the hard way.

In fact, I saw a Public Safety officer up ahead, pulling a tourist from the low-speed slide. She easily lifted the man into the air, making his eyes grow wide in surprise; and then she hopped over the low slide barrier and onto the unmoving floor beyond. She lowered him to the floor and inspected his leg.

By that time I had slid on past, so I did not see how bad his injuries were. I trusted Public Safety to handle it, as they had countless times in the past. They had an excellent safety record.

C

When I got back to the apartment, it was nearly 2100. There had been paperwork to file, reports to review, and reports to make to Anthony and Alonzo. I had let them know what Hogan had told me—without identifying him as the source, but they would figure that out easily enough. Anthony had been concerned, but Alonzo had just nodded as if he had expected it.

It was not the first time that I had come home that late, so I was not surprised to find Nick tucked away in the workroom, wiring up trees. I was a little surprised, though, at his choice in music. Like so many things since he was young, Nick's taste in music were strongly influenced by Brazil. His grandmother had worked there, his mentor had been born there, and he and I had both trained there in my homeland. Nick was as Brazilian as an Alabama hillbilly could get.

But usually he liked mellow songs or light, danceable tunes. That night he was listening to classic Brazilian thrash metal, Korzus. That was never a good sign. Nick had picked up his taste for metal from his brother, Derick—or Dek, as he called him—and it only came out when Nick was in a bad mood.

I sighed, and I went to the kitchen. I did not know what had upset Nick, but I knew better than to try to get it out of him. In our youth, I had tried to cajole him and cheer him up in his rare angry moods. I had learned the hard way: that never worked. Nick would come around in his time, and he would explain or not as he saw fit. Until then, I would give him some space.

I was lying in bed, reviewing the day's incident reports, when the music finally stopped. I heard Nick in the kitchen, finding some food. Then he came into the bedroom, carrying a plate of cheddar and a bottle of Martian Springs. He set them down on the bed stand and started to undress.

"Hello, Nico," I said. I did not question, I just let him set the tone.

"Hello, Rosie," he said. He tossed his shirt into the hamper; and then he picked up a slice of cheese and held it out, almost to my mouth. "Hungry?"

I smiled. He was over whatever it was. I nibbled at the cheese. "Thank you," I said, "but I did get dinner. I do not want to eat all of yours."

He shrugged. "I'm not that hungry," he said; but he finished the slice.

He seemed relaxed, so I took a chance. "Nick, can I help?"

"No," he answered. "You've got too much to do. I'll take care of it, don't worry."

That was part of it, I could tell. I was too busy, and he wanted my time, but he was too proud to ask for it. And now that he had taken a stand, I could not even offer without his stubborn pride making him refuse more strongly. I wished I had been more intuitive sooner.

☾

I woke up early, slipping out quietly so as not to wake Nick. I showered quickly and rushed to my office. Zeb's was not open at that hour, but we had the codes for the service door on a maintenance tunnel.

I needed the early start. I had a big task that I had to get out of the way before the shift began: a hole in my table of organization that had to be filled now that Flagg was gone. Three weeks in, we still were not up to full staffing as it was, and now I was down one in the command squad.

And my task was more complicated because I had *two* viable candidates: Brooks and DeHaven. Both had impressed me, Brooks for quick action, DeHaven for being willing to tell me uncomfortable truths. I did not have more than that on either of them, but that was not surprising. I still had a lot to learn about the patrol officers. Neither of them might be right for the position, but they were good candidates to start with. I pulled up their résumés and began to read.

Forty minutes later, I was no closer to a decision. Anthony's recruiters had done a good job: they were both excellent. DeHaven had a respectable record in Initiative Security, including commendations from Admiral Etough on Phobos Base for rescue work. Then he had transferred to port duty, where he had worked in both Customs inspection and surface rescue. Finally he had applied to emigrate to Maxwell City, where he had served admirably in DPS.

Brooks, meanwhile, was practically a native. She had emigrated as a youth with her parents, a team of agricultural researchers. She was one of the earliest children accepted as immigrants, and thus she had grown up under a microscope. Authorities had watched her and her cohort carefully in order to judge whether accepting children was a good idea. Some of the kids had rebelled under the scrutiny. Brooks herself had, for a while; but she had matured early, and she seemed dedicated to proving that she belonged on Mars. She took a series of jobs around the city, each seemingly chosen for the learning opportunities, ending up with a respectable record in Public Safety. And now in the police force.

There were other patrol officers with equally impressive records, no doubt; but these two had caught my attention, and I liked what I saw. Their résumés reinforced that; but they did *not* give me a good reason to decide between them. I liked Brooks because she had stronger roots in the community. It was a delicate consideration, but I wanted to reward DeHaven for his frankness, and I wanted to build morale. If I promoted

Brooks over him, it might even make him think I had passed him over because I had not liked what he had said. That could fester and make him clam up.

If possible, I wanted to promote both of them. And maybe I could.

I called Anthony. He was in early as well, so I told him I would be right over.

☾

"Vile? Are you serious?"

"She is good, Anthony." I poured some water from his wet bar, then sat in the mesh chair in front of his desk. "And we need somebody. The TO calls for *two* deputy chiefs, so we have a command officer for all shifts. Right now we have none, and I am stretched pretty thin."

"But Vile?"

I pushed her file to his desk, but he should already know it. "She was already a shift commander in Public Safety. She has surface experience, port experience, and a solid academic record."

"But she has no police experience."

I waved that away. "Who does? It is not like we have budget to recruit out from Earth. They are all learning on the job. Her record says she is a quick learner; and if we promote her, it will create another vacancy in the command squad. I can promote Brooks *and* DeHaven."

Anthony looked into space and shook his head. "Yes, it makes sense for the TO. And I agree, her record was good . . . right up until yesterday, when she was accused of taking a bribe."

"That is ridiculous! We already cleared her of that."

"I know." Anthony frowned. "But . . . I wish Alonzo were in. How's this going to look to the journos?"

I set down my cup, and I stood. "The journos? Anthony, do you want a police force or a campaign ad?"

He looked up and sighed. "All right, I deserve that. But have you seen the stories from yesterday?"

"No, I was working most of the night."

"They're brutal." He pulled up media feeds on his desk, and he pointed at them. "They make it sound like the whole force is under suspicion. Some of the editorials suggest that Vile and Monè's commendations are payoffs. Now you want to promote Vile?"

"Yes, I do." I could have said more, but I was angry. I was afraid what might come out. So I just stared at Anthony. And I fumed.

Finally Anthony nodded. "Okay. You're right. We can't let the journos run the city. Do it. I'll let Alonzo figure out the messaging."

16. WARRANTS

Vile beamed when I pinned her new badge on her. "I'll do my best, ma'am."

"You will work your butt off, Vile." I smiled. "I have sent you links to sites on Compact regulations, jurisprudence, investigative procedures, and criminal psychology. That is on top of your regular command squad training. Say good-bye to your free time, because your nights are now study time."

"What about my weekends?"

"You do not get weekends. Not until the TO is fully staffed and operational. Welcome to command."

"Yes, ma'am."

"Meanwhile you're my shadow. And my sanity check. I expect you to follow me around, learn what I am doing, and ask questions. *Any* questions. Make me explain what I am doing until you get it. And if you think I am wrong, say something."

"That's . . ."

"That is your job, Deputy Chief. I do not need a flunky, I need a stubborn partner who *thinks*. Is that you?"

She grinned. "I can be stubborn."

I grinned back. "Good. Let us go give Brooks and DeHaven the good news."

☾

With Vile by my side, I dug back into the insurance investigation. Thanks to Nick—and to Flagg's inept attempts to cover his tracks—we had a good way to identify at least some fraudulent claims: if the records on Earth said Flagg and the records on Mars said someone else, it was a lead; and already I had Sergeant Moore down in Digital Investigations working through city files to correlate those leads. Moore was dealing with Earth–Mars communication lag and the bureaucracies of seven different insurance companies, but the work was proceeding.

But too slowly! Yesterday Rockford had reported on the allegations and counterallegations of corruption within the force. Now she had more details, a broad picture of the insurance fraud case. Space her and her sources! Now, with these new stories, I could almost *see* evidence being burned and suspects fleeing.

It was not that easy: Mars was a set of confined environments with limited transports between them. But there were always ways; and every month small new settlements and bases popped up. Someone with enough money could buy secrecy and escape. Buy clean new records. I had to move fast.

"Vile, get on the line to Hogan and give him an alert for any of the persons on our suspect list traveling to orbit or to other settlements." I opened my comm, and I called Anthony. "Mr. Mayor, have you seen the latest news reports?"

Anthony looked harried. Alonzo was working behind him, not looking much better. "Yes," Anthony answered. "And we've got a flood of questions coming in about them."

"I am afraid you are going to get more. I am headed to Magistrate Montgomery."

"Montgomery? Do you have to?"

I reined in my temper. "Yes, Mr. Mayor. If I do not get some warrants, and fast, we will lose every bit of evidence we have in this case. I know this will not make me popular, so I wanted to give you a heads-up. But there is no time to argue. I have to go."

I cut off just as Alonzo was about to speak, and I headed around the Concourse to the Admin Center.

Magistrate Montgomery wasted no time. I had already sent across my request and my evidence so far, and she had reviewed them. Appearing before her was just a formality, one she might skip for warrants that involved imminent danger to lives or critical systems. But for warrants this sensitive, the officer pressing them had to appear in court.

Montgomery looked across her desk at me, and she shook her head. "You sure know how to make a splash, ma'am," she said. She was an older woman, one of the earliest Martian settlers. She had made a good start on a scientific career when an accident in the field had left her with time to kill during rehabilitation.

She had spent her downtime during rehab studying her other interest, law. She became fascinated with concepts of jurisprudence on another world where international coalitions governed. She went back into the field when she was healthy, but science no longer fascinated her like law did. She was older now, going gray, but her mind was as sharp as ever; and she had written the definitive text on the Compact. She had been on Mars almost since the beginning, and along with Nick was one of that small group that were hailed and respected as founders.

"You're not going to make any friends," Montgomery continued.

"I know, Magistrate. I do not need friends, I need to make a case."

She narrowed her eyes. "You've got a pretty good start." She signed her comp. "I'm approving all these warrant requests, subject to the limitations and super jurisdiction of the Compact. Go get your evidence, and your suspects if you can."

"Thank you, Magistrate." We both knew what she meant: suspects could cite the Compact, though evidence could not so easily be transferred. If this large group of prominent businesspeople all turned themselves over to Initiative authority en masse, it would be a media sensation.

But space it, I was *not* going to let them hide behind that, behind anything. I tapped my comm. "Sergeant Moore, we have authority. Start sealing the records. I have cc'd the Initiative inspector general, so let me know if you have any trouble getting them to cooperate." Then I changed channels. "Vile, we have the warrants. Execute immediately."

☾

The media explosion was every bit as bad as I had expected. The journos went wild, with story after story about corruption in Maxwell City. You could tell where the journos' sympathies lay: some played up the idea of corrupt businessmen on Mars who needed better government oversight, while others accused the government itself of being out of control.

Tara Rockford led the latter group, with zeal and guile. I suspect that she was camping at Carla Grace's campaign, because it did not take twenty minutes after word broke for her to air an interview with Grace. "So what is your reaction to the stories of rampant insurance fraud across Maxwell City?"

Grace looked down as if in sadness, but I could see her mouth turned up, barely concealing a smug smile. "I'm afraid it's business as usual in Maxwell City," she answered. "This is the way things have always been run, it's just that now journalists like you are bringing it to light." I cursed inwardly at that. How the hell did the journos get the credit? "This is why it's time for a change. Under my administration, we'll work more closely with Initiative Security and Initiative auditors."

"Your opponent would say that will only stifle growth and innovation."

At that Grace's eyes grew brighter and narrower. "My opponent has a long history of putting 'innovation,' as he calls it, ahead of good governance and the orderly development of Mars. If companies have to commit fraud to make Mars viable, then maybe Mars isn't viable yet."

The feed changed to another story, interviews with random people in the tubes, and I turned it off. Before my finger even left the comm, Anthony's line was blinking. It was going to be a very long day.

17. Horace Gale in Custody

It got worse from there. My day was occupied with interviews, arrests, and arraignments. I set up a temporary workspace outside Montgomery's court. I was in and out of there so often, it did not make sense to keep walking back and forth around the Concourse.

The arraignments were all pro forma, as every single person we brought in cited the Compact as soon as charges were read. But I was the police chief, the complainant, so I had to be there to stand and read the charges for everyone.

It was during the eighth arraignment of the day, or maybe the ninth, when a priority alert came on my comm. I discreetly tapped the audio button, and the text sounded in my subcutaneous earpiece: *Ms. Morais, contact me ASAP. Hogan.*

I did not respond. It would not do to disrespect Montgomery's court after all the trouble I created for her. But when the magistrate announced a lunch recess, I raised my hand to be noticed. "Yes, Ms. Morais?" she said.

"Magistrate, I have an urgent communiqué from the Initiative, and I have to meet with them. After the recess, Deputy Chief Vile will appear for the city."

"Understood, Ms. Morais. Court is in recess." She banged her gavel.

As soon as I got back to my alcove, I opened a comm line to Fort Hudson, and I asked for Hogan. When his face came on the screen, I could see annoyance in the set of his jaw. Before he could speak, I said, "Sorry for the added workload, Chief."

He shook his head. "Heavy hangs the head, you know the rest. We'll handle it."

"I am sure you will. How can I help? You have new information?"

"I have more than information," he answered. "I have a suspect."

I glanced at my comp, trying to figure out who on the list was unaccounted for. "Green? Lang?"

He shook his head. "No one from your watch list, but a person of interest. He won't talk, not to us. He says he wants to talk to . . . Aames."

"Nick?"

"Chief, it's Horace Gale. I think you'll want to talk to him."

☾

I found myself once again in the anteroom outside of Customs. I was not alone for long: Chief Hogan showed up only a couple of minutes after I did. He closed the door behind him, shook my hand, and sat down behind the desk. I sat as well.

Before I could say anything, he began, "I thought you'd want to talk here." He tapped his comm. "Off the record."

I tapped mine as well. It was already off recording. "Thank you, Chief. So between us, what is going on?"

"I did warn you that you don't have a lot of support on my side of Customs. There are those in the Admiralty for whom it's not just about the future of Mars. It's personal for them. They're still pissed at you and Aames."

"*You* are still pissed at Nick."

"Not enough for this. Ma'am, it's not in writing anywhere, but I've been urged to slow walk anything that helps you or Maxwell City from this point forward. Especially you. I think they'd like to see you fail as a result, so that your reputation will be blackened."

"They trashed my reputation pretty well as it is."

"On Earth, sure. In the services? Absolutely. That's why the fact that Maxwell City and Mars have taken you in, given you a home, given you and Aames authority—"

"Nick is a private citizen. No authority."

"Sure. He's *just* a founder. Nobody listens to him, right? Nobody except the old hands, the second generation, some of the third, everyone on the *Aldrin*, and half of Luna. Every malcontent who thinks the Initiative needs a black eye, well, Nick Aames is a hero to them."

I did not try to hide a smile. "Sometimes black eyes are instructive."

Hogan shook his head. "Not at the top levels. You know, you were an admiral. You might swallow a dressing down from above, but no admiral likes being shown up by the lower ranks. You know that."

"What does this have to do with Horace Gale?"

"I'm getting to that. There's another side of this, though, outside the Admiralty. There are investors, business interests, lots of those in commercial space who are no big fans of the Admiralty either. Maybe even on Aames's side. But more important, some of them have money and influence. Particularly the folks at São Paulo Mutual and a few of the other big insurance companies. Word is spreading through the industry about the fraud, and they want to know what we're doing about it. They complain about our rules and restrictions; but when they're facing a loss, they come yelling to us. And so they're putting pressure in the other direction: they don't care about your crimes or your internal matters, but they want lost items accounted for and responsible parties identified and made to pay. They don't want to be responsible for any losses."

"And so . . . ?"

"And so we have a lot of pressure to identify, locate, and confiscate items from your manifest report. To treat those items as stolen property, and to treat those in possession as felons. And we found some of the items."

"With Horace Gale?"

Hogan nodded. "With Horace Gale."

I shook my head. "Gale has not been inside Maxwell City."

"You can't know that. The city's too large. There's too much traffic, ship and surface."

"I could not know it an hour ago; but after our call, I ran a check for entry and exit records. There is no record of Horace Gale entering the city in over four years."

"Unless he used a fake ID. Or an unmonitored access. You know those exist."

I sighed. "Yes, they do. Our access control is imperfect. If we tried to monitor every airlock, there would be open revolt. So he might have been around. But I have my computers interrogating security systems and bars, restaurants, hotels, shops . . . So far no matches. Certainly no financial transactions. As best we can tell, he has not been there."

Hogan looked at his comp. "All right, let's assume that. But he definitely had items in his possession that were part of the insurance claims you're investigating." He swiped at his comm, and then he grinned. "I forgot: we're cut off. But I'll send the records to you later. He was found with chemical sensors, an analyzer, and a terahertz scanner, all with serial numbers from your manifests. He was trying to sell them in the Well."

"Of course." The Well was a free-form bazaar on the north edge of Port Shannon. Spare parts, surplus cargo, used equipment, and more could all be bought or traded in the Well. It did not surprise me to learn that stolen goods were trafficked there, but there was little I could do about it. That part of the port was in the Initiative control zone. "So does he say how he came to possess them?"

"He didn't say much."

"That is surprising. Gale was always a talker."

"Oh, he talked plenty, but he didn't really say anything. He tries to be really smooth with any guards or interrogators he talks to, show them he's cooperative. But on the subject of the goods in question, he'll only say he came by them honestly, and there's no evidence to say otherwise."

"That is an interesting claim," I said. "What jurisdiction is he claiming? The laws on stolen goods vary from one to another. In some, possession of stolen goods is presumptively a crime, with the burden of proof on you to show legitimate chain of possession."

"Uh-huh," Hogan answered. "And in others, you're presumed innocent, and the authorities have to show that you knowingly acquired stolen goods. But it doesn't matter. He hasn't cited the Compact."

"He hasn't?"

"Nope." Hogan shook his head. "So he's still under Initiative jurisdiction, with no instructions from anyone on Earth. I don't know if he's lucky or smart, but Inspector General Rand tells me that there's a loophole. The question of culpability for possession of stolen goods is never specified in Initiative regulations. There's case law on it, but conflicting opinions. So until I get an official IG opinion, Gale's in a gray area. And if I *do* get an opinion and he doesn't like it, he can press for an appeal."

"I never trusted the man, but no one ever said he was stupid." Then I thought back to the comm call. "But you said he wants to talk to Nick?"

"Yes. He was very insistent about it. I ignored him at first, but he didn't let up. Then I thought maybe it would make him cooperate if I at least asked."

"So you are asking me, not Nick."

"He's your husband, ma'am. I don't even know him, except by reputation. I thought it made sense to get your opinion first. I don't like it." The way Hogan said it, I knew he really meant, *I don't like him.*

"And my authorities won't like it either. But the business interests are getting loud. So I thought I'd ask."

"And you have him here?"

"I can have him here in a minute. Should I?"

I nodded, and Hogan tapped his comm. The recording light came on. As I activated mine as well, he tapped the call button. Not long after, the door slid open, and I heard a clanking sound of metal on tile.

I turned to look, and Horace Gale stood in the doorway, an Initiative Security officer behind him. Gale was thinner than I remembered, especially his face, and older. He had less hair, and it was grayer, though the same could be said of me. But worst was his body: his frame was scrawny, like he had been working hard and eating poorly.

And the one thing that had not changed was that he was still wearing an assist suit. Five years after the accident that had crippled him, he still wore the metal frame that supported his legs and arms and kept him upright.

"Gale . . ." I paused, but curiosity overcame courtesy. "What happened? More injuries?"

"No," Gale said. He smiled, but his tone was bitter. "Same ones."

I shook my head, but then I got up and held out the third chair for him. The man was a rat, but also disabled. Even rats deserve common courtesy. As he sat, I asked, "What happened to your rehab after the accident on the *Aldrin*?" I politely avoided mentioning that he had caused the accident.

Gale hesitated. "It . . . ended, Admiral."

"Ms. Morais," I said.

"Sorry, Ms. Morais. When we came down to Mars, I was bound for the Azevedo settlement, you might remember?"

I did. It had been a long time between Nick's hearing and our arrival at Mars, nearly four months. In that time, Gale had become, well, almost a fixture in the Aldrin City rings, as if he was unwelcome in the Admiralty space in G and H Ring. Which he certainly was. He had testified against

Admiral Knapp, ending Gale's career just as surely as Nick's and mine had been ended. The Admiralty had not discharged him at the time, but it was inevitable. And so Gale had come to Dr. Baldwin and her team for his rehab after the accident that had crushed his spine, destroyed his spleen, and broiled his lungs. Not to mention the damage to his legs. Connie Baldwin is one hell of a doctor, with one hell of a Hippocratic oath. The same accident—for which Gale was largely at fault—had almost killed her husband Chuks; and yet she had made sure Gale got the best rehabilitation that Aldrin City could give him. Just never when she was in the infirmary.

"Working for Azevedo was great, for a while," Gale said. "They knew me there. Margo and her team had work for me, a good-paying job. It was . . . I belonged, Ms. Morais. You know what that's like?"

"I think I do."

"But they're a small settlement, nothing like Maxwell City. Their hospital facilities . . ." He laughed dryly. "A clinic, no more than that. They did what they could, but I lagged behind." He swallowed. "And then Margo passed away. And their board appointed a new chair, someone who was more interested in commercializing than in the science. And someone with closer ties to the Admiralty, I suspect. It wasn't a week after she was gone that I was told my services would no longer be needed. And the air charges started mounting."

"I am sorry, Gale." And I was. Nick always said that Gale was a capable spacer, just a social and career climber. It almost sounded like once he had nowhere left to climb, he had gone back to what he was really good at.

Gale shrugged, and his harness rattled. "Mars doesn't care. You produce, you contribute, or you don't breathe."

"Or you go home."

He shook his head. "I have no home, now. What did they used to say? A man without a country? That's me. If Mars doesn't want me, no place does."

I could see how rough that life would be. Gale was not exaggerating. Aside from tourists, everyone on Mars learned it soon enough: nothing in the environment was free, you had to earn your way. The only biosphere Mars had was the result of hard labor.

But at the same time, I felt like I was being played for sympathy. The Gale I knew always had an angle. And I was reluctant to get played.

So I changed the subject. "Tell me about these goods in your possession."

Gale shook his head, and Hogan glared at him. "I just . . . pick them up," Gale said. "Scavenging, you know."

I stared at Gale. "Scavenging? This is not Earth. There are no dumps just lying around."

"There are more than you would think," Gale answered. "Ma'am, have you paid attention to the Earth–Mars traffic? Once, missions here were pretty restricted. That was when the Saganists had real influence in the Initiative. There were so many levels of approval and review, putting together a Mars expedition was expensive and difficult to push through channels.

"But that was old Mars. Today, we have Maxwell City, and Tholus Under, and Alpheus Base. Plus the Azevedo settlement, and dozens of other small settlements. There are many bases for expeditions to operate from. Not only that, but new voices in the upper echelons of the Initiative are more interested in permit fees, licensing, and other commercial considerations. There are at least twenty new expeditions a month arriving, some as small as a single person in a mini crawler, prospecting for water fields. But some are large enough to rival the Azevedo expedition, with plans to build new cities."

I had not realized. Nick and I had mostly worked insurance claims in and around Maxwell City, the most highly developed region on Mars. When an area gets that big, everything has to go through channels. There are plenty of layers of local bureaucracy to fight through.

I looked at Chief Hogan, and he answered, "Gale may be underestimating. Last month there were thirty-five expeditions that arrived. And twelve that gave up and left for home, plus five lost, for a net of eighteen new teams to monitor."

"You monitor them?"

Hogan hesitated. "Not as much as we used to," he finally said with a sigh. "There are just too many. We monitor traffic and distress bands, certainly. But we don't have the manpower to keep eyes on every mini crawler out there."

I nodded. No wonder the Saganists were becoming more vocal. "Five lost?"

"That's . . . complicated," Hogan said.

"What he means," Gale said, "is the Initiative doesn't much care. Mars has become routine. The public's not paying attention anymore, so neither are the politicians. If some settler never comes back, it might be big news here in Maxwell City, but it's barely a yawn back on Earth. Could you tell me how many people went missing in Hoboken last week?"

I looked Gale over. "So you . . . scavenged these parts?"

"It's what I do, ma'am." Gale spread his hands wide, as if asking for acceptance. "A man must breathe. It's not just scavenging, though. I'm . . . I'm old Mars, still. Nick beat that into me: you don't abandon people. You don't give up while there's a chance, and you don't forget that there are people behind those numbers, and they have people back home. So sometimes alone, sometimes with a partner if I find one I can rely on, I hang around the ports and the locks, following the news of lost expeditions. I've done a little search and rescue, when I could. Report and recovery more often, sad to say."

"And salvage."

"And salvage. Whatever it takes to keep air in the tanks."

I shook my head. "It is a wonder you've never gotten lost."

Gale smiled broadly at that. "Might happen someday, but I doubt it. Nick taught me better than that."

I paused, looking at Gale. "You keep bringing up Nick. What do you want from him?"

Gale shook his head. "I'd rather discuss that in private," he said. "Can you arrange that?"

I frowned. I did not know what Gale was up to; and through long habit, I did not trust him. His whole story seemed designed to garner sympathy. "I cannot promise anything." Then I had another thought. "But if you can be cooperative, maybe I can help. Tell us where you found these tools."

Gale looked away. "I . . . can't, ma'am."

"You do not remember?"

"I didn't say that. I just . . ."

"You just don't want to give up a bargaining chip, eh? Same old Gale."

"If that's the way you want to see it, ma'am . . ."

I turned to Hogan. "So what now? Am I taking him into custody?"

Hogan shook his head. "I'm sorry, ma'am. You've made no charges against him. And even if you had, there's no extradition in place. I wanted to give you a chance to talk to him, but he's ours for now."

"So you are charging him?"

"We're still going through the paperwork, trying to figure out who has jurisdiction. For now, though, he's going back to the stockade."

18. ARGUMENTS

I argued for several more minutes, but Hogan was not budging. *Orders from above,* he said. While I argued, he summoned a trooper, and Gale was led away.

Finally, I returned to the city, stopping by district offices as I did. They were lightly staffed, only a desk sergeant and a patrol officer in each. All of these arrests and seizures had my new department unexpectedly taxed.

And my messages reflected that: confirmation of five persons arrested, notifications of three still missing, and court notices of seven who had filed for stays. Two of those came from Magistrate Montgomery's court, but the rest came from other courts. Worse, these suspects were higher up the chain of the conspiracy, and hence more influential. They were raising more challenges in the courts. This case was overloading the system. I was not sure how I could keep on top of it.

And that was not all: there were requests for interviews from nine different media outlets, including three different requests from Tara Rockford. I sighed. When I had been an admiral, we had had a media liaison's office to handle this sort of thing. I had come to Mars to simplify a complicated life. Now I could use some of that complexity. I wished I could be out on the surface with Nick, exploring and building.

But I knew that was not to be. Mars was at a crucial stage of human settlement: we had growing pains, and we could not run away from them, or the whole project would collapse. Gale had gotten that part right. The growth of settlements made it possible for more people to explore and build a home on Mars, but somebody had to maintain the settlements. I had volunteered, and that meant it was my responsibility.

But I did not have to like it. And there was nothing wrong with asking for help. I called Anthony's office; but it was Alonzo who answered. "Yes, Ms. Morais?"

"Hello, Alonzo. I was hoping to talk with Anthony about media requests."

"I'm sorry, the mayor's tied up in his own interviews. And in city council meetings. There's some screaming going on in there." His eyes narrowed, and I could see he was irritated.

I let a little of my own irritation show in return. "What do you expect me to do, Alonzo? Turn a blind eye? Keep the corruption quiet? If that is what you want— If that is what Anthony wants, I serve at his discretion. He can fire me."

Alonzo shook his head. "Don't be ridiculous, Ms. Morais! I didn't say that. It just would've made my job easier. You could have been more discreet."

I counted to three before answering. "Once the media had hold of it, we lost control."

He glanced from side to side. "Never say that! If anyone heard—"

"It is true! Pretending does not change it."

"But that's—" He quieted and leaned closer to the comm. "That's not a message we want getting out to the public. If the damn journos heard something like that, it would be on every stream for the next week: 'Chief of Police says city is out of control.'"

"Space the journos."

Alonzo's eyes grew wide. "Do you want to lose this election, ma'am? Hand Mars back over to the Realists? Hell, why not to the Saganists? Shut down half of Mars!"

"I want to do my job, and my job is the truth, not good messaging. Shall I tender my resignation now?"

He actually flinched at that. I think he could tell I was serious. "Oh, God, no! That would be a scandal that would last through the election. 'Chief of Police resigns. Demands the truth.'" He shook his head. "No, Ms. Morais, I'm sorry. It's just tense here. Our numbers have really dipped overnight."

"That is your job, not mine."

"But you don't have to make it worse. You could . . . you could help out."

"Campaigning is not in my job description."

"No, but talking to the media is. All department heads have to be answerable to the public."

"I should have a media liaison."

"You will. Eventually. But we're growing too fast to staff your department now! And we don't have the budget yet. After the election, if we have a larger majority in the city council, maybe then. But to get there . . . I need you to talk to the press."

I sighed. "I can hold a press conference."

Alonzo shook his head. "You should. I'll set one up for this afternoon. But you really need to do some one-on-ones."

"Alonzo, I do not have time!"

"You have a deputy chief now."

"So Vile can talk to them."

"No, that would look like we're trying to hide something. She can take over your other duties, just for a few hours so you can do media interviews."

"She is too new at this!"

"We don't have time to waste. She'll have to learn. In the meantime, I'll set up some interview slots for you."

"Not today, Alonzo. There is simply no time. No time for a press conference either. There's too much going on."

"All right," Alonzo said, taking a heavy breath. "We can do the interviews tomorrow. But the press conference has got to be this afternoon. If we don't do that, they'll just start making things up."

"They will do that anyway."

C

I hurried back to my office, dropping off an order with Zeb along the way. It was going to be a late working lunch for me and Vile, and for the rest of the command squad as they checked in. It was time for me to start delegating responsibilities faster than I had intended. I was glad Anthony had made good hires and I could count on these people. Of course, I had thought that about Flagg too.

We started with a review of the situation so far. We had a double shift out serving warrants, making arrests, and seizing evidence. My command squad were distracted the whole time by reports in from the field; but for the most part, everything seemed under control.

Then I started laying out the strategy for the next two days of the investigation, knowing that if Alonzo had his way, I would be too busy to carry it out myself. Vile picked it up quickly, and the rest seemed to know their parts. This was still going to be chaotic, but I felt a little better about it. At 1700, we broke for the press conference. That is, I did. Vile and my squad kept right on planning and coordinating. After the press conference—twenty minutes of variations on *What did Mayor Holmes know, and when did he know it?*—I came back to check their work. They seemed to be progressing: not everything the way I would do it, but good work regardless. Maybe we were starting to form a team, with a team approach to things.

I kept on top of them halfway into second shift, when third shift showed up early, doubling up as planned. I dismissed first shift and went back to work.

But Vile tapped on my office wall. "Ms. Morais. Go home."

"I cannot, Vile."

"You have your comm. You'll take work home with you, I know that. But you're not doing us any good here now."

"How would it look if I were not at my post when something big came down?"

"How will it look if you had a nervous collapse? You're exhausted. And . . . well . . . you're not that young anymore, ma'am." I gasped, and she hurriedly continued, "You told me you wanted to hear straight from me at all times. Was that a lie?" I shook my head. "I haven't read your file, but I know Mars history. You're in great shape for your age, but you're not a young ensign anymore. You need your rest." Then she grinned. "Especially if you want to look good in front of the cameras tomorrow."

I sighed. "Vile, I hope you do not expect me to thank you for being blunt."

"No thanks necessary, ma'am. Just doing my job."

I grinned, and I left.

C

I had had too much of Zeb's fine food of late, and I was a little tired of it. Not to mention I had been getting too many calories, since Zeb didn't believe in small portions. So I looked around the Concourse for anything else that was open and appealing, but nothing caught my fancy. A check of my comm told me it was late, but maybe not too late for dinner with Nick.

So I went back to our apartment; but it looked like dinner was not in the offing, at least not right away. Nick was on his comm in the workroom, engaged in a vigorous conversation. I did not hear the words, and I was far too polite to eavesdrop; but I could hear his tone, heavy with sarcasm, and short, clipped sentences. He was chewing someone out. I had known him long enough to recognize the mood: the person on the other end of the comm line was not completely incompetent, and Nick thought they could be salvaged, if he badgered them into it. And if the badgering drove them away, then to hell with them. He would know that they were not good enough.

After ten minutes, I realized that it was going to be a long conversation, and there was no sense waiting for Nick. Instead I found my way to the kitchenette, and I looked in the refrigerator for something I could prepare. I would never be the cook that Nick was, but no one would starve on my meals either. I found some spinach and feta and slivered almonds, as well as some leftover chicken from three nights back? Four? I wasn't sure, but it still looked fresh. I diced a carrot and added that, and I tossed it all with a little bit of oil. It would make a light salad for the two of us. I was not that hungry anyway. If Nick needed more, he could find it after his call was done.

I dished the salad onto two plates, and I carried them out into the living area. I set mine down on the side table, and I carried Nick's over to the workroom. The door was open, so I did not knock, I just slid in to set the plate in front of him.

Nick looked up at me and nodded slightly. But he did not smile; he was still talking, still grilling the person on the other end. "It's your only choice, Gale," he said. My eyes widened. He noticed, looked at me, and shook his head. "We can make this work." He paused. "No! This line is not secure, don't keep talking. We'll handle this." Another pause. "Look, Gale, if you want to be an ass, that's your business. But you came to me for help. If you don't think I know what I'm doing, then go to hell." Another pause. "All right. Let me know."

Nick closed his comm line, picked up his plate and fork, and ate a bite of salad. "It's pretty good," he said, with a nonchalance I could tell was feigned.

"That was Gale you were yelling at?"

Nick straightened up, away from his plate, and looked at me. "Who is asking: my wife or the police chief?"

"Your . . ." I stopped. It was a complicated question, Nick was right about that. But I answered from the gut. "Your wife. What sort of trouble is he getting you in now?"

"It's not trouble for me," he answered. And then he grinned. "No more than I can handle."

"Nick!"

"I'll be all right, but he needs my help."

"He *needs* to cooperate with the investigation before things get worse for him," I said, storming out of the workshop.

Plate in hand, Nick followed me out. "I don't think he *can* cooperate, Rosie."

"You mean he does not want to. He is holding out for some leverage. He knows something."

Nick sat on the couch and set down his plate. "He knows something, all right, but he's not worried about leverage. He's afraid of something. He won't tell me what, not on an open line."

"He would not tell *me* today in a secure room."

Nick took a sip of water. "Did he know it was secure?"

"No . . ."

"And were you alone? No, you were with Hogan."

"So you already discussed this with him."

"I did. He didn't know who would overhear. And besides . . . Rosie, you're not me."

"What does that mean?"

"It means you're the police chief! You have . . . responsibilities that may not be in his best interests. And besides, he knows you don't like him."

"You are damn right I do not like him. Do not trust him. And I do not know why you do either."

"Rosie, he gave up his career for me."

I shook my head. "Five years ago he did one thing right, and that makes up for his entire career of screwups and toadying? That makes up for what he did on the *Bradbury*? And to Chuks? Ask Connie if *she* trusts him!"

Nick sighed. "He's made mistakes. Who hasn't? And he's owned up to them. And he's a damn good spacer, one of the best on Mars. Mars needs him more than it realizes."

"At this moment, we need him to fill in missing pieces in my investigation."

"That's not going to happen, Rosie. Not yet."

"Not yet?" I looked at him, eyes narrowed. "Nicolau Aames, what do you know?"

"Rosie, if there was anything I could tell you, you know I would."

"I know nothing of the kind! You would not lie to me, but you do not share everything you know either."

"Rosie . . . that's . . ."

In all our years, together and apart, rarely had I seen Nick's temper, and never out of control. He was too obsessive for that.

But sometimes, near his limit, he would count under his breath. When he started counting now, I worried. Not for my safety, but for us.

At five, Nick picked up his plate and stormed into the workroom. The door slid shut; but the soundproofing was not perfect, and soon I heard the sounds of Korzus playing loudly beyond the door.

19. Interviews

Nick never came to bed that night. In the morning, I found the couch cushions in disarray, indicating he had slept out there. I had hoped he would calm down. Now I did not know where he was; and as much as I wanted to, I did not have time to find out. I had another busy day ahead, and almost no time to prepare for it.

I did not have time to worry further. My comm had a message from Anthony, requesting an 0630 meeting. As if I did not have enough to worry about. There was barely time for a shower, but I had no choice if I was going to have media interviews that day. So I dashed under the water, cleaned up, and hit the tube.

When I got to Anthony's office, I had the satisfaction of seeing that he did not look any fresher than I did. Neither did Alonzo, nor the couple who sat in the chairs by the window, a man and woman. I did not recognize them, but their expensive clothing marked them as Very Important People.

"Good morning, Mr. Mayor," I said.

"Good morning, Ms. Morais," Anthony said, but I saw nothing good in his eyes. He turned toward the couple. "This is Leah Thomas and Jan Stehouwer of the Red Planet League."

I smiled at them politely. "Nice to meet you," I said. But they just glared at me, so I turned back to Anthony. "I have a busy day, Mr. Mayor. What is up?"

"A busy day harassing honest businesspeople," Thomas said.

Before I could reply, Anthony interrupted. "Enough of that. The police chief is doing her job."

"Her job is to catch criminals," Stehouwer said.

"And that is precisely what I am trying to do," I answered. "Is there something improper with my warrants? Then tell it to the magistrate." Again, I turned to Anthony. "The warrants are all signed and proper, *sir*." I emphasized the last word.

"I know," Anthony said. "We've reviewed them."

"We?" I looked around the room. "Who are *we* to be reviewing anything?"

"The warrants are public records," Thomas said. "And they're ridiculous. If you had questions, you should've come to the individuals involved to discuss things privately."

"This is a circus!" Stehouwer continued. "Our members will not stand for this."

"Your members—" I started, but Anthony interrupted.

"Now let's calm down," he said. "I'm sure we can make them understand—"

It was my turn to interrupt. "I do not care if they understand. I do not answer to them. I answer to you, and the magistrate, and the city council."

"And the council answers to us," Stehouwer said.

"I thought they answered to the people," I said.

Thomas's face grew redder. "And we—"

Anthony stopped her. "Enough! This is exactly why I didn't want to have this meeting."

I shook my head. "If you did not want to have it, then why did you, Mr. Mayor? Who is running this city, you or them?"

Alonzo stepped forward. "Please! This isn't helping." He turned to Thomas and Stehouwer. "I offered you this chance to talk to the police chief so you can express your concerns, but we have to keep calm. If we start fighting among ourselves, things are only going to get worse. The Libertists can't afford this sort of infighting."

"The Libertists?" I said. "Space the Libertists!"

Stehouwer rose at that. "I thought you of all people believed in Free Mars."

"I believe in doing my job," I answered. I turned to Anthony. "Mr. Mayor, is this a meeting or a campaign session?"

Anthony sat with a sigh. "It's not that simple, ma'am. If the Libertists lose power, everything changes here. I'm out, which means you're probably out. I wish I could just run the city, but it's become political now. And there's nothing we can do about that. For me to do my job—and for you to do yours—we need the Libertists united."

"And the Libertists need the Red Planet League," Stehouwer said, "our money and our voices."

Thomas caught her breath, and said in a quieter voice, "Sit down, Jan. Alonzo's right: this is getting too heated to get anything done."

Stehouwer glowered, but he sat. "You want heated, you should have been at the Steering Committee meeting last night. Mr. Mayor, the only thing that kept the members from rebelling is that the Realists would be worse."

"I'll talk to them," Alonzo said.

"You'd better do more than talk," Stehouwer replied. "Mr. Mayor, you need to release the members who are being held illegally."

Before I could answer, Anthony replied, "It's not illegal, Jan. Ms. Morais did her job by the book. Arraignment takes time. Bail proceedings take time." He paused, consulting his subcomp. "Two of those arrested have made bail already, and the rest will as well. Let the process continue."

"They made bail," Thomas said, "but these restrictions! This is ridiculous. Their passports confiscated, and their surface passes as well?"

"I didn't set the terms," Anthony answered, "Magistrate Montgomery did. But they're the right terms. We need to make sure the accused stay within our jurisdiction." Then he smiled, but without warmth. "Unless they want to cite the Compact, of course. Claim a different jurisdiction."

"They can't do that!" Stehouwer said. "They have too many holdings here. They can't give all those up."

"They wouldn't give them up," Anthony said, and his smile grew larger. "They'd simply be putting them under the jurisdiction of distant nations with . . . significantly higher tax rates. And of course they would still owe taxes and duties here as well."

Thomas visibly strove to stay calm, gripping her chair arms. "That would ruin them, Mr. Mayor. You're making them prisoners here."

"Not prisoners," I said, matching Anthony's smile. "They are just suspects. They shall have their day in court."

The conversation dragged on from there for a while longer, but nothing new was really said. The merchants and financiers of the city were unhappy, and some wanted my head; but Anthony had my back. For now.

But when Alonzo led Thomas and Stehouwer out and the doors slid shut behind them, I wheeled on Anthony. Before I could say a word, he said, "I'm sorry, Rosie. Alonzo hit me with it. I was as surprised as you."

"Sorry? You could have warned me!"

He shook his head. "They got here only a couple of minutes before you did. I had no idea until then how the meeting was going to go, and so I had no time to warn you."

"That did not mean you had to hang me out to dry!"

"I backed you up," Anthony said, glaring at me. "You're under a lot of pressure—"

"Pressure! I am hearing that a lot from you and Alonzo now. Pressure."

"That's the reality of this job right now, Rosie. This election's getting scrutiny like never before. You said yourself that outside interests were involved. Certainly, the journos are. I just . . . I just . . . don't know if I can hold it together."

Muscles clenched in his face; and for the first time, I noticed that Anthony was showing his age. He had come to Mars as a young kid, and he had kept his health and his youth through all the years of exploration and settlement and governing. But now, he was a tired middle-aged man.

I shook my head. "Maybe you should just walk away. You do not need this."

He closed his eyes and sat back in his chair. "I can't, Rosie. I know it sounds arrogant, but . . . I really think Mars needs me." He looked at me. "The Libertists are right, but we're fractious. We're right on the big picture, but no one can agree on the small. We need . . . Alonzo says we need visible symbols that Martian settlement is here to stay. People who've been here for the long haul, like me."

I nodded. "And like Nick."

"And you," Anthony insisted. "Rosie, don't sell yourself short. Yeah, Nick was a founder, but you served here for a long time. On orbit, but that still counts. People still think of you as old Mars."

I should not have answered, but I could not stop myself. "Is that why you wanted me for police chief? As a symbol?"

"Rosie!" His jaw gaped, and then he continued, "No! I wanted you—needed you—because you're the best person for the job. Not just the best police chief—Nick always says you're the best spacer in the business."

I sighed, and I sat. "This job does not need a spacer. I spend all my time down in the tubes. Visiting your office is the only time I see the surface."

"Well . . ." Anthony smiled. "That just means we're lucky. Our jurisdiction covers the surface around here, too, we just haven't had any crime there. Well, none until Jacob and Adam. Let's hope that's our last case on the surface."

I smiled back. "Yes, I suppose that is one way to look at it." I took a deep breath, trying to regain my calm. "I am sorry, Anthony. It is too early in the morning for me to cope with politics."

"I wish I could say the same. Lately, it's twenty-four hours a day."

"So you get a whole thirty-nine minutes free?" I said.

"On a good day. But I'll try to give you a little more. So are we good?"

I frowned. "Anthony, we are good for now. But you wanted a police force. You need the force, and not just politically. Do not let politics get in the way of that."

☾

My next appointment was a stop down in Digital Investigations to visit with Moore and her team. Things were progressing well there, better than I might have expected. Digital forensics was not my expertise, but it seemed that they had locked up most of the records we were going to need, at least the records from Mars's side, and were making good progress on the rest. It would take a lot of time and effort to sift through those, not to mention some court battles to get files unlocked; but we had the start of a digital case coming together. Already Moore had found additional instances of the fraud that Nick had identified. I thanked her and her team, and I left them to their work.

I wanted to cut around the Concourse to my office and look in on my team; but I saw on my comm that Magistrate Montgomery had added two early-morning arraignments to our docket. Vile had noted that she would attend, but I canceled that. She had been up all night. I sent her a note: *My turn to nag. Get some sleep.* Then I went to the arraignments.

Those ran longer than yesterday's. It looked like defense counsel had learned from the previous proceedings, and they mounted more effective objections and delaying tactics. Magistrate Montgomery had to spend more time tearing them apart and shooting them down; but shoot them down she did. One by one, the objections were overruled and set aside. And the arraignments went through.

So it was 1220 when I finally got to my office. My squad was busy manning comms and consoles, with only Wagner, Monè, and Ammon out. Vile was there, so I approached her and said, "I thought I told you to get some sleep."

"I did," she said. "Three hours under the desk in your office."

I left it alone. She really should have gotten more. But at the same time, while I was unready to concede the age factor, she was a lot younger. I had worked longer hours on less sleep when I was her age. She would survive. And I was certainly grateful to have her on duty.

Then I had to check myself in the mirror and head back around the Concourse. It was the middle of the day, so the place was thronged with tourists and shoppers and shopkeepers, about as busy as it ever got. The three levels had to have two hundred people crossing back and forth between the shops; and the slidewalks looked pretty packed too.

So it took longer than I expected to get back to Admin. I barely had time to duck into the lavatory and check my hair before hurrying over to the conference wing, where Alonzo waited impatiently, checking his comm. "You were almost late!"

"Almost late is still early," I answered. "Are they here yet?"

He shrugged. "No, but I expect the first one any minute. Pat Knighton. He's sympathetic to our cause, so try to be polite."

I was about to snap back at that; but just then, a thin, bearded man approached down the corridor. "Mr. Gutierrez," he said. "It's good to see you. Sorry I'm a bit early. Can we get set up?"

Alonzo smiled, concealing whatever he had been about to say to me. "Good to see you, Mr. Knighton." He turned to me. "You know Ms. Morais."

"I know of her." He held out his hand, and we shook. "We haven't been formally introduced, but I was at your press conference last night.

And also at your debut, of course. It's nice to meet you, ma'am. Pat Knighton, InterplaNet."

"We're glad you could take the time to talk to us," Alonzo said. He keyed open the conference room door. "Right in here."

We stepped in and found a room with six chairs around an oval table. As was typical for Martian architecture, no cubic was wasted. There was just enough room to squeeze around the chairs. I waited for Knighton to find a seat; but he pointed at the table and said, "Please, have a seat. There at the end will do. Let me set up."

I sat while he did something with his wrist comm. He looked at the wall opposite me, found a spot, and attached a comm pickup. Then he slid between the wall and the chairs until he stood near me, and he looked at his comm. "Not quite," he said. He went back to the pickup, moved it a few centimeters, and came back over by me. He checked his comm, and he said, "Good."

From the door, Alonzo said, "Can I get you any coffee or tea?"

"Water would be good," Knighton said.

"Water," I agreed.

"Sure," Alonzo said. "Just a moment." While Alonzo was gone, Knighton ran through some tests on his setup: sound check, transmission check, image check, tracking check. Alonzo was back with the glasses before the final check was done.

He set them down in front of us and then stood there quietly.

When the last check was done, Knighton said, "All right, I'm ready to begin. So . . ." He looked at Alonzo.

Alonzo raised his eyebrows. "So?"

Knighton smiled. It was a warm, broad smile, framed by his beard. I could see he was a charmer. "Mr. Gutierrez," he said, "I wanted an interview with the police chief. Not, my apologies, with the campaign."

"I won't say anything," Alonzo protested. "I just want to know what's said."

Knighton pointed at the pickup. "You can watch the live stream along with everybody else. And I'll get you a copy as well. I don't edit, not during the interview. Maybe in the analysis piece after. But I also don't need distractions. Unless you want me to mention in my report that you think Ms. Morais needs a minder?"

I could not contain a slight laugh at the look on Alonzo's face. "No!" he said. "Not at all. I . . . I'll go watch the live stream."

"Good," Knighton said to Alonzo's retreating back. When the door slid shut, he turned to me, eyes almost twinkling. "He seemed nervous."

At that, I did laugh. Then I looked at the pickup. "We are not live, are we?"

"Not yet," he said with a bit of a laugh himself. "He won't see that part. If you look at the pickup and you see a red light, we're reporting. Solid red means we have a good signal out; blinking red means signal trouble, but we're still recording. But relax. Concentrate on me, not the light."

I did not relax, exactly, but I felt more at ease. The man was a good interviewer. I told myself not to let my guard down; but so far, at least, I did not feel attacked. Knighton glanced at the pickup, then back to me. "All right, just like I promised Gutierrez, this is going to go out live exactly as it plays out here. Later, we'll do an analysis and summary; that will include your background, your accomplishments, and so on. And it will also include discussions of the background of some of the things we mentioned, the political situation and so on. I don't want you surprised later when all that comes in. The summary piece will have context, I owe that to my audience. But that would be dry, boring stuff here. Right now, it's going to be live video, uncensored, a chance for the audience to hear from you. Understand?" I nodded. "Good. We go live in five . . . four . . . three . . . two . . . one . . ." He tapped his comm, and the red light came on. "Good afternoon, according to the Maxwell City clock here; or good morning, good evening, good night, depending on where you're seeing this. This is Pat Knighton in Maxwell

City, Coprates quadrangle, Mars. With a welcome to my audience on Mars, and a time-delayed welcome to you folks back on Earth, Luna, Aldrin City, and wherever else you're picking up the sound of my voice. I'm here with Police Chief Rosalia Morais of Maxwell City to discuss the astonishing revelations coming out of the city in the past two days. Ms. Morais, welcome."

"Thank you, Mr. Knighton. I am glad to have a chance to talk to you."

"To me, and to the whole solar system," he said.

I smiled. "Your ratings are that big?"

That got a smile from him as well; and I could guess now that he had staged the scene so that the audience could pick up his expression, even though I was in the focus of the frame. "We do all right," he answered. "By now the audience has seen a lot about the big story out of Maxwell City, and maybe some of it is even true. Certainly the verifiable facts have come out on InterplaNet. But there are also a lot of rumors and questions and confusion. So Ms. Morais, I wanted you to get a chance to talk to the viewers directly and explain exactly what we know and what you can say about how things are going to proceed."

I shook my head. "I cannot explain everything, Mr. Knighton. There are privacy concerns. There is evidence that might not yet be confirmed; and if improperly revealed, it might incriminate innocent people."

"Or it might tip off the guilty and tell them how to evade the law," he said. "I understand. But tell us what you can—what's public."

"I shall try," I said. And I did. I had thought pretty hard about this: how to satisfy public curiosity while respecting privacy and the demands of the case. I had gone through what evidence we could not discuss, or should not, and I had come up with a bullet list of things we could safely discuss. It was all public information, things that could be pulled from court dockets and arrest reports. Anyone could have given the same briefing; certainly Knighton could. He seemed like a competent person, and I am sure he had a research team. But I guess he wanted to put a face to the information.

And I knew Alonzo and Anthony wanted to get the story out with a single face and a single narrative as well. Better to have one consistent version on record. It would not stop all the rumors, but it was the best damage control we could do.

So I told what I could, simply and truthfully, starting with the fire and the death of Ramos, and how that had raised questions that had inspired a follow-up on insurance claims. And how that, unfortunately, had led to the discovery of possible wrongdoing by one of my own force.

Knighton stopped me there. "You had to take that a little personally," he said.

I shook my head. "Getting personal is a bad idea in an investigation. It will cloud your judgment. I have had a lot of experience in this business. You put the personal in a little box, and you take it out later. Otherwise you will miss things. Or you will give people an opportunity to manipulate you."

"You're not a machine, Ms Morais."

"No, I am better than a machine. I am a professional."

He smiled at that, but only with the half of his face away from the camera. I think he liked that line. I continued on, explaining how we found the evidence against Flagg, and how that had led us to additional evidence and additional arrests. "I am not going to go into particulars about individuals. Arrest records are all public, of course, so anyone who is interested can look those up. But right now these are charges, not convictions, so it would not be right to discuss individuals outside of the court."

"I understand," Knighton said. "But it does seem to me"—his eyes grew a little more eager, as if he was searching for something—"that there is a piece here you haven't mentioned. You've talked about the police force, and it sounds like your people have done a very good job in their responsibilities; but my sources tell me that a lot of this work was done by the founder."

I did not frown at that, but I held my face still. "I would not say a lot. Nick Aames brought some facts to our attention at points along the investigation. And yes"—I held up my hand before Knighton could speak—"full disclosure, if anyone in your audience is unaware of it, that is Nicolau Aames, my husband. A *civilian*," I emphasized, "but with expertise in some of these areas."

"A civilian," Knighton said, "and the founder of Maxwell City."

I chuckled. "Let us not exaggerate his story. *A* founder, one of many. But he holds no official role within the city government."

"No," Knighton replied. "Not within the city government. Not anywhere, after the *Aldrin* mutiny."

"The inspector general ruled there was no mutiny," I said, my voice growing cold.

"I'm sorry. I used the popular term so my audience would get the reference. You're right of course, there was no mutiny. There were only allegations of mutiny. Just like there are only allegations of insurance fraud at this time."

"That is correct," I said. "An investigation was done then. An investigation will be done now. A court will get a chance to decide what to do from there. Until then, we have to let the process continue."

"And how will that play out?"

I shook my head. "I cannot see the future, Mr. Knighton." I checked my comm. "Well, not far into the future, anyway. My comm says that I have appointments in the very near future. So is there anything else?"

Knighton shook his head with a smile. "No, ma'am." He turned more directly toward the pickup. "So there's the straight story out of Maxwell City, folks. Remember, you heard it here first. And accurately. Thank you." He tapped the comm, and the red light went out. Then he turned back to me. "I'm sorry about the end there, ma'am."

"No apologies necessary," I said. I hoped I sounded congenial.

He shook his head. "You have a right to be upset. It's never fun to be on the hot seat. But I have a responsibility to bring out all the facts that are public."

"And the facts that will draw an audience," I said.

"And that," he answered. "Your husband's story is old news, but it's not forgotten. It *is* an angle people are curious about, so I had to bring it up. I hope you understand."

"I do," I said. "But I have some advice: if you ever interview Nick, do not bring up the founder business. He thinks it is a foolish title that he has not earned. He spent decades off Mars. There are people who earned the title, and he does not think that he is one of them."

"I understand," Knighton answered. "But legends take on a life of their own, and you can't stop them."

After Knighton was gone, I told myself that it had not been too bad. He had not been hostile, just thorough. He had given me the chance to say everything I wanted, and he had asked informative questions. And he was right: there were still those for whom Nick was a legend who added interest to a story.

That was the easy one, I told myself. I had only twenty minutes before my scheduled interview with Tara Rockford. That was going to be a challenge. So I ducked out to check my hair and makeup, even my teeth. Image was everything in media, and I wanted to show no weakness.

Unlike Knighton, Rockford was late. And she was not alone: she came with a videographer, a lighting technician, a sound technician, a legal assistant, and a producer. When Alonzo saw the size of her retinue, he shook his head. "My apologies," he said. "Let's find a larger room. If you could all follow me." I stood up and followed him as he led us down the hall to a large meeting room at the end.

As soon as we arrived, the technician set to work, mounting lights and cameras and microphones, rearranging chairs to get them out of their way. The producer looked at the big table. "This won't do, won't do at all," he said. "It's too big, dominates the space with a useless object. Can we get this out of here?"

No one moved. The producer looked expectantly at Alonzo; and finally, Alonzo said, "I'll get someone." He tapped on his comm. "Someone from maintenance will be right up."

Rockford checked her comm. "I hope they hurry," she said. "The key ratings window is coming soon."

I thought about pointing out that she was the one who was late, and her people were the ones creating further delay; but I bit my tongue. *Be nice, Rosalia,* I said to myself. *Smile for the camera.*

Once two maintenance workers had removed the table, the producer smiled. "Much better. Let's set up a two shot against that wall."

"It's a big empty space," Rockford said.

The producer shook his head. "It won't be on the stream. We'll blend in a video feed there, it'll look like you're talking in front of a monitor."

Rockford smiled. "Always taking care of me, Freddie." She pointed at the right chair. "Ms. Morais, have a seat." After a pause, she added, "Please."

I believed the "please" was phony, but I sat. I knew her work. She was good at sincere prodding, innocently provoking the subject into rash statements, all while she smiled as if she were doing nothing. I would not take the bait. I would match politeness with politeness, smile with smile, and I would stick to facts.

As I sat, the producer—Freddie—held up all ten fingers. "Here's our window," he said, and Rockford sat. She checked her long red curls on a monitor—a sure sign that she was from Earth, spacers tended to keep their hair shorter—and she adjusted herself, holding a tablet in front of her as Freddie's fingers slowly dropped. "Five. Four. Three. Two. One."

"Thank you, Bob, for that introduction. This is Tara Rockford coming to you live from the Administration Center in Maxwell City on Mars, for an important interview with Police Chief Rosalia Morais about the Libertist controversy. Ma'am, welcome."

"Thank you," I said.

The words were barely out of my mouth when Rockford continued, "Ms. Morais, as regular viewers know, is at the center of today's big scandal out of Maxwell City. The Libertist coalition is crumbling due to corruption in the highest ranks. Campaign leaders have been arrested. Accusations fly back and forth among others. Mayor Holmes has lost control of his own party. Ma'am, my sources tell me you're getting political interference in your investigation. What can you tell me about that?"

I kept my cool. "There has been no interference," I said.

"That's not what my sources tell me," Rockford continued. She turned slightly toward the camera. "Viewers, you've seen the leaked report from last night's Libertist Steering Committee meeting. It's getting bad here in Maxwell City. Top citizens are at each other's throats. There's a demand for action. A delegation from the Red Planet League met with Mayor Holmes and Ms. Morais just this morning. The League is part merchants association, part investment fund. Popular with small investors, it's run by some of the richest citizens of Mars. What transpired at that meeting, Ms. Morais?" She turned back to me.

I shook my head. "That was a closed-door policy discussion, Ms. Rockford."

"Closed door? What does Mayor Holmes have to hide? Hasn't he ever heard of open meetings?"

I stayed firm. "I am not an elected official, Ms. Rockford. I cannot cite the finer points of open meetings law. But an executive must be able to have private meetings with citizens. Not everything is an open meeting, only those where a quorum is discussing matters and making decisions."

"So you keep it under a quorum to evade the open meetings requirements?"

"If by under a quorum, you mean one public official, the mayor, with no council members present, then yes, it was under a quorum." I had started with a calm tone; but by the time I had finished the sentence, I could feel my temper rising. That would not do.

And Rockford had not missed that. "You seem agitated, Ms. Morais. Are you a little sensitive here?"

I smiled. I saw how to take control back. "I am sensitive," I said, "because you are verging into slander territory. And I wanted to make it clear that I was not going to be a part of slanderous allegations. If you have evidence of efforts to bypass open meetings regulations, I want to see it. I want to pursue it, and to charge it if the evidence stands up. So I am waiting: can you produce your evidence?"

Rockford actually sat back at that. I do not think she was used to subjects who fought back and who took the initiative. She was used to putting people on the defensive. "I . . ." She paused only slightly, and I saw Freddie make an okay gesture. She started again. "I made no allegations, Ms. Morais, I was just asking questions that any curious viewer would ask. That's my job, to ask questions for them." She half turned to the camera. "For you, viewers. What you want to know." Then she turned back to me. "But let's move on to a topic you might find less upsetting." I did not believe her for a second as she continued. "So your own right-hand man, Jordan Flagg, was part of this scheme."

"Lieutenant Flagg was not my right-hand man. I do not know where you get your information."

"Oh, everyone knows you were grooming him to be deputy chief. You replaced him with Vile; and hardly a day later, you appointed her as deputy chief. It's obvious."

I shook my head. "What is obvious is that you have received misinformation. Lieutenant Vile was already part of the command squad from the beginning, just like Lieutenant Flagg. She was not his replacement, Lieutenant DeHaven was. And Lieutenant Vile was a natural choice for deputy chief, because of her seniority in Public Safety before joining the force, and because of her accomplished record. I had every confidence in her from the beginning, and she is already doing a capable job in the middle of an unexpectedly busy investigation."

"A capable job? She's only been in it two days. How can you judge that?"

I glanced at my comm. "Because while I am here smiling for your cameras and answering taunts like this, I am not getting a hundred comm messages and emergency alerts. Vile is handling those in my stead. Things are running smoothly, and that's Vile's work."

Rockford grinned, but with no humor. It was predatory. "Then if she's doing the job so well, why do we need you?"

Oh, for—but I kept my outburst to myself. "Because as good as she is, I have much more experience, particularly in investigations. I set the course, she carries it out."

Rockford smiled. "You do have quite a career," she said, "if a bit . . . checkered. You were dismissed from the Admiralty in disgrace."

"I resigned," I said. "It is in the public record. Anyone who cares can look it up."

"Yes," Rockford said. "Misappropriation of material. Issuance of unlawful orders. Creating a threat to shipping. That's quite a list of charges."

I took a breath and carefully answered, "That is all in my statement with my resignation. The inspector general closed the matter."

"Yes, but it's not really that simple, is it? Admiralty sources tell me that you took responsibility to shield Captain Aames from the consequences of his own decisions."

"That is not what the inspector general found."

"No, it isn't. My Admiralty sources tell me that's yet another example of the corrupting influence of Nick Aames. He has quite a past. Losing the *Bradbury* expedition. Kicked out of the International Space Corps, until he found a loophole to get back in via the *Aldrin*. And his career there, well, he certainly cut corners and did things his way. I hear they're still auditing the books to try to understand where some of the money went to when he first led the mutiny and then stole the *Aldrin* from its rightful owners."

"He did not steal it, the inspector general granted it independence. And told him he could have no official duties there."

"Yes, thus bringing him to Mars, the site of his first big failure."

"He saved that crew."

"Most of them. If you don't count a few deaths here and there, and the loss of a $500 million spacecraft. And so he's back here where his chosen protégé is the mayor."

"Mayor Holmes is a respected, experienced Mars explorer who was duly elected by the people of this city and who serves at their pleasure because they trust him."

"A trust that some think is misplaced. And now here Nick Aames is again, right in the middle of this investigation. With his own wife in charge, where she decides what's evidence and what isn't. Who gets charged and who doesn't."

"Nick has no role in this department."

"Oh, I'm sure, you've practiced that line quite thoroughly. Some even might believe it."

"But you do not."

"It's not what I believe," Rockford said with a smile, "it's what my viewers believe. They're pretty good at seeing through lies. I just point out the truth for them, and they decide for themselves."

"The truth . . ." I paused. Rockford was getting to me despite my efforts. ". . . is that yes, Mr. Aames, a private citizen and my husband and an expert in the exploration and governance of Mars, discovered and turned over some of the evidence in this case. And cooperated in retrieving more evidence from his employers on Earth, São Paulo Mutual. That is the extent of his involvement with this case."

"Oh, really?" Rockford said, glancing at her comm. "Then perhaps you can explain the announcement made by Chief Hogan at Port Shannon Lopez?"

"What announcement is that?"

This time Rockford's grin showed teeth. "That your husband's long-time associate, Horace Gale, suspected of trafficking in stolen goods, has cited the Compact. And for his citizenship, he has claimed Aldrin City. And Chief Hogan has confirmed jurisdiction with Aldrin City, and they have designated as their representative to handle Gale's case . . ." She turned to the camera. ". . . Nick Aames."

20. Ambassador Aames

The interview went downhill from there. Despite my best efforts, Rockford had scored her big point, knocking me back. And from there, she had me on the defensive. She worked to put words in my mouth, question my motives, and paint me in the worst possible light. And I was unable to think quickly enough to stop her, because my mind was distracted. What the hell was Nick up to?

I could tell from Alonzo's face just how badly it was going; but there was nothing either of us could do. Rockford was uninterested in facts or logic. She was out for blood. And ratings.

Finally she wrapped up with a sneering allegation. "There's a lot more dirt buried here, Ms. Morais. If you can find it, we'll want to talk to you about it again. This is Tara Rockford, signing off for Maxwell City." And with that, the camera shut off. Without a word of farewell, she left the room; and as quickly as they could pack up, her technicians followed.

It was bad, I could tell that from the morose look on Alonzo's face. But I did not wait around to talk to him about it. I had to see Nick.

☾

This time I went through Customs. The agent there, a young Initiative trooper with a Dutch or German accent, scrutinized my credentials thoroughly before letting me through. "They're expecting you at Fort Hudson, Ms. Morais," he said.

Having no luggage, I bypassed the package inspection line and went straight to data inspection. The agent there took my comm and my comp and plugged them in for screening. When she declared them clean and handed them back to me, I proceeded to the slidewalk juncture. I took the right-most slide, and I headed toward Fort Hudson. A sign at the entrance to the slide said, *You are now entering Fort Hudson. All persons and packages are subject to search. Weapons will be confiscated.* I reflexively patted my holster, where I carried my pistol. It was an old-style semiautomatic, manufactured in one of the finest shops in Maxwell City. It had been a gift from Nick on our first anniversary on Mars; and I wore it now as police chief, just as I had promised the journos I would.

So when the slide deposited me in front of the big doors to the fort, I was ready. Three guards stood there in full matte-black Rapid Response Team armor. The closest stepped forward while the other two stepped aside for better coverage. The one near me said, "Hold. I'll need that weapon, ma'am."

I shook my head. "You know who I am. I am expected. This is my personal weapon that I carry in my duties. I am not turning it over without a receipt."

"I have no special instructions here, ma'am," he answered. "I'm supposed to confiscate all weapons that come through, save for Initiative forces carrying as part of their duties."

"And I am carrying this as part of my duties as police chief of Maxwell City. If you intend to confiscate it, then I shall turn around and leave, and you can explain to Chief Hogan why you have made an interplanetary incident about this. Or you can give me a receipt, check my weapon, and damn well have it here for me when I come back out."

"I'm not authorized to do that, ma'am."

"Then get authorized, or get spaced!"

He wasn't rude, he was simply following orders. No doubt there were others in the fort who would have enjoyed giving me grief, but this man did not. He winced, and then he tapped his comm and stepped away to talk in private. When he came back, he said, "Chief Hogan assures me that your sidearm is to be properly stored and returned to you. Here's a receipt." He pushed the receipt to my comp.

I nodded, checked the receipt, and then unfastened my uniform belt to slip off the holster.

"Thank you, ma'am," the guard said as he accepted it. "I'm sorry. Orders are orders."

"It is handled, Spacer," I answered. "We shall speak no more of it. Now where do I go?"

"You need to go to the stockade, ma'am. I can summon you an escort."

I shook my head. "Only if you have orders to keep an eye on me. I know my way around Fort Hudson."

"Oh," he answered. "I'm sorry, ma'am, I didn't know." He looked as his comm. "You have unescorted clearance except in marked secure areas. I assume you recognize those?" I nodded. "Then you are cleared to enter Fort Hudson, Ms. Morais." He stepped back and thumbed a switch by the door. It slid open, and the other two guards parted to let me through.

"I will see you on the way out," I said, trying to smooth some feathers there. Then I stepped through the doors to Fort Hudson.

It was a transition. Not just in place, but almost in time. It was my first time in the fort since inspection tours when I had been stationed on orbit; and yet little had changed. Underground facilities—and like Maxwell City, most of Fort Hudson was underground—do not change as quickly as surface facilities do. It is not as easy to just tear down walls and put up others, because walls might support a structure of the facility itself. So the layout tends to be unchanging; and that means the operations also change slowly.

But it was more than that. There was a neatness, an orderliness that I had forgotten after years of living in unplanned chaos. Maxwell City had a planned layout, four circular layers with radial symmetry; but within the broad outlines of that layout, side tunnels and chambers were arranged to suit the needs of thousands of different families and groups. In Fort Hudson, by contrast, things were rigidly planned, ordered, and *clean*. That is how you keep young spacers busy and attentive: you make them clean until it becomes second nature. Not that Maxwell City was dirty. It is never a good idea in space to let dirt get ahead of you. It can be bad for safety and your health. But even though cleaning got done in Maxwell City, it was casual. As needed. Order and discipline were not the job at Maxwell City, not the way they are on a military base. People had a lot of other work to do, and they fit in cleaning where they could. Here it was an ordered part of everyday routine.

Immediately beyond the big doors was what had been dubbed the Highway: a long stretch of high-speed slidewalks that could deliver troops in force to the gate. I remembered from my days in the Admiralty the reasoning behind these. There had never been a case of insurrection on Mars—not like some of the bad times on Luna—but the Admiralty had prepared for it. The Loonies had caught the Admiralty by surprise once, and they were not going to let that happen again.

So rapid delivery of force was part of the design. And not just force, of course, relief as well. Nine years back, there had been a major air system failure, an actual leak to Martian atmosphere from a processing plant out through a tunnel collapse. The Rapid Response Team had rushed out, both on the surface and through the tunnels, to render aid. The Realists still cited that case as an example. They said Maxwell City would not have survived without the Initiative that day.

They might have had a point. I was serving on Earth orbit by then, and I had not gone through the reports to see just how dire things had been and how much of a difference the RRT had made. Certainly, the troops drilled for that sort of emergency. But so did the locals.

The Highway was quiet now, with only two slides running each way, and none of the big cargo slides. I took a slide to the next checkpoint, where another trooper checked my ID and confirmed that I belonged there. She passed me through quickly, and I entered the crossroads, where smaller tunnels could take me to every part of the fort. I took a tube across and to the right, heading down in a spiral to the lower level where the stockade was.

At the bottom level, I stepped off the last slide, and I approached another guard.

"Ms. Morais," he said, as I approached, "right this way." After checking my badge yet again, he pressed the button on the wall, and a panel opened up. He leaned in for a retinal scan, then gestured for me to do the same. "If you please, ma'am."

I blinked several times, and then I stepped up for the scan, staring forward until the red flash had passed. A computer voice from the panel said, "Acknowledging Police Chief Rosalia Morais. Entrance granted. Proceed for security briefing." A door panel slid open, and I walked through.

Another guard stood on the other side, a young, solidly built woman in armor, but with her helmet off. "Hello, ma'am," she said. "I'm here to give you your security briefing." She grinned. "It's only fair. You gave it to me once."

I smiled back. "I am sorry, Spacer"—I checked her badge—"Powers. I briefed a lot of people in my time."

"I understand," she said. "It was ordinary for you, but my first day here. You happened to be down for some meeting or other, I think. I'm not sure what had you down here, but you gave me the briefing. Pretty much unchanged today. But you know . . ."

"You must go through the procedure," I said. "That is part of the briefing."

"It is." Then she got to work, reading off the regulations to me, showing me the video and still examples, quizzing me in all the right places to make sure I understood, and finally getting my signature that I had been briefed and was responsible for following the briefing. When I had signed, she took back the pad, and she said, "Thank you, ma'am. I . . ." She lowered her voice. "I never believed the things they said about you."

"Thank you, Powers." Her faith was touching. I wanted to tell her she was right, that I had not done the things I was accused of. That I had taken the blame to protect Nick, which was actually a bigger offense than what I was accused of, falsifying the record like that in a potential mutiny case. Rockford had not been wrong about that. But it was not something I could admit. On the record, I had to be guilty, to protect Aldrin City's independence. In a few years, maybe, Aldrin City would be secure, and no one would dare disrupt the arrangement. But we were not there yet.

The stockade, of course, was a high-security area. Unauthorized personnel could not wander around unescorted. So Powers summoned an escort—putting her helmet back on before the other spacer arrived, and winking at me over the slight infraction—and I followed the escort through the tight corridors of the facility. He led me to an interrogation room, where the door stood ajar so guards could look in. That indicated no interrogation was in progress, and they did not want any chance someone could hide in there.

But someone *was* in there. Nick sat in one chair beside the lone table under an overhead dome light. He sat erect, as he usually did in public. Relaxing did not come easily to him.

I stepped inside. "Mr. Aames," I said. I was not hostile, just formal.

Nick looked back at the door, which remained open with the escort standing just outside. Then he turned to me, and he rose. "Ma'am," he answered. He stood with his hands clasped behind his back, his way of keeping himself from making any revealing gestures—taking my hand, hugging me, shaking me; I was unsure what his mood was.

I did not want to have a fight, certainly not here in a public place with an Initiative spacer listening in. Nick and I did not get into it often; but when we did, I could be . . . fiery, and I knew how to push his buttons to get him angry too. And once angry, we might say things that just should not be said where others could hear. Things damaging to the case. Or to us.

But I had to know. "Nick, why didn't you tell me?"

Another man might have lied to me, told me it was Gale's idea to cite the Compact and claim Aldrin citizenship, even though it was such an obvious Nick move. Loopholes were his specialty. But where another man might have denied it, Nick could not even consider that. He might not respect arbitrary rules, but he was obsessed with the truth.

Instead he simply answered, "I didn't know if it would work. There was no sense getting in a fight with you if Gale was going to say no. Or Carver. I wanted to . . ."

"You wanted to put off the fight in case it was unnecessary." I lowered my voice. "And now we are here, where we cannot fight about it."

"We're here so I can take my citizen into custody."

"That is legalistic nonsense, Nick. You are not a citizen of Aldrin City. And besides, what about Inspector Park's order? You are not to have any position of authority in Aldrin City."

"Carver consulted Park," Nick said. "He can designate anyone he wants as his representative; it doesn't have to be a citizen as long as he authorizes my actions. Which he does. And Park concurs that a position as representative is not a position of authority and is not in Aldrin City. She is satisfied that her order has not been violated."

"But why, Nick? What do you hope to accomplish?"

"To get justice for my citizen," he said. Then he checked his comm. "And they should be bringing him around soon."

There was nothing I could say after that, so we stood in silence. Nick had some sort of plan—of that I was sure. But I could not see what it was. As his wife, I might ask what it was in the privacy of our home; but not as the police chief, not in public.

There was little we could say after that without getting into things that should be kept private. We sat and waited until a guard appeared, with Gale clanking behind her. Another guard stood behind him, and Gale was cuffed.

"You idiots," Nick said. "He's a weak old man in an assist suit. You two are young and strong in armor with weapons. Why do you need him cuffed?"

"Because this is a delicate case," Hogan said, stepping into the doorway. The rear guard made room for him. "Mr. Aames, I'm not taking any chances that a prisoner this important escapes or gets injured trying to escape while he's in my custody."

Nick shook his head. "I don't see what's so important about an old spacer mixed up in a petty crime."

Hogan looked at me. "If you don't, sir, I'm sure you're the only one who doesn't. This case . . . This man is a political hand grenade right now. Too many eyes are watching." He glared at Nick. "I know you were never too concerned about higher-ups, civilian authorities, and the media. But look what that did to your career."

Nick's face was stony as he answered, "I have no complaints. And I never let the journos tell me how to do my job."

I held up my hand. "That will do, gentlemen. We have business to take care of. Let us not waste time with irrelevant matters like this. We do not need this pissing match."

"You're right, ma'am," Hogan said. "My apologies. Other concerns are weighing on me. You understand."

I did understand. I understood what he had said earlier about not being able to speak openly without being recorded anywhere in the fort. So he could not talk about any pressures he might be under, but I could guess. "Understood," I answered. I expected no apology from Nick. By his standards, he had done nothing wrong, simply spoken the truth. That was never something he would apologize for. So I continued, "How do we proceed? I know the procedure for extradition from the Initiative to Maxwell City, and vice versa; but I do not know how this proceeds, or what I am doing here."

At that, Gale spoke up. "What *is* she doing here? I didn't ask for her."

"I did," Nick said. "I have to improvise procedures a bit here, since I am the only representative Aldrin City has on Mars right now. You might say I'm the ambassador and the embassy staff and the security all rolled into one. So I needed a little help."

"But . . ." Gale looked at me, then looked at the floor and went quiet.

Nick turned back to Hogan. "Chief Hogan, I have a receipt to acknowledge that you have transferred custody of Horace Gale of Aldrin City to me." He pushed it to Hogan's comm. "Is that acceptable?"

Hogan looked at his comm and signed it. "It is acceptable," he said. "And here's my acknowledgment." He pushed it back to Nick's comm. "Nicolau Aames, you are now responsible for the prisoner Horace Gale, citizen of Aldrin City. I'll have an escort lead you back to the port."

Then without explanation, Hogan made another push on his comm. I felt a slight buzz in my wrist, indicating a received message; but I had a hunch I should not look at it. Hogan wanted it kept quiet.

And quiet we were as the escort led us back out through the stockade. She did not stop there, continuing with us all the way out to the main gate to the port. Then she bid us good day as she cycled the gate open, and we walked through.

I stopped outside at the guard post, and I gave them my receipt. They brought me my sidearm. I smothered a laugh when I saw that they brought Nick's as well. He had less excuse, no official authority to give them a reason to ignore his being armed. But he was Nick, a force to be reckoned with. And who knows? Maybe being a founder carried weight even here among the guards.

As we rode the slidewalk back to Customs, I took the chance to examine the message on my comm. It was a simple security code, with no explanation. But I could guess. I ignored it all the way through Customs; but once on the other side, I walked over to the anteroom door, and I punched in the code. It slid open, and we stepped inside.

The door closed and locked behind us, no doubt a function of the particular code I had used. I sat behind the desk, and Nick and Gale sat across from me. I tapped my comm off and Nick did the same as well. "This room is secure," I said. "We are not being recorded."

Nick looked around. "Hogan told you that?"

I nodded. "And I trust him. He served under me for years, Nick. He is a good man."

Nick did not relax. "I'd prefer to check for myself," he said.

"Go ahead," I answered. "I would not expect anything less."

Gale and I sat in silence while Nick scanned the room. Gale glared at me from time to time, but I kept my expression blank. Nick eyed every inch, every corner of the room, including lighting and ventilation. He pulled out electronic and optical scanners as well. That made sense. No doubt he had wanted someplace that he could talk to Gale securely, so he had come prepared to scan an area.

Finally, Nick sat down. "If we keep it low, so no one can listen through the door, we should be okay."

"Good," I said. "Now tell me what the hell is going on." At least I said it in a low voice.

"You can't tell her anything, Nick," Gale said.

Nick sighed. "Gale, she's my wife, and I trust her. You can't expect me to keep secrets from her."

Gale shook his head. "She works for them."

"The city?" I asked.

"No," Gale said. "The . . . No."

Nick turned to me. "I'm sorry, Rosie. My hands are tied. I made a promise to represent him."

180

I shook my head. "That is not how this works, Nick," I said. "I know the Compact as well as you do. You do not represent him, you represent Aldrin City. Governor Carver and all the citizens who elected him. And their courts and their legal system. You are not his lawyer, you are his investigator and his judge."

"I'm . . . all of the above. I *am* Aldrin City for the purposes of this case. And that puts me in a complicated situation. I have to represent his interests and the city's and balance when they're in conflict."

I looked at Gale. "And you trust him to do that?"

Gale looked up, bags under his eyes, but also with a sense of . . . relaxation? Deliverance? "No one better," he answered.

I had to agree with that. Nick could sometimes bend the rules for his purposes, but his purposes were always about being right, doing the right thing. His psych profile said he was obsessed about it. Driven by it.

Of course I knew what was in his confidential psych profile because I *wasn't* so obsessed about it. When his profile had come up in the course of one of the many investigations he had faced in his career, I had gotten a chance to look at it. I had been weak, but it was important. I needed to know I could trust him.

Like Gale trusted him.

And so I should trust him now. "All right, Gale." I thought of telling him exactly what I thought about him: that I still did not trust him, that I found his change of heart to be suspect. But there was enough hostility in the room already. "You have cited the Compact, and you are now in the charge of your declared jurisdiction. That is all proper according to procedure." I raised an eyebrow at Nick. "It will be his responsibility to keep you in custody or let you out as he sees fit, to investigate any crimes you may be suspected of, to try you if charged, and to mete out punishment as appropriate. You have trusted yourself to this system . . . this man. And it was probably a smart move. I have no authority at this point, nothing I can compel you to do or not do. But I can *ask* you to cooperate in my ongoing criminal investigation where you might be . . . a material witness, let us say." Then I paused, leaned forward, and stared into his eyes. "And if you do, I can offer to testify to your cooperation before the person who has jurisdiction over you, and intercede to the degree that I can to see that you get favorable treatment and a light sentence if appropriate."

Gale looked at Nick. "Can she do that?"

Nick smiled at me. "There's no one else who can."

I smiled back at both of them. "I can."

21. THE LONG DAY CONTINUES

As soon as we were inside our apartment, I turned to Nick. "I am not happy about this, Nico."

"It's not about what makes you happy. It's about doing the right thing in a complex maze of opposing forces."

We were alone at last. With a line of credit from Carver, Nick had rented an apartment farther down India Tube and had declared it to be the Aldrin City embassy. It was only minimally furnished, but Gale would have a bed and food and water.

But he would not have the access key code to his own lock. Nick had conceded that much. Gale was under house arrest in the embassy.

I stared at the wall in the rough direction of Gale. "Space it! What does he want? I promised him cooperation. I know there is no love lost between us, but why can't he trust me? You vouched for me." Nick paused, and I could see he was struggling with how to answer. "Out with it, Nick."

"I have to think carefully before I answer, ma'am, so that my citizen's rights aren't violated unintentionally." He paused again, and then answered, "I think I can make him trust you, but not your bosses."

My eyes widened at that. "He does not trust Anthony?"

Nick shook his head. "He doesn't trust *Anthony's* bosses."

"Anthony is elected by the people."

"Agreed," Nick said. "And you trust him. Certainly I trust him to be his own man and to do what he thinks is right. He proved that to me long ago." He shook his head. "But not everyone can see that. They assume that Anthony answers to his party bosses."

I gasped. "Gale is afraid of the Libertists?"

Nick raised his hand. "I never said that. I never said what Gale thinks at all. I merely pointed out what some people believe. What conclusions you might draw from that are beyond my control. I gave you some facts and some impressions. But you don't guess."

"I investigate," I answered. "And you are not guessing whether any of these impressions might be accurate or not. Whether there might be any reason for someone to be fearful."

"I'm not guessing," Nick agreed. "But I *am* investigating. You have my word on that."

"And if you find anything in your investigation that bears on the safety and security of Maxwell City and the proper performance of my job, I hope that you will see fit to share it."

Nick nodded. "I will do my best, ma'am. As ambassador of Aldrin City, I have a responsibility to cooperate with local law enforcement as much as my other responsibilities allow. I'll share with you what I can, ma'am."

"Thank you . . . Ambassador."

I thought Nick was done; but then he added, "And Rosie . . . keep your eyes open."

C

I left the apartment and headed back toward my office. Between courts and media and prisoner transfer, I had done practically no actual police work today. Yes, that was all part of my job, but not the most important part. Vile had been carrying the load for long enough, and it was time for me to get back in charge.

The TO actually called for two deputy chiefs: one for second shift, one for third. Anthony and I had not even had time to discuss filling the third-shift slot. It felt like events were moving faster than we could possibly keep up. I knew from my days in the Admiralty that that was when mistakes happen. People think they can handle it, think they can keep pace, and do not see what they are missing.

My impulse in that sort of situation is almost the opposite: I slow down. I double-check everything. I fear those mistakes and how they can cascade. In an emergency, moving too slowly can be deadly; but my experience taught me that most emergencies are nothing of the kind, and you can figure that out if you take time to catch your breath.

So before I reached the office, I stopped for a quick bite. Not at Zeb's—I did not want to be seen there, and maybe drawn into a discussion. Instead, I went three doors down to Harrigan's, a small coffee shop with pastries and real coffee. Far too expensive for me to indulge often, but that day I needed it. As I sipped the dark brew, I could feel my muscles loosening. This small indulgence took me back to my hometown, made me feel fresh again. It gave me the strength to look over the day; and I needed the strength, because the day seemed pretty much a disaster in retrospect. The court session had gone as well as I could hope, but had taken too long. I could have gotten work done instead. And the interviews. I cringed at the thought of the interviews and how Rockford may have edited her stream to make things even worse by now. And then Gale and Nick . . .

I would not say I was still angry with Nick, but I was troubled. I understood his arguments, and they made logical sense, but I did not have to like them. There is a difference between private and secret. Nick was a very private man, and I felt special because he let me see inside his private world like perhaps no one has since his Grandma Ruth. When he lost her at such a young age, he had started putting up walls that kept people out, anyone he did not trust. And he did not trust many people at all. So to be let inside those walls, one after another, was a show of trust and faith that touched me inside so deeply that it overwhelmed me sometimes.

But secrets? Those were someone else's confidences. Those were different. And Nick could be trusted with those. He had been in the service long enough, he understood classified and secret information. He could cite the rules. And the same for privileged information. Gale had made an excellent choice there. Nick would be zealous in protecting his secrets and his rights.

But I could not shake the feeling that some of these secrets were things I needed to know. Things that might affect my work.

I sighed. I was taking it personally, because it was my husband. Again, I knew better rationally. Attorney–client privilege was recognized by every jurisdiction in the Compact, to one degree or another. Sometimes an attorney had information gained through privilege that might have bearing on a case. Or on public safety, even. Attorneys were tasked with weighing the ethical balance of rights versus safety. It was never an easy dilemma, but that was part of their job. That was the role that Nick was in now; and I trusted he would evaluate any conflict that came up, apply good ethical judgment, and act appropriately.

But I did not have to like it. He was my husband.

Refreshed from my coffee, I returned to the office. Ammon and Wagner were inside, along with the desk sergeant. Looking in my office, I saw Monè instead of Vile. "Where is Vile?" I asked. Monè stood, snapping to attention. "At ease, Monè," I said. "It has been too long a day for that. But where is she?"

"She's in arraignment court, ma'am. We made the last of the arrests for this wave, and Magistrate Montgomery hinted—"

"Hinted?"

Monè smiled. "Suggested, you might say, that the sooner we arraigned, the faster we would arraign. Process the suspects before they had time to mount yet more challenges."

"Probably wise," I said.

"Vile and I agreed," Monè said. "Somebody had to be there for the arraignment; and since I'm not the deputy chief, and you were occupied, that meant Vile. I told her I could handle the assignments here."

I did not miss the hint. "You would like to be deputy chief, wouldn't you, Monè?"

"I would not object, ma'am."

"Good." I clapped his shoulder. "I promise nothing, Monè. It is too soon. We have had enough changes here. I need to see how the department operates in the current structure."

"But you're not ruling me out?"

"But I am not ruling you out. And your honesty is a point in your favor." Then I thought about Gale's concerns about the Libertists, and I wondered if there was any validity there. "We need all the honesty we can get."

I looked over Monè's work, and all of the reports coming from the lieutenants and the patrol officers. There were glitches here and there, items that had not been properly followed up on. Simple human error, but they could do better. I pointed them out, and I made notes for additional training that would help in the future.

On the whole, it felt good to have something going right. Maybe the political side of the job was a burden. Maybe the diplomatic side too. But at least the actual police work was starting to come together.

I changed my mind about that when we learned that Philippe Trudeau was dead.

22. ANOTHER CORPSE

The comm call came in just after 0500. Once again I was alone in bed. Nick and I had not fought—more of a cooling-off truce—but he took his responsibility seriously. He had insisted that as Gale was in his custody, he would have to spend his nights in the embassy, planning strategies and making sure Gale did not escape.

I had not laughed at that. A capable spacer like Gale could escape if he really tried. The door lock was more symbolic than anything.

So when the comm sounded, Nick was not there to answer it. I picked up the unit from my desk, answered it, and got the word of Trudeau's death. After that I wasted no time on a shower.

The scene was a side tunnel off Foxtrot Tube on level 2, a district that was mostly filled with light industrial shops. I was on the site in eight minutes. I was pleased with the time I had made; but when I got there, I found that Marcus and his team had already beaten me to it. Vile had patrol officers blocking the area, keeping out journos and other curious people. We had yellow investigation tape up, of course, but Vile was too smart to rely on that. Journos only respect the tape if there is someone around to witness a transgression. Sometimes not even then.

As soon as Vile saw me, she came over. "Sorry to wake you up, ma'am," she said.

I pointed toward where Trudeau lay facedown in a service corridor. "Tell me the story, Vile."

"Yes, ma'am. We don't know much yet. A cleaning bot found the body approximately twenty-seven minutes ago. Those things aren't very smart, but they've got excellent image recognition built in, so they know what to clean and what to leave alone. Apparently that includes recognizing bodies in distress, and it signaled an alert right away. Public Safety dispatched aid immediately, but it didn't matter. His neck had been broken. He had been too far gone for resuscitation."

"Broken?"

"That's the opinion of the Public Safety officers who found him, ma'am. A couple of guys I've worked with before. They're no doctors, but pretty decent medics. They saw the twist, they found no pulse. Based on the images, they'd already sent for a doctor."

"Who was that?"

"Karen Knowles. Ammon's interviewing her now. She certified him as DOA. Cause of death is assumed the neck, until Dr. Costello files his report. My guess is he'll confirm it."

Reflexively I said, "Do not guess, investigate." Vile deserved better. She had this investigation well underway.

But she did not seem to take my comment as a rebuke. "Yes, ma'am. Public Safety blocked off traffic and summoned us. We got here as fast as we could, and we started investigating."

"Sorry, Vile. You have had less sleep than me, and I certainly have not had enough. You are doing a good job. I am just . . . irritated that we had this happen now. With everything else we have, the last thing we need is a sixth murder in two months."

"Assuming it's murder," Vile answered.

"Assuming. But it fits the indicators. Look around." I pointed up and down Foxtrot Tube, and then down the access tunnel. "This is just a simple throughway. Nothing to trip over, unless it was his own feet. And even then . . . healthy people do not break their necks just from tripping, not in our gravity. There are a lot of injuries he could have, but not that."

Vile nodded. "Dr. Costello said pretty much the same thing. He wouldn't rule out an accident, but he said not to bet on it."

"All right, Vile," I said. "Look at the scene. Costello and his team will put together a report, but I want your observations too. Tell the patrol officers I am going to expect reports from all of them. But from you, I want more. Speculate. Tell me what happened here."

"What happened to not guessing?"

"There is guessing, and then there is coming up with a theory to test. Give me a theory."

Vile paused. "It's a quiet district," she said. "Light industrial, not a lot of traffic overnight. No idea yet why Trudeau would be in an area like this—if he wasn't brought here."

"Costello's team should have an answer on that. For now, work it both ways."

"Well," Vile continued, "if he came here voluntarily, he had business here. It's nowhere near a main traffic area, and no one cuts through this district to get someplace."

I shook my head. "I could. There are access ways. Those are not used much now, but they have been there since early construction of the city. Someone might have come through here for that."

Vile shook her head. "You're not making this easy, ma'am. I'm trying to eliminate possibilities, and you're throwing them right back into the mix."

"Easy has nothing to do with it. Go on."

"All right. So one possibility is he was meeting someone and things went bad and there was a dispute that ended in his death. Another possibility is he was cutting through here to get somewhere else—I'm going to want to see a map, ma'am, so you can show me what we're talking about—and he ran into someone who killed him."

"Any other scenarios?"

"Sure. We're back to the possibility he was killed elsewhere and dumped here."

"So that makes three. Any more?"

"There's a slim chance of an accident. But that's all I have."

I nodded. "Pretty good. We might have minor variations on those, but let us accept those as what we have to work with. Now tell me what your theory is for each of them."

"The accident is easiest," Vile said. "If that's Dr. Costello's conclusion, then we document and store all of his evidence, get his personal effects to his next of kin, and stamp the death certificate. Easy work for us."

"Go on."

"If he met someone, or if he was coming through and got mugged, neither one speaks well for his purposes."

"How so?"

"If he met someone here, this far out of the way at that time of the overnight, he wanted not to be seen. That doesn't automatically prove wrongdoing, but it's suspicious. And if he was crossing through here to get to someplace else, the same suspicions are raised. I'll take your word for it that there's a path here; but it's not an easy path. There are more straightforward ways to get through the city. You only come through here if you don't want someone seeing where you're going."

"And what else, Vile?"

"Um . . . I'm missing it, ma'am."

"So he takes an out-of-the-way path because no one is likely to spot him there and yet he runs into someone who spots him and kills him. What are the odds of that?"

"Ah," Vile said. "I see. Too much of a coincidence. If he was passing through, it still wasn't a mugging is what you're saying."

"What I am *suggesting*. A theory. We cannot rule out a random mugging, but it is a low probability. So for either of those scenarios, someone he was connected to in some way committed the murder."

"I agree," Vile said. "That leaves us with our last theory, someone left him here."

"Dr. Costello will have some light to shed on that," I said. "But I do not like it. It is a stupid place to dispose of a body. Getting it here would be conspicuous. And any local would know it would be found by a cleaning bot soon enough. If you wanted to hide a body, this would not be the way to do it. There are lots of places in the city where you can hide one for a long time. Possibly forever. Dr. Costello will give us the final word, but I am not ready to buy the disposal hypothesis."

Vile rubbed her chin. "It's the same the other way, though, ma'am," she said. "If you killed somebody here, you'd have to know he would be found quickly. Why would you leave him out here for the first cleaning bot or passerby that came along to report him? You would want time to get away, make your alibi."

"Maybe," I said. "Maybe not. If you planned it ahead of time, maybe you also planned an alibi. But maybe . . . I think you have a point, but it will take some thought. Maybe this hypothetical killer panicked and just ran away. Or maybe not panic, maybe just saw someone coming and did not have time to dispose of Trudeau properly."

"We're getting a lot of maybes, ma'am."

"Too many questions," I agreed. "We *are* getting into guessing now. Let us see what Dr. Costello has to say. Vile, I relieve you. Get some sleep. At home this time."

"I'm all right, ma'am."

"Sleep, Vile! And I do not want to see you back on duty for eight solid hours."

"Yes, ma'am." She crossed under the tape and walked away. She weaved a bit, and I knew I was right in sending her to get some rest.

I made sure the patrol officers knew their responsibilities for the traffic block. While I was busy with them, Ammon finished her interview, and I put her in charge. Then I tracked down Marcus.

"My people have their orders, Doctor," I said. "They are to keep everyone out of the area until your team is done. You just let them know."

"I will, ma'am. Thank you."

"Anything to report yet?"

Marcus shook his head. "No. But we're being very thorough. If there's evidence here, we'll find it, ma'am." He gave me a slight grin. "This job is busier than I expected. I should have asked for more money."

"You and me both," I said, and he laughed as I walked away.

☾

So early in the day—before I would normally even be at my desk—and already I was off to a miserable start. I was heading back to my office when Anthony's line sounded on my comm. "Yes, Mr. Mayor?"

"Tell me they got the story wrong," he said.

"The story? Trudeau?" He nodded. "Who are 'they'?"

But I knew the answer before he said it. "The journos. Tara Rockford. Does that woman ever sleep? She's already filed a report, and she said she and her crew are on the way to the scene."

I shook my head. "She will not get near it, Mr. Mayor. We have it all cordoned off."

Anthony stared out of the screen with big, red eyes. "The next best thing to a dead body for a journo is a police line with a police officer blocking their access. That will be the top image on this morning's news streams, I can guarantee it."

"What am I supposed to do about that, Mr. Mayor?"

He shook his head. "Nothing. It's out of your control. It's out of *my* control. It is what it is. At least allow me a little stress relief by complaining about it."

And where was *my* stress relief? But I was polite enough not to ask.

☾

Later in the day, when Vile came in, it had been only six hours; but I decided not to quibble over it. Particularly because she found me in a good mood, laughing as she knocked on my door. "What's so funny?" she asked.

"It's . . ." I caught my breath. "It should not be funny, but . . . Wagner just filed a report of a drunken brawl in Port Shannon, including a couple of pockets picked while people were watching."

"And that's funny?"

"No, what is funny is . . ." I felt laughter building again. "I was so relieved to have a simple crime reported finally."

Vile laughed briefly as well. "Simple crime. Yeah, that's what I expected when I took this job."

"I thought we would work our way up to the more serious crimes," I said. "You know, riots. Parking violations. Do you know what it would take to get a parking violation in the tubes?"

"I suppose on the surface, maybe, landing a hopper too close to the tubes."

"Granted. So we would start with the simple stuff, and then work into . . ."

But suddenly it wasn't funny anymore. Vile continued, "Fraud, arson."

"Murder," I said. I tried to smile. "But no, we have jumped straight into the deep end of the pool."

"We're learning how to swim, ma'am. The hard way."

"I know. We had a rough start, but we *are* starting. Building. I think this crush of responsibility is getting through to people, making them take the job more seriously."

"I think so," Vile answered. "I . . ." She stepped inside and closed the door. "I think they're getting better. They see a duty, not a job. It's bringing some of your lessons home."

I shook my head. "Do not get complacent, Vile. This is all happening too fast. If it changes the culture, great, but it will not be a lasting change unless we build on it. I know everybody is exhausted, but we have to get some additional training in, fast. Reinforce what they have learned in the field. Get them to teach us from their observations. When it is their idea, the idea will stick."

"How do we do that?"

I checked my comm. Nothing major was on for a while. "Sit down, Vile. Let us throw some plans together."

We spent about ninety minutes finding time in the schedule for meetings, squad level and one-on-one. We developed a loose list of topics to walk the force through, but it really did make sense to let their observations and experiences be the agenda.

Then I noticed the time. "Sorry, Vile, I need you in the worry seat now. I need to go out and show my face in the squad rooms, so the troops know we are behind them. I have a city to inspect."

"Have at it, ma'am. I've got things here."

☾

So I worked my way from squad room to squad room, checking in, making pointers, issuing praises and corrections as appropriate. Eventually this would become routine for them. Some had enough experience either with the Initiative or DPS to know the drill already. The rest would learn.

Toward the end of the day, my circuit brought me back to Foxtrot Tube; and I figured I had better check in on the crime scene.

When I arrived, the tape was still up, and fresh officers were manning it. Ammon was still there, though, so I went over to relieve her. "Good work," I said, and she left with a smile.

I inspected the troops and their checkpoints, and I found nothing to critique. I made a mental note to congratulate Ammon on that next time I saw her.

Finally I checked on Marcus and his team. I was surprised how long they were taking. It was not like MMC, where they had had an entire building to investigate. All they had here was one isolated crime scene: a body on the ground and its surroundings. But they seemed to be examining that scene in minutest detail.

I walked up beside Marcus. "A challenging scene?"

He knelt beside the corner where the access tunnel met the side tunnel. "Surprisingly, yes. We're presented with a very important question here: Is this where the murder took place?"

"And you are sure it is a murder?"

He held a holographic caliper up against a scratch in the corner as he snapped an image with his comm. "I'm not *sure*, but sure enough. There was too much damage to the neck for any sort of fall. I'll confirm that with X-rays, but you're looking at a homicide, ma'am."

"So where the killing took place is a pretty important clue."

Marcus nodded. "And I don't want to get that fact wrong, because your future case could fall apart if we don't do our job correctly."

"What is your opinion?"

Again he shook his head. "I don't have one yet. It's premature. I can't rule out either hypothesis. There are scrapes in his clothing that match edges of the panel seams here, like there was a fight, and he banged against them. But someone really clever might have made those postmortem. There are matching bruises underneath those clothes, I'll bet. And tests may tell me if those bruises were pre- or postmortem. I think they were post, they had to be deliberate, and my bet is someone chose this spot deliberately. If pre, then this was a meeting place."

"That is how Vile and I worked it out as well," I said.

"I don't think dropping him here makes a lot of sense. Too risky. But I can't rule it out yet. You'll have to wait, Ms. Morais."

"I see." It was frustrating, but it was right. We had to follow procedure. "What about personal effects?"

"We've done a scanner inventory, but not a physical one yet. First we had to get every piece of evidence we could with the body in place. Then once we bagged him, we sent him off to the morgue. He should be under lock and key there—metaphorically, of course—while my team works here. We've got no one else to run the inventory. But it looks like what you'd expect: his comp, an earpiece, his clothes, shoes, and a belt. All of it ordinary."

"Ordinary?"

"Off the rack. Clothes you'd find in any shop in the Concourse. Or for heavy markup at the port."

"That does not sound like Trudeau," I said. "He fancied himself an important man. Important men do not shop off the rack."

"Now who's making assumptions, Rosalia?" Marcus frowned. "Sorry, ma'am. Rich people can buy plain clothes, but plain people can't buy rich clothes. It's not transitive."

"Sensible as always, Dr. Costello." I sighed. "I was just looking for some anomaly to latch on to."

"Besides the anomaly of a dead body in the tube, you mean?"

That earned him a grim smile. "Besides that."

I let Marcus continue working while I watched for a while. Then I circulated around the barricades again. At the north end of the main tunnel, the journos were piled up. Of course Tara Rockford was at the front, with her cameraman shooting video.

Rockford glanced up, saw me, and got a look like a hunting cat ready to pounce on a bird. "Ms. Morais," she called, "do you have any comment?"

Reluctantly, I walked up to the line. "We will issue a statement as soon as we know something," I said, addressing it to the crowd, not just to Rockford.

"But your team's been working all day," Rockford persisted. "You must have some answers by now."

I shook my head. "Ms. Rockford, real life is not some vid drama. Real evidence takes longer to gather than the time between segments, and far more time to analyze. We shall issue a report as soon as we have something concrete to report."

"Is that what you're telling Mr. Trudeau's research backers? Just shut up and wait?"

"My responsibility is not to his backers," I said firmly. "To his family, sure, I promise answers as soon as we have them. They will hear from us before you will. And to the city? I have a job to do. But I do not answer to his backers." I could not help myself from adding, "Do you?"

There was laughter from the other journos. It was petty of me, but I took some satisfaction in scoring one on Rockford.

Rockford turned away, adding over her shoulder, "Freddie, edit that out." She forced her way through the crowd, but the other journos persisted. Knighton found his way to the front and asked a question I was unready for: "So does this have anything to do with the fraud investigation?"

I paused. An ill-considered answer could create trouble; but not answering at all just left a vacuum for the mob to speculate in. So I said, "We have no reason to believe that at this time, but it is too early in the investigation to rule anything out. If there is a connection, Mr. Knighton, I shall let you know."

It was the best answer I could give. No doubt by morning, the story would read, "Chief of Police denies connection between murder and fraud." But I could not control what they said. I had to trust that Knighton sent my message out on his live stream, so my actual words would be out there on the record.

As the time dragged on past the dinner hour and into the evening, the journos started to give up. I think they had been hoping to break a scoop, and finally they realized there was not going to be one. No criminal revisiting the scene of the crime that day.

So by ones and twos they left. When the last straggler finally faded down Foxtrot, I went back to check on Marcus. "Not that I am rushing you, but do I need to schedule another shift?"

"No," he said with a smile. "Honestly, we've been filling in details at this point. My team informed me that the journos were giving up, so I figured if we dawdled long enough, they'd go away. I don't know how you put up with them, but I've got no interest in it."

I shook my head. "You cannot avoid them. There will be inquests and media reports. They come with the job of coroner."

"Yes, I know," Marcus answered. "But those are prepared remarks. Not impromptu mob sessions on the street."

"You never did like crowds."

"I'm not phobic," Marcus insisted. "I just . . . feel confined. Like they won't move fast enough, and like they have no idea where they're going. No sense of flow through an area."

"I have heard it before, Doctor. It still sounds like agoraphobia to me."

"Hey, who's the doctor here?" Marcus smiled. "You do the detecting, I'll do the diagnosing."

I grinned back. "*You* are doing a fair amount of detecting right here today."

"All right, you do the arresting and the marching off to jail. Or whatever it is police chiefs do." He looked around at his team. "Does everyone have what they need?" They agreed. "Good. Take all your evidence back, catalog and store it, and get some rest. We've got a big backlog now, so everyone's on overtime." Again he grinned at me. "Isn't Mayor Holmes going to love these expenses?"

I did not find it so funny, but it was true. They really had two ongoing forensic investigations: the arson, and the data forensics and other physical evidence from the fraud investigation. And now another murder on top of that. "When did this happen, Doctor? When did the crime in our city become so prevalent that your team cannot keep up?"

Marcus did not answer right away. Finally he said, "Maybe it was there all along, and we only just started looking. Maybe Mayor Holmes was right about us needing a police force."

"Maybe?"

He shook his head. "I'm sorry, ma'am. My mind is starting to wander. It's been a really long day, and a really long week. I spoke without thinking. I just . . . you know, I think we're growing too fast."

I knew. Even before Nick's effort to rekindle our own relationship, my relationship with Marcus had had one stumbling block. Marcus saw Mars as primarily a place for science. He was almost radical about it. I, on the other hand, wanted humanity to expand through the solar system. Through the stars. It had not been enough to prevent our engagement, but it had always been a small friction between us.

Marcus paused again, and then his eyes widened a bit. "Hey, what about Zeb's?"

"No, I—" But then I thought. I had missed another lunch, so I was hungry. And right now Nick was probably back in the embassy, strategizing with Gale over whatever his secrets were.

And I was just in no mood to go back to an empty apartment and sit alone with my thoughts from the past few days.

"Sure. Let us go to Zeb's."

23. Dinner with Marcus

This time I had the salad; but the salad I had made at home two nights earlier did not deserve the name "salad" compared to this. Greens and julienned vegetables and feta, so similar; but the dressing was Zeb's own spicy mix, and the whole thing was topped with Cajun blackened salmon, so good it could pass for real fish. Marcus had the ratatouille, and he sang its praises.

Both of us skipped the wine that time. I did not comment on that.

Another thing we skipped was discussing the body. I was not squeamish, but I was getting tired of it. Too many pointless deaths in my city. So I did not bring the subject up, and Marcus avoided it. Instead as we relaxed with the food and some Martian Springs, he said, "So how goes the other side of the MMC case? The whole insurance business?"

"Oh . . ." I looked around. The room was noisy, and I did not think we could be overheard; but I was careful about what I said anyway. "It is pretty much what I said to the media. I gave a thorough briefing yesterday, and today's arrest arraignments have not added up to anything new yet. Really, you can pull it up on the net."

"The Tara Rockford feed?"

"Space, no!" I put down my drink. "I would not trust a word she says."

Marcus's eyes grew wide. "Oh? She's got a pretty big audience. A lot of people listen to what she has to say."

"Not you?"

"Well . . . I've seen her show sometimes. I can't say I've ever fact-checked her, but she seems really good at asking uncomfortable questions and making people in charge scramble for answers."

"Uncomfortable questions based in fantasy," I answered. "She came at me with an agenda, and with her story already written. She was just trolling for quotes to fill in the blank spaces."

"I guess . . . I wasn't there. But she sure seems to know when somebody has something to hide."

"I have *nothing* to hide," I said. "And I resent the implication."

"Rosalia, please." Marcus put his fork down. "I didn't mean to imply that you did. I'm sorry, that wasn't what I meant at all."

"Well, it sure was what *she* meant. She was trying to trap me into admitting something when there is nothing to admit."

"I understand," Marcus answered. "That has to be frustrating."

I shook my head. "I am sorry. But yes, it is frustrating. And I had to sit there and take it, because Anthony and Alonzo want me to play nice with the media."

"That can't have been easy." He reached over and placed his hand over mine. "I'm sorry, I didn't mean to upset you." I gently pulled my hand away to pick up my fork, as if that were the only reason. He continued, "But you see, right there, you kind of implied she had a point."

"What?"

"You said the mayor and Gutierrez want you to play nice with the media. Present a good front. You don't have anything to hide, but maybe they do."

"Marcus!"

"Now, now, I know you wouldn't . . . I know you wouldn't be involved in anything illegitimate, but you're not the administration. They're . . . they're awfully cozy with the big business interests in town. And with . . ."

He did not continue, so I prodded, "And with?"

"With the Libertists," he said.

"With the party?" My voice rose, and he looked around nervously.

"Please," he half whispered. "I'm not trying to cause a fight. Of course he's the Libertist candidate, he's always been a proponent of Free Mars. No matter how impractical."

"Impractical? Marcus, are you a Realist?"

Marcus shook his head. "I'm a doctor, a man of facts and evidence and science. I don't look at the parties, I look at the facts. No party has a monopoly on those."

"But you do not think Free Mars is supported by the facts."

Again he lowered his voice. "Not yet, it isn't."

"So you do not think that it is realistic. Tell me how that does not make you a Realist."

"Party affiliation doesn't come down to this one issue."

"It does in this election," I said. "We are talking about the vision for Mars into the future. Are we supposed to be free, or are we supposed to be under the Initiative's thumb?"

"Of course we're supposed to be free! Someday, when we're ready. But not yet."

"Not yet. Not yet! It is always 'not yet.' I have never once heard a Realist answer to the question, If not yet, when? *When it is perfect,* they say. *When everything is right.*"

"What's wrong with waiting until we're sure it can work?"

"Because nothing is ever 100 percent sure! The only thing sure is that as long as we have to have every decision second-guessed by the Initiative, we cannot take actions that would *make* it sure. That would steer us in the direction of self-sufficiency and a second home for civilization on Mars."

Marcus looked around, and I did as well. I realized that the diners at several nearby tables were looking at me. What had started as a discussion had sounded even to my ears like a campaign speech. An elderly couple at a table across the restaurant smiled, and the old woman gave me a thumbs-up.

I tried to sink into the booth seat. Marcus did not help when he chuckled. "I guess you're a little more passionate about this than I am," he said.

"I cannot be," I answered. "Not in public. I am a public servant of the entire city, not of one party. People have to trust in the impartiality of my investigations."

"Relax, Rosalia," Marcus said. "I'm sure only half the restaurant heard you."

I felt my skin flush, and I pressed deeper into the corner. "Only half?"

"Maybe a little more. But I doubt any of them were recording for the journos."

I did not know what made Marcus so confident. It was a lesson they taught us all the way back in boot camp: assume anything in public is being recorded and will be played against you at the worst possible moment. Recording technology was everywhere.

"I know," Marcus continued. "I feel bad for you, really I do." But then he smiled. "Except for one thing."

"What is that?"

"For a moment, it was like the old Rosalia was back. You had . . . passion. I haven't seen you passionate in a long time. About anything."

"Marcus. Do not go there. It is not funny."

☾

After that, I cut the dinner short as soon as I could, claiming more paperwork. Which was true: when I stopped in the office, there were a half dozen minor reports for my review, along with the results of the day's arraignments and evidence gathering. Those took another half hour to get through.

Then I went back to my apartment, and I found the vid screen playing, running a loop from Tara Rockford's stream. It repeated her latest exclusive: "Police Chief Rosalia Morais Makes Her Electoral Stand." The backdrop of the story was a still shot of Marcus and I having dinner in Zeb's. A transcript of my little speech scrolled by, with computer-synthesized speech substituting for my voice. So whoever the snoop was, they had not gotten audio.

But it did not matter. Nick would recognize the rhythm and the word choice as mine, so he would know the speech was authentic. That would tell him that the photo was legitimate as well. And this loop was his reaction.

I hated the whole world that night.

24. THIRTY-NINE HOURS

I did not open my eyes when the comm sounded. I just reached over to the nightstand, found the button, and responded. "I am getting tired of these early-morning calls," I said, not trying to hide the disgust in my voice.

"I'm getting tired of making them," Alonzo said. "Get in here."

I opened my eyes at that. "For the last time, Gutierrez, I am not campaign staff. I do not answer to you, I answer to the mayor."

Alonzo paused. "I'm tired, too, Ms. Morais. I'm sorry. But if we don't get on top of this right away, you won't work for the mayor. Maybe I won't either. Maybe Anthony won't be the mayor at all."

That brought me fully alert. "What are you talking about?"

"The party Steering Committee met last night. They held a vote. They're still standing behind Mayor Holmes, but by only two votes. If things get any worse, they may put up another candidate."

"That would be crazy at this late stage," I said. "If they think Mayor Holmes cannot win, they have nothing left to lose."

"The Libertists will not go without a fight," Alonzo assured me. "Now I know you think that campaigning is beneath you; but the first thing a new candidate will do more than likely is to ask for your resignation."

"My resignation?"

"You precipitated this crisis by going all political last night. The mayor's ability to represent the city is in question now. And that could tip the campaign against us."

"I shall be there in thirty," I said.

"Make it— All right, thirty."

☾

Anthony's weak coffee was not helping, but nothing else would either.

As I had showered, I had watched the feeds. Rockford was not the only one raking me over the coals for my comments. Across every stream and network, the media were questioning my objectivity and using it to question Anthony's.

The same feeds were playing on Anthony's wall now. And as if questioning my objectivity had not been bad enough, Rockford was now attacking my integrity. "How could such an obvious staunch Libertist investigate the massive consumer fraud that's taking Maxwell City by storm when the accused are all leading Libertists themselves?" she asked. "It is this reporter's view that we won't see an objective investigation until Ms. Morais recuses herself from it or resigns."

Alonzo shut off the feed. "That opinion's becoming pretty popular," he said. "Recuse or resign. The Steering Committee's going to vote today about asking for your resignation."

"That is idiotic," I said. "I am the one who brought the charges in the first place. If I had wanted to, I could have hidden all of the evidence. Made the whole thing go away. She only knows about this story because of me."

From behind his desk, Anthony shook his head. "Show the rest of it, Alonzo." Alonzo's eyes looked pained, not calculating like they had for the past week.

"I was trying to spare her, Mr. Mayor."

"From what?" I asked.

"And for how long?" Anthony added. "She'll see it soon enough. Or Rockford will find a chance to shove it in her face. The police chief deserves to see it now, in private."

"Yes, Mr. Mayor," Alonzo said. He reopened the feed and selected a different time mark. "I'm sorry, Ms. Morais," he said as he tapped "Play." There was Rockford again. "My sources inside the police department tell me that the only reason this fraud was brought to light was because the famously apolitical, truth-telling Captain Nick Aames insisted on investigating it and on revealing what he found."

"That is not—" I started, but Alonzo held up a hand.

"Locals all remember how then-Captain Aames insisted on a thorough review of the *Bradbury* accident, even knowing that the result would be the end of his career with the Admiralty. *The man doesn't cover up,* they say. *Even when it hurts him.*

"And this reporter's sources in the Space Corps tell of another incident, early in Aames's career, when again he insisted on a full, truthful investigation that damaged his career for his mistakes. *And* that of his then-fiancée—Rosalia Morais.

"For all of his many squabbles with the Admiralty, even his critics acknowledge that Nick Aames believes in letting the chips fall where they may, as long as you chip away to the truth.

"So did Aames find evidence of a cover-up? No," Rockford continued, "I think we can be sure he didn't, or he would have told us of that too. But he found the thread, which is now unraveling.

"And that's causing trouble on the home front. As my sources revealed last night, Ms. Morais was seen in the company of her *other* former fiancé, the man she left for Nick Aames nine years back. The same man who she requested as coroner for Maxwell City. How convenient: the man who checks her evidence is the man she used to sleep with."

"Enough!" I leaned from my chair and shut off the panel. Then I turned to the two men. "Keep her away from me, or I may not be responsible for what happens."

Anthony's face grew pale. "Don't even joke about that, Rosie. If anyone outside this room heard you say that, it would be the end of your career, and probably mine. You do not threaten the media, no matter how much they ask for it. You let Alonzo and me handle her."

"Handle her how?"

"There's no good way," Alonzo said. "But there are better ways and worse ways. We'll start cutting off access, giving exclusives to her competition. We'll let her superiors know that our lawyers are combing her feed for actionable statements."

"You will revoke her media pass?"

"Can't do that," Anthony answered.

"That turns her into a symbol," Alonzo said. "We have to give her minimum access. But no more. We'll make sure that anytime we have a say, her competition gets the exclusives. And she'll get noncommittal answers."

"Knighton seems pretty good," I said.

Anthony shook his head. "He's no friend either."

"But he's honest," Alonzo said. "And he can't be bought, but he can be swayed. If I let him know there's a big exclusive coming along, but we need some breathing room to make it happen, he'll do what he can to give us that room. He won't be a booster, but he'll double-check everything. I think we can count on him not to run with anything that he can't verify from six different sources."

Anthony added, "And what he does run with, we back it up. We praise it."

Alonzo nodded. "We don't fawn over him, but we make sure to confirm his stories wherever they're true. Even if it hurts us. And no comment on hers."

"I have a few comments," I replied.

"Save them for your memoirs," Anthony said. "Which, if we don't get through this, you'll have lots of time for. That's how we'll handle the media; now how do we handle the Steering Committee?"

"I can delay the vote on the police chief tonight, Mr. Mayor. For one day. I can't promise two."

"All right," I said. "That's half a day in the future. So that is a day and a half. What are we supposed to do before then to change their minds?"

"Simple." Alonzo smiled at me. "Solve the case."

☾

Thirty-nine hours. Just over one and a half Martian days to piece together the full story behind the insurance fraud and the forces behind it. My first big case as police chief could be my last. I sat in my squad room, with the whole command squad called in. When they were gathered, I stood and addressed them. "This is the part of the job that you are going to hate," I said. "Politics." I looked them over. "Or maybe not. Maybe some of you are good at this, enjoy it. Maybe one of you would be better in this spot. And maybe you will get the chance very soon now."

At that, they gasped. Vile said, "Ms. Morais!"

"This is no joke, people." I explained the political situation, while trying to keep the personal matters out of it as best I could. When I was done, I said, "So that is where we are. If we do not know the true picture of this insurance scheme and who is responsible by the time the Steering Committee meets tomorrow night, I am out of a job, and who knows what happens to Mayor Holmes?" I was pretty sure I knew, but I was keeping that opinion to myself. "Even that may not be enough to save this department," I continued. "If the Realists take over the city council, they have made a promise to dissolve the police force and ask Initiative Security to take care of things here in the city. Now some of you come from there, maybe you would be more comfortable with that."

"Not a chance," said Wagner. "I'm a Martian. I left that behind me." The other former security officers nodded in agreement.

"All right," I said, "so none of us want that. We need to brainstorm, look at all the evidence and see what we are missing. I put a lot of trust in you nine, so now I am asking you for your help. Where do we go next?"

We spent the bulk of the morning going over the evidence. We broke into three groups, data, physical, and interviews, each attacking their part of the evidence. I bounced from group to group, listening to their discussions and throwing in questions.

And I realized: I was proud of my team—for as long as I could call them mine. They had raw potential, and they were coming together. I could really make something of a police force with them as my core. If I got the chance.

I treated the whole team to Zeb's finest out of my personal account. Who knew if I would get the chance to do that again? We stopped examining the evidence over lunch, but we did not stop the discussion. A theory of the case was starting to gel. I did not want to state it, because it might be a figment of my imagination. I wanted to see if they would reach the same conclusion.

So the discussion continued, arguments bouncing back and forth across the whole squad. We were halfway through dessert when I saw Monè's eyes grow large. "You have something, Monè?" I asked.

"A thought, Ms. Morais," he answered. "But . . ."

"Spit it out," I said.

"Not the cake," Vile answered, and everyone laughed.

"It's just . . ." Monè paused again. "I'm seeing something big, big enough to implicate even more of the Libertists."

"I do not give a damn about that, Monè. No matter what you may have heard on the media, in here, we care about facts, not ideologies. I was told to solve the case, not to make the Libertists look good."

"Well . . . it's not an answer, just a thought. We've been treating this as individual acts of insurance fraud, abetted by Flagg."

"And other opportunists in DPS," Ammon added. "Mr. Aames's clients have reported further fraudulent claims now that they know what to look for. Flagg wasn't the only one who approved the false claims, but the others seem to have disappeared. They're nowhere to be found in the city."

"Yes," I said. "We have alerts out for them."

Monè continued, "But I just thought, *What if we have it backward?* What if those committing the fraud are coordinated? What if Flagg and whoever aren't instigators, aren't behind it, but are just accomplices? Taking their cut, but answering to someone else?"

I thought about it carefully. Monè was starting to see what I had seen. But still, I wanted it to come from them, not to push them into an idea.

"It doesn't answer any more questions," Vile said.

"No," Wagner said, "but it simplifies some of them." He pulled up a data graph onto the big screen. "We've been imagining all of these little networks of collusion. We've been trying to see who interacted with Flagg and with the others, and where and how. But what if we posit"— he added an anonymous point to the graph—"coordinator one?" He added two more points. "One would be enough, but two and three might simplify it further. If we reapply a connectivity analysis now . . ." He punched in commands.

They could all see that the resulting graph was simpler, cleaner. A theory was not proof, but a theory was where you started looking for proof. Before, we had had a mesh of theories. Now we had just a handful. Maybe one.

I turned from the screen and looked at my squad. "We cannot be blinded by simplicity," I said. "Sometimes the answer really is complex."

"I understand, ma'am," Vile said. "But there's another consideration. Wagner, go back to the old diagram." Wagner did so. Vile got up and started tapping nodes in the network. "These are the places we'll have to investigate if this is the picture. Now the other, please." Wagner switched the picture back. "With this one, we have only a handful of places we have to apply leverage, people we have to pressure for information, places we have to search."

I shook my head. "That is still an argument from simplicity," I said.

"No, Ms. Morais, it's an argument from pragmatism. I know you don't want politics to have input into this investigation; but pragmatically, we won't have time to investigate the other picture. This one is all we have time to investigate before the Steering Committee. If we're going to solve it by then, we're assuming this is what we're solving."

"Space it, I will *not* have politics intruding!"

"Don't worry," Vile said. "It's only a day and a half. If it goes nowhere, the next police chief will have us try something else."

I had not even considered Vile's final argument. It made sense. With the resources we had and the available theories, this was the best use of our time. So I sent them out to pursue the simpler theory.

But I still was not happy about it. It smacked of desperation; and I just do not do desperate. I follow the facts. Cautiously, and completely.

And there was one set of facts that I knew was out there, but I did not have access to them. I left the squad room in Vile and Monè's capable hands, and I headed for the Aldrin City embassy.

25. GALE'S STORY

Nick ignored my comm signal. He ignored the door buzzer as well, and he even ignored me rapping on the door with the butt of my sidearm. He was sending the clearest message he could: *Stay away.*

But for once I was going to have to be more stubborn than he was. Too much was riding on this for me to let his wounded pride get in the way. And like Nick, I would never let a rule get in the way of getting the job done when it was urgent. So I used my police chief's access code on the embassy door.

For two seconds, I wondered if Nick had changed the security completely, and how he might have done that, so that my police chief code would not work. Then the door slid silently open, and I walked into the Aldrin City embassy.

It had more furniture than when I had seen it two nights before. Somewhere Nick had scrounged a vid panel, another couple of chairs, and a dining room table. And also dishes and food, since the two of them were eating a late lunch.

Gale looked up at me, eyes wide; but Nick stayed focused on the vid screen, some string of data scrolling past.

"Nick," Gale said, "get her out of here."

At that, Nick looked up at me. "Relax, Gale, she isn't here. That would be an interplanetary incident, and Ms. Morais would never do that."

I shook my head. "I am not playing that 'wife versus police chief' game, Nick. I am both, and do not expect me to ignore my job. For as long as I have it."

That got his attention, and he blinked. "As long as . . . ?"

"If I do not solve this insurance case, I am done. Out."

"Good," Nick said, leaning back in his chair. "About time. We can get back to survival school."

I strolled forward and loomed over his chair. "You do not get it, Nick. I am *not* giving up without a fight. You would not in my position, and you know I will not.

"I do not want to hear any arguments," I continued. "I already gave up one career for you, because it was the right thing to do. I am not giving up this one, because this city needs me. Staying in the job is the right thing to do. We will have time for survival school later, Nico, but not now. Right now Maxwell City needs its police chief."

Nick nodded slowly. "And they have got a damn fine one. Who has a lot of fight left in her."

"You are damn right I do. But I am fighting this one with one hand tied behind my back." I turned to Gale. "I need to know what you are keeping from me."

Gale shook his head. "Nick told you: the Libertists—"

"Space the Libertists! This is between you, me, and Nick. If my word is not good enough for you, Gale, I do not know what will convince you. Somebody has you scared, but it is not me. If you tell me what I need to know, we *will* bring them down. I do not care what party they are."

Gale shook his head. "They're more powerful than you."

"I am angrier than them. You have as much as admitted that they are Libertists, but I do not believe it. My city is under attack, and whoever is behind it is *not* a Libertist in my mind. They do not have the best interests of Free Mars in mind, whatever else they are after."

"Profit," Gale said.

"Hell, I could have guessed that. Of course it is profit. But I cannot see the connections. There is not enough money in insurance fraud to tempt people who are powerful enough to scare you like this. They do not deal in nickel-and-dime lots of parts."

"It's much bigger than nickel-and-dime," Gale said.

"Fine. Hundred lots, I do not care. You have implicated people powerful enough to tell Anthony what to do. He still owns a fairly large share of his father's empire, even if it is in trust to Aldrin University. He has voting control. Anthony Holmes is not a man to be bought, or he would never have come to Mars."

"I . . . Yes, I can see that."

"That implies that you are scared by someone even more powerful than him. Some of the movers and shakers of the Martian economy. Am I getting close?"

Gale swallowed dryly, and Nick poured him a fresh glass of water. Gale took a drink, and then said, "I think so. I'm not sure. But this . . . There's money behind it."

I shook my head. "But that kind of money . . . Penny-ante insurance claims are nothing at that level."

"We don't think it's about the insurance," Nick said.

Gale shook his head. "That fooled me at first. But Nick, he looked at it differently. He didn't look at the value of what was lost, he looked at *what* was lost."

"And that was . . . ?"

"Rare, hard-to-get items," Nick answered. "Expensive, yes, but rare was the key. These were instruments and equipment that were too noticeable. That were useful, but twice as useful if you had two. But if you bought two, people would *ask* why you needed two. They'd wonder what you were doing with all of the spare parts and equipment. But if you lost equipment and then replaced it, you could keep right on working with the 'lost' items."

"Working? On what?"

I looked at Nick, but no answer was forthcoming, so I looked at Gale.

And he answered, "Boomtown."

If you hang around the right parts of Maxwell City, especially some of the seedier areas of the port, you will hear talk of Boomtown. I am told that Boomtown tales are a lot more common in some of the smaller settlements, where life is harder. It is strange how in just a generation, Mars has developed its own mythology about a lost settlement somewhere out on the surface. And how if you find it and sign up, you make your fortune. No one ever has, of course, but that does not stop believers from dreaming about it.

In wilder versions of the myth, it is not just a lost settlement, it is a lost Martian settlement. *Real* Martians, nonhuman locals. The fact that we have never found so much as a fossilized microbe on the surface does not stop some people from believing that there are Martians hidden out there.

Whether they believe in humans or Martians, explorers near the end of their rope often dream of Boomtown: of finding it, signing up, and becoming the lords of all of Mars.

"Gale, you have lost it. You are crazy."

"It's not me." Gale shook his head. "I don't believe in the Boomtown myth any more than you do. But there's a project out there that sells itself to desperate explorers as Boomtown. It signs them up for work, secret work buried in the sands of Mars, and in secret hills, valleys, and crevasses."

Crevasses? I looked at Nick; but he raised an eyebrow, so I said nothing about crevasses. Instead I shook my head. "Gale, I need something more than a tavern tale. You are too experienced of a spacer to get scared by something like that."

Gale rose and started pacing, his assist suit grinding with the effort. Finally he turned back to us. "I know, ma'am. Because I was there."

I scoffed. "Sure, you went to Boomtown right after visiting Hy-Brasil."

"I'm serious, ma'am," Gale insisted. "I was hanging around the Gander settlement. It's a small place on the edge of the quadrangle, you might not have heard of it."

"I have." Before this police chief business, Nick and I had paid a lot more attention to what happened on the surface than locally.

"Well, I've done some work for two teams based out of Gander, but both went broke. It was the worst luck. I'd have been okay if one of them had fallen through, the other would have gotten me through to the next gig. But both within six hours of each other? That's the old Gale luck for you.

"So I was in a spot. My air bill was paid up for a week, my food and water for a little longer, and then I was going to be on the clock. Either sell to a labor combine or go back home to a world that didn't want me. Either way, I'd likely be in debt for the rest of my life. I was just getting ready to decide which, the farms or the long trip home, when I was approached by a man who bought me a drink."

I shook my head. "Because of course a man on his last credit is going to spend it in a bar."

"In Gander, that's where you're most likely to find work. It's not like Maxwell City, where the employment market is so organized. You go to the bar, you nurse a drink, maybe buy someone else one if it looks like he's having better luck than you, and you hope."

"And just when you needed it, an opportunity appeared."

"Of course," Gale answered, "that's how they work. They prey upon desperate people who are willing to work hard, but not ready to give up and haul slop. And I think . . . Well, I still have some reputation. I think they'd been keeping an eye on me. I do know my way around Mars."

"So you were recruited for this scam."

Gale shook his head. "Whatever else it is, it's not a scam. They took me out in a crawler with a half dozen other new recruits. They had the windows painted over, so we couldn't see where we were going. Not that their typical recruit could have guessed anyway. It was a sorry lot. Sorrier than me even. Hardworking, skilled even, but they would never make it on Mars on their own. Mars kills the unready. You know that, Nick."

Nick nodded.

"Hold up," I said. Gale had my interest, and I needed to hear more. I found a glass and poured myself some water, and I sat in the open chair. "All right, continue."

"They took us to Boomtown," Gale said. "Which is complete bollocks. It's no lost settlement at all. It's too well organized for that, and too new. They use the legends to rope workers in, but it's just a secret settlement. Getting built somewhere in Candor Chasma, not far from here."

"Ridiculous," I said. "It would be spotted."

"Not necessarily," Nick said. "If most of it's underground like Gale says, there'd be nothing to spot. The planetary surveyors got bored with Mars a long time ago. All the major features are mapped, and the geologists have their working models now. All of the interesting planetary science is happening in the Pournelle settlements around Jupiter, and even the moons of Saturn. After almost a century of exploration, Mars is boring."

I shook my head. "But the Initiative still monitors the surface."

"They monitor for ground-to-orbit traffic," Nick said. "And major surface flights. But they're so focused on customs enforcement that they pay no attention to other responsibilities, the original reasons the Initiative was put in charge of Mars space."

"Controlling development to preserve the environment," I said.

"Bingo. The Saganists, the few scientists who still care about Mars, are obsessed with Mars's nonexistent biosphere. They think if they can find evidence of life, they can bring attention back to Mars, and things will be run properly as they see it. They don't have a lot of influence, but what they have is loud and connected. Just enough that the Initiative and everyone in the Compact has agreed to the development restrictions. No new permanent development anywhere without certification by areologists that there is no impact on Martian life or evidence of the same."

"Which is ridiculous," I said. "If there had been any such evidence, we would have found it by now."

"Ridiculous is normal in politics," Nick said. "Somewhere out there"—he looked around—"somewhere right here in Maxwell City, probably, is someone who's bankrolling another city."

"I hate to repeat myself," I said, "but this is crazy. There is a hidden city in the chasma?"

"I am sure of the location," Gale said. "Because of my experience, they put me on some surface duties. I was out at night enough times to identify my location, give or take maybe thirty kilometers. I could have done better with more time."

"But this . . ." I stopped, trying to make sense of what I was hearing.

"Think about it, Rosie," Nick said. "We've seen the numbers before. We know the theoretical argument: one of the biggest things keeping Mars from being self-sufficient now is arbitrary limits to growth imposed by the Compact. There's enough wealth being generated here to make massive investments in growth. Some of that wealth is going back to Earth, but maybe not as much as we think. They say they're just waiting for Free Mars where we can write our own rules. But maybe they're *not* waiting. Maybe they're making the investment now, in preparation for the political change."

"They cannot buy their way out of the Compact," I said. "There are too many interested parties involved. But . . ."

"But they can buy an election," Nick said. "Swing more of the city, of all the settlements, toward the Libertist camp. Push us closer to declaring Free Mars. And when we do . . ."

"They are ready," I said. "Fait accompli. The settlement is already built, ready to mine resources, grow food, drill for water, and build infrastructure on top of what they already have."

"You see why I'm afraid," Gale said. "This . . . It's like a tsunami. I saw the water rushing out, and I see it rushing back. I just wanted to run for high ground and ride it out. I figured once your election was done, what I knew wouldn't make me a threat anymore, and they'd leave me alone."

I shook my head. "But Gale, why are you on the run in the first place? You had a job, suited to your abilities, paying you air and water and food, right?"

"Right," Gale answered. "If I'd been smart, I'd have kept my mouth shut. I'd have been on the winning side, it looks like, instead of a loser again. The Gale luck, one more time." He drained his glass. "But I couldn't stop asking questions. I . . . had to understand. I get restless when I don't know something."

Nick smiled at that, a rarity for him. "You're an explorer, Horace. You always have been. Even when you were a toady." I was surprised. For years when Nick had used Gale's first name, he had exaggerated it: *HORace*. It had been a subtle form of needling, prodding at Gale's sense of self-importance. Now Nick pronounced the name plainly. He sounded almost supportive.

Gale did not seem to notice, he only chuckled. "I had a good teacher." He turned back to me. "I got nosy. At first I was just looking for ways to make myself more valuable, get better assignments and better pay."

"Pay?"

"Absolutely! This wasn't slave labor. It wasn't even unskilled labor. They were selective. They wanted useful people, and they paid for the skills. Better than I've been able to get hopping around job to job across Mars. Anonymous payments, blockchips; but the rumor was that the payments came from the Red Planet League."

"The League!" I said. That was trouble. I felt the web of politics tightening around me.

Gale nodded. "And there were people getting paid better yet, people in higher positions."

It was my turn to laugh. "And your ambition bit you again," I said. "You are never satisfied if you are not climbing."

Gale spread his hands. "It's true. I can't change my spots. But can you blame me? Look at you, Ms. Morais. No disrespect, but you're just the same. You're . . . you're thriving in this new office. You're getting a chance to really change things, make a real difference. You grabbed it. You won't let go. Are you really that different from me?"

I opened my mouth to answer, but nothing came out. I had no answer.

But Nick did. "The difference, Gale, is she's getting there only through her accomplishments, not by playing the politics game. You were accomplished, but that wasn't fast enough for you. And apparently it still isn't."

"No . . ." Gale looked back and forth between us. "I've changed, Nick. In Boomtown, I wasn't trying to climb the social ladder, I was trying to be as good a spacer as I used to be. And find chances to prove it."

"And that made them nervous," Nick said.

"It did," Gale agreed. "One of the project managers, Merrick, finally decided he wouldn't work with me. I think he thought I wanted his job." Gale grinned. "I did, and I'd have been better at it. So he transferred me to another shift, with harder work. I didn't make an issue of it, I just dove into the new assignment. Soon enough, I was assigned outside work again, and I was able to narrow down the location. But I kept quiet about it."

"Oh?"

"Development restrictions weren't the only thing they were lax about," Gale explained. "They weren't that big on civil rights either. Three times, I saw workers hauled away for no discernible reason. The word among the workers was that they were spies of some sort, or maybe thieves. No one story was accepted by everyone, but everyone seemed to agree that we were being watched closely, and we should be careful to stay in line. I didn't really believe it until they took Jerry away."

"Who is Jerry?" I asked.

"I never got his last name, and I don't know if Jerry was his real first name. Names were a little fluid in the work rooms. Because of my reputation, I was stuck with my real name, but I might have been the only one. Jerry was . . . a friend, I guess. A bit of a dreamer, and curious like me. Not very bright when it came to keeping his mouth shut. He kept pestering me with questions about where we were and why we were doing this. He couldn't stop speculating.

"And the thing is, he was a believer! He wasn't sure what was going on there, but he was sure it was a good thing. A noble thing for the future of humanity. That was why I couldn't get him to shut up, no matter how many times I tried. He . . . he had the vision. And he had to know more.

"And then one morning, he just wasn't in his bunk. His roommates said one of the managers had called him out for a night assignment and hadn't brought him back. And that was it. We never saw Jerry again."

"He might have gotten reassigned," Nick said.

"Or . . . ," I said. "Or promoted. If he really was a true believer, maybe they rewarded that."

"I told myself that for a week," Gale said. "I kept an eye out, hoping to see Jerry in one of the manager jobs. But it just wasn't happening. And our work group stopped talking about Jerry.

"That was when the whole thing started to smell foul to me," Gale continued. "If they would disappear somebody as gung ho as Jerry because he knew too much, what would they do to me? I was smart enough not to show it, but I had a lot more answers than Jerry did. Enough answers to get disappeared, I was sure."

I nodded. "So you disappeared yourself."

"Exactly," Gale said. "But first, I hid some air tanks and filters and scrubbers. I had a long walk ahead, and air would be my limiting factor. Fortunately their inventory control systems weren't as secure as they thought, so no one noticed my scrounging. A few items at a time, I stashed my supplies in caches every time I had surface duty. I also socked away some valuables that might serve as trade goods. Or even . . ."

"Even bargaining chips," I said.

"Yes," he said. "That was in the back of my mind as well. But I wasn't sure how to put them to use. I knew the Libertist coalition controlled Maxwell City, so I thought maybe I could get the evidence to the Realists and tell my story."

"But you didn't," I said. "Hogan's people arrested you in the Well."

"Yes," Gale said. "But I'm getting ahead of myself there. Back in Boomtown, I built my stash, and I kept my mouth shut. But still they seemed to be keeping an eye on me. I'd been too friendly with Jerry, I think. I started getting dirtier, lower-level assignments, not things that would utilize my skills as I had proven them. I stopped getting surface duty entirely. I was afraid I'd missed my chance; but then I heard the news I'd been waiting for: a storm was coming. There had been an accident, and they lost three of their exterior team. Four more were laid up in the clinic. They couldn't afford to be choosy, and I was assigned to the exterior again.

"Once I was out on the surface, I volunteered for a surveying assignment, as that would take me farthest from the lot. I went out, taking mineral assays and locator sightings, doing exactly what I was supposed to do up until break time. They worked us longer and harder than on most jobs, but they were smart enough to know that you can't go forever without breaks. They stretched as long as they could, trying to beat the storm.

"But eventually they had to call a break. When they did, I checked the sky, and I remembered the meteorology lessons that Van der Ven had taught us. The storm would hit soon. I turned off my locator, and I also turned off the second locator hidden in my water recycler that we weren't supposed to know about. Then I turned off my suit lights, and I marched toward the storm front.

"The clouds moved quickly, making a dark Martian night; but I've seen darker, back when we on Nick's team were the only humans on Mars. Dark didn't scare me. Mars didn't scare me. Using dead reckoning, I found my caches before the sand completely buried them. Then I found my way to some rocks I had memorized, and I sheltered from the sand as best I could. When the storm let up, I started walking again."

Nick interrupted. "And Boomtown was far enough away that they couldn't expect anyone could walk from there to Maxwell City."

Gale grinned. "Exactly. Not just walking, climbing out of the chasma. I'm sure they didn't expect that. They probably thought I was lost in the storm; but even if they sent out search vehicles, I'm sure they didn't think anyone would try to evade them, or be smart enough to get away with it. Boomtown may have had some money behind it, but what it needed was some Mars experts."

Nick continued, "So you marched at night, and you dug into the sands by day, just leaving your solar collector out to help your batteries. You scavenged subsurface water, put it into your purifier, and let your suit turn some of it into oxygen. That wasn't even a challenge for you, Gale. You could walk halfway across Mars that way, and they'd never find you."

Gale shook his head. "I didn't have rations for that long, nor enough power for my assist suit; but I had more than enough to make Maxwell City. Well, Port Shannon, that is. Then I hung out by a field maintenance lock, and I waited for a service bot to go out to fuel up a lander. While the bot was focused outward, I came up behind it and then dashed in before the lock closed. That got me into the port, and it was easy from there. I'd heard about the Well, so I tried to look like I belonged until I could get into the common areas. From there I found the Well, and I traded a couple of items for a meal and some credits."

"So you had more than Hogan picked you up with?" I asked.

"I did," Gale said. "Don't worry, I have pictures and serial numbers. If anybody will believe me."

I did believe. I absolutely believed. Gale's story fit so many facts. I wished I had Wagner and his network analysis graph to plug this into. Maybe now it would pinpoint the people behind Boomtown.

But I could not draw anyone else in. Like it or not, this was not my call. I had agreed to Gale's terms, or I would not have known any of this. Sometimes you could bend the rules, but you did not bend trust.

Yet I was still on a deadline. Gale had been talking for over two hours. With that plus my morning and afternoon with the team, nine of my thirty-nine hours were gone. I had thirty left. What were we going to do?

26. RAIDS

If my life had been a vid, our next move would have been for Nick and me to lead an assault on Boomtown, with my whole squad behind me. Maybe the whole police force, the cavalry to the rescue, taking down the forces of darkness.

What rot!

We were a police force, not an army. We had not even trained in surface maneuvers, which would make us liabilities on the surface. And make us dead.

Instead Nick and I convinced Gale against his instincts that it was time to trust someone outside the embassy. I vouched for Hogan, and Nick did as well, if not as enthusiastically. Between us, we persuaded Gale to tell Hogan his story and give him the coordinates for Boomtown. The Initiative had the army, let them get shot at.

If it came to shooting. I was going to try to prevent that.

But suddenly I had a new appreciation for Nick's ethical dilemma. Between us, we now had a more complete picture than Nick had had when Gale had first taken him into his confidence. Complete enough to act; but also complete enough to possibly destroy Anthony. And Gale still did not trust Anthony, despite my assurances that Anthony was a good man. Gale conceded only this much: he let me call Anthony and promise him that I was doing the right thing, whatever happened.

"What do you mean?" Anthony asked.

"Mr. Mayor, I cannot say. But this is the right thing to do. I hope someday you will see that." I was prepared to go one step further: to call in Nick to back me up if I had to.

But instead, Anthony said, "Rosie, I trust you. You'll do the right thing."

He trusted me. This was not about Nick, it was all me. It warmed my heart, which was a nice way to feel as I headed out on what might be my last duty as police chief of Maxwell City.

☾

The Steering Committee was too large. I had heard Alonzo say that before. Too many people to make the tough decisions, too many opinions on trivial matters. They were large enough that they met in the auditorium in the Admin Center. It was a gray area in terms of the administration's official neutrality between the parties, but no one had ever turned down the Realists for using the facility. Of course the Realists had never asked.

My spotters told me there were at least fifty in the room. Alonzo was right: that was not a committee, it was a crowd. And my investigations had revealed that a significant chunk of that crowd were on the board of the Red Planet League. This was tangled, but I was starting to find the loose ends.

The bulk of my force was gathered at the main entrance—which was locked, of course. Private committees were not subject to open meeting rules. My other squads were gathered outside the side entrances, the Admin anteroom, even the service entrances. No one was getting in or out without me knowing.

We were not alone. Nick was with us. I had not even tried to argue with him about it. I was too tired for that; we could argue later. And as I promised, Pat Knighton was right behind me. "I sure hope this explanation is going to be good, Ms. Morais," he said.

"Trust me," I said. "It will be a ratings sweep. When the time comes, you start your monitor, and do not stop transmitting for anything."

And then we waited, until at last I got the comm signal from Chief Hogan: *In place.*

"All right," I said on my command channel. "Backup squads, watch your exits. We are going in." I keyed in my police chief code, the door popped open, and my police force entered the auditorium where we had debuted a month ago. This time, space it, we *marched*. I was sure it was a beautiful sight on Knighton's video.

Alonzo was up at the rostrum making some sort of speech. Again the holographic Mars globe hovered behind him. I did not get a chance to hear what he was saying, because he stopped at the sound of our boots. "Ms. Morais!" he said. "This is—"

Stehouwer walked up from the side of the stage. "This is outrageous, ma'am. Get these police out of here immediately."

"I cannot do that, Mr. Stehouwer," I said. I used the old command voice that I had not needed in years. I could still project, even in a room that was getting noisier by the second.

"Ms. Morais," Alonzo said, "you are ruining everything! I was just explaining why we needed to postpone the vote on your job for one more day. Now . . ."

"Now I think a vote is obviously in order," Stehouwer said. "I move that we vote to remove Ms. Morais from office immediately. Do I have a second?"

"You do not!" I said. "I do not serve at your pleasure. I was appointed by Mayor Holmes, with the backing of the city council, and only they can remove me."

Thomas came onto the stage from the other side. "The council will do what we tell them to do."

"I do not think so," I answered, "not once they learn that this entire committee is under arrest."

"That's outrageous!" Thomas said.

"You can't arrest all of us!" Stehouwer added.

"Maybe," I said. "Maybe only some of you, but we need to hold all of you for questioning, at least until I get my reports from Boomtown."

Stehouwer's face grew pale. Thomas was a better actor. "Boomtown? What's that?" But I did not buy it. These two had "ringleader" written all over them.

I marched up to the stage and over to the speakers at the rostrum. "That is what all of Mars is about to find out," I said. "And the Initiative. Their troops have got Boomtown surrounded."

Thomas took a step backward. "I don't— I don't know what you're talking about."

"I think you do, Ms. Thomas. And you are not the only one." I looked out over the crowd. "My apologies to those of you who are on this committee just because you like to hear yourself yammer. And to the true patriots among you, as well, my apologies. But some of you here are just in it for the power and the money, and you are the ones who know about Boomtown and are a part of that effort.

"So do any of you want to confess now, call your people and tell them to surrender before the Initiative has to go in shooting?"

"You'd never do that," Stehouwer said. "There hasn't been an Initiative military action in . . . since Luna!"

"This is not military," I answered. "For this operation, I have deputized Chief Hogan and as many Initiative Security troops as he needed."

That shocked Alonzo. "On whose authority?"

"On mine," I said. "Read my oath of office and the statement of my job responsibilities: *To preserve and protect the safety of the people of Maxwell City, and to ensure the enforcement of all laws of the city, and the Compact, and the Initiative where applicable.* Boomtown is a violation of the Compact, which makes it my jurisdiction, and I can deputize whomever I need to put a stop to it."

"But . . . ," Stehouwer said. "Shooting . . ."

"Shut up, you idiot!" Thomas said.

"That is close enough to a confession for me, Ms. Thomas. Do you want to give the order to stand down?"

I gave Ms. Thomas credit for her nerves of steel. She was ready to let things turn into an all-out gun battle rather than concede a single thing. Of course it was not her facing the guns.

In the end, though, it did not matter. As Hogan reported later, her money had bought loyalty, but not bravery in the face of Initiative troops. One shot was fired, an Initiative shoulder-launched rocket. When that took out the concealed dome of Boomtown's main lock, it took only seconds for Boomtown to signal surrender. The Initiative troops marched in to find workers standing stone still with their hands on their heads. The only casualties of the whole engagement were a handful of project managers. Hogan eventually reported that they had been beaten to death with fists and tools and other improvised weapons, before the Initiative ever entered the settlement. I was angry at that, and not just by the brutality. Those were probably people with a lot of evidence to share if pressured properly. But I remembered Gale's friend Jerry, and I understood why the men had been killed. In a base full of workers, the beatings had happened with no witnesses.

But that came later. All I knew at the time was that Hogan had signaled success, much faster than I had hoped for. This time, I used the microphone to make sure I could be heard clearly by everyone. "I have news," I said. "My Initiative deputies are in control of Boomtown. No shots were fired after the initial breach, and reports are that all evidence is intact. We are going to talk to every single person on this committee, and be aware that we will check your statements against every piece of evidence we find in Boomtown. We are going to have officers read you your rights"—in this regard, the Compact resembled American court precedent: suspects could not be compelled to testify against themselves and had to be advised accordingly—"and then you are going to be questioned. But I can tell you this: we are going to get a lot of evidence, incontestable evidence even, from the records at Boomtown. If what you have to tell us contradicts what is in those records, well, it will not look good for you in front of the magistrate."

That was a shot across the bow for any reluctant suspects. With a project as big as Boomtown, they could not know for sure what evidence we would find that might implicate them. Maybe the most brazen would remain silent, or even lie; but I counted on most of them to fold once they could see what was coming. If a conspiracy was large enough, some were sure to give us what we wanted before the evidence came up, just to get the best deal they could.

This was going to be horrible for the Libertists, and I felt bad for Anthony. And even for Alonzo: as much as I resented his politicking, I understood his reasons, and I had just sabotaged his campaign.

But I had done my job. I had upheld the truth. If that did not matter, then I wanted no part of any of this.

I headed toward the edge of the stage, contemplating my letter of resignation. It would be better than my last one, when I had left the Admiralty. At least this one would be the truth.

But before I could even reach the edge of the stage, Pat Knighton caught my sleeve. "Ma'am, do you have a statement for my viewers?" He nodded his head toward the door, and I got his point. Something like this would not stay secret for long, and the rest of the media would be here soon. And I had promised him an exclusive. He had not actually earned it yet, but a promise was a promise.

So I moved back to the rostrum, in front of that giant rotating globe. I wanted to give Knighton a nice visual for his report. Then, in brief but with all the basics, I explained about Boomtown, and the effort to circumvent the development restrictions of the Compact. I hit all the major points while leaving Gale out of it. Just in case we missed some conspirators, I did not want to make a target out of him. Just like a journo, I simply talked about my anonymous sources. Gale's identity would come out in court, but I could protect him for now.

When my story was done, Knighton smiled, again that broad grin with the beard. Rockford and her crew had just come in through the back entrance and had missed my entire story. He had his exclusive.

But he wanted more. "Ma'am, does Mayor Holmes know about this? What's his part in it?"

"These arrests"—I looked around the room—"required a high degree of secrecy, which I am sure you can understand. To protect my sources, I could not even inform the mayor. I acted on my own authority."

"But you could inform Chief Hogan."

"For reasons that will be explained in court, yes."

"So Mayor Holmes was not involved."

"Nor any of his campaign staff, we believe. This is not an operation of his campaign, it was the party Steering Committee. There *is* a difference."

"They're all Libertists," Knighton said.

"They are *not* Libertists," Nick interrupted.

Knighton turned toward Nick. "Audience, that was the voice of Maxwell City Founder Nick Aames. Mr. Aames, would you care to tell us of your part in this investigation?"

Nick looked flustered. He did not like dealing with the media. He was just not very good at keeping his mouth shut. But now he said, "No. Ms. Morais is the one you should be talking to. I was just a consultant, it's her operation."

Knighton turned back to me, and I responded, "Mr. Aames—for the record, my husband—provided valuable information for this operation and assisted in the planning.

"And he has a point," I continued. "These people behind this operation . . ." I looked out to make sure that Rockford had her system set up, and the other journos were filing in. She would probably get this wrong, but I wanted her to get it, space it! "The people behind this were not Libertists. They were profiteers from the Red Planet League." There. The League was in the story now. I could almost feel financial markets shudder, but it had to be done. "They were not interested in Free Mars. They were interested in *buying* Mars. There is nothing wrong with a little profit, but independence is about much more than profit. It is about self-determination, self-reliance.

And *then* a little profit." Knighton laughed. "Mars can be free," I continued. "Mars *will* be free. But under the Compact, following the rules and the precedents of Free Luna and Aldrin City. There are no shortcuts, and anyone looking for them does not have Mars's interests at heart. Free Mars is a long-term vision, not a short-term return on investment. I am not saying that people will not make money here, because what Martian doesn't hope to make their fortune? But there are *rules*. We want to keep the rules small. I know the Libertist platform is to cut them way back. But until that is done, we will not succeed by ignoring them."

I controlled my smile at that. Neither Nick nor I were sticklers for the rules, as I have noted before. But space it, there were principles involved here! The Compact was not arbitrary, for the most part. I thought the development restrictions were excessive, but I understood why they were there. Once we were independent, we could change them. But it was not the day to discuss that. Instead, I stuck to my theme. "So I tell you, these were not Libertists, they were opportunists."

"You sound like a Libertist yourself, ma'am," Knighton said. He grinned out toward Rockford. "You have been accused of that by other outlets. But they didn't ask you to your face. I'll give you a chance to answer: Are you a Libertist?"

I looked at Nick. Simple truth. "Absolutely I am a Libertist. Anyone who does not believe in a Free Mars is in the wrong place, in my opinion. I might be wrong about that."

That drew another chuckle from Knighton. "But what do you say to those"—again he glanced at Rockford—"who allege that you can't be independent then? Who say you can't be unbiased as a police chief because of your political views?"

For this one, I looked directly at Rockford's camera, not at her. "Look at what I just did to the Libertist structure. If after tonight you think I would go easy on *anyone*, on any suspect, because I happen to agree with them on politics, your own politics are blinding you. I follow the facts." I nodded toward Nick. "Let the chips fall where they may."

27. Damage Control

As we gathered in Anthony's office, I prepared myself for a fight with Alonzo. I was done putting up with his attitude, and I was ready to let him know that as clearly as I could.

So I was surprised when the door closed behind the three of us, and Alonzo sank against it with a long sigh. "That . . . could have been worse," he said.

Leaving well enough alone has never been one of my skills, so I said, "What does that mean?"

Anthony sat behind his desk, and he sighed as well. "I think he's saying that by any reasonable standard, that went well."

Alonzo shook his head. "There's nothing good about it, Mr. Mayor."

"And there wasn't going to be," Anthony answered. He looked at me. "We had already gone through every possible scenario." His eyes narrowed. "*Except* the scenario you actually pulled off. And we didn't see any good coming out of it. We didn't see any way for you to keep your job, and the odds of me keeping the nomination were pretty low. Winning the election, even lower. It looked like the Libertist cause was dead."

"But instead," Alonzo continued, "it turned out better."

"Better," Anthony agreed. "Unorthodox, but you may have flipped a few minds there, especially with that speech at the end. You took some campaign negatives, and you turned them into positives, simply by showing your integrity."

Alonzo went to the wet bar and poured himself a glass of water. "It could have been even better. If you had let us in on it, we could have prepared better statements and been ready for more questions."

I shook my head, and I sat. "I could not do that."

Alonzo drained half the glass. "And that's the problem," he said. "By surprising us, you made it look like you couldn't trust us. I give you odds that's what Rockford will be saying tomorrow. You should have trusted us."

"I could *not* do that," I insisted. "Gale trusts Nick, and Nick trusts me, but that did not mean that Gale trusted me. Once he did, that did not mean he trusted you just because I do. Trust is not transitive. It does not work that way."

Anthony leaned forward. "I understand that. But politically—"

"Space politics!" I said. "If I had played this any differently, the arrests might never have happened. The Boomtown people might have gotten away with it."

"And in the long run," Alonzo said, "the politics of that would've been worse." I started to object again, but he held up his hand. "It's all well and good for you to say, 'Space politics,' ma'am, but I have to think about it. Politics is the art of the possible. If we're not in office, our agenda can't get done."

I forced myself to sit back in my chair and relax. I knew the truth in what he was saying, but I did not want to have to think about that when I was thinking about how to do my job. But there was no sense fighting about it now.

Anthony, meanwhile, looked almost pleased. "You really think it could have been worse?"

"By election day?" Alonzo asked. "Absolutely, Mr. Mayor. It's like we discussed yesterday: all of this dirt was just waiting out there to be found. Better that *we* found it than the journos. Our so-called friends in the League shot the party in the foot. Ms. Morais put a bandage on it. And we may still limp to victory now."

"I don't see how," Anthony said. I silently agreed with him.

"That's my job, Mr. Mayor," Alonzo said. "I've got my team on damage control already. The police chief's speech will go a long way for that."

"Maybe turn it into a campaign commercial?" Anthony asked.

"Absolutely not!" Alonzo said. "She staked her claim as apolitical. We aren't going to make a liar out of her now." Alonzo turned to me. "And this should make you happy, ma'am. The one thing we must *not* do from this point forward is involve Ms. Morais in the campaign anywhere where the public will see her. That's a point of principle now. If we start using her as a PR token, everything she did gets undone. You or I might reference her speech, but we don't play it."

I was relieved at that. I had more than enough to do building a police force and investigating fraud and murders.

Then Alonzo leaned forward, hands on his knees, and added, "But what would help . . . would be if we could get the founder on board."

Anthony nodded. "He once said he would campaign if I needed him. Could you talk to him, Rosie?"

I hesitated. "You might want to ask him yourself, Anthony. I am not sure where Nick and I stand right now."

☾

I hesitated outside of the embassy door. This visit was not an emergency. Well, not a police emergency. It was personal, and I hoped it was not trouble. But in this circumstance, I could not justify using my police chief code.

But I did not have to. The door slid open, and Gale stood on the other side. "Hello, Ms. Morais" he said. "Come in."

I entered, and again I was surprised at the changes in the apartment. Now one of Nick's bonsai palms sat on the counter between the kitchenette and the living space. There was a dark-gray area rug on the floor beneath the coffee table. Pictures of nebulae hung on the walls, along with a scrolling display of spacecraft and Mars scenes. The bare, utilitarian space was becoming a living space.

Nick was in the kitchenette. It was smaller than our kitchen. This was an apartment designed for one, so he barely had room for the cooking he was doing. He was chopping onions and potatoes; and as I approached, he dumped them into a skillet lined with hot oil. They started to simmer.

"That smells good," I said.

"Uh-huh," Nick answered, opening the refrigerator door to pull out some soy eggs.

I recognized that noncommittal response. Nick was acknowledging my presence but not encouraging it.

But I was not giving up so easily. "It looks like we pulled it off, Nick," I said. I turned to Gale. "Thanks to you."

Gale relaxed within the frame of his assist suit. "That's . . . that's the first good news I have had since I learned about Boomtown."

"There is a lot of mopping up to do," I said. "Evidence to secure, cases to try. The prosecutor's office is going to have to add staff for this, attorneys and researchers. It is going to take months for these cases to wend their ways through the courts."

Gale's jaw dropped at that. "Months?" He stiffened again. "Months until I'm safe?"

"Gale . . ." I tried to think of what would sound reassuring. "Gale, you are safe now," I said. "The people behind this will be going down. They have already started turning on each other. If they have any vendettas to carry out, you are the smallest target. They probably do not even know your name."

"Good. Can we keep it that way?"

Sometimes telling the truth is unpleasant. "No, we cannot," I answered. "I will have to establish the complete chain of discovery in case after case. I can minimize your role. You were caught with stolen goods, and you told us where they came from. That should be enough for prosecutors to work with. But if the defense really tries to tear down our story, I shall have to tell more."

"And they will," Nick said, his first contribution to the conversation since I had arrived.

"They might," I said. "But if enough of them turn on each other, with enough evidence to back it up, we may never have to talk about how the case was made. That is what we are shooting for now."

Gale clanked into the living room and sagged down on the couch. "This will never be over, will it? The old Gale luck just keeps striking."

I was unsure how to respond to that. I understood: living under a threat is taxing, stressful. I really thought it would work out okay, but I was not the one caught in the middle of it.

Instead I turned back to Nick. "Anthony sends his thanks," I said, then turned to Gale. "To both of you."

Nick shook his head. "I didn't do it for Anthony. It was my responsibility to Gale."

"Well, he thanks you anyway. He also has a favor to ask. He would like you to campaign for him."

At that, Nick looked up, an eyebrow raised. "Not for the Libertists?"

I shook my head. "Only for him. But . . . would it make a difference, Nico? Have you given up on the Libertists?"

He added the eggs to the frying pan. "A party is just one more damn bureaucracy, another stumbling block for those trying to get things done."

"But . . . you still believe in Free Mars?"

"Of course I do. I just don't believe some party Steering Committee is going to make it happen. The people doing the work will make Mars free, not the people who think they're entitled to tell them what to do."

"All right." I hesitated. "Then just for Anthony. I will tell him that."

"Tell Gutierrez. He's in charge of the campaign. Anthony is just along for the ride."

"All right, I shall tell them both. You *will* campaign for them?"

"I did promise," Nick said. And then, in a lower tone he added, "I always keep my promises."

The way he looked at me made it an accusation. I should have left it alone, but I was just too tired after the past week. "I do not need that, Nick."

"And I don't need to see you on every news feed dining out with Marcus while I'm eating alone."

"Nick! It was a working dinner."

"Every night for the past two weeks has been a working dinner. How many of those were with Marcus?"

"We have had two murders and two long days. I can't *not* talk to him, he is the coroner! This was not fun, this was discussing cases."

"You have all day to discuss cases. You have email, comm messages. Once in a while, maybe you should try being at home."

"We have always worked long hours, whatever it takes to get the job done. You have never complained before."

"You've never gone out to Zeb's with your ex-fiancé before!"

"What do you want? Do you want me to give up my job? After I just made a point of how important it was on interplanetary media? Abandon the city now, abandon Anthony, when I just made the case for how much they need me?" Nick looked blankly at me, not answering. "Do you?"

Still he did not answer. After seconds of silence, I turned around and left the embassy.

28. JURISDICTION

After such a long day, I should not have been surprised that I was still tired when I woke up the next morning; but it was becoming a bit of a habit, and I did not like it. I was sleeping poorly, not getting enough rest, and I was starting to feel the effects.

Not to mention I was getting tired of waking up alone.

There was no sign that Nick had come back to our apartment at all. I did not know whether to get mad or sad, so I shoved that aside, checking my comm.

And already it was starting up: 0600, and I had a message waiting from Hogan. He wanted a meeting at my earliest convenience. The usual place.

So I quickly showered and made my way back to the port anteroom. Hogan was waiting. I sat down, and the door slid shut behind me. "Thank you, Chief," I said.

Hogan had trouble looking at me. "I . . . think you might want to hold off on thanking me until you hear what I have to say."

That got my attention. "What is it?"

He took a long breath before answering. "I have orders out from Earth that I'm to take jurisdiction of Boomtown."

"What!"

He shook his head. "Ma'am, it makes sense. Yes, you located them, but they're outside of Maxwell City territory. In clear violation of the Compact."

"I have jurisdiction over the Compact!"

He shook his head. "No, you have cojurisdiction. *Within* your territory."

"And on incidents that initiate within my territory."

"That has its limits," he answered. "Certainly you can't claim jurisdiction on Luna or Earth. And we don't *know* that this violation initiated within your territory." He paused, visibly trying to stay calm. "This is out of my hands, ma'am. And if you thought like an admiral for once, you'd see that too."

"I . . . You have a point. I am not thinking like an admiral, because admirals do not have a stake in what happens here. We have to manage our own affairs."

"The people in charge don't think you can. You made a pretty good speech yesterday, but they're not convinced. They don't think one honest police chief can clean up what looks like a corrupt town."

"But you would not even know about Boomtown if we had not dug them out."

"Damn it, ma'am, you think I don't know how unfair this is? How idiotic it is? We're not an investigative division. The Inspector General's Office up on Phobos is formally taking charge of the investigation, but they don't have the resources. If I had any say in this, I would lock the place down and let you run a proper investigation. But the decision's being made way over both of our heads."

I had to tell myself to calm down. Hogan was not to blame. It took admirals to be this stupid—admirals and bureaucrats.

Finally I was able to speak without bitterness. "So what happens now?"

"Now . . . we've locked the facilities down. When the inspector general finds the time and personnel, they'll go in to gather evidence."

"I need that evidence *now*. I have cases pending. I have prosecutors and magistrates ready to act, but they need solid evidence to back them up."

"I know!" Hogan slapped the table. "You have to give me a little time. Inspector General Rand knows what he's doing, he's prosecuted plenty of big cases. I've talked with him privately, and he wants you to have the evidence as much as you want it. He's ready to let you take an investigative team in, as long as it's supervised. But he has to get approvals from all of the higher-ups he answers to. With light-speed delay, and all the decisions that have to be made back on Earth, I can't promise any access. *Officially.*"

I looked up at that. "And unofficially?"

"Unofficially . . . he thinks he can get clearance for a small team by tomorrow."

"Then why didn't you say so?" I asked. "That is a whole different story. I would rather get started right away, but I can manage a one-day delay."

Hogan shook his head. "I didn't promise a day. That's unofficial, remember. Rand is trying to balance out several competing forces. There's a significant contingent in the Initiative who are ready to have the whole thing shut down until a security brigade can take charge. They're making noises that Martians can't be trusted."

"They are always making those noises."

"But this business gives them a much bigger megaphone. So he can't promise me, and I can't promise you. And if he can put it together, he might not be able to *keep* it together. So we need to move quickly if it happens. Have your best team ready to go in and gather everything they can as quickly as they can. I'll do what I can to give you time. But officially . . . Boomtown is off-limits."

☾

I made my way back to my office. This time I almost managed to beat Vile in. She was just opening our access door when I walked up the tunnel. "Good morning, Ms. Morais," she said. It might have been a good act—or maybe just a difference in years—but she sounded rested and fresh.

I hoped I did as well. "Not much good about it," I said.

"How's that?"

So I explained the lockdown of Boomtown. By the time that was done, we were both seated in my office. Vile responded, "We'll just hope for the best. It's all we can do."

"I know. We will have a team ready and wait for word."

"What are your thoughts on a team?"

I sighed. "That is a good question. At this point, it is about investigation, not interviews and policing. So we will have to start with Dr. Costello and the forensics crew."

Vile nodded. "That's what I expected. You'll still need some patrol officers, just as a backup, right?"

"Maybe," I answered. "Hogan will be sending a Rapid Response Team as escorts, but it would not hurt to have our own people too."

"So Dr. Costello and his team, Rapid Response troops, patrol officers. Anyone else?"

I paused for a deep breath. "I really should send Gale. He knows the locations. But . . ."

"But you can't send him. He's out of your jurisdiction, so you don't have a say in that."

"Right."

"So just ask Nick. That should be simple enough."

"I wish . . ."

Vile sat silently for several seconds. Finally, quietly, she asked, "Is that a problem, Ms. Morais?"

"Nick and I . . ." I had to say something. "We had a big fight."

Vile shook her head. "I'm sorry, ma'am. I shouldn't have asked. It's not my business."

"No," I said. "I . . . It is not right to discuss this with you, Vile. It is not workplace appropriate for a superior to discuss her personal life with the people she works with."

Vile leaned forward. "Ma'am, who cares about appropriate? You've got something you need to talk about. I'm here to listen."

"I appreciate that, Vile. I need to talk to someone."

And so I did. I unloaded. There were things I could not say, trusts I had to keep; and I had to respect Nick's privacy. But I told as much as I could.

When I was done, Vile asked, "So he's upset because you missed a few dinners?"

I shook my head. "It is not about the dinners. And it is not . . . it is not about Marcus. Well, it is, Marcus has always been a sore subject between us."

"But in the end, you chose Nick over Marcus."

"I did. But I chose Nick before, and then we broke up over career stress. And then he had his disastrous marriage to Hannah. I had other relationships. Our path has never been easy."

"So he's jealous. He's insecure."

"No . . . I think that is just what he latches on to. Nick Aames is not an insecure person. It is . . . São Paulo."

"Brazil?"

I shook my head. "No, São Paulo, Mars." I gave her a brief overview of our vision of someday striking out on our own on Mars. Our own research base, where we could do our own exploration.

"It sounds wonderful," Vile said.

"It would be." I sighed. "And now I think Nick thinks we are losing that."

"I can see that."

"It makes sense. He sees me suddenly becoming so involved in Maxwell City. We cannot very well set course across Mars when I am the police chief here."

"Then quit."

I managed to grin. "Are you after my job, Vile?"

She grinned back. "Not yet. Unless you need me to be. But you don't owe anyone anything, ma'am. You're doing what you think is right, and I respect that. But maybe Nick and your dream are more important."

"They are!" I said. "But that is why I *cannot* leave."

"You're confusing me."

"Don't you see, Vile? São Paulo cannot happen under the Compact's current development restrictions. And those restrictions will not be lifted by the Initiative. They will not be lifted . . ."

". . . until Mars is free. I get it."

"And so I have to do whatever I can to give Free Mars a chance."

"And you think that won't happen without a strong police chief on duty."

"Exactly. It is what I can do to make it happen." I looked over at the pile of virtual files on my desk. "Look at this. Yes, we broke a major corruption scam. But we still have two unsolved murders, with no real clues yet. The city is a mess. And that is becoming more obvious, more people can see it. People will lose faith in the administration. And they will *never* vote for independence then. The one thing I can do to make São Paulo happen is to get the crime in this city under control."

C

That discussion clarified things for me. I was grateful to Vile for it. The only way to get the future I wanted was to make it by crushing the crime. Starting with two unsolved murders.

Only it was three murders, two unsolved and one unresolved. Plus three other victims of Adam's plan. We had Adam's confession and concrete evidence that he had killed Jacob; but we did not know who had trashed his office looking for what evidence. I had been so busy with the docket of cases that had opened officially when the force started, that I had lost track of this case that predated us. And possibly others. I would have to work harder on culling those records.

Adam had disappeared; and Adam had left behind a message for Nick, one that the searchers had not found. Either they were not very good, or they had not had enough time for a thorough search. But they had been after something.

Or maybe they had found what they were after, and had stopped looking after that, and that was how they had missed Adam's confession. They had been quick and just thorough enough to get what they wanted, and then they had gotten out before they could be detected.

That made more sense, but it was still just a hypothesis. I needed evidence one way or the other.

I needed Marcus.

I knew how that would sound to Nick, and I just did not care. Space it! This was a professional matter, and we could act like professionals.

Well, I could. Marcus had been sending signals. I knew him too well to miss them. I had brushed them off, and I had told him to stop when he had kept going. But the signals were there.

And I had not told Nick. I could tell myself that that was because I did not want to instigate a confrontation between them. And there was truth to that. But was I ashamed of the signals? Had I somehow encouraged them?

Nonsense. That was the exhaustion talking. I thought over my encounters with Marcus, and there had been no signals on my part. If he saw any, he had imagined them.

Still, I would have to reinforce my barriers. I couldn't leave any room for doubt. Not on Marcus's part, and not on Nick's. We were professionals, and we had jobs do. Our past did not change that. I pulled open my comm, and I put in a call to Marcus.

He answered on the first buzz. "Yes, Ms. Morais?"

"Dr. Costello, I am pushing over to you an old file that we have not closed yet. It is a crime scene that could use another investigation. Simons Brothers Labs."

Marcus's eyes grew wide. "Simons. That case was a month ago. The scene could be hopelessly contaminated by now."

I checked the file. "No," I said. "Ownership is still tied up in probate. Adam has not been declared legally dead yet, and Althea has sacrificed her interests, as has Ilse. So ownership is still a gray area; and until that is established, the city has the place sealed. I cannot rule out the possibility that someone has broken in since our investigation. But if so, we will want to know that too." I explained the case and our search of the premises, and I pointed out all the relevant information in the current case file.

"I understand, ma'am," Marcus said. "My team and I will get right over there. We should have a follow-up report late tonight."

Another late night. "No, I said it is important, but you do not have to rush. I am sure tomorrow will be fine."

"I'm afraid we'll be too busy tomorrow," Marcus said. "Chief Hogan has commissioned us to do the forensics scan of Boomtown."

Oh. Of course. "All right, send it overnight then."

"We will." And I noted that he said *we*, not *I*. Maybe he was getting the message.

"Thank you." I disconnected, being sure not to show annoyance in my face. I kept my expression blank as I called Chief Hogan. "Chief, Dr. Costello says you have contracted his team for your investigation?"

"Wasn't I supposed to?"

How could I answer that? It was a smart move on his part. I had no reason to object. "It was just a surprise," I said.

"I checked with Inspector General Rand," Hogan explained, "and contracting local experts was their idea. As long as I could vouch for their reputation. Otherwise we're going to have to wait for their own team to arrive, which could be weeks."

"That makes sense," I answered.

"And Dr. Costello had a long, exemplary record with the Initiative, so he was easy to sell to the IG Office. And besides . . ."

"Besides what?"

Hogan took a breath. "Ma'am, there are matters of appearance here. Boomtown is a Libertist scandal, and Dr. Costello is a prominent Realist. There's no reason to believe that he would participate in any cover-up."

"Oh." How had I not known that? Marcus had voiced Realist sympathies at our dinner two nights before, but that was different from being a party member, known to the Initiative Security mission.

But I did not want to show surprise, so I nodded. "That makes sense, Chief. And they are certainly qualified."

Hogan paused. "And so are the . . . other additions to the team, ma'am."

"Other additions?"

"We really need an insider's perspective, ma'am. We've asked Horace Gale to join the inspection team. And he agreed on one condition: that Mr. Aames accompany him as escort."

At that, I am sure my surprise showed, my eyebrows rising and my mouth gaping. "Nick? But the Initiative hates him. For that matter, they do not much trust Gale."

Hogan shook his head. "You can't have forgotten: the Initiative is not one opinion. Your husband has plenty of supporters still. And Senior Inspector General Park is among them. She approved both additions to the team; and though Inspector General Rand looked like he just swallowed a lemon when he said it, he passed along Park's orders to approve the additions. I've already contacted Aames, and he and Gale have agreed. I . . . sort of expected you knew already."

"No," I said, but I did not go into details. Instead I said, "Chief, I need to be on that team. As a personal favor to me, if I can ask. And I think you are going to need me."

At that, Hogan seemed surprised. "I would've asked you first," he said, "but I assumed you were too busy."

"No," I answered. "Not too busy for this. If you will have me."

"Absolutely! I'll send you the assignment, and I'll see you at 0600 tomorrow morning."

I closed the comm channel. Hogan was definitely going to need me. Without me, Nick and Marcus might kill each other.

29. Entering Boomtown

The crawler was cramped. It was an Initiative model, and thus utilitarian. Seats and storage, all in the minimum space. It might have held fifteen, in an emergency; but wearing suits and carrying all our gear, the ten of us were cramped inside. Except for the driver up in his pod: he had room, but some of us would have to vacate if he wanted to climb down.

I was sure the other crawler was even more crowded, with a dozen Rapid Response troops in armored suits. Hogan was taking no chances. There might still be dangers hiding in Boomtown.

Once we were rolling, Hogan began his briefing. He pushed a map to our comms, and he pointed out surface features. "After we navigate the grade down into the chasma, we'll soon find ourselves among the Candor Colles: low, conical hills along the southeast flank of Ceti Mensa. It looks like they built among the Colles to provide additional cover. This is the main lock," he said, pointing at what showed on the map as a low, rocky hill, "as identified by Mr. Gale. It was camouflaged." He switched to a satellite reconnaissance photo at medium resolution, zoomed in enough so a person might be a pixel, or maybe half. The outline of the low peak was clear, and I could just make out edges and faces in the shape. "And this is after our bombardment," he continued, switching the image one more time. The rock lay in fragments around the hill, jagged clusters of pixels that hinted at the destruction. Where the hill had been was a metallic gray dome, riven by fracture lines. "We breached the outer lock," Hogan continued. "My people tell me the entrance was made for personnel defense, but never intended to stand up to heavy weapons."

Nick nodded. "Aside from the fort, there's not a lock in Maxwell City that could stand up to a sustained bombardment. We haven't needed one. And even if they had been that paranoid, the logistics of trucking in heavy armor and building the emplacement would've made it much harder to conceal."

"Agreed," Hogan said. "We examined the satellite maps. There are no obvious entrances. Everything had to be carefully camouflaged. So that guided our strategy: we could concentrate on speed and surprise, without having to worry about a sustained defense. With the maps that Gale provided from his memory, we identified two more likely locks; and then our analysts identified a handful of other likely access points." He tapped the comm, and it switched back to the original map, now with features circled. "There's also a crawler lock somewhere. We haven't found it yet, but we will. We blockaded the locks we *could* find, and we set satellites to watch for crawler traffic. Then we went in."

Gale shook his head. "There were more," he said.

Hogan turned away from his comm and looked at Gale. "Are you certain?"

Gale paused. "Reasonably certain, Hogan. I know there were at least two large locks, since I saw the second one. But only from inside, and the place was a bit of a maze. It was probably"—Gale traced a line on his own comm—"probably in these hills nearby."

Hogan whistled. "That's nearly ninety meters outside the extent that we mapped out. Are you certain, Gale?"

Gale frowned. "Not certain, Chief, but . . . as far as the distance, it might be off by twenty, thirty meters in any direction. But not more than that. So looking in that area, those hills are the only place to hide a lock. I can't give you a precise spot, but it's there."

Hogan's face tightened, his jaw clenched as he thought for a few seconds. Then he tapped his comm. "Crawler Bravo, this is Crawler Alpha. Check your loads. Repeat, check your loads. We may find some surprises." He closed the comm channel. "All right, it's time to turn around."

"Turn around?" I said. "Why?"

"We were wrong," Hogan said. "The area is *not* secure. I don't want to bring a bunch of civilians into a possible hot zone and have to watch your asses and maybe get mine shot up."

I shook my head. "You are being overly cautious."

"No," Nick replied. "He's being *properly* cautious, Ms. Morais." I glared at Nick, but he didn't seem to notice. "Standard Initiative Security doctrine: you don't bring untrained personnel into a hot zone."

Hogan's eyebrows rose. "Thank you, Mr. Aames."

"Except you're overlooking something, Hogan," Nick continued. "We're not untrained. Gale is still an active explorer and spacer. I should know, I trained him, and I'm the founder of Maxwell City. And Ms. Morais is better, the best spacer in the system. Dr. Costello has nearly fifteen years in surface and tunnel operations on Mars, including emergency medicine. Better than the medic you brought along." I did not ask how Nick knew. He had had all night to study the mission personnel records, and that would be just like him. "Out of the eight civilians, six of us are former Initiative, and the other two are seasoned Mars explorers."

I added, "And they are here under the authority of Maxwell City's executive, specifically under the police force. And that means me. I can vouch for this team."

Hogan shook his head. "Again, it's too risky."

"It is a risk trade-off," I said. "If there is someone inside there, they may be destroying evidence as we speak."

"We would see that," Hogan answered. "We planted monitors."

"Monitors can be spoofed," Nick said.

"Our security is excellent," Hogan said. "It would take a top expert to spoof our system."

"Experts can be hired," Nick answered. "And if there are hidden chambers, you won't have monitors there. You'll need your forensic team inside. You have no time to waste. And you need Gale to walk you through the layout, point out what your team missed. And Gale's not going without me, right, Horace?"

Gale nodded.

Hogan sighed. "And I'd probably better take Ms. Morais."

"You'd be a damn fool if you didn't," Nick said.

Hogan shrugged. "Donihue has top commercial scanners, as good as anything we have."

"Better," Donihue said.

"If there's something hidden," Hogan continued, "Donihue has the best chance of finding it and warning us. All right, Aames, you convinced me. But we're changing the infiltration plan. Instead of setting my troops up in zones, they're going man to man. Every one of you will be paired with one of my troops, with a virtual tether. If you get more than ten meters from your assigned guard, there'll be alerts screaming across the comm channels."

"Yes, Chief," I said. It was a standard escort protocol. It made good sense.

As the crawlers approached Candor Colles, we saw many more Initiative vehicles and personnel stationed in the vicinity. Hogan pointed out the guard posts and observation points on the map.

Nick turned to Gale. "Can you think of any other access points they should cover?"

Gale frowned. "I know I helped construct two. From the surface. One of them . . ." He tapped the comm. "It's probably that one. But I don't think the other is on the map here. My star sightings on that one weren't precise, but it had to be"—he gestured toward the north edge of the area—"somewhere up in here. It was a long way from the main part of Boomtown. The design was just a small surface access lock, like you might have for field maintenance. But I never saw anything out there to maintain."

I looked at the map where Gale indicated. "My money is on an escape tunnel."

Nick nodded. "That's a good theory. Escape from where? is the question. Gale, did you get down inside that lock and see where it led?"

Gale shook his head. "No," he said. "But it had to be south from here, didn't it?"

Nick frowned at Gale. "We're not guessing. That's a good theory, nothing more. We don't know what could be down there."

"If we find it," Marcus said, "we can use sonics and radar to answer the question."

Nick sneered. "If we find it, we can go down inside. Send down some of Donihue's drones to map it out for us."

"I know how to do my job, Aames," Marcus said. "I've got good people."

"I know you do, Costello. It's not your people who made the idiotic comment."

"It's not idiotic to—"

"Enough," I said. "I am beginning to think Hogan was right, we should all go back. You two have work to do, and there is no time for this petty rivalry. So stop it!"

"We weren't—"

"Enough!" *Men!* Did they think this was impressing me? Or would they be bashing their antlers against each other just as much even if I were not there? "We all know how to do our jobs. Shut up and do them, and stop arguing about them."

Hogan cleared his throat. "That's an excellent suggestion, ma'am. If we could have a little quiet so I can call my people . . ." He opened the comm line and issued redeployment orders for his troops on the surface, sending them out to cover the areas that Gale had suggested.

Then he turned back to us. "Helmets on, shields closed. We're almost to our destination."

Sealing our suits provided a good distraction from the bickering. Then we buddy-checked each other's seals, just like a drill.

But this was no drill. I felt every nerve jumping, anticipating action. The new revelations meant we could not be sure if there were still Boomtown holdouts down there. Seldom had I ever had to move into hostile territory, not in my service life and not on Mars. Initiative duty was mostly peacekeeping, and from a distance. I had occasionally had to inspect ships suspected of carrying contraband. Sometimes those had been armed and defended. So it was not my first time in a hot zone, but the first in nearly twenty years.

But Mars itself was a hot zone. Space was too. You paid attention to details, or you died. Sometimes you died even if you did pay attention, but drills and alertness could make a crucial difference. We would see how well I remembered my old drills.

After the crawler came to a stop, Hogan waited until the other team had unloaded and surrounded us before opening our rear hatch so we could come out. As we exited, each of us gained an escort, already assigned by Hogan. My trooper introduced himself as Oliver Matthews, and he pushed a tether signal to my comm. My comm acknowledged it, and then he said, "Hold still, Ms. Morais. We need to test." He marched ten meters away; just a little short of the distance, my comm started chirping, and I saw his blinking. "Ms. Morais, tethered," he said, and he marched back over to me. The other escorts tested their tethers as well, and all seemed good.

Hogan signaled on the all comm, "All right, search team and escorts, let's get to the main lock."

He led us over to the shattered rock of the hill, and he showed us a brand-new emergency lock that had been fitted on top of the old entry. It was the standard-model portable lock, sealed to the original entrance with weld tape. It stood above the original approximately one-quarter meter, easy enough to climb upon in Martian gravity. "Here's your procedure," he said. "The lock can take three at a time. We'll go down with two escorts and one investigator until all escorts are down. Then the rest of the investigators can follow. Dr. Costello?"

Marcus half turned, looking at his team. "Donihue, you go first with the scanners. Send out the drones, testing for physical and chemical risks, just like we did at the factory. Priest, you'll be next with video. Then data, then structural, and then me. Your people can come after, Ms. Morais."

"Nick and Gale and I can come down as a group," I confirmed.

Hogan added, "Then I'll come down last, and everyone should be regrouped with their escort by then. We'll assess the situation and break into search teams."

Marcus added, "Each team will take two drones, a shoulder mount and an aerial. The aerial drones will circulate as they see fit. The shoulder cameras will record anything you direct their attention to, and will otherwise scan the area."

Hogan continued, "There's a slight drop inside the lock, but there are ladders built into the sides. Once you hit the door below, just cycle through. There's another drop below that about five meters, and then you'll be in a big round vestibule. We've got maps from the raid to take it from there."

"Where you can trust them," Nick added. "Make sure we scan for joints, drafts, hollows, anything that might hide an exit. Hogan's people did a thorough search last time, but a quick one, more worried about apprehending personnel than about searching. Take your time, go slow, and notice details."

"Sounds good," Hogan said. "First group, up." Donihue and two escorts climbed up onto the lock. They cycled the air out, climbed down in, and let it close behind them. The cycle lock light turned green, indicating that they had full pressure; and then it turned white, indicating that the inner hatch had opened. Once it swapped back through green to red, Hogan ordered, "Next group."

One by one the groups dropped down. Soon enough, Nick and Gale and I stood on the rim of the lock, and Nick touched the cycle controls. When the light was red, he reached down and twisted the arm to open the lock. Six fitted panels dropped away, revealing a dark hole with another door and a control panel at the bottom, three meters down. He pointed to the three ladders, and we descended. At the bottom, Nick found the switch to close the upper hatch, and the button to start airflow. When the panel light showed green, he opened the next hatch, and we climbed through.

At the bottom, we gathered in the vestibule. It was a small space, maybe five meters across, and crowded with all the suited figures in it. The original lock had probably been faster, but this was not the best way to the surface for large numbers of people. In an emergency, this lock would only cycle maybe six people per minute if they were well trained and knew not to get in each other's way. Either Boomtown had no proper plan for emergencies, or there were other, larger exits still to be found.

Gale echoed my thoughts. "I hated this entry," he said. "A lot of the newer workers never thought what the design implied. They'd never been through emergencies. But I knew: if there had been a serious contamination or a breach, whoever designed this didn't care if we got out or not. We were expendable."

"That's a good indication that there are other exits," Nick added. "The engineers, the designers, the people in charge . . . they wouldn't see themselves as expendable." He looked around at the walls, the lighting, the floors. "This wasn't designed by idiots. Hogan, how many people did you arrest here?"

Hogan answered, "Eighty-one. Plus six casualties." He looked darkly at Gale.

Gale raised his arms in a half shrug. "I wasn't here, Chief, I have an alibi." Then he turned to Nick. "There should've been more people, Nick. Unless they reassigned or evacuated after I left, there were over 100 here, maybe 120. Eighty or so would've been the work crews, plus supervisors. Maybe some maintenance crew."

"We should have had you look over the arrest reports," Nick said.

"We will," I said. "As soon as the bureaucracy lets us."

"I'm working as fast as I can, ma'am," Hogan said. "My superiors want to review everything first before they clear it for release. I'm sorry, not my choice."

"All right," Nick said on the all comm. "Be ready for as many as thirty personnel here, hidden away somewhere. Or evacuated by now, and sneaking back into polite society, but we can't assume that. They could be trapped, and they could be dangerous. So keep alert!"

"Agreed, *Mr.* Aames," Hogan said. I managed to stifle a laugh. Then he continued, "Escorts, pay attention to motion sensors, and keep your eyes peeled. Do not let your charge go in someplace before you've checked it out thoroughly. Rely on drones, your scanners, and your eyes. Look for movement and concealment. And if any of your charges gives you any trouble"—he waved toward Nick—"restrain them physically."

Donihue declared the air to be clear, so we opened our face shields. No sense in wasting suit air.

But "fresh" was a relative term. The air stank of bodies, cleaning chemicals, and other industrial odors. "The recirculators are off," I said.

Hogan nodded. "We found emergency lighting, but we haven't found the batteries yet, so we don't how long the lights will last. My team took down the power plant. That's standard crowd and data control."

I nodded. As quickly as possible, you wanted to take machines off-line so there was no opportunity to wipe them. And people who had no air recirculators were more eager to get into custody so they could keep breathing.

Four tunnels branched off from the vestibule in the cardinal directions. I checked Hogan's map. "South looks like new construction," I said. "North looks like . . . some sort of communal area."

"We called it the Block," Gale said. "Someone joked that it was laid out like a cellblock. And I suppose it was. Three levels of small living quarters, arranged around an open central area where they held meetings and served food and such. There was room for maybe three times as many of us as were there. You could easily double or triple that, if you put more to a unit; but we weren't crowded, so we each enjoyed a private unit."

"My people searched the Block," Hogan said. "Just a quick run through to make sure no one was hiding in there anywhere. We videoed the whole thing, but we haven't had time to do a thorough search to gather evidence and personal effects. That's what . . ."

I nodded. "That is what my team would be doing right now, a swarm of us, if you had let us."

Hogan spread his hands. "If it were up to me, you'd be deep into it already."

"I know," I answered. "Orders." I looked back at the map. "Anything else to the north, Gale?"

He nodded. "Beyond the Block, there are storerooms, tool rooms, and labs. We workers weren't often welcome back there. That was for managers, techs, and VIPs."

"VIPs?"

Gale nodded. "It didn't do to ask too many questions. We sometimes had people in and out who we never saw in briefings or on work crews. They weren't supervisors or techs or mechanics. They acted like they ran the place, speaking only to our managers, never to us. I just thought of them as the VIPs."

"And they went back there?"

"Sometimes. Sometimes they headed over to the east from here, where the offices were. That was strictly off-limits territory, unless you got in trouble. Then you might be summoned back there for discipline. I was too smart for that, I kept my nose clean; but I heard there's dozens of offices back there, running all along parallel to the Block."

"Offices on level 1," Hogan confirmed, "and apartments down below." He tapped his comm, and a lower level appeared. "Nice and spacious, as you can see. Closer to a Maxwell City apartment than one of the units in the Block. That's where we found the casualties." He swallowed.

"Pretty bad?" I asked.

"I've seen worse," Hogan said. "I've worked accidents and boarding actions. There was a lot of blood, the bodies looked broken. Like somebody was angry. But there wasn't a lot of time between breaching the lock and us making entry. I think the responsible parties took what revenge they could in just a few minutes, and still had time to clean up so we couldn't identify them."

"We probably can," Marcus said, "with a thorough examination."

Hogan nodded. "We will. It's just taking my people time to do the processing." He narrowed his eyes as he looked at Marcus. "We *do* know how to do this, you know."

I gritted my teeth. Where was Vile when I needed her? Now I had yet another man trying to show who was the alpha dog. So I changed the subject. "And what is off to the west here? It looks like . . . a garage area?"

Gale nodded. "That's the crawler garage. From mini crawlers up to twenty-person transports. I never saw where the exit was. They never opened the doors until we were all inside under blackout."

"Hogan, how could you miss a crawler lock?"

"We haven't missed it," he said, "we just haven't found it yet. Our first priority was securing people and weapons and potential evidence.

After that, the IG ordered a lockdown until they could get here. We're the first ones in here since then."

"All right," I said, "let us work on that first. We need to find every access point into Boomtown. Until we know where those are, we will not have a secure crime scene." I shook my head. Security duty is not policing, so I could not fault Hogan for not locking down the scene. But his inspector general had dropped the ball there. Rand should have ordered that. "Donihue, what sensors do these drones have?"

"Acoustic, radar, IR, and terahertz scanning, ma'am," he answered. "The whole works, just not very smart. They feed back to my central unit for processing."

"And without the central unit? We might be cut off."

"All the data is there," he said. "You just need to interpret it manually."

I looked around at the investigative crew. They were smart people, they could handle that. "All right," I said, "let us split up and check the different passages. We will make better time that way."

Hogan raised his hand. "We're safer if we stick together," he said.

"You have given us escorts. It is their job to keep us safe, is it not?"

"Yes, but—"

"Hogan, this is your investigation, so it is your call. I just think time is critical here. If there are undetected passages, we do not know who could still be in here."

"That's my point," he replied. "We don't know what threats there might be."

"And we do not know what evidence they could be destroying. This case is going to tie up Maxwell City courts for years. *And* Initiative courts. But it will take even longer if we lose the evidence trail." Then I softened my tone. "I was out of line, issuing orders, I know." And I did know: it looked like I was trying to be alpha bitch, as bad as Nick and Marcus and Hogan. "But I really think it is the best idea."

Hogan sighed. "I don't like it. But . . . you have a point. Escorts, you're on high alert at all times. Patch into the aerial drone feeds to give yourselves an extra set of eyes. You're not looking for evidence, you're not exploring and enjoying the experience, you're just watching your charges. And watching for threats." He turned back to me. "All right, Ms. Morais, what do you recommend?"

There were nine of us plus escorts. Four directions to cover. "I would send Donihue and Swanson to the garage. They are our sensors and mechanical engineering experts. We know there are doors to be found there, and they will have the best chance of finding those. Our digital analyst, Taylor, should go to the offices and secure machines; and Hogan, you should accompany her. You have been through there already."

"Makes sense," Hogan said.

"Dr. Costello and Priest should head south from here for videography. If there is new construction . . . you had better go with your helmets sealed. Sometimes the seals aren't good in new tunnels."

"Understood," Marcus said, closing his helmet.

"That leaves three of us," I said, "Nick and Gale and me, to inspect the Block. That is a larger area, so we could use the extra person."

Again Hogan nodded. "That makes sense. Everyone stay on comms at all times. You see trouble, don't hesitate. Yell for help first, question second."

"How well do comms work down here?"

Hogan shook his head. "Spotty. The rock and the metal walls absorb some frequencies and bounce others so bad that there's constant noise. It looks like the designers never wanted over-the-air comms. Everything in here is secure wired connections. But my team put up repeaters as they went through the facility. There should be enough bands for what we need, unless somebody gets out of range of a repeater."

"So let us go."

30. THE BLOCK

Nick and Gale and I set out along the north tube with our escorts. Gale moved slowly. His suit was bulkier in order to accommodate his assist suit underneath. That meant more air, more pressure, so he had to work harder to move. He did not complain, probably because he was used to it. He had done surface work for years in the suit. But still, he was slower. I would have left him behind if I could have.

But Hogan had made the right choice. Gale was our local expert. He moved confidently through the tube, pointing out security eyes along the way. "It was never good to point them out to another worker," he said. "But they were obvious if you knew what to look for."

But *only* if you knew what to look for. They were concealed inside bolt heads, colored to blend in. Only if you caught them at the right angle could you see a reflection that indicated the surface was glass, not metal.

I got on the comm channel and sent out pictures of the lenses. "Watch out for these," I said. "Our scan drone says they are inactive, but do not assume that. We might be watched."

We continued along the tube until we reached a door with an alcove on either side. The door was slid open, and I guessed that the invading troopers had forced it and then left it. With no power, it did not operate on its own. The alcove was barely lit by the emergency lighting. I shined a flashlight inside. "Showers," I said.

"Yes," Gale said. "Though there was seldom enough hot water to go around. You'll find units like this on all three levels and on both ends. You'll find lavatories at every corner."

"No wonder you called it the Block," Nick said. "Either a cellblock or barracks. This wasn't luxury accommodations."

"No," Gale said. "But oh, the luxuries they promised. They were good at motivating us with the future of Mars and how someday we'd all be rich for it." He shook his head. "I never bought it. The VIPs and the managers were already doing pretty well for themselves. I didn't expect they'd be eager to share if Boomtown started paying off."

Because there were three of us, we had two of the aerial drones assigned, as well as two of the shoulder drones. One sat on my shoulder, and the other on Nick's. We sent the aerial drones out ahead to search for movement or other signs of occupancy. Nick and I checked our comms, and the drones were coming up empty. No sign of anyone there.

So our escorts entered the Block, satisfied themselves that the room was empty, and then motioned us forward. We stepped out onto the broad walkway of level 3 of the Block. It was a metal grid floor without anything to cover it. In Earth gravity, that can get pretty tiring to the feet. Here on Mars, it was bearable, it just looked ugly. Functional, but no more. And it was one of many ways that the Block stripped all privacy from its occupants. It was easy to look down and see what happened on the floor below, and even shadows from the floor below that.

The well of the Block was guarded by a rail and a mesh fence, a meter and a half high. A fall from here would not be fatal in Mars gravity, but you could certainly get hurt. Especially if you landed on something or someone. So the rail made sense. It just added to the institutional feel of the place.

But looking around the Block, that is where the resemblance to a prison ended. The units were small but private. Not bars but walls, with privacy doors set in them. I walked over and rapped one. It was a thin barrier, not enough to stop an intruder who wanted to come through, but padded with sound-absorbent foam. Inside there, the occupant would not hear any noise out in the Block. And probably vice versa. I went to slide the door open, but my escort put a hand on my wrist to stop me.

"Ms. Morais, if I may," Matthews said in a deep voice. Very business-like, and he did not wait for a response. He gently slid between me and the door while another escort took the other side. One high, one low, they slid the door open. Their rifles had lights mounted on the barrels, and they shined those around the room. Matthews said, "Go," and the other practically leaped inside. He said, "Clear," and Matthews followed.

It took them only seconds to secure the room. It was barely larger than a closet. "You can come in, ma'am," Matthews said; but I could not, not until he vacated the room. The other guard exited as well, and Nick and I stepped inside. Gale stood in the doorway, looking in.

"It is so small," I said.

"Not really," Nick answered. "We've gotten spoiled by all the cubic in Maxwell City. We think we're cramped there, but we've got more space per individual than almost anyone off Earth or Luna. On any ship but a cycler, they would double up in a cabin this size. Mars was settled by people who lived in rooms this small or smaller. This is just enough space for a hardy pioneer."

"You sound like one of the managers, Nick," Gale said.

"I assume you didn't mean that as a compliment, Horace," Nick answered.

"No; but . . . maybe? They had a . . . a zeal to them. And a lot of the workers bought into it. The ones fresh up from Earth, who still had big dreams. They fell for those pioneer speeches."

"But you don't think the managers believed them?"

"It was hard to say, Nick," Gale answered. "I think some did. I never got to talk to the bigwigs, certainly not the VIPs. But there was this sense that things were rough here because it was important, had to be done, whatever it took. Like people thought they were building something that mattered."

"It *should* matter," Nick said. "But not like this."

Gale laughed. "Nick Aames, defending the Compact? Thinking people should follow the rules?"

"It's never that simple, Gale. If a rule has a reason, you understand it, and then you decide if you should follow it. If it's an arbitrary dictate from thirty light-minutes away that has nothing to do with the situation on the ground, then ignore it. It's your life on the line, you have to decide."

Nick looked around. "But the Compact isn't arbitrary. It was hammered out over years, a balance between the scientists and the commercial interests and the need to set up a second home for humanity. There's a lot of dumb things in Initiative regulations, but the Compact isn't one of them. There's a time for this, for expansion far beyond this. For expeditions and settlements all over Mars. But these fools were too impatient to wait for that. And now it may cost us all our independence."

I did not know what to say to that. Nick was probably right, but I did not want to believe it. There were still six weeks before the election, six weeks in which we could make a case that the Libertist Party's goals were right, even if its backers were overzealous. Anthony believed we could make the case. Alonzo seemed certain of it. But I could see how it could all go sour.

We continued on to another room, and then a third; but they were not significantly different from one to another. Different clothes in the drawers, different pictures and mementos on the shelves, but the same layout and the same feel. This was a place where you lived identically to your neighbor in most regards.

By the fourth room, we decided not to bother. We set an aerial drone to circulate, looking for signs of any unit opening unexpectedly, while we made our way to the stairwell and down to the second level.

"The tube to the labs and workrooms is on the ground floor," Gale said, "but I'd like to stop here if I could."

"Here?" I asked.

"My cubicle," Gale explained, walking to the fourth one north of the stairwell. "If they haven't cleaned it out."

Again the escorts searched the room first before letting Gale enter. This time Nick and I both stood in the doorway, letting Gale have his space. Inside, he opened a drawer and pulled out a small duffel. Then he started pulling clothes from the drawers and stuffing them into it.

When the drawers were empty, Gale turned to three small shelves set beside the door over top of the drawers. He pulled down two items: a small plastic trophy, a soccer ball on a pedestal, less than four centimeters tall; and an electronic photo frame. He put both in the duffel, zipped it up, and turned to the door. "I didn't dare take anything with me," he said. "I couldn't afford them suspecting that I wasn't coming back. So I'm . . . Thank you, Ms. Morais, for letting me come back and get these."

I shook my head. "Thank Hogan. It was his idea."

Gale looked at the map, frowning. "I was only back in the work area a few times," he said. "I know there's an infirmary, I had to carry a wounded man back there once."

I pointed at a note on the map. "Maybe that was just this bio lab?"

Gale paused. "I really can't say, ma'am, but the tool room is in the right place."

Nick pointed at the map as well. "And what are these rooms against the back wall?"

Gale said, "Storage, we thought. Spare suits, machine stock, spare oxygen, power cells. It's one long storeroom, actually, with just dividers between sections."

"If there's something more through the north," Nick said, "it has to be through those rooms somewhere." Nick tapped the comm. "Hogan, have you found any access to the north?"

"Not yet, Aames. We're still searching."

Nick stared at the map. "Assuming there is a hidden section to the north, there will be a passage there, I'm sure of it. Whoever designed

Boomtown were no idiots. You want multiple ways out in case of a collapse or an air breach. We'll search down here. I'll bet we'll find multiple entrances."

Our escorts led the way into the tunnel network, and we briefly inspected each room, confirming that the labels on the map looked accurate. I really wanted a larger team and days to put into this search, not hours. This was far too much territory for such small groups to search so quickly.

But our immediate goal was simply finding the presumed hidden rooms. So we pressed on. We reached the storage corridor, and we approached the middle door. Like the rest, it was broken open.

"Your people were thorough, Hogan," Nick said into his comm.

But there was no answer. The comm sign was dead.

"What happened to the repeaters?" I asked.

"They don't always work in confined tunnels, ma'am," Matthews answered. "Tolhurst, go back to the Block and put up another repeater."

"Yes, Sergeant," another escort answered, heading back to the entrance to the network. As soon as he got outside the ten-meter tether limit, his escort alarm started chirping loudly. He tapped his comm to lower the volume, but the chirping continued.

Meanwhile our aerial drone circulated through the storage room. The section dividers did not reach to the ceiling, so it crossed from one section to the next, scanning the ground. Everything matched what we expected from the map, so the two remaining escorts stepped inside, and then nodded back to us. Nick stepped in, and Gale followed behind him. I was almost to the door when I heard a hissing sound.

Instinctively I stepped back. At the same time, Gale shouted, "Nick! Move!" I saw Gale grab Nick by the carry handles on his suit; and then he pivoted, tossing Nick through the open doorway and then leaping behind him. They were still in the air when the blast hit, slamming both of them against the ceiling of the tunnel. Then they slid along the corridor back south past me.

31. EMERGENCY MEDICINE

"Nick!" I screamed.

But if Nick was hurt, then Matthews and the third escort . . . I tried to pull up the aerial drone's feed, but I got only static. I saw Tolhurst running back up the tube. He leaped nimbly over Nick and Gale, landing just in front of me and stopping at the doorway. Beyond was a bright, yellow-white light and a wall of heat. I slammed my helmet shut and turned on suit air. I did not want to breathe whatever might be in those flames.

And I did not want Nick breathing it either, but this was time for triage for two escorts in there. Tolhurst checked all directions for more danger, and then he rushed into the flames. I followed behind him, led through the smoke by the sound of his escort alarm. Surface suits were lousy for fire protection, but we only needed seconds to find the two escorts and drag them out.

Not that there was much we could do for them. Their suits were charred, their faceplates cracked. Their limbs were at uncomfortable angles. They had caught the main blast.

The new repeater must have been working, as Hogan was on the comm. "Explosion! All units report!"

"Ma'am, it was the storeroom," Tolhurst said. "Four down. Repeat, four down. We're pulling back to the Block."

"On our way," Hogan said. "All interior units, to the storeroom. Surface units, be alert. Watch for any movement. If you see someone, stop them. Alive if possible, but don't let them get away. Pay particular attention to the field north of Boomtown. And send down some medics!"

Tolhurst and I continued dragging the escorts all the way back to the Block, where the remaining aerial drone flew in a tight patrol spiral. Tolhurst started back toward the tunnel, but I said in my Admiralty voice, "Take care of these men, I will get the others." I had not lost the voice. Or maybe he was just looking for someone to take charge. He started removing the men's suits.

I ran back up the tunnel, and I breathed a sigh of relief when I saw Nick crouching by Gale's side. He was trying to lift Gale up, so I took Gale's other arm. I could have carried the man myself, and Nick could have if he had been in better shape. But I saw spiderweb cracks in Nick's helmet, and he hesitated any time he used his right arm or just bent the wrong way. Probably cracked ribs.

Nick said, "It's a distraction . . . Someone's trying . . . to escape . . ."

"Hush, Nico, save your breath," I said. "Hogan figured that out already. He will get them. Let us get Gale to safety."

"They'll get away . . ."

"Hogan knows his job, Nick. Trust him."

I hoped this was just Nick's usual demanding personality. He always pushed. But the crack in the helmet, and the way he had hit the ceiling meant there could be a concussion.

But he did not argue further. We pulled Gale out and laid him on the floor next to the two Rapid Response troopers. Now that we had regrouped, the escort alarms went silent, one less irritant in our horrid situation. Tolhurst already had the men out of their armor and was applying mediskin to second-degree burns. Their armor had prevented much worse, but it looked like their air containment had been thoroughly breached. They had probably breathed hot gases.

I did not want to leave Nick, but the guards were in worse shape. Gale had said there was an infirmary here, so I ran into the tube network again. "Ms. Morais!" Tolhurst yelled, but I ignored him and that damnable chirping. My shoulder drone would be my lookout.

I found the infirmary/bio lab. It was not up to the standards of Maxwell City General, but it was a decent field hospital. I looked at intubation kits, but I shook my head. If there was enough damage to the lungs, intubation would only make it worse. Instead, I looked around for oxygen masks. I found them in a cupboard; and right behind them, I found even better: a portable oxygenator. This unit could be spliced directly into the bloodstream and directly oxygenate blood. It could keep the brain supplied, which was most critical for patient survival.

I did a quick search for other supplies. I found more mediskin, bandages, painkillers, and a few other things worth grabbing. I only wished I could find some scan nanos, which could be sent into the patient's lungs or into the bloodstream to look for damage. But I took what I could get.

When I came back to the Block, Nick was kneeling beside Gale, checking for broken bones. He looked up at me. He said only one word: "Sabotage."

I crouched down beside him. "I know, Nick." He was obsessed about the cause. A little too much, even for Nick. Now I worried again about a possible concussion. "Please . . . sit down. Back against the wall. You are hurt."

Nick shook his head, but he sat. "Gale," he said.

I nodded. "I will take care of Horace. In fact . . ." I looked up, and I saw lights approaching from the far end of the Block. They were clearly running; and as they drew closer, I could make out shapes outlined against the emergency lights. "Here comes Marcus, Nick," I added. "He will take care of Gale."

Marcus ran up, followed by Donihue, Swanson, Taylor, and Priest. First Marcus gave his attention to the two Initiative troopers. I could not argue with that; they looked pretty bad. Marcus saw the supplies I had brought, and he grabbed the masks and the oxygenator and went to work.

While Marcus cared for the escorts, I turned to Gale. Even dazed, Nick had had the right instincts: we needed to know if Gale had any broken bones or internal injuries. But manually feeling through the suit was not the way to go. I called Donihue over. "Can you give me internal imagery?" I asked.

"Give me a second to adjust the sensitivity," he said. "All right, sonics and radar should give a pretty good picture. Let's take a look."

Donihue pulled up the sensor data on his comm, and I looked at it. "That is not good," I said. "Four cracked ribs."

"Five," Donihue said.

"And these . . . dark areas. Are they spreading?"

"They could be," Donihue answered. "Internal bleeding? Dr. Costello, I think you need to look at this right away."

"Damn," Marcus said, standing up from the man he had been treating. "Hogan, are those medics here yet?"

"They're entering now, Doctor," Hogan answered.

"Tell them not to waste any time. In the meantime, keep an eye on that oxygenator. If it gets into the red, call me over." Then he came back and looked at the scanner image. "That's . . ." He tried to wipe his brow, but his helmet blocked him. "It's not as bad as it looks," he said. "That's swelling, not bleeding. It's still a problem, you're right to call me over." He removed a hypodermic from his bag, measured a dose, and injected Gale. "Keep on scanning," he said. "If that swelling grows, let me know immediately." Then he went back to the troopers.

I turned to look at Nick, and he was up on one knee, trying to stand again. "Nick," I said, "wait for Dr. Costello."

"They're getting away," Nick said.

"We do not know that," I answered.

"It's obvious," Nick said. "Slow us down. Distract us. They know the exits."

"They're not getting out, Aames," Hogan said. "We've got troops all over the surface out there, and we've got hoppers coming for aerial scanning. Phobos will be overhead soon, so we'll have orbital imagery as well. They hid from us, but they're not getting away."

"They know the area," Nick said; but despite his will, he sank back to the ground.

"We'll take care of them, Aames," Hogan said. "They tried to kill two of my men. They're not getting away."

Behind him, Marcus and his crew were loading one of the injured troopers up onto a stretcher. Swanson and Priest took the handles. "Ma'am," Marcus said, "lead me to this clinic."

I led them to the field clinic, and they set the man down on one of the two beds. The other bed was covered with gear. Marcus turned to me. "Get that clear, ma'am," he said. "We need to bring in the other trooper." While his crew ran back for the other man, Marcus searched the room, coming up with many more options than I had found.

I cleared the bed, as instructed. I was just in time for the next stretcher to arrive, and Marcus and his crew gently shifted Matthews to the table. The man uttered a feeble yelp of pain, and my eyes grew wide; but Marcus actually smiled. "He still has some strength," he said. "There's a chance. Rosalia, I need you on this monitor."

"I am not a doctor," I said.

"We don't have time for a doctor. I need you to watch this oximeter reading. It's going to beep incessantly, which isn't going to tell me a thing. I already know his O2 is low. I need to worry about critical levels. You tell me if it drops below seventy-five. And if it does, get the hell out of my way because I'm going to have to switch this oxygenator over quickly."

"Yes, Doctor."

Marcus set about slicing the oxygenator into the first man's carotid. He slid the two needle lines in, and pale red fluid started flowing out one line. Darker-red fluid came in through the other. Soon the man's oximeter stopped beeping, halving the noise level in the room.

"All right," Marcus said, "let's take a look at these burns." He turned back to Matthews, shaking his head. "Those troopers . . ."

"They did their best, in a hurry," I said. "That is all they are trained for."

"I know," Marcus said. "It's just . . . Mediskin is the wrong treatment for these burns. They need to breathe. And if I pull it off now, they'll tear." He opened his bag. "Rosalia, hold him down. I'm going to dissolve them, and it's going to hurt." I looked at Matthews. The burns were mostly on his torso and neck. His arms were unscathed, so I grabbed his shoulders.

Marcus started rubbing a solvent from his bag onto the man's burned flesh; and Matthews started to rise. "Hold him down," Marcus said. I leaned into his shoulders. Matthews was strong, typical for Rapid Response, but weakened by his injuries. Donihue grabbed the man's ankles, and between us we managed to hold him down.

Then I glanced at the oximeter monitor. "Seventy-three, Marcus," I said.

"Turn up his oxygen feed, I'll get right on it."

The oxygen tank was running at two liters. I turned it to 2.5, and I watched. His meter started to climb back up; so I bumped the flow up to three, and his O2 settled in at seventy-seven.

Outside I heard boots rushing by. Then we all looked up at the echoes of shots fired. "Hogan!" I said into the comm.

"Not now, ma'am." The comm line cut off. There were more shots in the background, but Marcus seemed not to notice, concentrating only on his patients. I tried to do the same, but it was not easy. I flinched at the sound of every gunshot. It had been a lot of years since I was under fire, but my reflexes were still there. When shots rang out, you found cover first. We were under cover, sheltered in the clinic, but my nerves did not get that.

Behind Marcus, I saw Swanson imitating his work with the solvent. The other trooper's burns were more extensive, from knees to chin. And they were darker. Marcus finished attaching the oxygenator from the other patient, and then he looked around the room, slamming through drawers. "Rosalia, did you see any antiseptic?"

"Yes," I said. "The cabinet under the sink."

"Under the sink? Idiots." He looked under the sink. "All right," he said. "And saline. Donihue, hold this hose over the sink. I have to flush the system with antiseptic, and then with saline, so we don't contaminate the other patient."

"Yes, Doctor."

After the tubing was flushed, Marcus began hooking up Matthews. Soon the machine was humming again, and Marcus said to me, "You can turn the oxygen back down."

With oxygen masks and judicious use of the oxygenator, Marcus coaxed Matthews's O2 back up into the eighty to eighty-five range, high enough that the alarms grew quiet. After they held there for a few minutes, he smiled. "I think the lung damage is manageable. If their oxygen stays up, I can give them a little painkiller." He frowned at the readings. "Very little, but better than none."

Just then, Hogan's voice came on the comm circuit. "Tunnels are clear, repeat, tunnels are clear." A few seconds after that, Initiative medics appeared in the door. "Doctor," one said, "could you use some help?"

"Thank God," Marcus said. "Yes, help and all the supplies you can bring." He smiled at me, then turned to smile at the others. "Not that I don't appreciate all your help. You did what I needed. Maybe you can transfer to the medics someday."

I shook my head. "Policing is easier, thanks. Let me get out of the way." Marcus's crew and I filed out of the clinic to make room for the medics. The immediate adrenaline rush was fading, so we ambled through the tube network and back to the Block.

When I got there, I yelled in surprise, "Nick!" Nick and Gale were gone.

Tolhurst was still there. He said to me, "The medics looked over Aames and Gale while waiting for the tubes to clear. They determined that the men were healthy enough for transport."

"Nick has a concussion, space it!"

"Yes, ma'am, they said that. They said he'd be better getting seen at Maxwell City General, so they evac'd both of them on a hopper." He checked his comm. "They should be on an approach path now. Probably be seeing the doctors as soon as they land." Awkwardly, the man clapped my shoulder. "He's in good hands, ma'am."

"Thank you, Tolhurst." I gave him a smile, but it was weak.

32. THE HOLDOUT

I stood motionless. Part of me wanted to run, move, do *something*. Run after Nick. Explore the tubes. Collapse on the floor. Hit something. For the first time in weeks—and it felt like forever—I had nothing to do. Nothing I *could* do. I was forced into inactivity. A small part of me wanted to just collapse on the floor, take advantage of this lull to sleep. Or maybe have a small breakdown. Too much was happening, too fast.

But old habits kept me going. I was on duty, and soon I would have to take action when the situation changed. I had to stay ready for that.

And so I paced, and I thought. Who could have still been hiding in Boomtown? And what were they hiding? Hogan had some of the answers by now. The firefight had ended, and his troops and drones patrolled everywhere, setting up more emergency lighting. The Block looked less closed in with lights everywhere.

While I paced, Hogan emerged from the tunnels. "It's over, ma'am," he said. "This wing is secure." He tapped his comm. "You're untethered now."

"Are you sure, Chief?"

"Yes, I'm sure, damn it!" Then he shook his head. "I'm sorry, ma'am, but I'm angry."

"You are just pumped up from the fight."

He looked back toward the two tunnels. "No, I'm angry! At myself, for letting you civilians get attacked."

"We knew what we were doing," I said.

"It was my responsibility! I should've never brought you in here. Not until we knew every inch was secure. I was . . . I screwed up."

I shook my head. "Chief, you acted on the best information you had, and in compliance with instructions from above."

"But . . . two of my men are in there. They may not come out alive."

"I know that," I answered. "But they have Marcus and the medical team. That is the best chance they could have."

"I should've sent in a sweep team."

"And then you would have your sweep team in there," I answered. I put my hand on his shoulder. "Chief, I know how you are feeling. You are talking to an admiral, remember? I have sent people into hot zones. Sometimes I sent people in, and they did not come back. But they were doing their job, and you were doing yours. Were these your first casualties under your command?"

"No . . ." He looked down at the ground. "But . . . does it ever get easier?"

"No," I said. "Not if you deserve that command. But for now . . ."

"For now, set it aside," he said. "I know the drill. I'll get drunk about it later."

"Later," I agreed. "Maybe I will join you." I took a deep breath, and then changed the subject. "So what did you find?"

"Not as much as we'd like," he said. "There were a dozen holdouts in there, I think maybe Gale's VIPs. The ones we got alive—"

"Alive? So the shooting . . ."

He nodded. "Firefight in the tubes. It's never easy, but we trained for it. They had sabotage and ambush points, but strictly amateur stuff. I don't think there were any veterans in the group. So the ones we got alive are talking. Well, they gave their names and cited the Compact, different jurisdictions on Earth. So we're pulling up the records now. Industrialists, financiers, and one scientist. More of a bureaucrat than a researcher. Then there were five dead. We're still waiting to identify them."

"And you are sure that is everyone? No one escaped?"

"After last time, I'm not going to say I'm sure," Hogan said. "But we found four hidden access tunnels. We're reviewing surveillance for where the exit points are. So far, no sign that anyone got out. At least, not once we tightened the perimeter."

"I see," I answered. "Now what?"

"Now . . ." He looked around at me and the forensics team. "Now, I think we still need to gather evidence. And we have our experts right here. I hate to ask, after what you've been through."

Donihue said, "If you're sure it's secure, we've got a job to do."

"Thank you," Hogan said. "It's secure. Follow me."

This time we searched in a group. Hogan may have secured the facility, but he was still taking no chances. Our escort was twice as large, surrounding us front and back. They might trample on some evidence, but we would be *safe*.

Hogan led us back to the ruins of the storage room. "The blast suggests that someone rigged a power cell to overload by remote. It was set to trigger an explosion, some solvent combined with oxygen tanks. We saw no sign of this rig when we secured the facility, so it was probably assembled later. Our monitors missed it. Aames was right: somehow somebody spoofed them. The monitors showed us a believable sim of an empty room. We did a frame comparison." He pushed an image from his comm. A tank with a bulge had been circled. There was no bulge in the other frame.

I had to concede the skills. Hogan was right, there were not many who could crack Initiative Security protocols. That itself might be a clue. I sent a message to Moore down in Digital Investigations: *Gather a list of the top computer people in Maxwell City.* Maybe we could find some hidden connections to Boomtown.

Hogan continued to a door that had been concealed behind an air-scrubbing unit. The blast had mostly blown away the cover, and Hogan's team had done the rest. Beyond was a similar tube network, but larger, with larger compartments. These looked mostly like living quarters, storage rooms, a dining facility, a trio of conference rooms, and some offices.

I looked around at the walls. There were bullet holes and laser rifle burns. The angles indicated that the shots came from deeper inside the network. "They fought back," I observed.

"Five of them did," Hogan answered. "They were probably a rear guard, trying to give the rest cover to escape."

"Probably?"

Hogan shook his head. "Such a waste. They refused to be taken alive. They had to know they were outnumbered by superior troops. They were fanatics, or threatened, or . . . It didn't matter. We captured all the others."

I frowned. "You're sure?"

"We are now. We've found the escape tunnel entrances and followed them; and they match to surface sites where we made arrests. There was fighting there, but . . . not so intense. These defenders were the true believers." Hogan pointed through one shattered door. "Especially this one. He held us off the longest. Then . . . we had him surrounded, and we'd already passed his position. He was behind cover, but he couldn't hurt us. We could wait him out. We tried to talk him down, but . . ."

Hogan stepped aside, and I looked at the office within. A desk had been overturned to make a barrier. There were burn marks on the desk, and on the walls behind. A cracked display screen hung from a single hook. I looked over the desk, and I saw the body. The head was a barely human mess of blood and flesh and teeth, shattered by a bullet from the high-powered pistol that lay next to the figure's outstretched hand.

I shook my head. "He did not want to live. He had something to hide. To die for. Do we know who he was?"

"Not yet," Hogan answered. "Facial recognition is in progress. We got a picture before he died, when he popped up for a shot. It's a bad angle, but we'll find him." He pushed the image to my comm.

I paused. Finally I said, "I will save you some time. That's Adam Simons."

☾

Marcus's team was far behind us, still gathering evidence in the blasted storage room. When we found Adam's chamber, I called back and asked them to search it first.

I was surprised how much Adam's betrayal still hurt. Jacob's murder had been bad enough. This just added to it. Adam must have been more involved with the Red Planet League than I had ever realized. He had always been a vocal proponent of Free Mars. In the end, maybe it was all he had really believed in. He had died for it.

And killed for it, it appeared. And more than once. Marcus's team found evidence that led to no other hypothesis. After three hours of searching, they produced a set of data chips. Taylor verified that they were secured, and then I inserted them into my comm. The contents were encrypted, and Taylor had not been able to crack them; but there were dates and other identifying metadata that painted a disturbing picture. The first folder contained records of a core survey that Jacob had performed, commissioned by Trudeau—but never stamped with his acceptance code. The second folder contained the core survey Nick and I prepared for Trudeau—and the metadata showed different location codes from Jacob's. Adam had sent us to the wrong place. There was something that Adam had not wanted found.

The clincher was the third folder, a request for another core survey. There were no result files, but it had been commissioned by Manuel Ramos—after Adam's disappearance.

How had Adam acquired this request? Had Ramos completed it before his death? And if so, where were the results?

Ramos's death had acquired new significance in my investigation. Maybe he had not been killed over just the insurance fraud. Maybe somehow Adam had returned to Maxwell City unobserved—it should not be possible, but we already knew that security systems had been compromised—and slain Ramos to conceal whatever secret Trudeau sought.

And Ramos had died for that secret.

"Dr. Costello, do you have any findings from the Trudeau investigation yet?"

Marcus shook his head. "Only preliminaries, ma'am. Our caseload is backing up just like yours."

"So you do not know where he was killed yet."

"No, we don't. I believe he was moved, but I don't know how the killer hid it."

Another mystery. Another suspect moving through the city undetected—or maybe the same suspect, since Adam seemed to have had an ongoing concern with Trudeau. Coincidence did not prove a connection, but it was a strong hypothesis.

That meant the Trudeau investigation was part of the Boomtown investigation; and from what we knew right now, Adam did not have Trudeau's report from Ramos.

I asked Hogan for an external comm channel. When it opened, first I sent an update to Anthony's line, though he did not answer. His subcomp would inform him. Then I called Vile.

"Ma'am! You're all right," Vile said. "We heard there was shooting."

"I am OK, Vile. Nick is in the hospital. I shall explain later. But I need you to get over to the courts."

"On my way. What do you need?"

"Warrants. I am sure Magistrate Montgomery is getting tired of us, but we need warrants to search the home and lab of Philippe Trudeau. I will send her the probable-cause papers, but do not waste any time. Send officers to the sites *now*. Make sure they are people you trust, and tell them not to let *anyone* in until you arrive with warrants."

33. RETURN TO THE TOMB

When Vile disconnected, I found myself standing and trembling. It was not the sort of post-crisis shakes I knew so well from Nick. Nearly the opposite: I trembled with the need to *do something*, and there was nothing I could do at that moment.

Nothing *there*. I returned to a local channel. "Dr. Costello, is there any way I can help?"

"Just let me do my work, ma'am."

"Sorry." I had forgotten how short Marcus could get when he had a patient in trouble. How obsessive. How Nick-like.

I did not need to pursue that thought. I turned to Hogan. "Chief, there is nothing for me to do here. Dr. Costello's team knows how to investigate. Can I get a hopper back to Maxwell City? I am just one more civilian here for you to guard."

"About time you realized that," Hogan answered, but he smiled. "Sure, but you'll have to share the ride."

"With whom?"

Hogan nodded at the office with Adam's corpse. "Costello's team tells me they're done with the body. We need to get it into the morgue." Before I could speak, he added, "*Our* morgue, ma'am. You're here as consultants, but this is still our crime scene. We'll turn the body over to your interment department once our medical examiners release it. You can hold ceremonies then."

I shook my head, remembering Adam's fraudulent last wishes: no rites, no last respects for a killer. That still seemed good enough for the traitor now. "No ceremonies. All he is good for now is compost."

C

Thus I found myself and Adam's remains sharing a hopper. Once we launched, we would be locked into an arc, letting Isaac Newton pilot us until we braked for a soft landing. It would be less than ten minutes once we were in the air; but I did not want to spend even that long staring at Adam's body bag.

So I strapped in, lying down in my couch with the nose of the hopper above me. When there was a lull in the launch checklist, I asked the pilot for an external comm channel. When he opened it, I put a call through to Maxwell City General.

"MCG," a cheery female answered. "How may I direct your call?"

"This is Rosalia Morais." I pushed my identification through the call. "My husband Nicolau Aames should have been admitted to Emergency in the last two hours."

"Ms. Morais!" The woman said. "Yes, the founder is in the ER. Let me patch you through to that department." Then she leaned closer to the screen, lowered her voice, and added, "Free Mars!"

The image switched to another face, a dark-skinned man in scrubs. I introduced myself again; and after he confirmed my identification, he smiled. "Nick is fine, Ms. Morais. The doctors have relieved pressure on his brain, and they expect a full recovery. He's resting comfortably now."

Then, at last, I cried. Relief swelled through me. But before I could respond, the pilot cut into the line. "I'm sorry, ma'am, but we're ready for launch, so we're going to lose this comm channel. You can reconnect when we're ballistic. Launch in five . . . four . . . three . . . two . . . one . . ."

It was a gentle kick in the back, maybe 0.6 G—or 0.2 net G. I had ridden rendezvous shuttles for the Mars cyclers. Compared to that, a suborbital Mars launch was almost leisurely—even if it made me weigh 50 percent more than I was used to in my daily life.

It took around thirty seconds for the engines to cut off. A longer trip would mean a longer burn at higher G, and a lot more fuel use; but Boomtown was only three days' walk from Maxwell City, at least for an experienced spacer. It hardly made sense to travel by hopper, unless you were in a serious hurry. Which I was.

As soon as the hopper went silent, I reconnected to the hospital; and they put me straight through to Nick's bed. "Nico, *meu amor!*" I said, tears flowing.

"I must look pretty bad." Nick smiled.

"You look handsome and fit for duty," I said, trying to match his smile. But I lied. His face was covered with cuts and bruises. One large dark bruise showed through his mussed red hair, much of which had been shaved on the left side.

And worst of all, he looked *tired*. Nick *never* looked tired, not like this. "Rosie . . . ," he said. "Horace . . . didn't make it."

"Oh, Nico!" I reached my hand out, touching the comm screen. Nick reached out to his as well, touching my fingers across the kilometers.

"I wanted a quick ceremony at the Tomb," Nick said, not really seeing me. "They said . . . as soon as it clears . . . we can consign him to Mars."

I found myself sobbing, big gulping sobs. I had not even *liked* Gale. But even with all the man's flaws, Nick had seen something in him. Had trusted him, when Nick trusted so few people. Had lately seen him as one of Nick's few friends.

Nick could not cry about Gale, not yet; I could see that. So I cried for him.

I could not cry for long, though. The hopper was already starting to tilt for its descent phase. Finally I was able to speak. "Nick, it was Adam."

Nick nodded. "I wondered. You know I never believed his disappearance."

"I know. It is starting to piece together." Quickly I explained what I had learned and what my hypotheses were.

Nick frowned. "If Adam somehow snuck into the city unobserved—"

"He might have, Nick," I said. "He was an old Mars hand. He knew paths and tubes from the early construction phases, ways that are older than the current maps. And he might have known of new construction that has not been mapped yet."

"He might have," Nick agreed. "But he would still need a way to spoof cameras or erase records. Adam wasn't a data expert, he wouldn't know how to do that."

"Jacob would have," I said. "Maybe he made something, and Adam took it?"

"Not impossible," Nick said, "but unlikely. I learned a bit about data security from Carver. I'm no expert, but I know our security measures are adaptive. Any such device would have to be adapted as well, recalibrated and even reprogrammed by a skilled programmer. If it's static, our security will lock onto it and counterattack."

"So it is back to my first idea: he had an accomplice, somebody with the skills. Moore should track them down."

Nick shook his head. "Someone with those skills might clean up their own record to erase that information."

I sighed. "That makes sense. So we need another lead. Maybe Marcus can find something in Trudeau's autopsy."

"Maybe," Nick said; but his eyes seemed to look past the comm. Then he looked back at me. "Rosie . . . about Marcus . . . I . . ."

I read his face. He was about to apologize, something which did not come easily to him, and usually took a long time.

A look at my comm showed there was no time right then. The braking rockets would soon cut in, and I had other calls to make. So before Nick could continue, I interrupted, "It is all right, Nico. We are all right. *Nunca mais*, Nick."

He smiled; and just like that, I had my old Nick back. I fought back tears as he said, "*Nunca mais.* Get 'em, Rosie!" He closed the call.

I checked time on the comm. There was just enough flight time left for one or two quick calls. First I tried Anthony again. This time instead of getting his machine, Alonzo answered. "Can I help you, ma'am?"

"I was hoping to brief Anthony, and also make a request."

Alonzo shook his head. "You're not paying attention to the campaign, so you wouldn't know. Grace challenged him to a debate; and our numbers are so precarious, he had to accept. He's in the auditorium now. It's bad, ma'am."

I did not need to know this; but curiosity made me respond. "Bad?"

He nodded. "He might pull it out, but instant polling shows him holding steady. Maybe losing ground. Here, let me share."

I was going to protest that there was no time; but before I could protest, the screen switched to a live stream of the debate. "A city of fifty thousand people doesn't need a year-long election," Anthony said.

Grace answered, "What a city of fifty thousand needs is a mayor who understands that it's a different city now than it was when it was five thousand people. It needs new blood with new vision, not the same old insider business as usual. Your League is out of control, Mr. Mayor."

The screen switched back to Alonzo. "It keeps going like that. She's trying to tie the mayor to the League and Boomtown. We've already put out the evidence to counter that, but—"

I checked the clock, and I cut Alonzo off. "Sorry, there is just no time. I need to make another call. Alonzo, we need a security audit.

Someone is changing our records. As soon as the mayor is off that stage, ask him to order the audit."

"I can do better than that. I'll kick that off immediately, ma'am."

"Good. Pay particular attention to preserving copies of all evidence. Gotta go!" I closed the call.

Then I opened another call to Vile. "What have you found?" I asked.

"You guessed it, ma'am," Vile answered. "Monè's at the lab, and it's a mess. I'm in Trudeau's apartment with three officers, and it's worse. There was a fight here, ma'am. And the place has been ransacked. So has the lab."

I nodded, trying to visualize; but Maxwell City is a three-dimensional maze, and it is hard to keep it all in your head. Instead I split the screen on my comm, and I plotted both locations on the map. Then I had the system plot out possible routes between them, highlighting low-traffic routes preferentially. It took three seconds for the algorithm to work.

One of the brightest routes ran right near Foxtrot Tube on level 2, the light industrial neighborhood where Trudeau's body was found.

At that time of night, Adam might have avoided human eyes, disguising his burden in a cart and himself as a maintenance worker; but he would have shown on *some* of the surveillance videos along that route. Yet Moore's searches had come up empty.

"Good work, Vile," I said. "Keep searching." I closed the call.

I did not believe Vile would find anything; or at least not *the* thing, the reason Adam had risked coming back to Maxwell City. That *had* to be Ramos's report for Trudeau. If it had been in Trudeau's apartment, Adam would have found it, and he would have had no need to search the lab.

Nor to bring Trudeau's body with him. That only made sense if he thought there was a chance that the information was *on* the body. He would have searched the man's pockets, surely; but maybe Trudeau had a subcomp. They were common enough today, not as rare and expensive as when Anthony had gotten his. Most people did not see the need to implant a computer that could only be upgraded surgically. It was easier to wear a comp on your sleeve, or just fall back on a comm. But some people, including many scientists, preferred instant access to data.

If Adam had suspected a subcomp, he would have wanted to find it and extract it—a bloody bit of work that would take time. *But it would go faster and easier in a lab!* And Adam's own lab was locked down for auction. But Trudeau's lab might work.

So Adam had searched the home but had not found the report. Maybe he found something else, the key code to Trudeau's lab. He had packed the body into a trash cart. Maybe he had brought one as a part of a disguise for roaming the city, or maybe he even had the foresight to know he might need it. Adam was pretty smart.

Then, heading to the lab, he had for some reason abandoned the body. Perhaps the search had taken too long, and there were too many people in the tubes. Perhaps his mysterious accomplice had warned him that it was getting late, and he needed to move quickly, so he had left the body where the accomplice could blank the cameras and no one was likely to notice.

And then he had continued to the lab, searched it quickly, and found nothing. He had gotten out of Maxwell City through a maintenance lock and headed back to Boomtown.

Or maybe he had searched the lab, found the report, and dropped it in the Martian sands between here and Boomtown; and the winds were busy burying it now, and we would never find it.

Maybe. That would fit. It would mean that the only two people alive who knew what Trudeau had commissioned were Adam and his accomplice. And when he knew he might be captured and might be compelled to tell, Adam had chosen to prevent it the only way he could.

We were so close. I could feel the answers *just* out of reach. Yet they could all be lost already.

I would not accept that. I remembered a lesson from command school: *acting as if.* If your options were limited, act as if they were the *correct* options, and do what it took to get the maximum results from them. If they were wrong, then your actions did not matter anyway. You were defeated before you started. But if they were right, then acting as if was the only way to make them pay off.

I breathed easier then. The only option that could possibly work was if Trudeau had a subcomp with all our answers on it. Marcus would get back from Boomtown, I would ask him to do an immediate autopsy, he would find the subcomp, and we would have our answers. For once the right path was simply to wait.

But I did not like it. Something nagged at me. Something I had heard just recently. Something more urgent than I had realized.

Nick had said: *I wanted a quick ceremony at the Tomb. They said as soon as it clears . . .* Why did it need to clear?

Before I could pursue that thought, the pilot called back. "Ms. Morais, I have to cut off comms now. We're ready to start braking."

"No!" I said, instinctively slipping into command voice. "Do not land yet."

The voice still worked. Instead of ignoring my nonexistent authority, the man started to explain. "We're ballistic. We *have* to land now. Unless we boost back up again."

"Then boost," I said.

He scanned his instruments, and he seemed to realize he was answering to someone who was not in his chain of command. "We have enough fuel for it, but it's highly irregular."

I softened my voice, going from command to reasonable person. "This is important for the investigation, Lieutenant. I need you to boost back up long enough for me to make one more call; and then I need you to land at the new coordinates I am pushing to you."

The pilot read my new flight plan, and he scratched his head. "I can't do that, ma'am. We'll be landing nearly empty. And nowhere near port service. It'll take a pile of paperwork, time, and a lot of expense to get this hopper fueled for another launch. Plus it's against regulations to land that close to the tubes."

"Do not worry," I said with what I hoped was a reassuring smile. "I am the police chief of Maxwell City. I can fix a parking ticket."

I did not tell him that no matter how this worked out, I might not be police chief for much longer.

C

We landed near a little-used maintenance lock on the western edge of town. Adam was not the only one who knew the nooks and crannies of Maxwell City!

Adam. "Lieutenant, I need one more favor. Keep an eye on this body. Do not let anyone near it except me, Dr. Costello, or Chief Hogan. Refer all questions to the chief, and tell him I will explain soon."

The pilot glanced back at Adam's body bag, and then he looked out the port at the Martian surface. "Neither one of us is going anywhere until you get me refueled, Ms. Morais. I'll watch the body."

"Good man," I said, clapping the lieutenant on the shoulder. Then I sealed my helmet, worked my way to the airlock, and cycled through.

Had we landed at the port, there would have been a gantry to help me down. Instead I looked at the dusty plain down below. It was about a nine-meter drop. I would be moving about five meters per second when I landed. Not the worst fall I had ever taken, but extra difficult in a suit.

I really had no choice, no time. I let go of the hatch, and I dropped.

It was a long, slow fall, over one and one-third seconds. Plenty of time to get my legs curled under me in a crouch. I bent over as well, forearms bent to take the impact if my legs were not enough. Just like in survival school.

The forearms made the difference. My left knee gave out, a sharp, painful jolt running through it, and I tumbled forward onto my readied arms. If I had not followed the drill, I might have landed face-first. Helmets are pretty strong compared to the early days of space travel, but you still take care of them if you want to live to be an old spacer.

And I *was* an old spacer. I was too tired, my knee hurt too much to lie to myself. I was not the young lieutenant anymore, I was not even the admiral in the prime of her career. Healthy lifespan had extended greatly in the last century, but I was still too old to be jumping out of spaceships anymore.

But I had had no choice, and I still had no choice. There were only a few people I could still trust, and the most important one was in the hospital. But he always told me I was the best spacer on Mars. I always laughed when he said it; but it was time to stop laughing and believe Nick. Believe in myself, and do this.

Gently I pushed myself back to my feet, taking care not to topple backward from the weight of my environment pack. I tested my knee and found I could stand on it without screaming. Just wincing. A stiff, cautious step produced a whimper, but I could do it. I could walk. Give it a day and my knee might swell up like a soccer ball, but I could walk.

So I started for the lock. My police chief code granted me access, and I cycled it open. It was a vertical lock, a smaller version of the one at Boomtown. Those were less convenient to use, but less work to construct and maintain. I climbed down the ladder, using two hands and one foot, and I cycled it closed.

Then I opened the inner hatch and climbed down into a side tunnel on the west side of Maxwell City. No doubt by now Port Shannon Traffic Control was asking the lieutenant why he had landed in a restricted zone; but it was too soon for anyone to look for me belowground—I hoped.

I took off my helmet and set it against the wall. Then with a few painful gasps, I managed to shrug off my environment pack and set it beside the helmet.

But when I tried to take off my suit, *then* I finally screamed. The suit was too snug, like a well-fitted suit should be, nearly a second skin but with a layer of air space. I could not even free one arm without tugging painfully on my left knee. If I wanted to remove the leggings, I would have to bend that knee, and that just was not going to happen.

So I kept the suit on. Pressure suits are more restrictive than tunnel attire, but my knee was the bigger restriction. I gave up on the seal, but I took my gloves off so I could work unencumbered. Then I headed northwest through the ring tube. It was nearly a hundred meters before I reached a small access shaft. Again my police chief code opened it, and I started climbing down.

I had chosen that airlock because of its proximity to that shaft; and I had chosen that shaft because it is one of the few that descend all the way to the Services level of Maxwell City.

All the way. Every jarring rung. In the low gravity I could easily descend the ladder using only three limbs; but every time my foot swung against a rung or the wall, a little jolt of pain ran through my knee. And the more it hurt, the harder it became to control the swinging.

By the time I reached level 3, I had to step off the ladder for a rest. I was breathing so heavily, I was sure someone would hear me; and I was sweating so badly, I was afraid I would lose my grip. I doubted I could take another fall, even with just one level left.

I wanted to sit, but I knew that could not work. I would never be able to stand again. Instead I just leaned against the wall, propped on my right leg with no weight on my left. I wished for a towel, but all I could do was wipe my hands on my sealed, moisture-resistant pressure suit. That was useless. My hair? No, that was sweat-drenched as well. All I could do was smear my palms back and forth on the plastic wall panels. Those did not absorb sweat, either, but there was a lot of surface to smear. Eventually my palms were dry. At least dry enough to manage one more level. I finished the last level faster than the first. In fact, my knee hurt less.

It took me several seconds to realize that that was not a good sign. Field-medic training told me that endorphins were kicking in. The good side of that was the lack of pain; the bad side was I might do more damage without even realizing it. And I might even experience euphoria, dulling my reactions when I needed them to be sharp.

I hurried back south through the ring as best I could, past the hydroponics tunnels, trying not to think what I was doing to my knee. The trip seemed to take too long, and the side tunnels seemed all the same. I could have checked my map, but I was in a hurry. Besides, I knew the way.

I hoped that was not the endorphins talking.

Then I passed a familiar elevator, and I knew I had reached Lima Tube. Beyond that elevator, the plastic wall panels and floor tiles ended. I stepped onto raw Martian rock, carved into a tunnel and polished smooth. The lights were softer in this corridor; and only red emergency lighting showed through the open door to the funeral chapel. But beyond that I saw the bright, indirect, false sunlight of the Tomb. I drew my sidearm, and I stepped into the darkness.

I moved slowly. My leg did not hurt, but it moved . . . oddly. I did not want to stumble and alert whoever was in the light beyond.

The stone pews, red shadows in the red light, were so tempting. I could sit. Rest. Catch my breath. Give my knee some relief. Maybe even pray for guidance. It was a chapel, right?

But that was fatigue and stress talking. Every second increased the risk that the evidence would be destroyed. And if I sat, I might not get up in time.

Instead I made my way toward the rear of the chapel, away from the light, before crossing between the pews. I thought the words of a prayer, half-remembered from *mamãe's* knee, but I kept moving. I made my way forward again, moving cautiously to the edge of the doorway.

All that quiet, all for naught. As I crouched low (the knee suddenly reminding me it was there) and leaned my head halfway around the edge, Nick's voice sounded from my comm. "Rosie!"

Immediately I ducked back, right before a shot echoed from the rock walls and a bullet ricocheted off a pew. The shot had been way high. The shooter had fired at the sound, he had not seen me.

But I had seen a familiar profile "Nick!" I risked another glimpse, not the entire chamber, just the nearest area by the big recycler.

Nick was there, crouched behind a hospital gurney with a shape on it. There was a rotting smell in the air, making me want to gag. The Tomb was open, and the shape dripped decaying organics. "What took you so long?" Nick asked, leaning forward as if to be sure it was me. I saw blood oozing from his left shoulder. His own sidearm was in his right hand.

"Nick! You are bleeding! Again!"

Another shot sounded. This time, the bullet sank into the mulch-encrusted body of Philippe Trudeau. Nick again took cover behind the Tomb.

"Of course I'm bleeding," Nick replied. "Alonzo shot me!"

I tightened my grip on my pistol. "That is because Alonzo is an idiot." I was ready to kill him. So many deaths he had caused. And now he threatened Nick.

But I controlled my temper, and I shouted louder, "Alonzo! It is over!"

"No!" Alonzo's voice came from the far side of the Tomb. "It can't be over. Mars must be free!"

I tried to imagine how he felt. Sure, I believed in a Free Mars. Nick *believed*, as much as he believed anything. But neither of us would kill for the cause. Did that mean we did not believe enough?

"It's too late," Nick answered. He gestured with his pistol, pointing over the big bulk of the Tomb. Then he moved to climb up on the gurney.

I took over the conversation, shouting to cover any noise Nick might make. "No, Alonzo, it is too early. It might have been the right time, but the League ruined it. For years, maybe tens of years, the Libertist cause is tainted."

"No!" Alonzo was pleading now. "We can still win this election. My projections don't lie. It's close; but with the League locked up, *I* run the Libertists now. I have the winning strategy."

As Nick clambered to the top of the Tomb, I saw more of Alonzo's scheme. "You *knew*. You knew about Boomtown. You wanted me to find out."

Alonzo chuckled drily. "With a little help from Flagg. A *real* Mars patriot, willing to accept punishment and exile on Earth for the sake of Free Mars. Someday we'll have a statue to him."

I saw Nick creeping closer, so I wanted to keep Alonzo talking. "You set him up," I said. "And he let you, just so we would find the evidence against the League."

"It should've been Vile or Monè," Alonzo said. "Neither one is a true Libertist. Not like Flagg. But when you saw through the case against them, Flagg didn't try to flee. He saw it through, for the sake of the cause."

I leaned out a little farther, drawing Alonzo's attention—and a shot, but I ducked in time. "But if your campaign plan is that good . . . ," I said. "If you have the people on the Libertist side, then you do not have to do this. Turn yourself in, we can handle things quietly, and the campaign will be run according to your plan."

Alonzo paused before answering. "I can't take that chance," he said. "The evidence . . . the subcutaneous comp . . . It *must* be destroyed. We can't risk what it might contain. We'll lose the Saganists for sure."

"I do not understand," I said, though I was beginning to. I just wanted to keep Alonzo's attention on me. "What could be so dangerous that it would break the coalition? What don't you want the Saganists to know?"

"I—" Alonzo started; but he stopped when he heard the sound of Nick leaning over the edge of the Tomb, pistol aimed and ready. Alonzo slowly raised his hands.

Nick said, "Martian life, of course."

I heard Alonzo's gun clatter to the stone floor, and I limped forward, my own gun raised in his direction. "No," I said. "It is probably fossil microorganisms, not life itself. We would have detected the outgassing of living cells." I did not take my eyes off Alonzo, but I said to Nick, "What brought you down here?"

"Same thing as you," Nick said. "Once my head cleared and I was able to think again, I wondered why the Tomb needed to be cleared. We don't have that many deaths around here, one every few days. There shouldn't have been a body in the early stage of decomposition, so the Tomb should've been available for . . ."

I shook my head slightly. "So you checked out against medical orders, and you went to the morgue to check on Trudeau's body."

Nick shrugged with his free hand, but his gun never wavered. "I'm not the police chief. I couldn't just call and get that kind of answer, like you did."

"But they assured you that Marcus had finished the autopsy, written the cause of death, and released the body for delivery down here."

"For an anonymous atheist interment," Nick said.

I hobbled closer to Alonzo. "You hoped the body would be down here long enough for early decomposition to get to the subcomp. Or maybe you would even sneak down here yourself and cut it out, so you would know what the report really said."

"It was encrypted, of course," Nick said, "but a software artiste like yourself could break that eventually."

"Those software skills are not in your personnel file, I am sure," I said. "But whatever Trudeau had, it could not have been conclusive proof. If it had been, he would have already made the announcement. It was only enough to convince him to keep looking. So you and Adam stopped him."

Alonzo turned toward me. "I'm sure it's nothing, ma'am. It might still be something we could . . . lose. We can find it again once Mars is free. We're scientists, many of us. We want to know the facts about Mars as much as the Saganists do. But we want to do that research under *our* rule."

"It was never going to work once we were on to you, Alonzo," I said. "You were going to have to kill us. And what would *that* do to the campaign? If Anthony's chosen police chief and the founder ended up dead? Or missing, hauled off to some hidden place, never to be seen again? Either way, it would be one more scandal—one too many for the Libertist campaign to survive."

I saw Alonzo's lips tremble, as if he was about to sob. "Ma'am, it's not too late. The Libertists can still prevail, if you just turn your head. Bury this business. For another six weeks."

I looked at Nick, and there was only one answer I could give. "I could not do that, Alonzo. That would be a lie. Mars will be free someday, but not this way. Not all this death, and not these lies. The Libertists do not deserve to win *this* election. Not yet. Everything the League has done, everything *you* have done proves that. The cause is right, but the Libertist structure is all lies. I stand with the truth."

Nick nodded. "I believe in Free Mars, Gutierrez. It has to happen someday. For the sake of humanity. But not yet."

I took another painful step forward. My endorphins were crashing, and I might follow pretty soon. I did not want to get in the way of Nick's shot, so I said, "On the ground, Alonzo. Facedown." He complied, like a broken man. He lay down, put his hands behind his back as ordered, and waited for me to pull out my cuffs and put them on him.

Then, with a final spark of defiance, he looked up into my face and said, "My name is Alonzo Gutierrez, and I am a citizen of Maxwell City. *Mars.* I demand to have my case heard by a representative of *my* government."

Epilogue

I was finally out of rehab. My knee was almost as good as new, with just four small scars to show from the surgery. I had done all the proper therapy, and I had behaved myself. I had not pushed, and I had not tried to get off my crutches too soon. I had not tried to walk a patrol too soon either. Nick had made sure of all that. There he was with a shoulder wound and a concussion, and *he* was the one playing nursemaid.

But that day, I was alone. It was a professional responsibility; and I would be spaced before I would take anybody's help or use any crutch to stand while I got fired by the new mayor elect. I had my pride.

Francis Merced, once Grace's campaign manager and now her chief of staff, let me into the office. It was still technically Anthony's office. The inauguration was not until the weekend. But Anthony had not seen the sense in making Grace's transition difficult. After the Saganists declared themselves the leaders of a new coalition with the Realists, the election was a mere formality. Carla Grace would be the next mayor of Maxwell City.

But the Saganists *were* the leaders now. They had been empowered by Trudeau's finding: the report showed nearly conclusive proof of fossil microorganisms in certain parts of the quadrangle, and it was only a matter of time before the final piece of evidence was found now that so many researchers were out looking for it. Life on Mars was about to change, as more researchers arrived, and as the planetologists brought their focus back to the Red Planet. There was nothing we could do about that. Maybe once I was free, Nick and I could sign up as researchers ourselves. It would not get us São Paulo, but it would be nice to be out in the field again.

I stood at attention before Grace, and I waited for her to look up from her comp. Finally, she did. "Ms. Morais," she said.

"Madame Mayor," I said. No sense waiting for the title to be official.

She consulted notes. "I hope you don't expect me to thank you," she said.

"Excuse me?"

"For your help in getting me elected. I ran a great campaign. I think I would've won even if you'd never solved Trudeau's murder."

"I was not helping," I answered. "I was doing my job, letting the chips fall where they may. Or at least that *was* my job."

At that, Grace looked up. "Yes, about that." She tapped her comp. "After everything we've seen, I've changed my mind. Mayor Holmes was right, we do need a police force. And a police chief. And you've demonstrated that the department can work well with Initiative Security, which is very important to my administration."

I nodded. "There is no reason why it cannot."

"There's plenty of reason," Grace said. "With the wrong person in charge, friction with the Initiative is inevitable. They say personnel is policy. I haven't filled the police chief position yet, but I know what I want: someone I can trust to work with Chief Hogan and his people as Maxwell City requires."

At that, my eyes grew wide. "You are asking *me*? Madame Mayor, I am a confirmed Libertist. That has not changed. I think you are wrong about your entire platform."

"Good," she answered. "The last thing I need is a bunch of sycophants who think and do only what they think I want them to. Look at you, Morais! You burned down your entire party because it was the right thing to do. Who can I trust more? Who else can I be sure will do the right thing, even when I'm in the wrong?"

"*Especially* when you are in the wrong, Madame Mayor."

She grinned. "Oh, this is going to be fun." She pulled a virtual file onto her desktop display. "I received your resignation letter this morning. Do I take it, or do I toss it?"

I paused. "I . . . need to think on that, Madame Mayor."

C

Nick was waiting at Zeb's. I sat down at the table across from him. He looked up as I sat. "So how's it feel to be a free woman?" he asked.

I shook my head. "Nick . . . she wants to keep me."

Nick's eyebrows rose. "Grace is smarter than I thought." Then he smiled. "So what did you tell her?"

"It would mean no São Paulo—"

Nick raised his hand. "We know that's not going to happen, not for years now. With the Saganists holding the reins, there's no way that individual settlements will be opening up anytime soon. They're not going to forget Boomtown." Then he took my hand, wrapping it in both of his. "I can wait. São Paulo isn't a place, it's my life with you. Wherever that is. Everything else is bonus."

I wrapped my other hand over both of his. "It means no survival school either. The city needs a whole lot more policing than I had ever realized."

But Nick kept smiling. "I understand Anthony's going to be looking for work pretty soon. I might see about taking him under my wing. He's had some good training. With a good mentor."

"The best spacer on Mars," I said.

Nick shook his head. "No, second best. The best is the police chief of Maxwell City. And they need her."

ACKNOWLEDGMENTS

This book started three years ago as I write this in late 2019. I didn't know if my first book, *Mutiny on the* Aldrin *Express*, would ever be published. (Eventually it was, of course, as *The Last Dance*; but that was after my second novel, *Today I Am Carey*, was published. So I have *two* first novels—and now this third.) Nevertheless, I was convinced that I had to write a sequel. So on the trip down to MidAmeriCon II in Kansas City, I started dictating this book. Four years or more later, you hold it in your hands; but it didn't get there without a little help from my friends.

First, as always, I must thank my friend "Editor" Bill Emerson, along with my Brain, fellow authors Kary English and Tina Smith. (Kary and Tina are also among my favorite writers, and I highly recommend their work. We're still waiting for Bill to decide that he's a writer . . .) They didn't get to see as much of this book in progress due to deadline pressures. They read that first story, "The Adventure of the Martian Tomb" (chapters 1–7 in this book); but when I picked the project up again in 2019, I was too rushed for my usual feedback loop. They read snippets and served as vital sounding boards; but much of this book will be a surprise to them. I can't wait to hear their reactions!

Jack McDevitt, one of my favorite authors, has been a fount of encouragement and support. Of all the many rewards this career has brought me, it's hard to top the day I received fan mail from Jack for my first Carver and Aames story, "Murder on the *Aldrin* Express." As much as any check for a story, that email made me feel like a real author, and in it, he suggested that he was looking forward to a sequel, "The Adventure of the Martian Tomb." Here it is, Jack!

Another reason this book exists is that my editor, Jason Kirk, believed in *The Last Dance* so strongly that he pushed for a sequel as soon as I mentioned it. He championed the sequel within 47North, and he and my agent, David Fugate, made the deal happen. Jason and the entire 47North team have again been a joy to work with. Thanks to David and Jason and the team.

Tina Smith introduced me to her friend Meghan Murphy. Meghan is a fellow author and editor . . . when she's not working as a spacesuit designer for NASA. She provided an excellent edit, including checking my future science. Laura Montgomery, an expert in space law, also advised me on legal matters as they pertain to other planets. And Dr. Robert Finegold advised me on Jewish traditions as they might be observed on Mars. All three are excellent writers, and you should check out their books. Any errors that remain are mine, not theirs.

A number of friends have served as sounding boards for ideas in the book and have provided moral support, some without even knowing it. A full list would fill another small book, and would take a better memory than I have; but among them are: Sarah A. Hoyt; Daniel M. Hoyt; Robert A. Hoyt; Blake Smith; Marshall Hoyt; Brad R. Torgersen; B. Daniel Blatt; Patrick Richardson; Tom Knighton; Tully D. Roberts; Sarah Clithero; Paul Clithero; Jonna Hayden; Erik Wingren; Wayne Blackburn; Jim Bellmore; David Burkhead; David Pascoe; Sarah Pascoe; Jeb Kinnison; Larry Bauer; Amanda S. Green; Nicki Kenyon; Jonathan LaForce; Brian de Almeida; Elyse Frances; Julie Pascal; Ian McMurtrie; Rita Smith; Jim Curtis; Amanda Fuesting; Jason Fuesting; Danielle Hecht Slack; Scott Slack; Benjamin Olsen; D. Jason Fleming; Xe La;

Vindaloo Diesel; Amanda Spriggs; Kal Spriggs; Scott Bascom; Dawn Smit Miller; Laura Runkle; Jason Dyck; Melissa M. Green; Stephen Green; Jeff Duntemann; Jesse Barrett; Dorothy Grant; Francis Turner; Nitay Arbel; Sabrina Chase; Pam Uphoff; Cindy Couch Cannon; Michael Hooten; Paula Bunny Handley; Brad Handley; Zachary Ricks; John Kincaid; Travis Lee Clark; John S. Spomer; Joel Chesky Salomon; Kate Paulk; Charlie Martin; Shira Tomboulian; James Snover; Julie Doornbos; Dave Freer; Kortnee Bryant; Richard Chandler; Barry B. Longyear; Mia Kleve; Gama Martinez; Melanie Meadors; Jim Holmes; Greg Vose; Wulf Moon; David Farland; Mike Resnick; Bryan Thomas Schmidt; James Artimus Owen; Lazarus Chernik; Lauren Lang; William Ledbetter; Arlan Andrews; Dana Jack; Emily Jack; Richard Fowler; Amy Fowler; Thomas Trzybinski; Rachel Orzechowski; Steve Poling; Trevor Quachri; Emily Alton Hockaday; Lezli Robyn; C. Stuart Hardwick; Marianne J. Dyson; Thor Dyson; Emily Godhand; Ronnie Virdi; Dave Butler; Julie Frost; DawnRay Ammon; Jenna Etough; John Goodwin; Joni Labaqui; Kevin J. Anderson; Jeffery D. Kooistra; Lawrence M. Schoen; Grieg Pedersen; Nancy Pedersen; Aurora Celeste Pedersen; Martha Pedersen; Deana Weibel-Swanson; Glen Swanson; Luke Swanson; Amy Venlos; Russ Venlos; Steve Harrison; Starla L. Stocking; Alex Miller; Kathy Miller; D. A. Marshall; Eric Janulis; Debbie Morrow; Deborah A. Wolf; Anne-Mhairi Simpson; Duane Collicott; Tom Lavey; Laurie Gailunas; Bryan Donihue; Rob O'Neil; Russ Slater; Peter Welmerink; Christian Gross; Alex Shvartsman; Elektra Hammond; Mike Brotherton, Christian Ready, and the members of the LaunchPad mailing list; and the members of the Grand Rapids Region Writers Group.

My family members, as always, have been incredibly supportive over the past year. Some writers have families who aren't so supportive, or who even undercut their careers. So I appreciate how great my family is, especially my siblings: Stephen Shoemaker and his wife, Laura;

Joel Shoemaker and his wife, Clarine; and Anita Buckowing and her husband, Mark. We've needed to support each other more than ever this year, because we lost Mom in August. Mom (Dawn Shoemaker) was my best first reader, and I'm so glad she got to see my first published novel, *Today I Am Carey*, dedicated to her and to my late mother-in-law. I wish she could've seen *The Last Dance* and this book. I owe my love of reading to her and to Dad. We miss her every day.

And to my wife, Sandy: *Brigas nunca mais.*

ABOUT THE AUTHOR

Martin L. Shoemaker is a writer and programmer who, as a kid, told stories to imaginary friends. Fast-forward through thirty years of programming, writing, and teaching. He wrote, but he never submitted anything until his brother-in-law read a chapter and said, "That's not a chapter. That's a story. Send it in." It was a runner-up for the Jim Baen Memorial Short Story Award and earned him a lunch with Buzz Aldrin. Programming never did that!

Shoemaker has written ever since. He is the author of *The Last Dance* in the Near-Earth Mysteries series, and numerous short stories and novellas, including *Murder on the Aldrin Express*, which was reprinted in *The Year's Best Science Fiction: Thirty-First Annual Collection* and in *The Year's Top Short SF Novels 4*. He received the Washington Science Fiction Association's Small Press Award for his *Clarkesworld* story "Today I Am Paul," which continues in *Today I Am Carey*. Learn more at www.Shoemaker.Space.